# THE HOUSE

# THE HOUSE
## A NOVEL

*Teresa Waugh*

Weidenfeld & Nicolson

LONDON

First published in Great Britain in 2002 by
Weidenfeld & Nicolson

© Teresa Waugh, 2002

A CIP catalogue record for this book is
available from the British Library.

ISBN 0 297 82917 3

Typeset at The Spartan Press Ltd,
Lymington, Hants

Printed by Clays Ltd, St Ives plc

Weidenfeld & Nicolson
The Orion Publishing Group Ltd
Orion House,
5 Upper Saint Martin's Lane,
London, WC2H 9EA

*For Michael and Alistair*

# 1945

## *Sydney Otterton's diary*

Yesterday afternoon we buried my father in the awful family vault. There aren't many places left in it – one for myself and a couple more. All Priscilla says is, 'Don't you dare put me in that frightful place.' I think she despises my family and wouldn't want to be buried with them, which isn't altogether surprising, considering the way my dreadful mother has treated her. Then we all drank rather a lot and when I went to bed I dreamt I was back in the Western Desert.

In my dream it was as though I were in some safe haven, yet missing the excitement of a line of German shells bursting only thirty or forty yards away, missing the beauty of the desert and missing my comrades in arms. On waking, I was reminded of a time on leave in Cairo when four of us had smartened ourselves up and gone out on the town, initially full of high spirits, only to find them soon flagging. That night none of us slept and, on comparing notes in the morning, we discovered that we had all been kept awake by thoughts of the desert, of its incredible beauty, and by visions of tanks and armoured cars and all the heroic and sordid incidents of battle. We were not used to being safe. Waking this morning, I thought long and hard about what we had all been through only so very recently – North Africa, Italy, Normandy – and I wondered how any of us would ever manage to settle back into anything like a normal existence. I know that for a long time to come I will miss the thrill of war and the companionship it brings. Nothing will ever be quite like it again.

Back in the safety of England, I was hardly expecting my father to die so suddenly. After all, he was still comparatively young. My first reaction was one of irritation; it was

3

inconvenient of him to die now, just when I was hoping to be selected to stand for Parliament and so to start a new life. Perhaps I am anaesthetised by war, but I feel quite indifferent to his passing. I have seen so many young men die, that the death in his mid-sixties of my father, with whom, in any case, I never got on particularly well – my mother saw to that – leaves me quite unaffected. But at least it means that *she* won't go back to the house. It will be Priscilla's and mine and we will be able to move in with the children and make it our own safe haven.

Mind you, we'll probably need a haven if the Bolsheviks get in – which most people seem to think they will. Even Priscilla says she's going to vote for them. As for me – if I go into politics now, it'll have to be the House of Lords.

It's funny how often I thought of Cranfield when I was abroad, especially during those last months in gaol in Germany. I used to play games in my mind, counting the rooms and imagining that there was one I had never discovered which was always somewhere between the white stairs and the West Room. Like it or not, a house like Cranfield Park works its way into one's system; it can't fail to become a part of one, regardless of whether or not one has been happy there. As it is, it was built by an Otterton, back in 1730 – admittedly with a Jamaican heiress's money. I don't doubt he married her for her dowry and probably made her very unhappy. She died young and they say her ghost haunts the house. Perhaps she lives in that undiscovered room between the white stairs and the West Room, pacing up and down from dawn to dusk.

JUNE 25TH

There's no damn money and Priscilla isn't sure she wants to live in the house. She says we can't afford to and that it reminds her of my parents. I'm having nightmares every night about my mother, the war, money, ghosts, undiscovered rooms. You name it.

I'm sure I will be able to persuade Priscilla to change her mind in the end. She will grow to love the house. I know she will. I will make her. Of course she can't see it the way I do and keeps complaining about the mess. She says it's full of junk and that my parents had no taste. I've told her she can do what she likes with it when we move in, arrange it as she pleases. She just says that the war has changed everything and that anyway the house is too big. Of course the bloody thing's big but I have no intention of spending the rest of my life in a cottage.

As soon as all the public records which have been stored there for the duration of the war have been taken back to Chancery Lane or wherever they belong, I'll get Priscilla to come round the house with me again. It'll look different then – and better. She's quite right about the place being full of junk – things which have been accumulating for generations. We'll have to sort it all out somehow and store away what we don't need. It's not as if there weren't plenty of room.

I bought a golden Labrador puppy this afternoon. She's called Peggy. Priscilla was rather annoyed, but the children are pleased.

JULY 5TH

My mother, thank God, has announced that she intends to go and live abroad. She doesn't say where, but I should imagine she ought to be ashamed to show her face round here after the way she has manipulated my father into leaving all his free money to her. No doubt she would have got the house too and the farm in Essex if they hadn't been entailed and then she would certainly have ended up leaving the whole lot to a cats' home.

Peggy is making quite a nuisance of herself, chewing up everything in sight. Priscilla is still unwilling to commit herself to moving into the house. I told her that Peggy wouldn't be so much under her feet there. Anyway, I mean to send the puppy down to the keeper's cottage and get Summers to train her.

## Letter from Annie to her sister, Dolly

Dear Dolly,

Thank you for your letter. I'm sorry I have been so long in writing, but what with one thing and another I have been very busy. What with the relief of the war being over and now that her son is safely back, Mrs Gower has got all sort of plans. We've been spring cleaning the house from top to bottom and turning out all the cupboards.

I went home last week-end. Father was his usual self and very pleased to see me, but I think he misses you all, not that he complains. You know Father.

Now listen to this. While I was there the new Lord Otterton came to see me. It was at about six o'clock on Saturday evening. I have to say that I had a feeling he would be around before long. Anyway he must have heard that I was home for a few days. Father was down at the milking shed and I was ironing a few of his shirts when there was a knock on the kitchen door. Mister Sydney (as was) always comes round to the back door. I don't doubt you can picture him. He had this naughty little puppy with him which came straight in and made a huge puddle right by my feet. His Lordship just laughed and said, 'I want to talk to you Annie,' then he started on about his father dying and the house and his mother. He was going on alarming about his mother, calling her every name under the sun. I didn't say a thing, mind, but you can hardly blame him. No one's got a good word to say for her. I reckon his late Lordship is well out of it. It seems that the new Lady Otterton will only move into the house if I go with them. I told his Lordship that I'd have to think about it, but I could see he was full bent on persuading me. He's never been one to take no for an answer. To tell the truth, I can't quite make up my mind what to do. I'm supposed to return to Mrs Gower's on Sunday. Although I would like to come back here eventually, I don't want to leave the Gowers suddenly and neither did I really mean to leave so soon. I've been with them a long time and they've been good to me. I didn't mention anything to Father when he came in from milking. I wonder what you think? Then, of course, there's always Bert to consider too.

I hope Fred and the children are keeping well.

Love from
Annie


## Sydney Otterton's diary

I saw Annie at the week-end. If only she would move into the house with us, I feel everything would be all right. It's just a question of persuading her to leave those wretched Gowers. I've always been fond of Annie ever since I was a boy when I used to play down at the farm with her brothers and sisters. I'm sure Priscilla likes her too and I think that if she agreed to come, it would make all the difference. When I saw her she was ironing Jerrold's shirts and wouldn't give me an answer, but just giggled and said 'We'll see.'

# Letter from Dolly to Annie

Dear Annie,

Just a quick reply to your letter. I think the idea of your going to live at Cranfield is very exciting and it would be lovely for Father to have you nearby. But don't do anything too hasty, you know you have been with the Gowers for a long time. It's a decent job and you have been lucky to be with such good people. Then of course there's Bert to worry about! But that's up to you! To tell the truth, Fred and I never really thought that Bert was good enough for you.

Fred and I were thinking that if you do go to Cranfield, you ought to keep a diary about the goings on at the house. The *servant's*-eye view! We enjoy all your letters and read them over again. When all's said and done, you always were the bookish one and the one who should have stayed at school. I expect you would have done too, if Mother hadn't died and left you with the rest of us to look after. Who knows, your diaries could make you a fortune one day! And you could become a famous writer!

Fred and the children are well. Little Fred is growing up so fast that he's always hungry and it's sometimes difficult in these hard times, what with rationing, to give him enough to eat.

I enclose a letter for you to pass to Father to save on the postage. Let us know when you have decided what to do.

Love from
Dolly

# Annie's diary

Fancy Dolly thinking I should keep a diary! Well, to tell the truth, it won't be the first time, not that I ever managed to keep it up for very long before. I can't get the house out of my mind. Why the house, I wonder, when I might be expected to be thinking of Bert or Father? I know Father would like me back at Cranfield Park to be near him as I'm the one he's always relied on since Mother died and am really the one who replaced her. Besides, he's very much alone now the others are all married. But it's not Father, it's the house that I keep thinking of, and the idea of living there, upstairs on the top floor I presume. Perhaps my room will look out over the copper beech avenue, down towards the farm where I grew up and where Father still lives. We used to go into the house at Christmas time only, when there was always an enormous tree in that huge marble hall with presents for everyone on the estate. Something for the children and a bottle of port for Father. I used to wonder what the rest of the house was like and I still do. I suppose it must be ever so grand inside, but cold, I should think. The girls that worked there always thought it rather frightening, but that could be because of her Ladyship. They say she drugs herself and shuts herself away in a darkened bedroom all day, shouting at anyone who crosses her. She and his late Lordship moved out during the war and lived in what they called the Dower House. She's still there now although they say she's going away soon which I should think will be a relief for everyone. She hardly ever goes out, but I have seen her from time to time stalking around the place, striding by with a long, forked stick, her pointed face as white as death and looking through you as if you were nothing. And when his Lordship was alive, they said he was afraid of her. No wonder Mr Sydney carries on so about her.

The house is very big indeed and none of my sisters has ever wanted to work there. They say they think it is haunted and they'd be frightened to live in. I see it differently. It's rather like the centre of our small world, the centre of everything we have known since childhood, a place full of mystery that draws you to it despite all the unhappiness that has gone on inside and despite its imposing, even forbidding front. I can imagine a kind of independent life there. I would have a big room, and if Lord and Lady Otterton really need me so badly, I'm sure I would be able to do things my own way without any difficulty.

To go back to Bert, the trouble with him is the usual thing of course. He wants me to marry him. But I'm certainly not going to do that and end up spending the rest of my life in a horrid little tied cottage with an outside w.c. and rising damp in the kitchen. No fear. He thinks I must want children by my age, and I do love children, mind, but what he doesn't understand is that I spent my youth bringing up my brothers and sisters after Mother died and I don't want to be doing all that again. And Bert, well, he's nice enough but he's a rogue really. A bit of fun, but a rogue. Not half as good-looking or as hard-working as Father. My father is one of nature's gentlemen.

## Sydney Otterton's diary

Nobody can think of anything except the results of the election, which we won't in any case know until next week by which time they say they should have collected all the armed forces' votes from abroad. Priscilla carried out her threat to vote Labour because, she says, she really believes they will do something about housing and unemployment. She seems to be beguiled by the popular phrase, 'Labour can deliver the goods.' She must have been reading the *Manchester Guardian*. Anyway, it rather looks as if the Bolshies will have carried the day, although some people still seem to think that Winston could get back in with a majority of as much as eighty.

I still haven't heard from Annie about whether or not she'll work for us, although I think I've persuaded her, but she may have cold feet about telling the Gowers she wants to leave. I saw Jerrold this morning down at the farm and he said she would be coming home again at the week-end, so I'll look in and see her then. I've already told Priscilla that she *is* prepared to come, so I hope she won't let me down. Priscilla definitely does like Annie very much (I've verified that) and is, I think, beginning to envisage living in the house, despite her misgivings.

We spent the morning at the house yesterday and began to go through some of the things, to decide how it would be possible to arrange everything. There is such a lot there, some magnificent things of course, but a good deal of rubbish too. I never really knew that one half of it existed. It was a funny feeling really, going through so much stuff – some of which is so familiar and some of which means nothing to me – and realising that it's all mine now.

Priscilla says (and I suppose she's right) that if – always 'if' – we move into the house, we'll have to do something about the kitchen. She says that these days we can't expect to find people who are prepared to carry food up to the dining-room from the basement, and that, in any case, the food in my parents' day was 'perfectly filthy' because it was always cold. But I don't know what she has in mind.

The basement is a problem in itself. The only part of it that is even remotely presentable is the flat in the corner where the caretaker from the Public Records Office lived during the war, and even that is pretty dilapidated. The rest is dark and damp with the plaster crumbling off all the walls. I suppose we'll manage somehow, but even I sometimes think that I'm

biting off more than I can chew. Not that I'll admit that to
Priscilla.

## Letter From Zbigniew Rakowski to Lord Otterton

1 Robin Hood Way,
Wimble-on-Thames,
Surrey.
JULY 20TH 1945

Dear Lord Otterton,

On perusing this letter you will no doubt cast your hands up
in dismay when you discover that it comes from an
unknown, humble writer who begs you of your generosity to
bear with him a while and to listen to his modest story. My
name, as you will observe, is Polish and I was born under
Austrian rule in the town of Przemysl in South Eastern
Poland, where at the time my father practised as a doctor of
medicine. When I was but a mere boy of some ten summers,
my poor mother died and my father, appalled by the
Russification of Eastern Poland and wishing his only son to
be educated in neither Russian nor German, decided to
move to London where, in the early years of this century, he
was fortunate enough to be able to establish a small practice
and to educate his son.

You will doubtless be familiar with the role played by
Przemysl in Eastern European history. Having been founded
in 1340 on a trade route from Ruthvenia to Poland and, later,
in the 15th and 16th centuries, having served as a frontier
post to defend the country against invasion from the Tatars
and Hungarians, Przemysl is a town full of significance to
which its many elegant and interesting medieval and
Renaissance buildings bear witness. It is a hill town,
occasionally beset by mists and rain, but I will not trouble

you further with details of this kind, having mentioned them only that you might appreciate from whence my lifelong passion for history sprang. My purpose, then, in writing to you, could you but indulge me one moment longer, is to beg of your kindness, permission that I, in my humble capacity as a chronicler of facts, might consult some documents which I believe to be in your possession.

In recent years research has led me to concentrate my modest endeavours, such as they are, on eighteenth-century England and thus I am now engaged on a study of the Whig aristocracy in that century. It is my belief that amongst your family papers you may have some letters from many distinguished figures which might be of help to me in my researches. Yours is, indeed, an illustrious family.

I beseech of you, in your kindness to an impecunious widower, to accept the enclosed copy of my most recent work which I send as a token of my deepest respect. In it you will find a complete list of the earlier works which it has been my privilege to publish.

Pray, Sir, excuse a mere scribbler from daring thus to intrude upon your time.

I remain, Sir, your humble and obedient servant.
Z. A. Rakowski

## *Sydney Otterton's diary*

JULY 22ND

Annie has agreed to give the Gowers a month's notice and to move into the house with us. Hurrah! We couldn't manage without her. Priscilla is attempting to appear aloof, but she, too, has agreed. Not because of me but because of Annie.

Despite her affected aloofness, Priscilla has of course taken charge of everything to do with the move, which is just as well. She's very competent and doesn't allow herself to be pushed around. The more she takes charge, the more I feel the house will get into her system and the happier she will be to move in.

The children were all very excited when they were told the news. I took them to see the house this afternoon and showed them round. Even little Georgina appeared to be delighted and not at all discountenanced by the size of the place. I think the children must have been to the basement flat once or twice during the war, but otherwise they've probably never been inside the house at all, except as babies before the war. Jamie wasn't born until '40 so he wouldn't have been there then anyway, and Georgina who was born in '38 certainly wouldn't have been old enough to remember it.

## Annie's diary

Father was delighted when I told him that I'd made up my mind to come home, to live in the big house and work for the Ottertons. His whole face lit up and his blue eyes twinkled more than they have done for a long time. He kept on saying with a smile, 'So I'll have my Annie back again.' That always sounds funny to me of course because of Mother's name being Annie. But I was glad to see Father looking so happy. As I say, he must be lonely at times now all the others have left home, but with me only two hundred yards away up the drive, it will be different.

Neither Bert nor the Gowers took it quite so well. Mrs Gower did say that when she heard that the late Lord Otterton had died, she was frightened that the new Lady Otterton might try to steal me. I felt like saying that I was hardly an object to be stolen but I thought I'd better mind my p's and q's, so I said nothing. It's funny the way the gentry when they employ you seem to think that they own you. In any case Mrs Gower was quite distant with me for a few days after that. Then she melted and began to say how much she would miss me which I dare say she will. Mind you she's been good to me over the years.

As for Bert, he worked himself up into a right tizwas. But of course he was only thinking about himself and worrying about who was going to wash his shirts and who was going to cook his Sunday dinner for him. He didn't like it at all when I said he'd better start to do a bit of cooking himself. And surely he could learn how to sew on his own buttons. But I began to feel quite sorry for him at one point so I took away a couple of pair of socks that needed darning.

Of course Bert's mother always spoilt him, waited on him hand foot and finger so that when she died he didn't know how to do a thing for himself. Bert's worked for the Gowers ever since he left school, in the garden and around the place. He stayed on in that same cottage after the death of his father who was head gardener there for years, and then again when his mother died. She was the scullery maid in days gone by. Because of all that I didn't quite dare tell him that I have an idea that I might be able to persuade his Lordship to take him on. There's an empty cottage down at the farm, just next to Father's which would do Bert nicely. I don't know if they have anyone in mind for it and, in any case, I'll have to have a think about what job he could do. I don't know if they need another farm hand, or an under-gardener perhaps to replace that lazy Stanley. I'll have a word with Father. He knows everything that goes on. Not that he'll give anything away, mind. Father is a very careful and peace-loving man. He hates any kind of trouble and doesn't like to interfere so I'll have to look how I go about it. Then, when I know how the land lies, I'll talk to Bert, by which time he may be beginning to miss me.

## Georgina's exercise book

Yesterday Father took us to see the house were we are going to live. It is very very big and red. He showed us the stairs and the hall. There are lots of pictures and things and a stufed bear in the hall. Father says we can have it in the nursry. Nanny is leaving and we are getting a guvernis.

## Sydney Otterton's diary

Priscilla is busy interviewing governesses for the two younger children. She's delighted to be getting rid of Nanny who she says has a face like a horse and with whom she has never got on. She wants the children to learn French, so she's interviewing French governesses and is keeping on old Major Doubleday from the village who's been coming in to teach them the three r's. I nipped out of the back door when I saw him coming this morning. He's like the Ancient Mariner. Once he gets hold of you, you can never escape. In his imagination he's never left India; it's Poona this and Ootie that, and what do I think of the Mahatma? And he remembers this and he remembers that and he remembers what happened when they passed the Government of India Act, and what do I think about the Punjab and what about the Muslim League? He really is an awful old bore who has a way of asking you a question in order to answer it himself at great length. But, according to Priscilla, he's an excellent teacher and Georgina certainly seems pretty good for her age at reading and writing. Anyway, I had to get away from him. I wanted to go down to the farm to see the vet who was coming to look at one of the carthorses which has gone lame.

Somehow we're going to have to beg, borrow or steal the money to buy a tractor before much longer. I'm still having nightmares.

A frightful bloody fool of a Pole came to lunch yesterday. He's writing some sort of history book and wants to look at a few family papers. There didn't seem any very good reason to refuse although it's rather a bad moment for him to turn up. Priscilla was very keen to let him come; she rather likes these writer fellows and got quite cross when I described him as an old humbug. She says she knows all about him and he's very well regarded, but even she could hardly deny that he's ridiculously affected and pompous, addressing everyone as 'Sir' and 'Ma'am' the way he does, and speaking in the most pedantic drawn-out tones. But you have to give it to him that to some extent he seems to be sending himself up all the time. In any case Priscilla played up to him, laughing a lot at his facetious jokes, and I could see that he was quite delighted by her. I told him what I thought there was in the way of papers and he has agreed to come back after we have moved in, but Priscilla still insisted on walking up to the house with him after lunch to show him the muniments room which for the moment is still under dust sheets. He's like a kind of gnome, all buttoned up in a worn-out jacket, with the utility label showing on his floppy sun hat.

I had to go and see the agent about the farm. It's running at a dreadful loss and we seem to be employing an awful lot of people. God alone knows how we'll ever sort it all out. I hate the thought of sacking men who've been here since before the war, but with the agricultural wage at around £8 a week, I can't see how we can afford to keep them all on, and I don't suppose things will get any easier under Mr Attlee. Everywhere I look there are problems; the stables are falling down, the cottages are all in a bad state of repair, the horses are lame. Sometimes I think that life in the Western Desert was simpler. Even the prospect of living in the house seems daunting when I wake at night, and yet it's the only thing that's really keeping me going. Priscilla is being wonderful about it and I daren't tell her that I occasionally get cold feet. She seems to think we'll manage with a butler, Annie, a cook, a governess and daily help from the farm and the village. She's probably right, but it seems odd when I remember all the people my parents used to employ. Butlers and footmen, tweenies, scullery maids and God knows what. Mind you, they all caused a lot of trouble. I'll never forget when my crazy old father discovered that the footman had been in bed with the butler. He worked himself up into a terrible rage and I can see him now, banging that big gong outside the dining-room with all his might and yelling, 'There are buggers in the house!' The pair of them were out by lunchtime the next day, poor devils, and I'm afraid I think the police were informed.

## Zbigniew Rakowski's notebook

JULY 30TH

Lunched with Lord & Lady Otterton. I think they have papers which will be invaluable for my research, and I am kindly invited to return in the autumn by which time they will have moved into what at first sight appears to be a forbidding great barrack of a place. There was a good deal of talk about the new government. Lord Otterton who, having been captured in Normandy, spent the last few months of the war as a prisoner in Germany, regards what he chooses to call the Bolsheviks with a jaundiced eye. She, on the other hand, is delighted that they have been elected and voted for them herself. I sat on the fence. His Lordship and her Ladyship are in fact a most unlikely couple. He is small and dark with a round head and a round face, quite foreign looking, with a raunchy humour and displaying mostly a devil-may-care attitude. At times, though, he appears almost unsure of himself, glancing around with huge, dark, almost negro eyes, trying to catch an approving look from her Ladyship's hyacinth-blue ones.

We ate rabbit and stewed gooseberries. A more or less daily fare, her Ladyship told me, whilst proclaiming their luck at having the farm to live off in these hard times of rationing. She is tall and willowy, elegant with light brown hair tied loosely in a bun at the nape of her neck, a large nose and, despite her youth, a commanding presence. She clearly prides herself on her good taste and, unlike his Lordship, she appears to have some interest in literary matters. They live at present in the grounds of Cranfield Park, in a small gabled house with hanging tiles (a bailiff's house perhaps).

After lunch Lady O. insisted on walking with me to the big house. His Lordship seeming relieved to entrust me to her capable hands, mumbled something about having to go and see someone about something and quietly departed with a cat-like tread. We had walked up the rutted drive for barely a couple of hundred yards when, suddenly, around a bend, across a handful of fields, the great house appeared at an angle, large, oblong, a warm gleaming red, against a background of heavy summer woods. A first impression of this noble structure is never to be forgotten.

Built in around 1730, the house was designed for the second Lord Otterton by the Palladian architect, Giacomo Leoni. The exterior displays an exquisite reticence of decoration on which much of its beauty depends, but on entering the marble hall, a forty-foot cube which rises to take in the first floor of the house, the visitor will catch his breath at the magnificent opulence of this Palladian dream. Here is some of the finest plasterwork in England, but, as her Ladyship was only too ready to point out, gesticulating dramatically with her hands as she did so, the recent incumbents had little, if any taste. They had carpeted the magnificent white marble floor with heavy Persian and

Turkish carpets and furnished the room with, as her Lady-ship said, 'every conceivable bit of junk'. At present the carpets are rolled up and the 'junk' is covered with dust sheets. When she moves into the house, Lady O. plans to empty the hall, to leave it alone in its splendour that the proportions, the plasterwork and Rysbrack's two marble chimney-pieces on opposite walls may speak for themselves.

I must confess that it was a delightful afternoon I spent with Lady Otterton. She took endless trouble in showing me around the house, a tour much enlivened by her wit and charm. When we reached the muniments room (or the Red Drawing-Room as it is properly called), where I have been invited to work, she showed me a locked cabinet containing family papers which she assured me would be put at my disposal. The Ottertons, she told me, were not a literary family, indeed she regarded them as somewhat Philistine in their leanings. Their humour was slapstick, their occupations unrefined, their intelligence pedestrian, but for all that, she trusted that I might find something of interest for my researches among their papers. And for all that, they had caused this perfectly extraordinary monument to the eight-eenth century to be built.

I had much to ponder over on my bus ride home. And I have much, I feel, to look forward to. The locked cabinet in the Red Drawing-Room is indeed full of promise. By September I shall need my muffler and my mittens, but I nevertheless envisage spending many a rewarding hour in that dark red room, beneath its delicate stucco ceiling. In truth, I also nurture a hope that I may have the chance further to enjoy some hours of her Ladyship's company. The Ottertons of today threaten to be quite as intriguing as their Whig ancestors.

Back home in my own modest abode in Robin Hood Way, I turned on one bar of my electric fire, for despite it being July, the evening was chilly, and made myself a cup of tea. Having eaten so royally at luncheon, I had no need of tea or supper, but took up my book immediately, only to find that Athens of the fifth century B.C. which had so engrossed me only twenty-four hours earlier, no longer had the power to enthral me. My mind kept returning to that great red house, that marble hall and to her Ladyship's hyacinth-blue eyes.

## Annie's diary

Today her Ladyship took me around the house. I was quite fascinated. Even the rooms on the top floor where I shall have my room and where the children will live, seem huge to me, most of them with black patches on the ceiling where the water comes through when it rains. My bedroom which is not really as nice as the one at the Gowers' is, thank goodness, a little smaller than some, but next to it I will have my own sitting room. I don't have that with the Gowers. At the moment, everything's in a dreadful mess and needs a thorough cleaning. There is a huge landing on the top floor with a great, long table (I think they call it a refectory table) in the middle and a little spiral staircase going up onto the roof. We can have a washing line on the roof and dry the clothes there. From outside, it looks as if the roof is flat, but when you get up there, you find rows of small pointed roofs running parallel to each other, down which the rain flows into a series of gutters. It's an extraordinary place, that roof. I would never have imagined it to be like that. Round the edge is a stone balustrade much of which is broken. It would be very dangerous to allow the children up there.

The children's rooms, the governess's room and the nursery (or rather the schoolroom) all open onto the landing, from one side of which a long passage leads off to the other end of the house, to the servants' rooms and what will be the butler's flat. Mind you they haven't found a butler or a cook yet. Or a governess for that matter, as far as I know.

There's one very funny thing at the end of that big landing, against the outside wall. At first I thought there were just two large bookcases sticking out into the landing space to form some sort of a corner cupboard. Up to a point I was right. Well, I couldn't help laughing when her Ladyship made me look a little closer. One of the walls is filled with real books, but the other one is made up of false ones and there's a door in them that you certainly don't notice at a distance. And all this to hide the fact that there's a w.c. in there. And in one of the rooms on the first floor, there's a bath inside a wardrobe and another w.c. in a big chest. You open up the lid and then you open the two front doors and Bob's your uncle! So long as no one's in a hurry!

It's going to be an awful job sorting everything out. At the moment there are things piled up everywhere, some of which have to be stored away and some which just need putting in the right place. Her Ladyship has all her own ideas. She wants everything moved around. Mind you, it looks as if no one has cared for the place for donkey's years. I think his late Lordship probably just gave up, it all being too much for him what with her shut in her room all day having hysterics. Mister Sydney says he can't ever remember seeing his mother on the top floor. She had no idea what went on there. It'll certainly take some cleaning up and they'll need to get the men in to move the furniture.

They're going to put a kitchen in one of the corner rooms on the first floor and have the dining-room off it, which is a darn good thing, if you ask me. I don't think I for one would stay if I had to spend any time down in the basement. That basement is more like something out of a Victorian slum than anything in a gentleman's residence.

When I got home and told Father about it all, I think he was quite horrified. He'd prefer to live in the bothy with an outside w.c. and a tin roof I shouldn't wonder, rather than up at the big house. But he never said anything. Typical Father. He just looked and smiled. I asked him if he thought they needed any extra men on the farm. Again he just looked, but I reckon he knew why I asked. And when I mentioned the empty cottage next door, he said he knew no more about it than I did, except that it wasn't in very good condition and he wouldn't want to keep a cow in it. Father loves his cows.

I've got till the end of the month with the Gowers and then I'll be back, staying with Father for a week or two before we move in and while we get the house in order. I still haven't dared tell Bert that I'd like him to come here. I'll have to find out if his Lordship will give him a job before I say anything.

AUGUST 6TH

After I'd cooked Bert's tea, he started on about me leaving. Why wouldn't I marry him and stay put? In that dingy, damp old cottage, cooking his tea and darning his socks for the rest of my days? I've heard it said that they don't marry you with the same face they court you. So why would Bert be any different? In the end, I made the mistake of telling him that he might be able to get a job with the Ottertons and come too. That didn't please him one little bit. It crossed my mind then that he would be afraid to leave the place where he's always been and the cottage where he was born.

## Georgina's exercise book

AUGUST 6TH

We are getting a French mamzel when we go to the big house. She came to see Mummy yesterday and is very fat and old. Mummy speeks French to her so we cant understand. Mummy thinks she is *marvlous*.

# Sydney Otterton's diary

Priscilla seems to think she's found a suitable governess. The old bat didn't look much fun to me but Priscilla who interviewed her for quite a long time, says she has excellent references. I think I've found a butler through a fellow I used to know at Sandhurst whom I bumped into the other day in London. Priscilla doesn't like the sound of him and thinks my pal is just trying to offload him. In any case he's coming to see us next week. So you could say that in one way the house is filling up, almost coming back to life even before we've moved in. The public records have nearly all been taken back to London now, so when that's done, we'll be set to go.

The Americans have dropped an atom bomb on Japan. It should mean the end of the war in the East, but I can't get it out of my mind. I dreamt I was driving round the farm in a tank with bombs dropping on every side.

They've dropped another bomb on Japan.

Thank God for Priscilla. Now she's really got the bit between her teeth about the house. She can't wait to move in and I feel that without her I would be totally useless. There are so many problems that I sometimes don't know where to turn. Of course we haven't got probate yet, so I've no idea what the death duties will be. The thought of them makes me ill. Whatever happens, we'll have to sell something and borrow huge sums from the bank as well. I'm sleeping badly and drinking a lot.

The house is beginning to look quite empty since Priscilla really began to move everything around, and an army of cleaning women is due to move in any day under Annie's stern eye. We should be in by mid-September. Then I think I'll feel better. I'll put the Essex property up for sale as soon as I can. But no one has got any money. Perhaps I'll feel better when I know the worst where death duties are concerned. But it won't be good news and it's not as if Mr Attlee's likely to make things any easier for the likes of us.

I wish my mother would go away. She's been talking about going ever since my father died, but she's still here. At least I have managed to avoid seeing her for some time.

I might go up to London and see Tony one of these days. He's a bit like me and can't get used to being back in civvy street. For years our day-to-day experiences in the war were everything to us. The war was all that mattered. The time in the desert haunts me especially. More than Italy, Normandy or being in gaol. It was such a strange and different life, one which no one who was not there can begin to imagine. It's so difficult now to concentrate on tumble-down cottages and widowed mothers, sales and governesses and solicitors. I sometimes feel like two people, almost as if the life I am leading back here is unreal, and that the real me has been left behind in a sandstorm with my Honey tanks in the Djebel. I also want to get hold of Johnson and take him on here. I somehow feel I can't really manage without Johnson. Life is incomplete without him. His flat, north-country manner and limitless courage made him the best troop sergeant we had in the desert, and I was damn lucky to have him as my driver. I shall never forget him on the day poor old Bill Martin was killed, opening the driver's hatch, standing up there without any cover and yelling at me, 'The buggers are trying to murder Mr Martin.' And they succeeded.

## *Georgina's exercise book*

I am having a 4 posta bed. Mummy says it is only an ugly one and there is a lavatry inside the book case on the landing. Nanny has gone and Mamzel is here. She has got to teech us French. Boring. She looks at you with horrid eyes. Jamie thinks she is a german spy but Mummy says she's swiss. Lucky Thomas is at bording school so he wont have to see her much.

## *Zbigniew Rakowski's notebook*

There is a distinct chill in the air in the Red Drawing-Room, which is compounded indeed by Lilian Otterton's icy stare as she gazes down from Laszlo's fine three-quarter-length portrait of her which hangs above my left shoulder. Lord O. speaks openly and scathingly about his mother, a woman who, to judge from her portrait, would not be out of place in a tale of Gothic horror. I do not like to feel her eyes upon me as she silently fingers her long necklace and as I peruse letters from Horace Walpole, Newcastle or Pitt, for the cabinet, once unlocked, has revealed a wealth of treasure. On the wall beside the portrait of Lady Otterton hangs its pair. The late Lord O. is far less mesmeric than his spouse. An ordinary-looking man in whom the artist has captured an expression which reveals both pomposity and hesitancy, even a certain brazen determination not to apologise. While I sat there, I was repeatedly tempted to allow my attention to wander from my work, to look up again and again at this strangely haunting couple who for so many years presided over this great mansion, allowing it quietly to decay under their stewardship. As I scrutinised their faces I attempted to divine their natures and through them to understand the present Lord O. who, together with his mother's dark looks and full mouth, has inherited his father's broad brow and slight build. But from whence came his jaunty manner and iconoclastic humour which at times amounts to insolence almost?

At luncheon, between mouthfuls of rabbit and vegetable marrow, I looked discreetly at Lord O. with the same question in mind. We lunched in the new dining-room on the first floor. The old dining-room on the ground floor, re-decorated as it was in 1801 for the Prince of Wales, is now no more than a museum, richly dark, heavy with mahogany furniture and louring family portraits.

There were present at luncheon with us, the three young Ottertons. Two pale boys with floppy locks, the older of which is due to return to his preparatory school at the end of the week, and a solemn girl with a round face like her father's and a bow in her hair. There is a Swiss woman employed to take care of these children. I did not like her in the least and wondered at Lady O. having thought to employ her. She speaks in the silvered tones of a practised hypocrite and has no light in her eyes. There is something soft and cruel about her, like a cat waiting to pounce. I fear for the children in her care, but then, I am nothing but an old fool with no understanding of the young and an over-active imagination which has only been enflamed by my morning spent watched over by the late Lord O. and his lady.

Lady O. was as gracious and as delightful as ever. She asked me kindly about my morning's work and I, in turn, congratulated her on the wonderful transformation she has so swiftly effected of the house, turning it from an exotic, dusty warehouse into an elegant abode. She seemed much gratified by my praise. Her eye is sure and her style unmatched. With the delicacy of her certain touch, she has most especially resurrected the hall in all its glory. Gone are the tables and chairs and carpets that could only have confused the eye, distracting it from the stupendous beauty of the proportions and the details of the carving. One chimney piece depicts the sacrifice to the goddess Diana and the other the sacrifice to Bacchus. Many an hour I would wish to spend in the now uncluttered beauty of the hall, gazing at these two admirable pieces of work.

Around the walls of the hall at the level of the ceilings on the rest of the ground floor there runs a narrow ledge, and opposite the front door, above this ledge, is a row of window embrasures through which it is possible to look down on the hall from a gallery running the length of it on the first floor. Her Ladyship told me that there is one small monkey of a man on the place (the estate carpenter, it would appear) who volunteered to skip fearlessly along this ledge with a bucket of soapy water and a scrubbing brush, in order to clean away the years of encrusted dirt. As he performed the task the whole household, with bated breath, admired him from below. His antics have earned him considerable recognition with the children for whom he has now become some kind of hero. The funny thing about him, Georgina opined when asked, was that he kept a small round hat on his head throughout the performance. For the most part at luncheon the children were seen and not heard, as was the governess.

After luncheon I thanked the Ottertons as graciously as I knew how for their kindnesses to me and, having confirmed that I would be more than grateful to return next week, I withdrew downstairs back to the Red Drawing-Room and to the uneasy company of Lilian Otterton and her husband. I expected to let myself quietly out of the house later in the afternoon and to wend my weary way home. It was a great surprise to me then, when about an hour later, the door of the muniments room suddenly opened, causing me, I have to admit, to start. Lady O. had come to see how I was getting on and to ask me if I was comfortable, whether I was warm enough or whether I would like Annie, her maid, to bring me a cup of tea. I thanked her profusely and explained that I had brought a thermos of tea with me. In these times of rationing, I feel that it is enough to be kindly invited to luncheon and that the least I can do is to provide my own tea.

Lady O. did not then immediately retire, but expressed an interest in my work. She flatters me by clearly having read the book I sent his Lordship. She did not know, she said, what papers the cabinet held and would be most interested to find out. So it was that instead of pursuing my research, I spent the next hour explaining to her Ladyship the contents and context of some of the letters which I had already seen before lunch. It was a delightful hour the memory of which I shall treasure.

At home I spent a quiet and thoughtful evening and, having a good deal to dwell on, felt contented in my own company, yet, as I eventually climbed the stairs, wearily carrying my old stone hot water bottle under my arm, I pondered on the fact that although I have much reading to do and my notes to sort out during the intervening days, next Tuesday seems so very far away.

## Sydney Otterton's diary

SEPTEMBER 25TH

Priscilla is furious with Peggy. She's threatening to ban the poor puppy from the house since it made a mess on the Aubusson carpet in the saloon and that bloody old fool Rakowski went in there without looking where he was going and walked in it. She didn't think it at all funny when I suggested that she ban Rakowski. I don't know what he was doing in the saloon in the first place. Apparently he went in there to admire the tapestries, when I thought he was meant to be getting on with his work in the muniments room. Priscilla seems to be so taken by him, she's forever showing him this and showing him that and laughing extravagantly at his jokes. I'm not sure I really trust the fellow. But I suppose Priscilla did have a right to be annoyed; after all she spends hours on her hands and knees mending that carpet and anyway I was already in bad odour because I'd gone and bought an African grey parrot called Julia. She lives in my dressing-room.

## Annie's diary

Her Ladyship's not at all pleased about the parrot. His Lordship has got it stuck in a great big cage in his dressing-room. It makes a dreadful mess, throwing seeds around and dropping them outside the cage on the floor. Her Ladyship says it will encourage mice and rats, but he just grins. Mind you he always has liked animals, but her Ladyship grumbles because she says he doesn't know how to look after them properly since Peggy made a mess in the saloon and *that* Mr Rakowski walked in it. We had the devil's own job trying to clean the carpet which is a very old and precious one, according to her Ladyship.

Anyway what with the new parrot and the new butler, this week has been all go. Mr and Mrs Cheadle moved into the flat with two children on Wednesday. Mr Cheadle looks like Mr Punch to me, with a bright red nose. As for Mrs Cheadle, I can't quite make her out. She doesn't say much and isn't prepared to work in the house. If you ask me, she looks a bit downtrodden, with black hair tied in a tight knot at the back of her head and an unsmiling, grey face. The children seem nice enough. There's a well-mannered girl who goes to the grammar school and a little boy. Then there's another girl who won't be here for long. She's married to a G.I. and is waiting to get to America. I don't much like the look of Mr Cheadle to tell the truth. I'd say that he was a bit too keen on the bottle. Her Ladyship snorted when she saw him. I heard her tell his Lordship that *she* should have been allowed to interview him before he was hired and that she'd very much like to know why he left his last place.

I was rather hoping his Lordship might have taken Bert on as an odd-job man but now it turns out that he has found someone who was in the war with him. I think he was his Lordship's driver and his Lordship is full bent on having him. Although he's more than likely soberer than Mr Cheadle, I don't think Bert would have been quite up to the job of butler, even with me supervising him. In any case, I wouldn't have wanted him living in the house.

SEPTEMBER 30TH

I can't say I'm really missing Bert. I know he wants me to go up there on my weekend off, but I think I'll have to make some excuse. If he won't come down here, he may have to find some other woman to do all his washing and ironing and darning. If he's lucky, he may find someone who is even prepared to marry him.

Father asked me at dinner time how I was getting on up at the house. He's obviously pleased to have me here to cook his Sunday dinner but I think he's surprised at my liking living in that great big cold house. I certainly have a kind of feeling there of independence in a way that I haven't properly known before. I have made my own rooms quite nice really. Mrs Gower gave me a lovely clock as a leaving present which I've put on my sitting-room mantelpiece and Mr Sydney has let me have some nice water-colours of the house. It's a little cold to be sure, but I see to it that one of the chars lays the fire for me every day. There's a huge old lift with a pulley in one corner of the house which is used, among other things, for bringing the logs up from the basement. I caught the two children trying to play in it the other day. In fact I don't suppose that even if he were here, Master Thomas who has gone back to school now, would be strong enough to pull it up with all three of them inside. I didn't want to tell his Lordship or her Ladyship what the children had been up to because I knew they would be for it. And I certainly wouldn't tell Mamzelle. She'd murder the pair of them as likely as not. All I did was to ask them if they were *supposed* to be playing with the lift. They knew darned well they weren't. Master Jamie just gave me an old-fashioned look and off they both went. I expect they'll be worrying in case I tell their parents.

## Georgina's exercise book

SEPTEMBER 25TH

Anie found us playing in the lift. I hope she doesn't tell Father. Mamzel killed Jamie's pet mous. She squoshed it behind the cubord to punish him. We think she's horrid. She says she is a frend of Queen Mary but Mummy says there must be some mistake. She says she's got a foto of some fairys which we can see if we are good. Jamie said it was a bluddy lie so she squished his mous.

## Sydney Otterton's diary

OCTOBER IST

I saw my mother yesterday and told her that I had decided to take my seat in the House of Lords. I really don't know why I bothered to tell her, perhaps just for something to say. She of course just gazed at me with her usual cold, unfocused stare. I wish I didn't have a mother and I wish the one I have would bloody well go away. She keeps saying she is going abroad and when she does go, we may at least be able to get something from letting her house.

When I come across my mother unexpectedly as I did

yesterday, walking stealthily through the hall like some ghastly predator, I feel as if I've been kicked in the gut. Give me the Bosch any day. I don't know what she was doing in the house, but Priscilla, of whom I have a feeling that she may even be a little wary, would have been furious if she had found her. Why is it that I would far rather come under enemy fire than confront my witch of a mother?

## Georgina's exercise book

OCTOBER 4TH

Mamzel chucked a French book at us this morning because we dont understand it. Major Dubbleday is much nicer. He makes us do sums and reading. He tells us a lot about India. Jamie wants to go there. We dont dare tell about the mous. I dont think Mummy would believe us.

## Zbigniew Rakowski's notebook

OCTOBER 24TH

If I were truthful, I would surely be obliged to admit that my weekly visits to Cranfield Park have begun to take over my life. My research there is proving to be both fruitful and interesting, but it is Lord and Lady Otterton themselves and the peculiar world which surrounds them that I find most deeply fascinating. It is as if I had entered an unreal country peopled with mad hatters and white rabbits, a country somehow divorced from the rest of the world, in which all the rules are different and where the bizarre holds sway. It is not just Lord and Lady O. who create this atmosphere, but the extraordinary galaxy of characters by whom they have managed to surround themselves, the apparently hermetically sealed society in which they all exist and the way they interact with each other, all somehow absorbed into the house and all in some curious manner dependent upon it, enclosed as they are in its all-embracing vastness. The children seem as natural and as normal here as they would be in any suburban villa or tied cottage, blissfully unaware of the strangeness of their surroundings, regarding their home, and no doubt their parents, as quite run of the mill. It is as if they and everyone else in it were part of the house, or at least belonged to it, just as the pictures on the wall and the Mortlake tapestries do.

I have not yet had the opportunity to make the acquaintance of Lilian, Lady O. whom I am told inhabits a dower house on the estate, and perhaps the occasion may never present itself, but as I sit in the Red Drawing-Room, watched over by her and her somewhat quaint-looking husband, I find my thoughts only too frequently wandering from a proper contemplation of the second half of the seventeenth century, from the scandals surrounding Wilkes and from the scurrilous behaviour at the time of one George Otterton, to the consideration of the house as it now is and of the peculiar assortment of people living there.

I have already said that Lord and Lady O. seem to me to be quite unsuited to one another, and the more I see of them, the more persuaded I am of the rightness of this judgement. In another, but similar fashion, I perceive Lord O., in his heedless quixotism, as being quite unsuited to the elegance of the surroundings in which he finds himself. Some might call him vulgar, as many of his ancestors have been, yet his quite unusual wit and maverick disposition would make of this a misnomer. Imagine a man laughing at a puppy fouling an antique carpet; imagine him furthermore laughing at a humble guest who has the great misfortune to step into the deplorable leavings of this unenlightened hound. Her Ladyship and her faithful maid, Annie, were fulsome in their apologies, and came rushing with newspaper for my shoes which I had so carefully cleaned that very morning, and with soapy water for the carpet.

Her Ladyship is, of course, ever delightful, intelligent, courteous and witty. Annie, her maid, appears to hold a position of the greatest importance in the house since she is undoubtedly in the confidence of both his Lordship and her Ladyship. She, I would wager, is the power behind the throne. She it will be who, in the years to come, hires and fires. She is a good-looking woman of about forty years old with a firm tread, a quiet confident manner and a twinkle in her hazel eyes. There is nothing at all servile about Annie and, whilst being clearly relied upon and liked by Lady O., she appears to share a conspiratorial sense of fun with Lord O. I even suspect that I caught her, bucket and cloth in hand, exchanging a humorous glance with him, which I will find hard to forgive, although to me she is always the personification of good manners. Or do I on occasion detect an underlying irony in her tone?

The butler who, I believe, should by tradition be the head of such a household as this, is not a man I would trust, and he is, I would opine from my superficial observation of the situation, somewhat in awe of Annie. He shambles around the table when he waits at luncheon and I aver that on one occasion, I heard him hiccough in my left ear as he offered me the dish of baked apples. It would be fair to describe his breath, emanating as it does in uneven gusts from a mouth half open, as rank, if not putrid. Her Ladyship, I fear, is a little short with him, almost haughty, although she can hardly be held to account for this, since the man is clearly wanting in refinement and must test the patience of one so well-bred as she. His Lordship looks unconcerned and would no doubt have found the hiccoughing tremendously droll had he been aware of it, since he clearly appreciates the incongruous, not to say the grotesque, and the Hogarthian appearance of his butler may well be an added source of amusement to him.

With this cast of characters, the children, the governess

and others with whom I am as yet unfamiliar, who can doubt the fascination that this household has for me? Who can doubt that, as I return to my labours on a Tuesday morning, I feel a little elated, curious and somewhat excited to know what may have happened during the past week, and eager to divine the future? What is going to happen next? What indeed?

Her Ladyship has made a sitting-room for herself in a corner apartment. It is a delightful room, known, on account of the magnificent scenes of the chase depicted on the eighteenth-century English tapestries adorning the walls, as the Hunting Room. This is one of the most delicate rooms in the house, and the smallest on the ground floor. When I had finished my work yesterday, I was most kindly invited to partake of a cup of tea in that exquisite room. As I crossed the threshold a little warily, I felt obliged to enquire as to the whereabouts of the recalcitrant cur. 'Ma'am,' I ventured, 'I tread in trepidation lest his Lordship may have allowed his young dog to step this way before me.' The dog, she assured me, was under no circumstances allowed in the Hunting Room.

Over tea, Lady O. enquired kindly about my writing and appeared to be particularly interested in the modest novels I have penned. I made a mental note to bring her, on my next visit and in the nature of a grateful offering, my most recent work of fiction. We then became engrossed in what was, for me, a most stimulating discussion of the merits of various new writers, when, all of a sudden, the door burst open and in came his Lordship, preceded of course, by his bounding puppy dog. I saw the interruption as a sign that the time had come for me to take my leave.

# *Annie's diary*

My room is really looking very nice. Her Ladyship found a pretty faded blue brocade bedspread in the old linen press on the back stairs. I think she hardly looked at it, but handed it to me, saying it was for Mamzelle who had been complaining that she didn't have one. I didn't much care for the one on my bed so I gave that one to Mamzelle and kept the blue one for myself. It goes much better in my room and it can't make any difference to anyone else. Beside my clock on the mantelpiece, I've got some photographs of the Gower family in a nice leather frame they gave me, and one of Father in his Sunday best, taken at one of my sisters' weddings. Yesterday afternoon I went for a walk. It was a beautiful day and I picked some autumn leaves which I have put in a jug on the table. Her Ladyship has done a beautiful arrangement in a large white urn she's put on a tall column in the hall. She takes endless trouble with the flowers and they are always lovely and very natural.

Now I have had a letter from Bert. He must be really missing me because he even suggested that I should find out if there is a job for him here, just as if the idea was all his own and that I hadn't suggested it in the first place. The only trouble is, I think he may have left it too late. I suppose he could have had Mr Johnson's job, but nothing would make his Lordship get rid of Mr Johnson when he's only just arrived. In any case his Lordship seems to spend half the day lolling about down in the boot room, talking about the war with him. Mr Johnson thinks the world of his Lordship and says he was very brave, which I don't doubt. They remind you of a pair of schoolboys when they're together. Of course his Lordship must be the younger of the two by a long way.

I quite like Mr Johnson. He comes from Yorkshire and is very blunt, but he likes a joke and seems to get on with his work despite his Lordship talking to him all the time. And he had a thing or two to say about Mamzelle. She was very rude to him, expecting him to clean her shoes as if she were the lady of the house. He soon told her where she could get off and advised her to clean her own b— shoes. I couldn't help laughing to myself about that.

As for Bert, I'm not quite sure yet what to do about him. I certainly won't answer his letter for a day or two. I can't think about him at the moment anyway because I've got too much on my mind. There's Lilian, Lady Otterton, for instance. She gave me the fright of my life the other day.

I'd just been in my sitting-room, doing some ironing for her Ladyship and was about to take it down to her room when I heard someone walk past down the passage. At first I didn't think twice, but supposed it was Mr Cheadle or Mamzelle or one of the children, but then I looked at the time (it was half past eleven in the morning) and I realised the children would be doing their lessons and, by rights, Mr Cheadle should have been in the butler's pantry, cleaning the silver or getting ready for lunch. In any case I felt a little unnerved because I thought the footsteps stopped for a moment outside my room. Now, if there is one thing I don't like, it is the idea of being watched or spied on. After a moment I decided to open the door and see who it could be, and there she was, as white as a ghost, walking back towards me down the passage. I said, 'Good morning, M'lady,' and she just stared at me, leaning forward a bit, with her head on one side, and after a long time said, 'Ah, Annie. I thought it was you. I should like to talk to you some time.' Then she turned on her heel and walked slowly away along the corridor towards the schoolroom. I don't know if she went in there, or if she just went downstairs and left the house. Neither his Lordship nor her Ladyship mentioned anything about her having been here, but if his Lordship had seen her, I'm sure we would all have heard about it.

Yesterday afternoon when I came in from my walk I found a note pushed under my door. I have no idea how it got there unless *she* has been back again. It crossed my mind that Mr Cheadle could have put it there but he says he didn't. Not that I would necessarily believe anything he said. I went into the dining-room the other day for her Ladyship, to fetch a handbag she had left in there and I caught him drinking port straight out of the decanter. He put the decanter back on the sideboard as quick as winking when he saw me and began to polish it with a grubby handkerchief. Then he said he was very busy, as if I had gone in there on purpose to get in his way. I didn't say anything and I won't say anything.

So I found this note in Lilian, Lady Otterton's spiky handwriting, written in purple ink. She has summoned me to go and see her one afternoon but she doesn't say why. There will be no need, she says, to tell anyone that she has been in touch with me. I'm wondering whether I ought to tell his Lordship or her Ladyship, but it would only make them angry. Her Ladyship says her mother-in-law is a terrible woman and that because of her, Master Sydney (as was) had a dreadful childhood. Mental cruelty, her Ladyship calls it, and then she says there was no love and no discipline. She doesn't have to tell me about that, and as for mental cruelty, the poor lad used to be whipped by the servants for nothing if *she* was in one of her tempers. Everyone on the place knew about it and we all felt sorry for Master Sydney, and for his late Lordship for that matter. I think most of us would forgive Master Sydney anything.

Perhaps I'll wait and see what Lady Lilian wants before I say a word to anyone. Mind you, I can't say I'm looking forward to going to see her. It crossed my mind to pretend I never found the note. If she gave it to Mr Cheadle, I could get away with that, but not if she put it under the door herself. I thought of going down there this afternoon, but it was a lovely afternoon, so I decided to go for my usual walk instead. I may go tomorrow.

It was raining today, so I still haven't been to see *Lilian* as I stayed in to write a few letters instead, and to mend a couple of Father's shirts. I think that rather than go this week, I'll talk to Father about it on Sunday and see what he says. He's very wise, but then he doesn't say much.

## Georgina's exercise book

OCTOBER 30TH

We don't see are grandmother very offen. She is fritning and looks quite like a wich. Jamie says she's spooky. Mr Dubbleday makes us learn tables *all the time*.

## Sydney Otterton's diary

OCTOBER 30TH

The best thing to have happened lately is the arrival of Johnson. I don't know how long he will stay though, because he keeps talking about emigrating to Australia. I would have thought he might be a bit old to think of doing that, but he says there is nothing for him in this bankrupt country, and he seems pretty resentful about the war which he was damn lucky to survive. He certainly had one or two close shaves. He feels that it took the best years of his life and that he received scant thanks for his efforts. Then he came home only to discover that his woman had deserted him for a German P.O.W., so with no wife and no family to tie him down and only a sister he never sees in Skipton, he has nothing and no one to keep him here. I'll miss him dreadfully if he goes. It's bloody useful having him about the place as, not only is he able to do almost anything from stoking the boiler and mending the car, to plastering and wiring, but if I get a pair of parakeets I've seen, he is going to do up an old Victorian birdcage I've found in the basement. It's a magnificent thing shaped like a pagoda with a fountain for the birds to drink from. I haven't told Priscilla about that yet. I think she would be rather annoyed. As it is, she thinks I spend too much money on animals and too much time talking to Johnson. He's someone to talk to about the war so we are bound to spend quite a lot of time reminiscing, but Priscilla insists that I'm preventing him from doing his work, besides which she thinks I've got enough animals. She seems to think that animals stand in the way of my doing other things which she regards as more important. It's true to say that she does work very hard to keep the house going. I sometimes feel quite useless beside her. Despite her earlier reservations, it is quite clear to us all that she loves the house and it is quite clear to me that without her, it would never have been possible to make the move. She is wonderful. Only last week, she had the brilliant idea of hanging two of the Barlows on either side of the double doors between the hall and the saloon, where they fit exactly and counterbalance the windows opposite. That huge ostrich and the cassowary with the monkey on the pedestal behind him both look as if they were made to go there. Perhaps Priscilla thinks that with so many painted animals, we don't need real ones. I like both.

Still no sign of my mother leaving. And not only has she not left, but she has taken to wandering around the house whenever she feels like it. I've told Cheadle not to let her in. I've no idea what she wants, whether she just wants to help herself to a few things, which I somehow doubt, or whether there is some more sinister motive. I can't help blaming her for the fact that I'm finding it so difficult to settle down. I know it's partly because of the war, but still, it's strange because I was so sure that if and when we moved into the house, all my restlessness would disappear and I would begin to be able to concentrate on it and the farm. The truth is, there are just so many problems involved in both, that it's hard to know where to begin. And yet the thing about the house is that it acts like a kind of drug so that when I'm feeling really hopeless, I'll either have a gin and tonic, or I'll walk round it, drinking in its atmosphere, looking in long-forgotten cupboards, climbing up to the roof to admire the view. It gives me a peculiar sense of freedom and an extraordinary feeling of security although God alone knows why when the rain is coming through everywhere, so much plaster is crumbling and there are damp patches in half the rooms. If I concentrated on the dilapidation, I'd want to shoot myself, but then Priscilla has got the ground-floor rooms looking splendid. Better than they ever looked in my childhood. She instinctively knows how to hang the pictures and arrange the furniture to best advantage.

I've proved my legitimacy and had my writ of summons and am beginning to look forward to taking my seat in the House; perhaps things will get better then and life will seem more real. At the moment nothing appears to be solid or permanent and I sometimes feel as if I were only a figment of my own imagination.

## Annie's diary

NOVEMBER 4TH

I couldn't get Father to say much at dinner-time about what I should do about *Lilian*, but I got the idea that he didn't really want me to go and see her. Then Father has always been one, as I say, to walk away from trouble. He admits as much himself. In fact he frequently claims that he makes *tracks*, as he would say, at the first sign of an argument. All I could get out of him was that I should remember who my employers are and who is not my employer. That's right, I suppose, but then in one way, I'm quite curious to know what she wants. And then again, I don't want to find her suddenly wandering about outside my room, which I probably will if I don't obey her. His Lordship says he's told Mr Cheadle not to let her in, not that that will make any difference. She'll come in through the basement or any way she wants. In any case, I doubt she'd pay any attention to Mr Cheadle. As a matter of fact, I wouldn't mind seeing the pair of them together. Mr Cheadle with his big red nose and all that nasty spittle in the corners of his mouth, and her Ladyship with her white face, black hooded eyes and ghostly stare.

The other day Mr Cheadle wanted to know what the matter was with Lady Lilian. He had the nerve to ask me if she drank. I wasn't saying anything. Talk about the pot calling the kettle black.


## Zbigniew Rakowski's notebook

There is no doubt about it that the house has a hold over each and every one of these people. And dare I suggest that it is even beginning to exercise a mysterious control over myself. I who regard myself as beholden to no one, enslaved to nothing, a poor immigrant from a beleaguered country to which I shall now probably never return. I have ever seen myself as unattached, impartial and have indeed considered this to be a peculiar advantage, most especially so to one of my chosen profession: a writer, and most particularly a historian must needs retain his detachment. Yet now, here I sit, eternally, it seems, watched over by Lilian, Lady Otterton, and what do I do under her very nose, under her disapproving eye? Instead of working as I should, instead of poring over and examining minutely the wealth of letters which have so fortunately fallen into my undeserving hands, the study of which would be so richly fruitful for my *œuvre*, instead of doing thus, I spend the time fantasising about the lives of the present Lord and Lady Otterton, dwelling (a little too lengthily, some might even submit) on the contemplation of her Ladyship's periwinkle eyes, as the French would say, her swan-like neck and sparkling wit. I, poor, humble gnome that I am, am hardly used to the attentions of so fine a lady, nevertheless, when at home last week, I was not a little disconcerted to discover on checking through my notes for the Whig aristocracy, that these are far too generously interwoven with musings on Cranfield and, as one might say, those who sail in her. Yet here in the Red Drawing-Room, do I find myself once again at their mercy.

It has however crossed my mind that whilst I am at work, it is possibly no waste of time to make notes on whatever it is about the place that might capture my attention. It is not beyond the realms of possibility that I might, at some later date, consider using not merely the historical notes I have collated, but also the material I have recorded with regard to the present day. Thus I might use it in creating some slight work of fiction. Perhaps even, the thought passes through my mind as I write, a murder story. This is not a genre at which I have so far tried my hand, but everything in this house is conducive to thoughts along these lines. *The Corpse on the Carpet* might I entitle my work. Or perhaps, *The Body in the Bathroom, Bloodstains in the Boudoir, Murder in the Mansion, Death in the Drawing-Room* . . . The imagination races. In my thick-coming fancies I can already see that blood-stained Aubusson carpet, and Annie, always Annie, quiet and enigmatic, laughter in her eyes, a bucket of cold water and a cloth in her hands, ever ready to wipe away the evidence of something about which she knows far more than she should. Indeed, with a study of the Whig aristocracy and a murder story simultaneously researched and published in the same year, I could truly claim to have killed two birds with one stone, and, no doubt, would be the less impoverished for it.

NOVEMBER 7TH

I have to confess to having perhaps been a little too extravagant in my thoughts whilst I was at work in the muniments room at Cranfield yesterday morning. At lunch Lord Otterton appeared to be very much concerned with taking his seat in the House of Lords and consequently most of the conversation turned on that subject. As I looked at her Ladyship, I could not help but recollect the ugly imaginings that had been mine so shortly before, as I envisaged her poor mangled body spread-eagled on the Aubusson carpet in the saloon, her blood so mercilessly spilt. So strong was my emotion at this remembrance, that it almost behoved me to take her hand and reassure her that she was of course in no real danger. But she quite naturally was unconcerned and certainly appeared heedless as she chattered gaily about his Lordship's arrangements or offered me a second helping of rabbit. After lunch, somewhat chastened by the contemplation of my own impertinence, I returned to the muniments room and was able to concentrate on some very interesting letters of Horace Walpole's which can only be of great benefit to my work in hand.

## Annie's diary

NOVEMBER 16TH

There's a dreadful row going on between Mamzelle and Mr Cheadle. I'm not saying anything, mind. It's all about a tray which has been left on the table on the landing outside the schoolroom for four or five days now. Mamzelle says that it's Cheadle's job to take it back to the kitchen, but he just calls her every name under the sun and refuses to take it. I've seen the children giggling about it. I think they must hate that Mamzelle because she's never very nice to them. To tell the truth, I think she's as mad as a March hare. She's always so polite when she sees her Ladyship, but I can't help thinking that her Ladyship must see through her soon. I feel really sorry for the children. She fills them up with a lot of funny stories. The other day Georgina asked me if I believed in God. Now I wasn't telling anybody about whether or not I believe in God, so I just asked her why she wanted to know. And she came out with an extraordinary story.

That Mamzelle took the children for their walk one afternoon and they ended up going into the church. Now she told the children, that if they were very very good and went behind the altar with her, they would be able to see God. See God, my foot! But, on the other hand, if they were wicked, they wouldn't be able to see Him. Only good people could see God. So they all went behind the altar and of course they didn't see any god, or gods or goddesses, but that terrible woman fell on the floor and began to wail and to chant, claiming that she had her arms around God's ankles. Apparently Master Jamie whispered to his sister that Mamzelle was a b— fool and that she was only pretending, but I think Georgina was really worried that she might not be able to see God because she was too wicked. Then on Thursday morning her Ladyship happened to ask me to take the horologist to the schoolroom where there's a grandfather clock, and there was Mamzelle, for some reason telling the children that she had a photograph of some fairies she might or might not choose to show them. I felt quite foolish standing there and I can't imagine what Mr May can have thought. In future he is to come once a week to wind all the clocks in the house. Anyway, I was given to understand that Mamzelle was supposed to be teaching the children French, not telling them a lot of twaddle about fairies. I can't help noticing that most of the time, the children escape from the schoolroom as soon as they can and disappear somewhere in the house. Then it can be very difficult to find them and I've seen that woman pounding up and down the stairs shouting for them, purple in the face and puffing. I dread to think what happens when she finds them. I doubt she'll think it very easy to control Master Thomas when he gets back for the holidays. I should think he'd play her up something awful. And serve her right, to my mind. Anyway, I wonder what the outcome will be about the tray. I'm certainly not going to take it down for any of them.

In fact, I find there's something creepy about both Mamzelle and Lady Lilian. It's hard to know which of them is the worst. In the end I did go and see Lady Lilian. I went one afternoon like she said, not that I wanted to, so I put it off for a while. When I arrived at the back door, I found Doris, her maid, in the kitchen. She's a queer one that Doris with her scrawny figure and long face and all that, what I call common, peroxide hair. I wouldn't be surprised if the pair of them didn't dope themselves together. So Doris looks at me when she opens the door as if I had no business there. Well I could tell Doris a thing or two and I could tell her, furthermore, that my father has been at Cranfield far longer than she has so she needn't think she can come one over me. Doris came shortly after Lilian and his late Lordship were married. I seem to remember that her Ladyship always had difficulty in keeping servants which was hardly surprising. No one could ever understand why Doris Batty stayed so loyal. Two of a kind I suppose.

I expect her Ladyship must have heard someone at the back door, or else she heard voices, in any case, there *she* was, all of a sudden, in the kitchen. 'Ah Annie,' she says, just like she did when I met her in the corridor. Then she beckons me with her bony finger to follow her through to the front of the house. I don't know who is supposed to do the cleaning there, but I couldn't help noticing that the house was in a dreadful mess. We went into what must be her sitting-room. There were papers, old envelopes, dirty glasses and half-filled ashtrays everywhere and so many ornaments and so much furniture that there was hardly room to swing a cat. Never mind cats, as I came into the room, a fat old corgi with one eye growled at me from an armchair covered in dog's hair. Her Ladyship sank down into a great big sofa, stretched out a thin white hand and slowly stroked the cushion beside her. I felt quite a shudder run down my spine when she said, 'I'd like to have you next to me.'

I wasn't going to sit next to her on that darned sofa and have her stroke me, not for all the tea in China. Instead, I sat on an upright chair opposite her and as I sat down I heard the floorboards creaking outside the door. I have very sharp hearing and I wouldn't mind betting my bottom dollar that Doris was out there eavesdropping. I needed some Dutch courage so I just kept thinking of Father, and him saying, 'Remember who your employers are.' I thought of Dolly too and her telling me to keep a diary.

And all the time she goes on stroking the cushion beside her and sort of staring through me without ever smiling. Then she suddenly says in a grand voice, 'I'm leaving here you know.' Then she starts to tell me how ill-used she's been by Master Sydney after all she has done for him. She adored her son, she said, worshipped him. Not that I believe a word of it. And now, she told me, he had turned against her, and all because of his wife. She narrowed her eyes when she said that. 'And you work for her Ladyship, I gather,' she said icily and all sarcastic. I wanted to get up and walk out. To tell the truth, I began to wish I had never gone to see her in the first place. Anyway, the long and the short of it was that she wanted me to spy for her and to send her what she called a regular 'bulletin', only she pronounced it as if it were a foreign word, for which she would see that I was 'hand-somely rewarded'. I could hardly believe my ears, but then, after all the talk there's been about her, I shouldn't really have been surprised. I said I wasn't sure I ought to do that, and then, as I was leaving, she caught hold of my wrist, pushed her face right up to mine and said, 'Do as I tell you child,' before adding mysteriously, 'There are things to be looked for.' Then she pressed a piece of paper into my hand on which I later discovered she had written the address of her bank! I couldn't get out of the place quickly enough and, as for the expression on Doris's face as she saw me out again through the back door, well, if looks could kill!

## Sydney Otterton's diary

NOVEMBER 23RD

On Tuesday I took my seat in the House of Lords. They were debating demobilisation and on Wednesday Lord Methuen spoke on the preservation of historic buildings. I can hardly have been the only person in the place who felt a knife turning in the wound when he said that present-day taxation makes the occupancy of large country houses virtually impossible and that if they are to survive, they will have to be put to a new use.

It was a funny feeling really, being there, stepping into my father's shoes in yet another way. His was a modestly distinguished career and there are a lot of his friends still in the House who were kind enough to put themselves out to welcome me, the new boy. I certainly felt like a new boy but hope that as time goes by, I shall be able to live up to my father and to achieve some minor success myself.

On Tuesday the House rose at around half past five and then two pals of my father's, old Bodger Florey and Bumpkin Exebridge, asked me to go and have a drink with them; they both seemed far more concerned about the inconvenience of sitting in the Royal Gallery while the Commons occupies the Lords, than they were about affairs of state. No doubt it'll be a year or two before the lords get back to the Lords and all the bomb damage to the Palace of Westminster is repaired. I hate the sight of bomb-flattened London, it's terrible to see. So, feeling a bit flat after swearing my allegiance to King and country in such high-flown language and then listening to Bodger and Bumpkin banging on about nothing much, I decided to go round and see Tony. He was his usual cheerful self and we went out on the town. I'm afraid we got dreadfully drunk and I slept some of it off on his sofa before driving home in the small hours. Priscilla was not best pleased.

The next day I had a bloody great bill from my solicitors for nothing much that they had done, as far as I can see, and then, on Thursday, I had an unbelievably gloomy meeting with my bank manager. The farm in Essex still hasn't found a buyer. I have to admit that in the Lords that afternoon, I found it pretty difficult to listen to what was being said; my mind kept on returning to my appalling financial situation and wondering how the hell it's ever going to improve. No wonder I feel like going out and getting drunk with Tony. In actual fact I was glad to get back to Cranfield, despite Priscilla's frosty welcome. It is a private haven for all the problems that attend it.

A most extraordinary thing happened while I was in London on Thursday, and perhaps it was because of this that Cranfield felt so safe on my return. It was Annie who reported seeing a furniture van outside the Dower House when she walked down to the farm to see her father after lunch. When she got back she told Priscilla who made a few enquiries and discovered that my mother had just left, like that, without so much as a word to anyone, presumably taking the monstrous Doris with her. God alone knows where she's gone, but it feels to me as if a huge black cloud has lifted. I don't expect to hear from her for some time and certainly hope not to. Of course Priscilla is immensely relieved too and has quite forgiven my earlier misdemeanours.

I asked Annie if she had seen my mother at all recently. It

struck me that she gave me a funny look, but all she said was, 'Now you know I wouldn't have anything to do with *that* Lady Otterton.' My mother is the sort of woman who might easily have tried to put Annie against us or even to take her away. But then she doesn't know Annie as I do. Annie is a very intelligent woman and I trust her completely, even if she is a bit of a dark horse. She's always stood up for me which my mother probably knows and which is why my mother would, I suspect, so love to destroy her and to turn her against us.

## Letter from Annie to Dolly

NOVEMBER 25TH, 1945

Dear Dolly,

I'm sorry to have been so long in writing but I think you can partly blame yourself for not having heard from me. Do you remember telling me that I ought to write a diary? Well, that is just what I have been doing and I'm afraid it rather puts me off letter-writing because I feel I've already said everything there is to say in the diary. Mind you, with all the goings on here, there is a lot to tell. Besides, there is something odd about the house that makes me want to keep a diary.

Lilian, Lady Otterton has left Cranfield at last. She didn't even tell his Lordship when or where she was going, but I think we are all very relieved now she has gone.

Bert is quite cross with me because I haven't been back to see him since I left the Gowers. I expect I'll go up there before Christmas, but what with one thing and another I've been very busy.

There's a Mr Johnson come to work here now. He was in the war with his Lordship and seems very nice. He comes from Yorkshire.

Father is keeping well as I hope you and Fred and the children are. Do write soon with your news.

With love from
Annie


## Sydney Otterton's diary

It wasn't possible to get the shoot off the ground this year, but I should very much like to get it going again next year, if only in a modest sort of way. Whatever happens, one of these days I'll have to face up to doing something about Summers. I suppose he spends his days breeding ferrets and killing rabbits, but with precious little to do during the war and pheasant shooting suspended, I think he just got idler and idler. I sent Peggy to him for a while; he was supposed to house-train her and train her as a gun dog, but I rather think he failed on both those counts. Despite their having been left in peace for the last few years (or perhaps because of it), there are precious few pheasants around. My father used to raise quite a lot of them before the war but the stock is sadly depleted, and, as for next year, well I certainly haven't got any spare cash to spend on putting pheasants down. I don't like Summers's sly look, and never have. The children do a very good imitation of him riding his bicycle with both knees pointing outwards at a ridiculous angle. But I'll have to be careful how I handle him, because his mother-in-law, his wife and his sister-in-law all work in the house and Priscilla, who finds all three of them invaluable, doesn't want them upset. I sometimes panic at the thought that all these people, whether I like it or not, are dependent on me. I can barely afford their wages and I'm not at all sure how to cope with them, especially people like Summers who were employed by my parents before the war. I can't just kick them out. Thank God for the likes of Annie and old Jerrold who loves his cows, and for Johnson.

Annie has found someone called Miss Wheel whom Priscilla has employed to do some sewing. God knows where she hails from, but she sits all day with a sewing machine in a room on the top floor, cutting up old curtains and making them into new ones, fabricating cushions out of my grandmother's wedding dress and covering dressing-tables with worn brocade. Priscilla is delighted with her. Although she joins us for lunch and is round and smiling and rosy, she never speaks but to say please or thank you, and she reminds me of some sort of benign sorceress, working away silently in an upstairs room. What happens to her in the evenings, I have no idea. Apparently she is to be with us for a fortnight and may return again at a later date. From where, I wonder, did the all-powerful Annie whistle her up?

I feel a bit more cheerful since I've started going to the Lords. If I stay here all the time, I begin to panic about everything as I see myself drawn daily further into a quicksand of debt and decay. Then I go to London, spend a bit of money, which cheers me up, go to the Lords, see a few friends, and come back here refreshed.

## *Zbigniew Rakowski's notebook*

DECEMBER 4TH

This evening I find that there is a great emptiness in my crabbed old soul and indeed I have no difficulty in divining the cause of this most gnawing malaise. Love is like a canker that eats into man's very being and where that love must be hidden, subsumed, suppressed, there must be exquisite pain. For the last two months and more, I have had the good fortune to be a regular visitor to Cranfield, there quietly to pursue my researches not only into the past, but also into the present. There I have repeatedly eaten rabbit and gooseberries and stewed apples at the table of one who must be the most elegant, the wittiest and the most intelligent lady in the land. Lady Otterton has graced me with her friendship, she has been so kind as to listen to the meanderings of a dreary old Pole, nay, she has laughed at my jokes, encouraged me in my work and inspired in me a passion quite unsuited to the occupancy of my old frame. If I am to be truthful, I must admit to having lingered over my work in the hope of prolonging my tenuous relationship with this most enchanting lady. But, alas, and woe indeed is me, the time has now come to an end when I can reasonably expect to continue to visit Cranfield on a regular basis.

With her usual kindness, Lady Otterton, when I bade her farewell this evening, assured me that I was always welcome to return should I require any further examination of the Otterton papers. 'And I do wish you would call me Priscilla,' she added. I, with a lump in my throat, could only reply, 'Thank you, Ma'am.' 'Any time you like,' she added vaguely so that I was unsure as to whether she referred to my calling her by her first name or to my continued visits. She insisted that she would be delighted to hear how I was getting on with my book and begged me to keep in touch which I, with some degree of presumption perhaps, take to be an invitation to write to her. This I shall surely do since there would certainly be no harm in the exercise and the correspondence would unquestionably allay, if not entirely alleviate the ache in my poor shrivelled heart.

For it is with a truly heavy heart that I now contemplate the long winter ahead, shut up as I shall be in my small hovel, with no outings in view, but the occasional visit to the public library, the occasional trip to town, there to pursue my researches, and the twice-weekly bicycle ride to the shops. To make matters worse, at this time of year the day barely breaks ere the night draws in. Similarly, in the fanciful mood in which I find myself, I imagine a weak winter sun rising within me to spread its watery light over the rejuvenated landscape of my soul, a light to be so soon, so swiftly, drowned by darkness. I know that I am an old fool whose brain has probably been addled by years of loneliness, and it is this loneliness which provokes me to write as I do, for what is there to look forward to now, but the Christmas visit of my bossy daughter with her mewling child and tiresome husband? Why should I not indulge myself a little with flights of delicious imaginings?

But it will not be only her Ladyship whom I shall miss, for I shall miss the house itself, that large mass of red brick, so deceptively clumsy at first sight, so subtly elegant on further examination. Only the monstrous *porte cochère*, that clings to the front of the house with the tenacity of a misshapen barnacle to the side of a boat, destroys the simplicity of the original design. It was most unfortunately put there in late Victorian times by the present Lord Otterton's grandfather, so that her Ladyship's carriage might in inclement weather drive right up to the front door. In order to make way for this horrible protrusion, Leoni's gracefully balustraded steps were removed and placed incongruously below the *porte cochère*, where they appear to be at a loss as to their purpose.

How can I, after so short a time, have come to love this magnificent great house almost as though it had become part of me, or I of it? I shall even miss the late Lord Otterton and his lady, watching over me as I work, for I have begun to feel at home in the Red Drawing-Room where I had made a comfortable corner for myself and which seemed to welcome me anew each week as I arrived. Of the hall, I will surely dream.

# *Letter from Annie to Dolly*

Dear Dolly

This afternoon the tree was put up in the hall. Just as it used to be before the war. It took three men to fix it in place. I couldn't help thinking of you and Wilfie and Cis and the others, and of days gone by. You should have seen his Lordship. He was all smiles. I don't think I have ever seen him look so happy. He seems much more cheerful since his mother left, and I can't say I blame him. He must feel that at last the house is really his.

I'm not sure how they would have managed without Mr Johnson. He was the one who worked out what to do, with his Lordship walking around behind him in a right state of excitement, talking about mending tanks and saying that anyone who could mend a tank, could find a way of putting up a b— Christmas tree! Mr Johnson didn't say a word mind you, but just got on with the job. He looks like a very strong man.

I'll write again after Christmas and tell you all the news. I just had to tell you about the tree. Father is well, but I'm worried about what will happen when he retires next year. He'll certainly miss his cows, but I suppose he'll spend more time in his garden.

Happy Christmas & New Year to you all.

Love from
Annie

# Sydney Otterton's diary

Our first Christmas in the house. God knows how Johnson and the others managed to fix the tree, but they did. The children were thrilled; they'd never seen anything like it and Priscilla managed brilliantly with the decorations and the estate party on Christmas Eve, and everything else for that matter. With two huge fires lit on either side of the hall, the place looked wonderful; you could have said it was just like old times except that it wasn't because my mother has at last been exorcised. It was like a proper, old-fashioned family Christmas such as I have never seen. Quite a lot of drinking went on, but then you'd expect that at Christmas. I think Priscilla was very pleased with how well she'd managed on a shoe-string and by how much everyone seemed to appreciate it all; in fact she was so pleased that she even melted a bit towards Peggy and allowed her into the library on Christmas Day. I reckon old Jerrold had a tear in his eye when he thanked me for his perennial bottle of port. He wished me luck. I don't care to think about him retiring which I'm afraid is due to happen at the end of this year and will be just one more problem. But never mind, I've decided to go into the New Year feeling optimistic. I can't help thinking that one way or another it will all work out, and in any case, it's hardly worth being kept awake about death duties night after night when it looks as if it will be months or possibly years before we even get probate.

# 1946

# Annie's diary

Everything here seems to have been running quite smoothly since Christmas. There don't seem to have been any silly rows with Mamzelle, like the one about the schoolroom tray. Lord knows how long that tray stayed on the landing. It was her Ladyship who took it down in the end, making it quite clear as she did so what she thought of both Mr Cheadle and Mamzelle. I don't suppose the pair of them have addressed a word to one another since, though. No one can stick Mamzelle. Even Miss Wheel, who is a very kind person, was quite put out by her when she was here. She thought she was cruel to the children. And as for Mr Johnson, he just pulls her leg whenever he sees her. He generally says something about his being no more than a bootblack and she looks ready to burst a blood vessel.

Of course there was one thing that didn't work out very well over Christmas and that was my visit to Bert. He was quite upset that I hadn't been up to see him sooner, although he must understand that what with the bus fare, the train fare and then another bus fare at the other end, it costs me quite a bit to get there. It was different when I was coming back from there to see Father, because Mrs Gower used to pay my fare. I suppose I should be sorry for Bert as he is quite lonely. He won't go down to the pub for company because he says it's a waste of money, so he sits on his own in that cottage every evening and all week-end. In any case, he brought it up again about getting a job at Cranfield and I didn't know how to discourage him although I tried. I don't want Bert hanging around me for the rest of my life. I told him that if he was lonely, he'd better get along on and find someone else. But he didn't like the idea and then, blow me down, if he didn't ask me when Father was due to retire. So now he's thinking of applying for Father's job, which I call a bit of cheek. I doubt he knows one end of a cow from the other. Anyway he wasn't very pleased with me by the time I left, so perhaps he'll change his mind.

Mr Johnson is talking about going to Australia. He says they haven't enough people over there, so they're encouraging British ex-servicemen to emigrate. It'll be a shame if he goes though, because he's a very nice man and a hard worker. I expect his Lordship will do his best to dissuade him, but he keeps telling me about these assisted passages the Australian government are offering. He says it would only cost him £10 to get there and when he got there, they'd find him a job. It all sounds like so many castles in the air to me, and I've told him as much.

Then this morning I had a nasty shock. As I say, things have been running quite smoothly since Christmas. His Lordship and her Ladyship have been seeing eye to eye and even Peggy seems to have come to heel, but this morning I had this horrid letter from *Lilian* with which she enclosed a cheque. I was just thinking that we had all really begun to forget about her and to behave as if she didn't exist, but of course she's out there somewhere making her wicked plans. I know it's awful to think of such a thing, but I honestly suspect that his Lordship would be quite glad if she died. His Lordship's cousins came up to stay over the New Year and Mrs Coppleston (that's his Lordship's first cousin) said to me, 'Annie, my aunt is an evil woman, you must never do anything she asks.' It was almost as if she knew what was coming. But she said she could tell me a thing or two about his Lordship's childhood which would make my blood curdle. And I don't doubt it.

I really don't know what to do about this letter. I could show it to his Lordship, but then it would only cause an awful to-do. Or I could tell her Ladyship or wait till I see Father and discuss it with him. That is what I will probably do.

Meanwhile I'll keep it with this diary locked in a drawer in my bedroom. I don't want it to be found by any prying eyes. There are so many people around in the house all the time that you can never be sure. That dreadful spiky, violet handwriting on the envelope. I knew at once it was from her.

JANUARY 16TH

Father, who doesn't usually say much, thinks I should tell his Lordship about his mother's letter, but I'm not quite so sure that it's a good idea. He also says that I must return the money at once, which of course I have already done. I had to send it to the bank in London which is where the letter came from and the only address she gives. I'm just a bit worried about what she'll do next when she finds out what I've done. Father doesn't think I should answer her letter at all. 'Just you keep out of trouble my girl,' was what he said. He claims that nothing Lilian, Lady Otterton might do would ever surprise him. He didn't think Cranfield was going to be shot of her as easily as all that. She'd be haunting the place for a while to come in his view. He didn't think she could ever have been a happy woman and she could certainly not have been happy at Cranfield, and yet the place seems to have as strong a hold over her as it does over everyone else. I never heard Father talk so much.

## Georgina's exercise book

JANUARY 16TH

Mamzelle is horrid and we hate her. She's allways nasty to Jamie because she hates him so she broke a baloon he got at Christmas on perpous. She spent ages sqashing it on the bed with her hands and then it burst in her face. Jamie laughed. He is very daring. We wish she would go because she spoils everything. Thomas told her she was fat so she ataked him

63

with the toasting fork and stopped him having tea. I think Annie hates her to. We like Annie best. She's nice to us.

## Sydney Otterton's diary

My spirits have been wonderfully buoyed up since Christmas; even the eternal grey weather has failed to get me down. The house is looking better than I can remember it and Priscilla is happy, permanently occupied with further improvements; the children are jolly, and everything seems to be getting better. In spite of rationing which I suppose will last for ever, we've had several friends to stay, each bearing pathetic little parcels of butter and sugar, and the house is alive again. But best of all, I've lost my mother. I haven't heard a squeak out of her since she left. I don't even know what country she is in. For all I know, she's still in London. The only address I have for her is care of her bank, not that I have any desire to get in touch with her. Perhaps this is just the lull before the storm, although I can't quite imagine what kind of a storm it will be.

I'm hoping to get a loan off the bank for a tractor which would make a hell of a difference to things here. It's time those two old horses were put out to grass, although I'm afraid it may have to be the knacker's yard for them. It'll be sad to see them go, but we can't run a place like this these days on two old mares, one of which goes lame every time there's a bit of harrowing to be done.

Of course there are still problems but all of a sudden I feel better able to face them. Not, in fact, that I really want to face up to the problem of Cheadle whom Priscilla wants me to sack because she says he's always drunk. I'm not entirely sure that's fair although he obviously does have a weakness in that direction. He seems to do his job and, after all, he's only been here for a few months so I feel I ought to give him a chance, despite the fact that I couldn't help noticing the port disappearing with amazing rapidity over Christmas. His daughter, who's having a baby any minute, is being taken off next week to a camp for G.I. brides at Tidworth where she'll have to stay until they can arrange some kind of transport to America for all these women. Poor old Cheadle, he looked quite red-faced and rheumy-eyed about it when I saw him this morning. I could hardly give him the sack on top of that.

Never mind Cheadle. I think that old Swiss cow in charge of the children is the one who ought to be shown the door. Priscilla doesn't believe the things the children say about her, but Annie said to me darkly yesterday, 'And her Ladyship doesn't know the half of it.' Priscilla says that children always invent things and that it would be very difficult to find anyone else suitable.

Another problem is the kitchen garden. Denman came to me the other day saying we needed another gardener. He says we can't possibly manage with just him and Stanley. He says the whole thing's gone right downhill since before the war when there were six gardeners. When I told him I couldn't afford to employ anyone else, he remarked sourly that he wasn't getting any younger which was manifestly the case as he limped away, muttering about his arthritic hip. I went and had a look at the garden later. It didn't look too bad to me, but as Priscilla remarked sharply, January is hardly the right time to be looking at gardens. I saw Stanley leaning idly on a fork, complaining that the ground was too hard to dig and in fact I did feel a bit sorry for poor old Denman. The garden used to be immaculate when I was a child and it must be sad for him to feel it getting out of control. Perhaps Johnson would lend him a hand. Johnson can do anything. They'll manage somehow between them.

I've been giving quite a lot of thought to my maiden speech in the House, not that I intend to be making it just yet, although I'm pretty sure it'll be about agricultural labour since that is a subject close to my heart.

# *Annie's diary*

Mr Cheadle's daughter went off at the beginning of the week. She's got to stay in a camp with all the other G.I. brides until she eventually goes to America. Mrs Cheadle is very upset. Mind you the woman hardly ever speaks to me, but I bumped into her on the stairs yesterday and she blew her nose loudly and looked as if she had been crying. Or perhaps she has just taken to the bottle like her husband.

Mr Johnson thinks that Mr Cheadle beats his wife and that the reason Mrs Cheadle was crying is that her daughter is her only ally. Mr Johnson wouldn't put anything past Mr Cheadle. He says he's told his Lordship that Cheadle helps himself to bottles from the cellar. The trouble with his Lordship is, he doesn't really want to know. He just laughs and goes off with that dog of his. It makes her Ladyship wild.

I haven't heard another word from *Lilian*, but I dread the post every day because I somehow don't think she is going to leave it at that.


## Letter from Zbigniew Rakowski to Priscilla Otterton

1 Robin Hood Way,
Wimble-on-Thames,
Surrey.
FEBRUARY 3RD, 1946

Dear Priscilla,

It is, Ma'am, with a degree of trepidation that I take up my pen to write, for I fear that you will only find it in your heart to despise a bewildered old man who in his senescence, is obliged to admit that despite the most generous help afforded him by yourself and Lord Otterton, he has merely frittered away the hours and not therefore advanced as he had hoped in the work in which he is engaged. I have written some twenty thousand words of a work which should run to at least one hundred thousand and which is due with my publisher by the autumn. I fear that I have been side-tracked and thus have been engaged on a work of a more frivolous nature about which I will not bore you at the present time.

The expression of my gratitude to your good selves for the kindness and forbearance with which you received a tedious old man when you had but barely arrived at Cranfield, can only ever be inadequate. When, Ma'am, I wrote to thank you, before ever the evils of the festive season descended upon us, the fruits of my research were fresh in my mind and thus I hoped to be full of vigour with which to undertake the task in hand. Perhaps it was a visitation from my daughter which sapped that vigour. She is a good Catholic woman, and a conscientious person of little imagination who sees it as her painful duty, once or twice a year, to travel from her home in Liverpool to call upon her sad old widowed father, to instruct him about his diet, his clothing and any other matters which she considers as pertinent to his well-being.

Let me not however make excuses, for the fault, dear Brutus, is indeed not in our stars, but in ourselves, that we are underlings.

I have now, I fear, Ma'am, to implore of you to be merciful to me in my incompetence, for I have to admit that I have failed to make sufficient notes concerning some of the papers in Lord Otterton's possession: there are in truth one or two matters which I must clarify if I am to do justice to my subject. I hesitate to bother Lord Otterton with what for him must be so trivial a matter, for he is a busy man, and thus it is that I humbly turn to you with a request that I might, at some date suitable to yourselves in the not too distant future, be allowed to return to Cranfield, further to examine the aforementioned papers.

I have the honour to remain, Ma'am, your humble and obedient servant.

Z.A.R.

## *Sydney Otterton's diary*

Rakowski's written to Priscilla asking to come back again. God knows what he needs to do that for. I was surprised that he took so long over those papers in the first place and fully imagined that he might have almost finished his book by now. Anyway Priscilla's quite delighted at the prospect of seeing the old humbug again. She's written back and asked him to lunch in a couple of weeks. Well I won't be here; I'll be in the House of Lords which I don't doubt will please him, as I suspect he's much more eager to see Priscilla than he is to get on with his book. She gets very cross when I say so, but in fact I think she's quite flattered by him. He's a wily old devil and I sometimes wonder what he's up to, nosing about the place. Annie giggles whenever I mention him and says, 'I reckon he rather *likes* her Ladyship.' Annie's regarded him as a comic figure ever since he walked in that dog mess in the saloon.

## *Extract from Zbigniew Rakowski's work in progress*

*. . . As a faint breath gurgled in her throat and a thread of saliva tinged with blood trickled from the corner of her Ladyship's beautifully formed mouth, she turned her hyacinth-blue eyes to look at the masked face of her would-be murderer who, in an instant and with a flamboyant gesture, defiantly ripped the stocking from a distorted face, to reveal the*

*dreadful truth of an assassin's identity. But there was not merely breath in her Ladyship's body yet, but courage to feign death and strength enough for her survival.*

*'It was you,' she whispered faintly as the door closed behind the fleeing figure of her assailant.*

*Confident in the assumption of a deed well done, her attacker had swiftly withdrawn the dagger from the wound in her side, thus allowing the blood to gush and flow until it formed a dark, sticky puddle on the Aubusson carpet on which she lay, spread-eagled and lovely. The murderous villain then placed the dagger in the lady's outflung lily-white hand so that she might be thought to have inflicted the wound upon herself, and tip-toed quickly from the room, blissfully unaware that the blood-stained weapon had miraculously failed to attain a vital organ . . .*

## Georgina's exercise book

Mamzelle has been packing all day. She says she's going to stay with the King and Queen. Poor them. Annie took us for our walk this afternoon and we picked snodrops. She says she's not shore the King and Queen know Mamzelle. Mamzelle says there very sorry for her plite. When I told Mummy she just said What Bosh!!!

## Sydney Otterton's diary

At last it dawned on Priscilla that that bloody Swiss woman was barking. Thank God she's been sent packing. I think what finally persuaded Priscilla was the woman banging on about a mixture of fairies and the Royal family. She was certainly never really convinced of how nasty the old bag was to the children. I also suspect that Priscilla was reluctant to admit to her own bad judgement and to having hired such a lunatic. The woman definitely gave me the creeps and reminded me more of my mother than of anyone else. In any case the children seem much more cheerful with the new French governess who's tiny and looks like an old wizened walnut under a thin grey bun.

But we've still got Cheadle although I haven't dared tell Priscilla that I found him in a stupefied slumber, snoring his head off on the pantry floor the other morning. I got out of the room before he woke up but I must have disturbed him because a moment later when I was still in the passage outside, he came to the pantry door and I heard him say, 'Who's that? Can't you see I'm busy?' Priscilla would be furious. She was pretty cross with the way he announced dinner on the evening the Bishop and his wife came to discuss the future of the cathedral. He put his head round the saloon door, as drunk as a newt, and said, 'Your din-dins is ready M'lady.' It was incredibly funny because that's the way he talks to Peggy when he feeds her. I suppose Priscilla is right and we ought to get rid of him but he doesn't really do much harm and I can't face the bother of looking for someone else. There are so many other problems that need solving.

I've written to my mother, c/o her bank, telling her that since she has left the Dower House and emptied it of furniture, I presume she no longer wishes to lay any claim to it and that unless I hear from her to the contrary within a month, I will set about letting it. Of course I haven't heard a word from her as yet. And Priscilla has come up with another good idea for raising a little cash. She thinks we could make a viable flat on the first floor, with the West Room as the main bedroom. We don't really use that part of the house and there's a bathroom there already and a smallish room that could easily be made into a kitchen. Whoever lived there could use the white staircase and the back door in the basement and we would hardly ever see them.

Priscilla is incredible. I don't think anyone else could have anything like her energy and enthusiasm for reviving the house. She is full of good ideas and without her I would be absolutely done for. She's always trying to enthuse me about things and to encourage me and to dissuade me from thinking things are impossible. She can also be quite sharp, but I suppose that's a good thing. Annie laughs and says, 'Her Ladyship keeps us all on our toes.' She probably needs to especially now, as I'm afraid I haven't managed to keep up all that good cheer I felt after Christmas. I had quite a lot to drink last night and felt a bit better, but then I felt like hell this morning. Priscilla says I'm incompetent, that I drink too much and that I ought to concentrate on one thing at a time. I hope she realises that I couldn't begin to manage without her, although I don't think she quite appreciates how bloody difficult it is to try to run this place with no money. Neither do I think she quite understands about the war. I don't see how anyone can just come home after all that and get on with life as if nothing had happened. Johnson feels the same. Thank God for him is what I say. He reminded me only the other day of the camel I'd had shot for the men's Christmas dinner back in 1940. We were advancing to Saunnu and one of the fitters had just shot some kind of wild cat which one of the men who was a butcher in peacetime, skinned for the officers' dinner. To shoot the camel was strictly against orders, of course, and I got into a bit of hot water with my colonel afterwards, but as I saw it, it was those boys' first Christmas away from home and they might have been going to be killed the next day, so why couldn't they have some mild jollification at the expense of a camel?

Still, I can't blame the war for my inability to sack Cheadle. In an awful sort of way, I think I'd miss him if he went because he provides so much entertainment. You never know what the fellow's going to do next.

71

# Georgina's exercise book

The new mamzel is much better than the old one. She's very little and Jamie is nearly as tall as her. She keeps a huge bottel of green stuff in the schoolroom cubbard. She's allways taking spoonfuls of it for her cough. It must be good because she never seems to cough. She is French.

## Zbigniew Rakowski's notebook

I should indeed be ashamed to admit, even in this my personal notebook, how gladly last Thursday morning, despite the bitter cold, I set out for Cranfield, how light was my tread, how full my heart. Her Ladyship, I trust, is unaware that an old man's heart can be so vulnerable. Sighing like furnace, with a woeful ballad made to my mistress' eyebrow did I travel. Or rather, should I say, if I were completely honest, with a woeful tale of murder. Once my novel which I shall have the temerity to dedicate *To Priscilla* has been accepted by my publisher, I shall feel that I have in some degree freed myself from the stranglehold of my sweet passion and thus will be able to continue to work on matters of a more a serious nature. I do not at present wish to tell Lady Otterton what it is that I am writing for fear that she might well misinterpret my intentions and might also hesitate to invite me so willingly to Cranfield in the future. She will, I feel, when the book is published, be both dazzled by its jauntiness and flattered by the content. However, I fear that when I wrote to her, I let slip that I had not recently been devoting my efforts entirely to Whig history, and at luncheon on Thursday she, not unnaturally, with her usual spirit of enquiry, was curious to know what it was that I had been writing.

I think she was not a little displeased by my reluctance to discuss my novel with her. I surmise, however, that she guessed it to be a work of fiction in which I am involved, as, laughingly, but with a touch of hauteur, and an autocratic glance from those blue eyes, she remarked that she sincerely hoped that 'we' weren't all in it. It is extraordinary how vain the general public is; the least of human beings has but to meet a novelist once, to presume himself of sufficient interest to be instantly transposed to the pages of fiction. Of course in the case of Lady Otterton, she has every right to make such a presumption. I laughed inwardly as I looked at her across the luncheon table, chastising the children for not eating their cabbage, and imagined her as she has recently been in my mind's eye, *spread-eagled and lovely*, her blood staining the Aubusson. Then for a moment I felt a twinge of pity. How could I treat her so? But then the true artist must have a heart of stone and thus I must not be moved, but stick to my original plan.

There is a new governess; a small French woman with bright eyes and a brusque manner. She looks very old indeed and is, I trust, kinder than her predecessor who is to be immortalised in my novel.

To be frank, I practised a minor deceit in order to return to Cranfield on Thursday. I needed, for the purposes of the book I am engaged upon, to examine more closely the saloon and its furnishings. I was, furthermore, uncertain as to whether, between the Green Silk Room to the north and the Red Drawing-Room to the south, there were two of those beautiful mahogany doors, one behind the other, or if there was only one, set deep into the embrasure of the wall. I had entertained the idea of my murderer lurking for some while between two doors. To be sure, I can, in a work of fiction, design the doors and indeed the furniture to my own liking, do precisely as I please, but there is something about

Cranfield so magnificent and so imposing, that I would feel it an impertinence to tamper in any way with Leoni's great design, or indeed with the arrangements made inside the house by Priscilla Otterton herself.

Once again, I was aghast at the splendour of the hall with its fine proportions and the beauty of its plasterwork ceiling. Opposite the main entrance, a handsome pair of double mahogany doors open into the saloon through which can be seen French windows that in summer must be wonderfully opened onto a graceful flight of stone steps, and beyond them the garden and the lawns across which can be seen an incongruous, slanting may tree. One of the charms of this house is that, for all its grandeur, it has the capacity to accommodate the simple and the ordinary. The fine marble busts of negroes over the main doorway of the hall and the doors to the saloon had temporarily escaped my memory. Her Ladyship tells me that they were put there as a tribute to the Jamaican heiress whose money built the house. How bewitching a house it is! What a hold it appears to have over those mere mortals who pass through it. We mere mortals who, destined so soon to become dust, will be long gone before Cranfield crumbles. For, saving a bomb or an earth-quake, Cranfield will surely survive to exercise its enchant-ment over generations as yet unborn. I wax lyrical, but I shall surely have to find some further reason for returning there. Bother the Whigs, I need to look again and again at the house and, indeed, I need to know what fate befalls those who live there now. I note that the drunken butler is still in residence.

Fortunately for my purposes, the doors are as I had imagined them. I shall have no trouble concealing my killer.

# Annie's diary

It is bitterly cold in the house, or, as Father would say, it's cold enough to freeze a brass monkey. I reckon the only place where one could keep really warm would be in front of one of the two big fires in the hall. They're kept burning all day in this weather, but of course you would only freeze the minute you stepped back. Mamzelle is complaining about having chilblains for which she takes cough mixture. I couldn't help laughing when her Ladyship told me that she thinks Mamzelle has a peppermint liqueur in that bottle. All I can say is that she's a good deal better than the last governess and the children seem to like her more.

I've been helping her Ladyship get some rooms ready on the first floor to be let as a flat. The main bedroom is a huge, icy corner room with two windows on one side looking down across the lake and another two overlooking the garden. Because the floor has been raised to make room for a sunken bath, the windows come right down to the ground, which, I have to admit must be lovely in the summer. I couldn't help laughing when her Ladyship first showed me where the bath was. It is completely covered by floor-boards forming a lid that is lifted by means of brass handles which hook back to hold it to the wall.

Goodness knows who we'll ever get in that flat. I told his Lordship that I thought they'd better wait until the weather was a bit warmer before trying to find a tenant. I can't imagine anybody moving in there now. They'd probably freeze to death. We are quite lucky on the top floor really with the rooms being smaller and the ceilings a bit lower, although the school-room's big enough and cold enough. When I was in there the other day, the children were pushing each other about in front of the fire, trying to get near it. I told them that if they weren't careful, they'd fall in one day and then there'd be hell to pay. I didn't add, especially if it happens when Mamzelle's been at the cough mixture.

Mamzelle's only been here a couple of weeks, but she is forever telling me about this thing and that thing that she thinks needs fixing. Yesterday, it was a snapped sash cord in the window, and the day before it was a door with a broken latch. I thought Mr Johnson could mend both those things, but she won't have anything to do with him. I don't know why unless it is because she's taken a rather sudden fancy to the estate carpenter. Perhaps she broke the window on purpose! I wouldn't be surprised as Mr Kipling's always up there, laughing and talking to her on the top landing. I shouldn't wonder if she lets him have a drop of her cough mixture from time to time.

MARCH 8TH

There's a lovely picture on the paper this morning of the banana boats arriving here for the first time since before the war. I should think we could do with a banana or two each, what with the state of rationing. I thought that was all supposed to be getting better now, but rations have just been cut back again to what they were in the middle of the war, with only seven ounces of margarine each a week. I suppose we're lucky to be here with all the extra things off the farm, not that I fancy the idea of eating squirrel pie which is what the government is busy telling us to do. You won't catch me taking to that. No fear. Mamzelle takes the children out every afternoon to look for dandelions to make salad for their tea. There'll be plenty of them around, I should think, but she says they're not quite ready yet, not sweet enough. Would you believe it!

# Letter from Annie to Dolly

Dear Dolly,

I wonder if you saw the picture on the paper yesterday morning of the banana boats arriving. I thought to myself, what wouldn't I give for a banana right now? To tell you the truth, I wasn't in the least bit bothered about bananas, not until we couldn't get them.

When I was writing my diary last evening, it crossed my mind that I should really have been writing to you instead, because you would be so interested in all the goings on. One of these days I will have to give you my diary to read to make up for all the letters I haven't written.

Anyway, I think I ought to tell you that I had another letter from Lilian, Lady Otterton this morning. I don't know what makes her so sure that I won't mention anything to his Lordship. I suppose I'll have to if she goes on, although Mr Johnson advises me to do nothing. Least said, soonest mended, is what he says. She didn't send me any money this time. In fact, I thought the letter was downright rude. She said she was disappointed in me and she wanted to know where my loyalty lay. All this in her dreadful spiky writing.

I only told Mr Johnson about it because he knows his Lordship well, is fond of him and would be on his side. Besides he (Mr Johnson) is a very kind man and sensible.

Father's really looking forward to your bringing the children to see him, but what with Easter being so late this year, it seems a long way off still.

Wilfie and Ethel came over for the afternoon on Sunday which was nice. Father was pleased to see them and they both looked well.

Love from
Annie

# Georgina's exercise book

Mamzel makes us eat dandylions, but aksherly there quite nice. She says they eat them all the time in France. And they eat snails. Ugh!! Jamie wants to try them. He would. She's been caching them in the garden for him. There are some new people in the flat but Mummy says were not allowed to bother them. Ive seen them in the garden. They are very odd and have a big dog and a funny name and don't smile.

# Sydney Otterton's diary

Priscilla's found a very rum fellow with an equally rum wife, to live in the flat. They answered an advertisement she put in the *Surrey Advertiser*. I suppose we won't have to have much to do with them, so it doesn't really matter what they're like so long as they pay the rent. Apart from anything else, they've got a pretty strange name. He says it's Channel Islands, but I'd have thought it was more of a bogus crook's name. Legros dit Courrier. It's certainly a new one on me. To be fair to her, Priscilla doesn't think much of the so-called Legros either, but unfortunately people weren't falling over themselves to live in vast, freezing-cold rooms in the corner of a dilapidated stately home. Legros looks like some kind of robot as he walks, staring at the ground in front of him and without appearing to move any other part of his body but his legs. He has bright brown, dyed hair in a thick mat, like a wig, over his head (it probably is a wig) and a very high colour. I should think he must be nearly seventy. In any case, he looks as if he might die of apoplexy any minute. Mrs Legros is one of those faceless women whom you cease to be able to imagine once they are out of sight. For all I know, she does cease to exist once she's out of sight. She walks silently beside her husband (if he is her husband), always holding on to the leash of their vast Pyrenean mountain dog and never looking up when you speak to her. The only thing one can't help noticing about her is the make-up which she cakes all over her face.

Priscilla thought it a bit odd when she took them round the flat in the first place because when she asked them where they'd been living before, they wouldn't answer. She's convinced that they have some kind of shady past, in which case, perhaps we shouldn't have let them have the flat. Let's just hope they don't rob us. I asked Annie what she thought about them, but she only giggled and said they were most extraordinary. Johnson was pretty annoyed about them and told me that they looked like trouble and that if he had a house, he wouldn't want to share it with them. Then he started saying something about Australia again, which depressed me.

Julia is beginning to talk which annoys Priscilla. She says that there are enough human beings talking nonsense without parrots having to join in. I think she's really annoyed because Julia gives a passable imitation of Priscilla calling my name. The children think it's very funny which I suppose she finds even more annoying. Annie's minding her p's and q's, as she would no doubt say.

I spent an evening with Tony MacIntosh in London last week. I couldn't help feeling rather sorry for him. He's completely on his uppers, without a bean to his name and with an ex-wife and a child to support. He's found some sort of a job in the City but earns a mere pittance. It crossed my mind that I might be able to help him by letting him have a room on the top floor here until he sorts himself out, but I haven't mentioned it to Priscilla yet, not that I can see why she should object. Tony is one of my friends she has always liked.

# Letter from Bert Farthing to Lord Otterton

Cinder Path Cottage,
Battle-by-Stitch,
Sussex.
APRIL 5TH, 1946

M'lord,

Please excuse the liberty I take in writing but I would like to
apply for the job of cowman as I have heard that Mr Jerrold
is to retire soon. I am single, forty-two years old and have
been working here for Mr and Mrs Gower since I left
school. Mr Gower would give me a reference.

    I am hard working and in good health and I look forward
to hearing from your Lordship in the near future.

Yours respectfully
Albert Farthing


## Annie's diary

APRIL 7TH

I don't know what has got into Bert. He's gone and written to
his Lordship asking for Father's job when he retires. His
Lordship showed me the letter and wanted to know what I
thought about the idea and I think he may have wondered if I
had anything to do with the matter, which of course I assured
him I hadn't. But I had to be tactful although I wasn't quite
sure what to say. For one thing Bert had no business writing
that letter without consulting me, and, for another, I doubt
he knows a darned thing about cows. I haven't dared say a
word to Father yet. Apart from anything else, he doesn't
really like his retirement being mentioned and what is more,
he loves his cows and wouldn't want them to be looked after

by anyone who didn't know what they were doing. For my part I'm not really sure whether or not I want Bert here. I have been getting along quite nicely without him, but then when I think about him, I do feel sorry for him, all alone in that cottage. But one thing's for certain. If he comes here, it's not going to be like it was before. To some extent I came here to get away from being his housemaid. In any case I doubt I would have the time now, what with all the work there is here, and Father and Mr Johnson's washing to do and one thing and another. Of course I could just tell his Lordship that Bert would be no good with the cows and that would soon queer his pitch. I might have a word with Father.

I think I am going to have to write a letter to *Lilian* (just a short one mind), saying that I am very sorry but I can't help her. That may put a stop to her writing to me. It's begun to bother me, seeing her writing on the envelope. I think it would be easier than telling his Lordship about her letters because he might easily go into a towering rage and he might anyway think that it was all somehow my fault. He might suppose that I'd already been talking to her before she left here or that I had told her something that I had no business to. Nothing makes his Lordship angrier than the thought of Lilian, Lady Otterton, and, there's no denying it, but he has a nasty temper when he's roused. I wouldn't want to tell her Ladyship either. I think it would only cause trouble as there always seems to be a row when the subject of Lilian comes up. I think her Ladyship accuses his Lordship of not standing up to his mother. He just says that her Ladyship really doesn't know what his mother is like and that he has had to put up with her spite and her moods, her lack of reason and her tantrums all his life. It makes me quite sad to think about it. He was a dear little boy, we all loved him on the farm, and we knew that *she* was downright unkind to him. It's his late Lordship who should have stood up to her, if you ask me, but then, they say he was terrified of her. The butler before the war was a Mr House from North Devon where Lady

Lilian's family came from, and he had a story or two to tell. Perhaps she's gone back to Devon. No one knows where she is, except the bank I suppose. All I can say is that it would certainly give me the heebie-jeebies if I suddenly bumped into her around these parts.

I didn't want to say anything to his Lordship or her Ladyship about Mr and Mrs Legros either for that matter. But I can't say I like the look of the pair of them. I heard her Ladyship say that it didn't really matter what they were like because she wouldn't be having very much to do with them, but Mr Johnson is really annoyed. What he says is that his Lordship must be out of his mind to have a pair of b—s like them in the house. I think he thinks that they'll steal all the silver and pictures and God knows what, and he has decided to make it his personal responsibility to watch what they get up to. Mr Johnson says that he sometimes thinks that life made more sense in the Western Desert than it ever does at Cranfield with what he calls this 'daft bunch'. I'm afraid he's still thinking about going to Australia. I hope he changes his mind. Perhaps he's too old to go now.

## *Sydney Otterton's diary*

The daffodils are all out. I've always loved Cranfield at daffodil time. So much so in fact, that I remember dreaming about it once when I was in Cairo on sick leave recovering from dysentery and lying in bed sweating in some grimy hotel. I kept falling asleep and then being woken up again by a damned fly landing repeatedly on my face. Every time I went back to sleep this dream recurred. Just a simple dream that I was at home down by the lake and the daffodils were in bloom. Priscilla just laughs when I tell her about it. I think she imagines I've invented it, but I can't think why. She says

I'm ridiculously sentimental, which doesn't stop her from filling the house with huge bowls of daffodils and saying that she's never seen lovelier ones than those in the field sloping down to the lake, 'fluttering and dancing in the breeze,' she says. *She* is allowed to quote poetry.

A peculiar thing happened yesterday afternoon. I'd been down to the farm to have a word with Jerrold about this and that and I was walking back up the drive with Peggy and looking across at the daffodils and down at the lake and wishing that I had enough money to dredge it and to renovate the old boathouse that's lurking there, mouldering among the bamboos, both of which things are sadly low on the list of priorities, when Legros appeared, buttoned up in a British warm and wearing an Anthony Eden hat. He had with him his wife, equally unsuitably dressed for a country walk, who was, as usual, hanging on for grim death to that huge hound leashed to a chain. The two of them were coming up from the lake, out from what is literally an impenetrable jungle of overgrown weeds and shrubs. There was something eerie about the way the pair of them suddenly materialised from nowhere and, heads bent, walked on up to the house without apparently having noticed me as I watched them from the drive above. As I went on up the hill and into the house through the front door, I was wondering what exactly it was that made the appearance of those two with their great white dog seem so sinister. I had the instinctive feeling that they had not wanted to be seen and that they had been snooping. But what on earth is there for them to snoop about down by the lake? Anyway as I crossed the hall, I thought I heard voices in the saloon, so I went over and opened the doors, expecting to find Priscilla and curious as to whom she might be talking, but there was no one in the saloon, although the door to the left, leading to the muniments room, was just quietly and mysteriously closing. I quickly nipped back into the hall and out of the other door, expecting to meet whoever it was coming through the library since there is no other way out. Sure enough, as I stepped into the library, I heard a low, ferocious growl and there was that damned white dog, lowering its huge head and baring its horrible teeth at me, with Mrs Legros hanging on to the lead as tightly as she could with both her hands. Legros stood beside her with his hat still on, which I have to admit he had the good grace to remove as I appeared with Peggy idiotically cowering at my heels.

The Legros have no business whatsoever in the library, let alone the saloon and they must have felt embarrassed by my finding them there. As for me, I have to admit that I was rather shaken by the sight of them and pretty angry, so I asked them what the bloody hell they thought they were doing and added rather unceremoniously that I didn't want them or their effing dog wandering about the house. Legros apologised obsequiously and made some ridiculous excuse in that flat whiny voice of his about the dog having slipped its leash and run away from them. I didn't believe a word of it and furthermore I don't trust the bugger a yard, with that broad, expressionless face of his and those shifty eyes.

When I told Priscilla what had happened, she was furious and pretty concerned about what they might have been up to. I did look round after they'd gone to see if they'd nicked anything but nothing seemed to be missing. I can only imagine that they were casing the joint. Priscilla was a bit worried that I might have been rude to them because she says that if I was, it would only put their backs up and make matters worse. I decided not to tell her exactly what I'd said. Then she calmed down and began to persuade herself that they had been telling the truth about the dog all along. Johnson's furious about the Legros and I'm beginning to think he may have a point.

Jerrold's due to retire in the summer, so I wanted to ask him what he thought about my taking on Annie's friend, Farthing. I know he didn't want the matter discussed but in the end, I got him to admit that he wouldn't want to hand the herd over to anyone who wasn't used to cows. So I'll let it go at that. After all Bert Farthing already has a job, and there'll be plenty of people coming out of the forces any minute, crying out for work on the land. I might even be lucky enough to find a decent cowman among them. What I can't quite make out is whether Annie really wants me to employ Farthing or not, and one thing we simply cannot afford to do, is to lose Annie.

Another problem is that you can't get a tractor for love or money. Apparently they're making plenty of them, but they all go abroad, along with the combines and the beet lifters that are made in this country. So this winter the poor landgirls will still be having the job of pulling by hand all the mangels and sugar beet that the government encourages us to grow. If ever there was a filthy job . . . then that is jolly well it.

## *Georgina's exercise book*

Mummy stands on the landing and talks French all the time to Mamzelle. They talk for ages and ages and I dont no what they are saying. Now Mummy wants us to colect snails for her. She says she knows what to do. Im not going to eat them. So there.

## *Annie's diary*

APRIL 15TH

Now there's an awful kerfuffle going on about the snails. You won't catch me eating snails, mind, but her Ladyship and the children and Mamzelle have brought dozens of them in from the garden and her Ladyship says they're going to be delicious and that Mamzelle knows all about them. Well she may, but what about poor Mrs Laws in the kitchen, trying to get on with her work? There's a great big wooden box right there on the floor ready for her to trip over, and full of darned snails crawling around in flour which is supposed to clean their insides out. Mrs Laws says that when she came down to the kitchen this morning, they'd got out and were walking all over the place, up the walls and along the draining board, and then his Lordship found one on the stairs which he thought very funny, but her Ladyship was furious. She said Mrs Laws ought to have known better. She should have put a lid and a heavy weight on the box to keep them from escaping. Mrs Laws was livid. She said she thought Mamzelle was supposed to be in charge of snails. In any case she's refusing to cook them and I can't say I blame her. Her Ladyship just said that nobody should look a gift-horse in the mouth in these hard times. Never mind the gift-horse's mouth, I'm not putting any snails into my own. That's for sure, and no one's ever called me fussy. Her Ladyship was in there in the kitchen this morning, pulling the wretched snails off the walls and off the oven door and carrying on alarming, talking about the French and how wonderful they are and how stupid the English are, just as if she wasn't English herself. Well I never noticed the French were so wonderful in the war, but I didn't say a thing. Now her Ladyship says the snails have got to stay another week in that box and then she'll cook them herself.

Mamzelle and Mrs Laws don't get on at all well which only makes matters worse. I suppose Mrs Laws has caught on to the fact that Mr Kipling spends half his time up in the school-room talking to Mamzelle. I feel sorry for Mrs Laws. We had enough trouble finding her and I know she's got Lorraine settled at the village school, but all the same, I doubt she'll stay if she has to spend her time chasing snails. I felt like telling her Ladyship she ought to be tactful, see.

I don't know what to do about Bert. Nothing I suppose, but I think he'll suspect me of not putting in a good word for him with his Lordship. In fact his Lordship asked me point blank what I thought about Bert coming to work here and that was after he said he'd already asked Father. Father never said a word to me, mind, but I doubt he would have encouraged the idea. I certainly didn't know what to say to his Lordship because the more I think about it now, the less I like the idea. I'd have thought Bert would have got used to being without me by now in any case. Then his Lordship mumbled something about not needing him to look after cows, but he might be wanted in the garden.

I haven't written to Lilian, Lady Otterton yet. I don't know why I keep putting it off.

## Sydney Otterton's diary

Those bloody Legros are beginning to get on my nerves. I went down to the farm yesterday afternoon in my old van and when I wanted to come back, I couldn't get the damn thing to start so I walked up to the house with Peggy and went to look for Johnson who was taking a mowing machine to pieces in the back yard. He said he'd go and see if he could do something about the van for me. Then, feeling generally fed up, I went to the Japanese room, gave myself a gin and tonic, shut the doors and sat down to brood. Some of the cottages on the farm are in such dreadful condition, I can't imagine any man being prepared to live in them, let alone one with a wife and family. I don't see any way round it as I don't begin to have the money to do them all up. There'll have to be some kind of government help, particularly if what they want is to boost agriculture and encourage people back onto the land. Then I went on to think about my poisonous mother and, not unfairly, as far as I can see, to blame her for everything, all of which immediately made me want another drink and then I began to worry about Bert Farthing and Jerrold and Annie and the kitchen garden. We certainly need more help there. The whole place is overrun with docks and ground elder and I really don't see how poor old Denman can manage any longer without a bit more help. I was wondering about giving Farthing a job in the garden and then I just went back to worrying about the cottages again. There seems to be no way out.

It was about half past five and I was sitting there engrossed in my thoughts with Peggy, who's become quite biddable at last, lying peacefully at my feet, when all of a sudden I heard footsteps coming from the Palladio room next door. Priscilla had gone out for the day to see her aunt, so I supposed it might be Johnson coming to say he had mended the van, or that drunken fool, Cheadle, coming to help himself to a drink, but as I got up to go and see who it was, I heard soft voices. Who on earth would Johnson or Cheadle have been talking to? Just as I opened the door on my side, someone else opened the door on the ballroom side, and there I was, standing nose to nose with the nightmare couple and their dog. I have to say that it was a great pleasure to see the horrified looks on both their faces and to see them jump out of their skins. A sly expression momentarily crossed the old boy's face which reminded me uncomfortably of someone else, not that I could think who, but I thought he might be about to have an apoplectic fit. Pity he didn't. I was so angry and I suppose I'd had a drink, so I just bawled at them to get out, while Peggy stood beside me, ludicrously wagging her tail at the Pyrenean brute which was growling in a menacing fashion.

Thinking about it afterwards, I decided that they must have snooped about and seen that neither my van nor the car was anywhere around, so presuming that Priscilla and I were both out, they thought they could have a field day. I'm also certain that they must know that I use the Japanese room as my own private study and that I have my desk and all my papers in there.

Priscilla made me angry when she got back because she would keep going on about my shouting at the Legros, and complaining about my temper. Anybody would lose their temper with that grisly pair prowling around. I think they ought to go, but Priscilla says we can't do without the money and, because they were the only people who answered the advertisement, she's convinced that we'd never find anyone else. She didn't think it at all funny when I said I'd rather meet a fucking snail on a staircase than that pair of monsters in a ballroom. This morning she brought the subject up again rather coldly. She said that she would have to go and appease them because I had obviously been so rude and then she announced that she was sure they had a perfectly good excuse. After all, it was only natural for them to be curious about the house and they were probably only having an innocent look at the plasterwork. If they were so interested in the plasterwork why didn't they stay in the Palladio room or the hall? And, if they're so interested in plasterwork, why, as they walk, do they both always stare so fixedly at the floor?


## Zbigniew Rakowski's notebook

JULY 25TH

These are bleak times indeed. Only few weeks ago we were being threatened with bread rationing, and now the latest news from Mr Shinwell is that we do not have enough coal to see us through the winter. With day after day such woeful tidings, imagine, amidst the ensuing gloom, my joy at the unexpected arrival by the morning post of a delightful letter from my *Beatrice*, my *Laura*, my very own *donna angelicata*, the exquisite blue-eyed angel of my dreams. Lady Otterton bids me lunch at Cranfield next week. She wishes to introduce me to Lord Otterton's aunt who may have some papers which could be of interest to me. Alas, if only she knew how slowly *that* work is progressing, whilst *Bloodstains in the Boudoir* comes on apace, and will indeed be shortly finished.

I hastily wrote a note accepting her Ladyship's kind invitation, so that now an old man's life suddenly seems worth living again. Indeed I have concocted a plan whereby it may be possible for me to continue visiting Cranfield on a more or less regular basis for a while at least, but I shall wait until I have broached the matter with Priscilla before allowing myself to become too hopeful. This I think I shall do by letter after I have lunched there. I will not, I do not think, as yet, discuss my detective novel (*roman à clef* that it is) with her, for it has to be admitted that in the small hours, I have begun to toss and turn, to ask myself quite how her Ladyship will react to my little *bétise*, my humble *jeu d'ésprit*. Will it tickle her as it is designed to do? Will she see it as my own modest *Divine Comedy*? My hymn of love to Priscilla? At times I fear that once she has read it, she may banish me for ever from her sight, but surely not. Surely she will be flattered. Surely with her unique humour, unparalleled wit and peerless powers of perception, she will receive my dedication for what it is, an act of homage. Nevertheless, I will not discuss it prematurely.

## *Extract from Zbigniew Rakowski's work in progress*

*. . . The governess crept stealthily up the oak staircase, the murder weapon concealed beneath her cardigan. At this hour of day she felt confident of meeting no one. Her ample body quivered as one pudgy foot caused a polished board to creak ominously beneath her weight, and, unnoticed, a silvery hairpin slid from her white bun and fell to the floor,*

*landing noiselessly on the red patterned carpet that covered the centre of the stairs.*

*She knew exactly where she would deposit the blood-stained weapon, where indeed it would be quickly found and to the best possible effect. His Lordship, she thought, narrowing her pig-like eyes, will hang for this, and I, with my hand on the* Sainte Bible, *will swear to his guilt . . .*

## Sydney Otterton's diary

Priscilla asked Rakowski to lunch the other day because she wanted Aunt Lettice to meet him. He looked even smaller and more gnome-like than ever, but otherwise he was his usual self. You can't help quite liking the fellow despite all his humbug because, although he's always playing some damn silly part, he seems to know it, and he can be quite funny. Anyway he was obviously tickled pink to meet Aunt Lettice and she was quite delighted by him and said he was *moost* interesting. He seems to be taking an awfully long time to write his wretched book. It even crossed my mind that he might be spinning it out as an excuse to keep coming back here. Not only does he always gobble up his lunch, but he is obviously completely infatuated with Priscilla.

We're still being haunted by the Legros although I have to admit that I haven't found them snooping around the house again. All the same I hate the feeling of their presence.

I've finally agreed to take Farthing on to help in the garden as from next month, and on the farm if needed. He came to see me and seemed a decent enough sort of fellow. He's going to move into that almost derelict cottage next door to Jerrold. He seemed satisfied with that and is quite ready to do a bit of work on it himself, but I've said I'll get Kipling to have a go at it first and then Johnson might give it a lick of paint. He appeared to be quite pleased and is definitely keen to come. He's certainly got a good reference from the Gowers who will obviously be pretty sorry to lose him. Funnily enough, Annie hasn't said a word about it. Next week I've got a possible cowman coming to see me and Jerrold hasn't said much about that either. I think it'll break his heart to retire. As a matter of fact he looks as if he could go on for another twenty years.

Tony came down from London last week-end. He's certainly got his problems too, so I ended up offering him a room here. After all we've got this bloody great barracks of a house, half empty, and commuting to the City would be easy for him from Cranfield. He seemed very interested by the idea and is going to think about it, although I'm afraid Priscilla was doubtful about how well it would work out. Perhaps she gets fed up with the pair of us sitting up all night, reminiscing about the war, particularly about jollifications on leave in Cairo. Last week-end I suppose we did bang on a bit about the time we were on reconnaissance at Alamein when, with absolutely no warning, our jeep suddenly sank chassis deep into the sand. A huge Bedouin caravan had just arrived and as we were trying to get the jeep out, these great big white sheep-dogs began to attack us. Luckily the Arabs were very friendly and called the dogs off, but we had a nervous moment. Perhaps that bloody Pyrenean sheep-dog of Legros's reminds me of those dogs, which may be why I take such exception to it.

It's funny but it still seems that in spite of the discomfort, the fear, missing one's wife and so on, life was easier crossing the desert in a 'Honey' tank, than it can ever be in peacetime. I think Tony feels much the same. For one thing, we've seen too much, and feared too much, and lived on our nerves and, luckily for us, survived, but we can't put the whole damn thing behind us just like that, which is why, at the moment, everything seems to require such a monumental effort. In comparison to what we went through then, nothing now seems worthwhile or even very real. Our sensibilities were heightened in those days, now they are dulled, and at times one can feel almost despairing. Thank God for people like Johnson and Tony. Without them one might feel one was going quite mad at times.

## Georgina's exercise book

We were playing in the garden and Thomas was anoying me because he said I had to be a german and be killed and I was crying. Then a car came and two men got out and asked for mr Legro. We were terryfied and Thomas took them to find Father. Jamie said they were germans who wanted to murder Father.

## Annie's diary

AUGUST 16TH

There was a terrific to-do here yesterday afternoon. It was about three o'clock when I left by the back door to walk down to the farm. I had a letter to post and I was going to look in on Father. I'd just seen the children from my bedroom window. They were all three playing quite happily in the garden, but as I came out of the house, I found Thomas talking in rather a grand way, I thought, to two policemen. They were pulling his leg a bit, but when they saw me, one of them asked for Lord Otterton. I wasn't sure if his Lordship was in, but I directed them round to the front door. Thomas went striding off with them, ever so keen to know what was up, I don't doubt. I did wonder myself what they wanted, but, to tell the truth, by the time I'd posted my letter and got to Father's, I'd forgotten all about them. I was more worried about Father.

His Lordship has told him that when the new cowman and his family come, he will probably need Father's house, which is fair enough, I suppose, and the cottage at the lodge is plenty big enough for Father on his own, but it's not in a very good state of repair and Father will hate it after being in the same place all these years. He was looking a bit down in the dumps, but he didn't say much. 'It's drier where there's none,' is what Mother used to say when we children complained that the bread was stale. I rather think that that's the way Father sees most things in life. He's never been a great complainer. He never even said much when Mother went, but just turned to me instead. He used to say, 'You're my Annie now.' Poor Father, I reckon he must have been lonely at times.

He did ask me how I felt about Bert coming to Cranfield. I just told him that it won't make any difference to me, so he didn't say any more, only that he hoped they'd manage to make his cottage fit for human beings. Then he took me out to his garden to admire his marrows and his sweet peas. Father always loves his sweet peas.

By the time I got back up to the house, it seems that I'd missed most of the drama. Her Ladyship told me later to keep out of his Lordship's way because he was in a thundering rage. Apparently the police had been and after they'd spoken to his Lordship, they went along to see Mr and Mrs Legros and, blow me down, if they didn't arrest Mr Legros, but no one is saying what for. Her Ladyship was dreadfully worried because of the children. She hadn't wanted them involved, but then they'd been there when the police arrived and young Thomas had been marching around the house with them, looking for his father. Well somehow they were all sent packing back up to the school-room and Mamzelle was told to keep them inside for the rest of the afternoon although it was a lovely day and Thomas was full bent on looking for tadpoles. Her Ladyship said it was too late for tadpoles and he wouldn't find tadpoles anywhere in August. I'm not sure she was right, mind.

Anyway no one seems any the wiser about why the police took Mr Legros away. Apparently Mrs Legros was in floods of tears and quite hysterical. She left for the station soon after, in a taxi with that darned great dog. Her Ladyship doesn't think we'll see her again. She told me she didn't want me talking about what had happened to anyone. 'You know me,' I said to her. Now would I say a word? Well I certainly wouldn't say anything to Mrs Laws or the Cheadles, but I did have a word with Miss Wheel. She's back for a week, using the sewing machine in my sitting-room. She's covering a sofa with some old curtains her Ladyship found, and mending the curtains in the Peacock Room. It's wonderful what she can do and I'm certain she wouldn't be one to repeat anything.

I saw his Lordship when I went to turn down the beds. He wasn't in a rage then, in fact he looked as if butter wouldn't melt in his mouth. He probably wanted me to clear up the birdseed that blasted parrot had scattered all round his dressing-room. Anyway he asked me if I'd heard about the drama and what had happened to Mr Legros. He was chuckling about it as if it was the funniest thing that had ever happened. 'Do you know, Annie,' he said, 'I always hated the b—.' Then he went on about various times he'd found him prowling around the house with Mrs Legros whose face was as white as the dog's. Then he was stalking round the room, imitating the pair of them. You couldn't help laughing. Her Ladyship was quite annoyed when she came in. 'Annie,' she said, 'don't you realise this is quite serious?' And his Lordship said, 'Don't blame Annie.' I just quietly left.

I expect her Ladyship's worried because they might have stolen something and because she let them have the flat when his Lordship never wanted them here in the first place. Mr Johnson is sure to know all about it. I wonder what he'll have to say.

Priscilla's desperate to find someone else to take the flat now the Legros dit Courriers have gone. I presume we really have seen the last of them. I expect he'll be behind bars for a while as the police apparently had a list of charges as long as your arm. Of course they still owe quite a lot of rent, but judging by the fact that, as she left, she was begging us to lend her the train fare to London, I don't suppose we'll ever see a penny of it.

I do feel sorry for Priscilla though, because, to be fair, she took a lot of trouble to make that flat half-way decent and it was hardly her fault if a pair of crooks turned up to rent it. We haven't found anything missing yet, but I can't help feeling that we may before long.

I was talking to Johnson this evening and he told me something which has left me feeling a bit uneasy. Everybody in this village knows everyone else's business, partly because the post office is a centre for gossip, and partly because of the telephone exchange. If you ring someone and the line is engaged, the people at the exchange tell you that Mrs So-and-So's talking to her mother or her auntie . . . And as if that weren't bad enough, it now appears that the postman who empties the box at the farm has told the postmistress in the village that he's surprised by how many letters he collects from that particular box which are addressed to my mother. He'd heard that my mother and I didn't get on, so he took it upon himself to wonder who could have been writing to her. I think he was quite right to wonder. I would certainly like to know who, on this place, is busily keeping in contact with her, and why. I haven't written to my mother for months and Priscilla certainly wouldn't write to her. Of course the postmistress would love to know too, but where she made her mistake was in talking to Johnson about it. Even if he knew, he'd never tell her. He won't even tell me who he thinks it is, because, he says, he can't be certain.

## Annie's diary

I was quite cross with Mr Johnson yesterday. We were having a cup of tea in my sitting-room and I'd just sat down to enjoy my one cigarette of the day. I always have my one cigarette with my cup of tea in the afternoon. Anyway, he looked at me as bold as brass and asked me if I had been writing to Lilian, Lady Otterton. I looked at him and I thought to myself, now, there's no good you gazing at me with those big brown eyes of yours, and making suggestions like that.

Of course he knew that *Lilian* had wanted to pay me to spy for her, but he must have known perfectly well that I would do no such thing. Furthermore I'd already told him so. Of course, like all men, when I gave him a piece of my mind, he tried to sweet talk me. 'Go on Annie,' he says, 'don't take on so . . .' I couldn't help wondering, though, why he was asking me about *Lilian* all of a sudden. Then he told me this long story about the postman who empties the box at the farm, finding all these letters to Lilian. Neither of us could imagine who on earth might be writing to her, but it's horrible to think that someone here is spying on us all. Mr Johnson is determined to find out who it is, even if it means putting off going to Australia, he said, with a twinkle in his eye. If you ask me he'll never get to Australia. In any case he'd do better to stay here.

It wasn't until I got to bed last night that I suddenly remembered that when I did eventually write to Lady Lilian, which I should have done way back, I posted the letter down at the farm. In fact, I'd been putting off writing and keeping my fingers crossed that she had forgotten about me when I suddenly had another nasty little note from her, written, I reckon, when she was out of her mind with drink or the Lord knows what! It didn't make very much sense as far as I could see. I don't know why, but I never mentioned that note to anyone, not even to Mr Johnson. I just tore it into little bits and put it straight down the w.c. Then, ever so quickly, I wrote a letter back and posted the wretched thing at the farm last week. I think it must have been the same day that the police came for Mr Legros. And now I don't want to tell Mr Johnson about that letter or he'll think I was fibbing yesterday. In my head I have been going over and over what I wrote and cannot imagine that anyone could read anything into it that was not meant to be there, yet the whole thing worries me. I only wrote the one perfectly innocent letter of which I made and kept a copy and which certainly doesn't explain who has been sending the others.

## Letter from Annie to Lilian, Lady Otterton

Cranfield Park.
AUGUST 15TH, 1946

M'lady,

Thank you for your letter. I hope your Ladyship can appreciate that I am unable to give you any information about what passes at Cranfield. I am employed by the present Lord and Lady Otterton about whose private affairs I know nothing and to whom I owe my loyalty. Please do not ask for any further help from me.

Yours faithfully,
Annie Jerrold

## Georgina's exercise book

Father wants to by us a pony but Mummy says there too xpensive. Mr Kipling is always in the school-room making mamzel laugh. He likes her cough mixcher and is always winking and pretending to cough. I hope we get a pony.

## Zbigniew Rakowski's notebook

To what folly does an old man descend when his ancient frame is shaken as mine is by a passion more suited to the lusty heart of a younger Romeo? When I lunched earlier this month at Cranfield, so dazzled was I by her Ladyship's magical presence and so flattered by the kind attentions of Lord Otterton's gracious aunt, that I failed to remember to take my umbrella home with me. When I left my hovel in the morning, rain threatened, but the radiant sunshine of Priscilla's dazzling personality soon chased the clouds away, leaving a bright, light afternoon and a hyacinth-blue sky to match, need I say it, her Ladyship's sapphire eyes.

I did not think that Annie could reasonably be asked to make a parcel of so unwieldy an object and (let us not deceive ourselves about the matter) I somewhat relished the idea of an excuse to return as soon as I might to Cranfield, and thus I wrote to Priscilla to thank her for the delicious rabbit pie of which we had partaken, suggesting that I might, in the not too distant future, call to collect my carelessly mislaid umbrella. I have to admit that it was not without a little disappointment that I received her Ladyship's reply. Gladly she welcomed me to collect my umbrella at any time convenient to myself, insisting only that I inform Annie of my intentions. There was no invitation to share further exquisite ragouts of *oryctulagus cuniculus*, of carrots and turnips, only, or so it felt to my sick heart, instructions to collect my possessions and *scram*. Ah me, they are not long indeed, the days of wine and roses.

However, I did not wish to hasten too soon back to Cranfield, but rather preferred to relish the anxious days of sweet expectation leading up to my visit and carefully to plan it in such a way as to increase the likelihood of an encounter with the object of my dreams – nay, of my desire. So it was that yesterday morning I betook myself to Cranfield. It was about midday as I walked from the station up through the village to the park gates, bearing my small basket in which I had packed a book, my sandwiches and a cushion, for I thought to find a pleasant spot within sight of Leoni's *capolavoro* where I might sit and picnic and indulge my fancy.

As I walked up the drive and rounded the bend to see the great house away across the park, stark and red against the dark green, heavy summer background, I was reminded of my first visit to Cranfield just over a year ago. Such is the hold that this place has exerted over me since that very first day that I, a formerly sagacious old man, have been metamorphosed. I have become foolish and fanciful, but not for one moment do I regret my folly, for now I do not, as I did formerly, suffer from tedium nor from the inevitable *ennui* of the sceptic. Now there is excitement, intrigue and joy.

Yesterday, as I sat on my cushion under a tree, eating a fishpaste sandwich and gazing across at Cranfield, I could not be sure whether it was Priscilla or the house which truly held me in thrall. I had encountered no one on the drive, nor was I observed as I picked my way through nettles and thistles and up a gentle slope to the middle of a small field where a lone oak peacefully spreads its boughs. The day was hot and sultry, lazy insects hovered around my picnic, bold, daytime rabbits lolloped in and out of the hedgerows, some long-faced Guernsey cows stared soulfully at me across a rusty iron fence and somewhere a thrush sang. I was in an idyllic setting at an idyllic moment. When I had finished my picnic, I returned to the drive and walked on up it towards the house. At one point I came across a hundred tiny frogs crossing the road, leaping, hopping, jostling one another, heedless of the flattened bodies of their many peers so recently squashed by a passing vehicle, as, full of hope, they hurried on towards their destination.

Perhaps Annie had seen me approaching from a window, for no sooner had I reached the front door than there she was with my umbrella held out towards me. She did not suggest that I come in, but merely commented on the warmth of the weather and wished me good day. I can only say, that of a sudden I felt forlorn and unwilling to return immediately from whence I came. Thus it was that before betaking myself back to the village by way of the front lawn and the path that leads through the wood to the church, I wandered down towards the overgrown lake where I came across the three children attempting to capture frogs. The girl, Georgina, was, I noticed, in tears, bewailing her incompetence at the sport in hand. It crossed my mind to wonder if she might not be in danger of falling into the water and drowning, but considering her childish troubles to be none of my business, I simply doffed my sun hat, and went on my way.

Wishing to linger in the neighbourhood, for I was still hopeful of a chance encounter with her Ladyship, I found some trifling excuse to visit the village shop and post office where I happened to run into Mr Johnson. Johnson is a fine-looking fellow, a self-assured north countryman of some fifty summers, who joined the war with the 11th Hussars as a reservist and subsequently became Lord Otterton's driver. I have never been quite sure exactly what function he performs at Cranfield now, but his Lordship evidently holds him in the highest esteem and he in return is apparently devoted to his

Lordship. Perhaps his function is in some degree to act as a father figure to his indisciplined young employer.

I think that Mr Johnson was not immediately aware of my presence, for he was engaged in a curious exchange with a postman and the spinster lady who keeps the shop. I could not help but remark that, even in this warm weather, Miss Gooch, as she is called, was wearing her usual grey, knitted mittens. Her poor hands are twisted with arthritis. The postman stood between her and Johnson, one elbow leaning casually on the counter, with his hat held behind his head between the thumb and forefinger of his other hand, thus permitting himself to use the ear-finger, not for the purpose for which it was named, but rather with which to scratch his balding pate. After a moment, Miss Gooch, sensing my presence, interrupted the conversation to wish me good afternoon. It was then that Johnson first noticed me, but not before I had partially divined the nature of the discourse in which the three of them were involved.

It would appear that they had been discussing calligraphy. Mr Johnson, in possession of various samples of handwriting, was, to my amazement, being advised by Miss Gooch and the postman as to whether or not they were familiar with any of them. 'I seen that one,' I heard the postman say ungrammatically, as he continued scratching his head in the manner I have described. Miss Gooch meanwhile looked a little puzzled. She is a gentle old lady who always wears her snowy hair tied into a roll at the nape of her neck by a blue ribbon attached around her head. This ribbon and her overall both seem designed to match the thick rich, waxy blue of the paper bags used by grocers everywhere. Despite her spectacles, she appears to be a little short-sighted and so was bent like a small mouse over whatever it was that Mr Johnson had placed on the counter, her grey paws placed carefully side by side.

I may be an old man, but as a professional writer, it is ever my business to observe. It sometimes occurs to me that whatever quaint mannerisms may be mine, they have the effect of bamboozling others as to my real nature. Thus I do not suppose for one moment that it crossed the mind of either Johnson or Miss Gooch that I was even remotely aware that what they were involved in was no ordinary commercial transaction, yet, as soon as Johnson became conscious of my presence, he hastily snatched up various pieces of paper and stuffed them into his pocket. He gave me a somewhat cursory nod and a flat, north-country 'good-afternoon', before swiftly leaving the shop with a few muttered words to Miss Gooch and a sidelong glance at the postman. A rather flustered Miss Gooch then hastened to attend to my requirements.

On reflection, there was something so strange about the whole episode, that it was as if I had entered the pages of my own novel. *The Poisoned Postmistress*, I instantly thought, or perhaps *The Soldier Servant's Revenge*. But what, I wonder, can verily lie at the root of all this mystery?

I haven't yet put my new proposal to either Lord or Lady Otterton. I shall do so forthwith, as indeed I must.

## *Georgina's exercise book*

AUGUST 30TH

Yesterday Mr Rkofsky cort us down by the lake. Were not supposed to go there becaus me and Jamie cant swim. Thomas said it was all right becos he could save us if we fell in and he wanted to get some frogs to put in mamzel's bed. Acsherly we only got one and it escaped. Mamzel was livid. She said she saw us out of the window and we wernt on the lawn but we said we were. Mr Rkofsky looks funny. I think hes very old. He's got a beerd and a sun hat and talks like an old old man.

# Annie's diary

I cannot understand how Mr Johnson knows that I wrote to Lilian, Lady Otterton. Of course he may be simply guessing, but it's most peculiar him being so sure. Naturally I've said nothing, I've only told him that he has no idea what he's talking about. 'Now come on Annie,' he says. 'You can come clean.' He makes me quite cross, and to tell the truth, I suspect he's being difficult just because of Bert's arrival which will have put his nose out of joint no end, I should think. Anyway all he can think about these days now the football has started up again for the first time since the war, is winning the pools and dashing off to the other side of the world. Thousands of people were so excited about the football, that they all turned out the other day in the pouring rain to watch some match or other. As for me, I'd sooner stay at home and do my ironing, or go for a quiet walk through the fields.

His Lordship's been in a bad mood lately too, so, between the pair of them, I've been pretty fed up. Mr Kipling hadn't finished the work he was supposed to have done on the cottage by the time Bert appeared, which is hardly surprising, since he spends all day up on the school-room landing with Mamzelle, laughing and giggling. Anyway the fuss about the cottage made his Lordship see red although he just thinks it's funny about Mr Kipling and Mamzelle, so he doesn't say anything to Mr Kipling but lets him get away with murder. It's a wonder what that man sees in Mamzelle, if you ask me, but I couldn't help laughing to myself the other day when I heard Mrs Kipling say that she was welcome to have the lazy so-and-so for all she cared.

Then there's Father who's staying on till October now because his new cottage isn't ready either, and, in any case, he's all of a dither about moving. Not that he ever complains, but I can tell. And naturally he's worried to death about his blessed cows. We don't know anything yet about the man his Lordship has taken on, but Father thinks the yield is sure to go down as soon as he retires. And I don't doubt it.

Bert's been at me too of course, because I haven't been seeing him as much as he would like, but I told him that what with Father and one thing and another, I haven't the time. I don't think he's cottoned on to Mr Johnson yet.

### *Sydney Otterton's diary*

SEPTEMBER 15TH

Blasted Kipling is never anywhere to be found although Priscilla tells me he spends half his time in the school-room with that French woman who apparently calls him *le petit homme au châpeau rond* and fills him up with *crème de menthe*. I don't know what Mrs Kipling has to say about it, but I should think he must be pretty desperate if he's after Mlle. She must be twice his age. Anyway, it's quite annoying because he hasn't finished the work he's supposed to have done on Bert Farthing's cottage, so Bert's living in something like a slum. The window frames are all splintering and the whole place is riddled with rot. In fact Bert's been pretty good about it and has been doing some work on the place himself. Priscilla gets cross because she says she can't think how I commanded a regiment or led a column across the desert, if I can't even sort Kipling out. What am I supposed to do? Go up to the school-room and tell the pair of them to stop boozing?

Johnson's making a bit of a nuisance of himself at the moment too. I don't know why he has to go on so much about all these letters he says someone's been sending my mother. I don't want to hear any more about it, but he's determined to get to the bottom of it. He told me point blank that he didn't think it had anything to do with Annie. It's never ever crossed my mind that she might be involved in any way with my mother. Now he wants to know if I can find a sample of Legros's handwriting because the nosy postman has a theory that the letters have stopped. It's ridiculous to suppose that I can control who writes to whom. In any case whoever it is that was writing could be posting their letters somewhere else for all I know, or care. You can't go around suspecting the Legros; the frightful pair didn't even know my mother.

Much more to the point is my maiden speech which I'd rather given up thinking about but which I will be making some time in the autumn. Obviously it'll be about what most concerns me which is the agricultural industry and housing. Everything to do with all that is chaotic at the moment and I'm sure I'm not the only landlord with such insoluble problems on my hands, even if I am the only one with an estate carpenter who spends his time poodle-faking with a geriatric governess.

In fact I find that with the House of Lords not sitting at the moment, I become quite restless spending all my time here. Perhaps it's just because nothing ever seems to be settled and Priscilla who does so much so well makes me feel pretty useless at times. I can't help thinking things will get a bit easier once we do finally get probate, whenever that will be. At least, then, I'll have some idea of how things stand.

I thought of buying a horse and a pony for the children but foolishly mentioned it to Priscilla who announced categorically that I couldn't afford either. There doesn't seem to be much point in living in a place like this if you can't even have a horse, and the children were delighted by the thought of a pony but now we'll just have to see how things go next year.

One good thing is that Priscilla has found a respectable widow who certainly ought to be a better bet than the Legros to take the flat. But on top of that particular success, she's begun to get really very fed up with Cheadle. She insists that he has to go, and I can't deny that he was absolutely blotto when Priscilla's aunt came to lunch. He couldn't begin to walk in a straight line and at one point I really thought he was going to fall over, but I still can't help feeling sorry for the old boy. With that great big red hooked nose of his, he looks more like my parrot than anything else, and I don't suppose for a moment that he'll find another job very easily. Mrs Cheadle looks like a real martinet; she probably cracks a whip at him to keep him in some sort of order. No wonder the poor fellow has taken to the bottle, living with a woman like her. I've promised Priscilla I'll talk to him at the end of the week but I can't say I'm looking forward to doing so, although I suppose I'll have to. After all, I know Priscilla has a point; apart from anything else the bugger's getting through my port at a terrific rate.

I've been having rather unpleasant nightmares lately so in order to put off the hour of going to sleep, I've been sitting up late and consequently drinking rather a lot myself which may explain why I'm not very much in Priscilla's good books at the moment.

## Annie's diary

SEPTEMBER 19TH

Mr Johnson told me in the end how he knew I'd written to *Lilian*. Apparently he's been talking to the postman who empties the box at the farm. I wasn't very pleased with him and haven't spoken to him for a week which not only serves him right, but is just as well because it's given me a chance to see a bit of Bert who's feeling rather down in the dumps since coming here. I told him it was his own damn fault. No one asked him to move. It's hardly surprising if he misses the cottage he's lived in all his life which, in any case, is a darned sight nicer than what he's living in now. That cottage has been empty for any number of years so no wonder it's full of damp and falling to bits. He wasn't very pleased either when I made it quite plain that we weren't picking up where we left off. 'Oh, Annie,' he said, 'I only came here because of you.' 'More fool you,' I said. It's not that I mind keeping him company of an evening from time to time, but he needn't think I'm being his unpaid housekeeper-cum-wife. He can look elsewhere for a fool who's prepared to play that part. I don't really know why I didn't stop him from coming here in the first place. Mark my words, there's bound to be trouble.

There's a new person coming into the flat which her Ladyship's very pleased about. We've had to go and clear it up behind the Legros. They left a shocking mess and it took Mrs Kipling and Mrs Summers all morning to make the place look half respectable. You'd have thought it hadn't seen a duster since before the Legros moved in. The oven was covered in grease, there was some sour milk left in the Frigidaire, the bath and the w.c. were filthy, there were dog hairs all over the place and there was even a bowl full of stinking dog food in the middle of the bedroom floor. It was quite peculiar. Considering how neat and tidy the pair of them always looked, you would have thought that Mrs Legros would have been most particular. Her Ladyship and I were just taking the loose covers off the chairs to get them cleaned when Mr Johnson turned up to see if her Ladyship needed him to mend anything or move some furniture. I just let him get on with it and didn't pay him a blind bit of notice, although I did hear him say he'd take all the rubbish down, and there was plenty of that. I doubt the Legros had so much as emptied a waste-paper basket during the whole time they were here.

What with one thing and another, I sometimes wonder how long his Lordship and her Ladyship will be able to keep going here. There seem to be so many difficulties in every quarter, not to mention all the personal intrigue that goes on and, if his Lordship doesn't give Mr Cheadle the sack shortly, I think there'll be a hell of a to-do. I keep my mouth shut but

I do know Mr Johnson said something to his Lordship about all the empty port bottles that were put out last week. He didn't say anything about Mr Cheadle though, but only passed a comment. His Lordship can draw his own conclusions, but I think he'd have a bit of a shock if he went and looked in his cellar which is supposed to have been well stocked since before the war. I really don't know why his Lordship keeps Cheadle on. Either he can't be bothered to do anything about finding a new butler, or he really thinks the whole thing is just funny. And I wouldn't put that past him. He always thinks everything is funny.

## Sydney Otterton's diary

SEPTEMBER 28TH

I sacked Cheadle yesterday morning. All Priscilla could find to say when I told her was, 'High time too!' Of course she's right up to a point but when I thought he was about to blub I couldn't help feeling sorry for the miserable old so-and-so. For one thing, it's impossible to imagine what will happen to him now. I don't suppose he could stop drinking if he tried, so even if he gets another job, he won't keep it for long. He's probably been at the bottle all his life and you can hardly blame him for that, with a wife like his. Well I soon stopped feeling sorry for him when he turned on me and called me every name under the sun. Luckily Johnson was around down in the basement after that. I don't know what he was doing, but he found Cheadle in a terrible rage, getting ready to pour all my best port down the drain as an act of revenge. Johnson managed to calm him down and when he told me about it later, he said that even he felt sorry for Cheadle. The man's got a wife and two children still at school and now he'll have nowhere to live. I felt so guilty about it that I started drinking rather earlier than I should have myself.

After that I began thinking about my mother again. I suppose that when one is a child whatever happens seems normal since it is the only norm one knows, but by Jove it was peculiar living on the top floor of this house with a mad mother who either screamed at one or ignored one and of whom I was certainly afraid. The servants were terrified of her too. I used to lie in bed at night petrified lest she should decide to come roaming around the house seeking whom she might devour. Sometimes she would come into my room and stare at me crazily without saying anything and then turn and leave as suddenly as she had come. At other, rarer but in some ways more awful times, she would put on a tremendous show of acutely embarrassing and quite artificial maternal concern, boasting to whoever was around about her marvellous son. The very memory of her mad, vacant stare is enough to make me shudder. I can't think why my father didn't have her locked up, as she occasionally threatened to do to me when she disapproved of something I'd done.

I suppose that I initially came to understand how mad and bad she was when I used to be sent to stay with my cousins in Devon. Their mother was so kind and sweet and always appeared so concerned for me when the time came to pack me off back home. Nowadays the more I think of my father living in this house with a woman like that, the more I pity him although I can't really forgive him for having been so weak. I remember now, that whenever she was out or away, which wasn't very often, he would become quite a different man. He would relax and become mellower, laughing a lot. He made good jokes, but beyond that, I don't think we ever had a serious conversation. I think we were wary of each other. Now that it's too late, there are a lot of things I would like to be able to ask him.

Thomas went back to school last week which was just as well as Mlle can't begin to control him, but all the same, I couldn't help feeling a pang when I saw him go. He was quite subdued, not at all his usual cocky self. In fact he looked quite forlorn as he got into the car and I couldn't help wondering what the future held for him, or indeed what there will be left of this place by the time I kick the bucket. Nothing, I should think, to judge from the way things are going. The other children both seem remarkably jolly as if they didn't have a care in the world. Mlle has them out there every day picking food from the fields and hedgerows – dandelions, blackberries, sorrel, mushrooms, wild carrots. She'll be feeding them on bird's-nest soup before she's through.

Johnson's still going on about those letters to my mother and his latest idea is that they definitely were from the Legros. I told him not to be a bloody fool. How could the Legros have anything to do with my mother or know anything about her, let alone how to get in touch with her? And in any case, what would they have to say to her? They came out of nowhere and, according to someone, had been living abroad in Switzerland all through the war. Anyway, he says that when the flat was cleared out after they left, he found some samples of their handwriting in the dustbin which he then took up to the Post Office where both Miss Gooch and the postman swore that it was the same as the writing on the envelopes addressed to my mother. If you ask me the whole thing's getting quite out of hand, but Priscilla is a bit uneasy about it all and can't quite dismiss the thought of Legros. In any case, I don't see that there's very much we can do about it either way since the fellow's probably in jug by now.

## *Georgina's exercise book*

SEPTEMBER 29TH

Poor Thomas had to go back to school. He says its beastly and they beat you all the time and give you no food. Weve started lessons again. Major Doubleday is boring. He makes us do spelling and tables all the time. Mamzel makes us talk French at tea. Jamie just giggles.

## *Sydney Otterton's diary*

I don't know what Johnson expects me to do about the blasted Legros. Everyone's talking about the Nuremberg verdicts and all he can think about is Legros, as if the fellow were some sort of monster on a par with Goering or Ribbentrop. He even seems to think that I ought to write to my mother and ask her if she knows anything about the Legros. I've told him that that would be perfectly pointless because, subject as she is to insane delusions, she'd only lie. She might not even answer my letter. As far as I can see, the sooner the whole matter is forgotten, the better. Priscilla thinks that Johnson has a point for once. She thinks that if we were being spied on by a crook, we ought not merely to try to find out what has been going on, but to make it absolutely clear to my mother that we won't put up with any more of it. She also thinks that the Legros must have stolen things from us and that we should go through everything very carefully to see if anything is missing. There is so much junk in this house and there are so many pictures and snuff-boxes and trinkets everywhere that probably even I don't know exactly what we've got. Besides everything has been moved about so much since before the war that it's impossible to remember where some pieces of furniture are, let alone all the damn bibelots. None of the best things appear to have been touched, some of which would have been easy to take. I somehow don't think that whatever the truth about them may be, those Legros were thieves.

Rakowski is back again. I must say I was even quite pleased

to see him. But no doubt not as pleased as Priscilla. She makes a lot of fun of him behind his back but I think, like me, she finds him funny and unusual, besides which he flatters her a lot and makes her think she's very clever. She is perfectly clever, but she gets fed up with me because I'm so unintellectual and is furious when I tease her for reading French books. In fact I rather admire her for being able to, but I'm not going to say so. Anyway Rakowski and she bang on together about Proust and Gide and Flaubert which seems to make them both happy. Funny thing about Rakowski is that, for all his affected mannerisms and all his archaic turns of phrase, he's not really intellectually pretentious. Probably because he has such an acute sense of the ridiculous which he depends upon to present the ludicrous image he does of himself. An image behind which he hides so that none of us probably knows the real Rakowski. Anyway he's back again. I wonder what he'd think if he knew that at one time Johnson suspected him of being the secret letter-writer. But he's apparently been exculpated. Johnson saw him in the Post Office one afternoon which, for some reason, he found very suspicious. I can't imagine Johnson having a good word to say for Rakowski whom I've often heard him refer to as that 'pansy writer'. Next to Legros, he'd probably be most delighted to see him incriminated.

This time the pansy writer has an idea that he wants to write a history of the Otterton family. Of course there are masses more papers for him to go through here and my aunt, who took to him when she met him at lunch, has been, as she would say, *moost* enthusiastic about the idea. She has got quite a few family papers and she not only knows a great deal about the family, but, despite evidence to the contrary, she firmly believes that the Ottertons are the greatest blessing that the Good Lord ever happened to bestow on this country. They're certainly a rum bunch which is probably what appeals to Rakowski about them. I don't really know what the fellow thinks he's doing, though, because he hasn't finished his book on the Whigs yet and, according to Priscilla, is being chased by his publisher.

## Zbigniew Rakowski's notebook

So it is settled that I am to return on a regular basis to Cranfield. Lord and Lady Otterton and indeed his Lordship's gracious aunt, Lady Isley, have all encouraged me most generously in my new undertaking. Not wishing to put too high a value on my poor self as a writer, I am somewhat tempted to suspect that neither Lord Otterton nor Lady Isley felt entirely indifferent to what they may both have perceived as a flattering request on my part. They may have been not a little surprised that an old Polak such as myself should become so interested in a family abounding with rakes and turncoats, with angry men and eccentrics, that he would wish to devote some two or three hundred pages to their antics, not to mention the many hours required to research those antics. Whatever surprise they may have felt, however, they kept concealed and purported to regard it as only natural that their family should be of inordinate interest to anyone who might pause for one moment to consider it.

There are, of course, as well as the rakes and turncoats, one or two deserving members of the family whose deeds are worthy of recall. Not least of these is the great Sydney Otterton, the eighteenth-century Speaker of the House of Commons, renowned unlike, alas, too many of the family, for his integrity and devotion to duty, and who at the end of a long life, suffered a protracted and painful death which he is said to have borne with courage, good humour and breeding! I have to say that Lord Otterton is himself less anxious than his aunt to promote the respectable members of the family. He, with a wide grin, would rather dwell on one Tom

Otterton whose passion was to drive a four-in-hand and of whom it was apparently said that he possessed an infinity of wit that not too infrequently degenerated into buffoonery. Lord Otterton, I conclude, is more than likely sensible of an affinity with this character.

Although I am of the opinion that I will delight in the undertaking on which I will shortly embark, of course it is not the integrity and wisdom of Speaker Otterton alone, nor is it the tomfoolery of his descendants that draws me back and back to Cranfield, that house which has so infiltrated my soul as to have now become almost a part of my very being. My frivolous work of fiction is all but finished, yet I have decided that for the time being I must put it aside, most particularly because I sense that with my return to the house, I may feel the need to alter it and develop it in directions that had not hitherto occurred to me. As for my other work, I fear that I am still lagging behind with it. It will be long overdue before it reaches my publisher's desk but I mean to make a start on my further research whilst completing the work in hand. Perhaps I will allow myself a visit to Cranfield as a reward for finishing a chapter, thus providing my idle old self with a carrot when what I truly need may be a stick.

Priscilla, not altogether surprisingly, is somewhat sardonic with regard to my project. 'They're a very dull family, you know,' she says. 'Not one of them ever read a book and their taste has always been quite appalling.' 'Ah, but Ma'am,' I reply, 'they caused to be built one of the great houses of England, something of which they can be justly proud. Think Ma'am,' I begged her, 'of Rysbrack's exquisite chimney pieces, think of his garlanded grapes, of his sacrifice to Diana, his sacrifice to Bacchus, and let me hear no more of this nonsense.' 'I can only imagine that the Ottertons were very vulgar at the time,' she retorts, 'vying with other rich families as to who could have the biggest or the grandest house. Or as to who could spend most money. Cranfield was just an accident dependent on the circumstance. Consider,' she says, 'the monstrosity they would have built had good fortune attended them a hundred and fifty years later.' 'Ah, the ifs and buts of history,' I sigh. Yet no one is more carried away than she by the enchantment of the very house she affects to denigrate.

## Letter from Annie to Dolly

NOVEMBER 3RD, 1946

Dear Dolly,

Thank you for your letter. I'm sorry not to have written for so long but we have been very busy here what with one thing and another and then I have been helping Father move as well. He seems quite happy at the lodge and says that it suits him at his age to have a smaller garden. Mind you he has already started digging it. He says that no one has looked after that garden since before the war. Well, I wouldn't be surprised because for one thing the house has been empty. It's not in too bad a condition though and the w.c. is just by the back door. I wish it was inside, but at least it's not right at the end of the garden.

The new cowman has come. He is a little red-headed man with a very big wife. They have several children who make a lot of noise and get on Bert's nerves next door. Bert has cheered up a bit which is just as well but I suspect he's really regretting having made the move. Not that he'd admit it, mind.

There's also a new butler. A Mr Mason. He and Mrs Mason keep themselves to themselves so I'm not sure what to think of them yet. I rather think his Lordship misses Mr Cheadle, for all his faults, and the children are always singing a song he taught them about a brown-faced sailor. Rather a drunken song, if you ask me. Not that I've said so.

His Lordship has bought a pink and white cockatoo which lives with the parrot in his dressing-room and makes a frightful darned mess and a lot of noise. Her Ladyship was none too pleased when that put in an appearance.

The house is very cold and we are all hoping that we don't have too hard a winter.

Well that's all the news for now. Give my love to the children.

Love from
Annie


## Sydney Otterton's diary

Having spent the evening with Tony, I got home pretty late last night and needless to say have an almighty hangover this morning. I think he's agreed to come and live here after Christmas. I know he likes the idea and only hesitates for fear that it might not work out and we might regret it. Priscilla agrees with me that it's an easy way to help an old friend and that, in any case, it would be nice for us to have him here. He can pay a peppercorn rent, if he feels like it.

I'd been at the House of Lords all afternoon where they were debating the rise in the divorce rate. The Lord Chancellor kept talking about a tidal wave of divorce sweeping the country, but, as Tony said, what else can you expect? He came back after the war to find his wife disappeared, as no doubt hundreds of other men did (Johnson for one) and I don't really see what the government or any other government can do about it. In my view it would be quite impossible in any case for a man to come back from fighting or from being a prisoner of war and to pick up with his wife as if nothing had happened. Apart from anything else, you've hardly seen each other for six years.

Anyway next week I've got my maiden speech to make, which is causing me a lot of trouble. I know what I want to say but I want to be sure of doing it well, but still, I don't quite understand why the prospect of standing up and saying what I have to say seems rather more terrifying at times than the thought of a line of German tanks. I'll be glad when it's over.

## Zbigniew Rakowski's notebook

DECEMBER 10TH

Today I visited Cranfield for the last time this year. It was bitterly cold in the Red Drawing-Room despite a small electric heater with one bar that Annie very kindly saw fit to provide me with. Next time I go there I shall remember to take a rug to wrap around my knees. I doubt that I could gladly suffer such cold again, even for a glance from her Ladyship's blue eyes or for the pleasure of lunching with her.

Lord Otterton at luncheon was much concerned with the House of Lords and his maiden speech which he apparently delivered with aplomb yesterday afternoon. He seemed quite elated by what had clearly been a success for him. I enquired as to the subject on which he had addressed the House. It was indeed a subject that must be dear to his heart, concerning the housing of the rural labour force and the renovation of old cottages, which he claims would be considerably more economical than the building of new houses. I feel that to a certain extent we were treated to a repeat performance of yesterday's speech, with his Lordship ending his oration with a flourish of sentiment, for we, he says are merely trustees for the future, whose duty it is to protect the beauty of our villages and countryside and not destroy them with indiscriminate building for which future generations will curse us. Lord Otterton appeared to have the full support of his consort in this matter.

So I shall not now return to Cranfield until the New Year but hermit-like will withdraw to my small dwelling where I shall slave over the final chapter of the Whigs, interrupted briefly only by the annual Christmas visit of my poor daughter and her tedious husband. At least I shall have the consolation of knowing that it will be easier for me to keep the frostbite at bay in my small room than it ever would be in the Red Drawing-Room at Cranfield.

## *Sydney Otterton's diary*

DECEMBER 10TH

Priscilla is wonderful as usual. God knows how she keeps this house afloat as well as being so very nice and encouraging as she was to me about my speech which, I have to say, went off very well. Several people congratulated me about it after-wards so that I felt quite pleased with myself. It seemed like the first thing I'd done at all well since the end of the war, so that all yesterday evening and this morning I was quite fired up by the prospect of some kind of continuing political involvement.

Then old Rakowski came to lunch and asked how the speech had gone and by the time I'd talked about it to him and gone through the whole thing again, I suddenly felt very flat and deflated. It's freezing cold and quite impossible to keep this place warm. I know we're lucky to have our own logs, but we need coal as well, so let's hope we have a mild winter as it appears that the country's already running out of fuel.

Poor Priscilla's keeping an amazing smile on her face and doing her very best about Christmas which is a nightmare that none of us can afford. I admire her energy and her level-headedness. It's hardly surprising if she gets a bit fed up with me at times as I seem to go from the heights to the depths without any warning. A depressing letter from my solicitors this morning didn't help either. I'll be glad when Christmas is over.

## Georgina's exercise book

No more lessons. Goody-goody gumdrops! Thomas is coming home tomorrow and theirs only a week till Christmas. Goody-goody gumdrops!

# 1947

## Georgina's exercise book

Poor Thomas had to go back to school today. He looked sad and now he's gone me and Jamie have to start lessons. Boo-hoo. We prayed for snow so we'd get snowed in and he wouldn't have to go but it didn't work. Jamie's always singing a briliant song Mr Cheedle taught us about the brown faced sailor lardy dardy da. Father thinks its funny but Mummy says its silly. Anyway Mr Cheedle's gone and now we've got Mr Mason who is boring. Mamzel keeps teaching us French songs about o clair de la looner. I heard her singing them to Mr Kipling and he was laughing. Father's got a friend called Tony whose come to live with us. He's awfully nice.

## Annie's diary

I can truly say I have never been so cold in all my life. What with the fuel shortage and now a shortage of food as well, it'll be a wonder if any of us ever survive this winter. The meat ration was reduced again yesterday from one and tuppence worth a week to a shilling's worth and now they're even talking of rationing bread. No one's going to be getting very fat with that.

Mr Rakowski was here yesterday, working away in the Red Drawing-Room with a rug wrapped round his knees and a hot-water bottle which I filled up for him a couple of times by his feet. I can just see him struggling on and off the bus with that great heavy stone thing under his arm and his rug and all his bits and pieces of paper. He was wearing mittens while he worked but he told me that by the time he left at three o'clock, he thought he might have frostbite on his fingers. Never mind frostbite, but I'm sure he'll have chilblains. His fingers looked blue with the cold. I said that I wondered at him venturing out in weather like this. 'Ah Ma'am,' he says, 'but a man has a living to earn.' You can't help laughing.

It's just as well really that Father has moved. The lodge with that tiny kitchen is much easier to keep warm than the other house was, but I don't like the idea of him at his age having to go outside to the w.c. in the dark in this freezing weather. I would hate to think of him slipping on the ice and breaking something and then lying there alone all night. I told him to keep a chamber pot in the bedroom but he pretended he hadn't heard. He just sat there with his eyes twinkling and never said a word. I know he hates to admit that he's getting any older. He doesn't think much to the new cowman, but then he wouldn't, would he? And he certainly disapproves of the thought of a new milking machine. What he says is that it's always been the case that a cow needs milking by hand, and it always will be.

Mr Johnson annoys me. He's still talking about Australia as if he was likely to be off there any minute. 'I'd be on that boat tomorrow if I could,' he says. Then he goes on about it being summer over there and he laughs and looks a bit soppy and says, 'Wouldn't you come with me, Annie?' No fear, I told him. Wild horses wouldn't drag me to the other side of the world, summertime or no summertime. Then he says he's not talking about wild horses but kangaroos. 'Think of all that sunshine, sweet Annie,' he says. I quickly told him not to 'sweet Annie' me and that it would soon be winter again as like as not, once we got there. So then he goes on about the blasted kangaroos. Now I ask you, what would I want with kangaroos? I suppose he's just pulling my leg because I'm sure he's too old really to think of emigrating, although he does say he's applied for the papers. But I have to admit, I was a bit worried when his Lordship asked me the other day what I really thought about Mr Johnson going to Australia. 'I don't know what I'd do without him, Annie,' he said. 'You know he was my driver during the war.' Well, we all know that. Then his Lordship goes on praising him up to the skies, saying you don't find many like him, so brave and trustworthy and loyal. On and on he goes. He thinks the world of him. All I could say was that I couldn't imagine him going, and his Lordship looked quite relieved. 'You do your best to persuade him to stay, Annie,' he said. Well, I'll do that, whatever happens.

## *Zbigniew Rakowski's notebook*

As her Ladyship's faithful Annie would say, it is cold enough to freeze a brass monkey and has indeed been so for many days. The good Annie was kind enough to replenish more than once the hot-water bottle which I had had the foresight to take with me on my last visit to Cranfield. Without it I fear I might, like Captain Scott, have been found huddled up and frozen to death despite the fire which had been generously kindled on my behalf in the Red Drawing-Room and which made not the slightest difference to the icy temperature in which I found myself. It is quite hard to imagine how all those good people survive in the Arctic conditions which they are obliged to endure in the house of my dreams. They have plenty of wood from around the place to keep the fires burning, but it is coal or coke that is needed if any heat is to be given out, and with the crisis deepening in Mr Shinwell's newly nationalised mines, it hardly seems that there will be very much of either commodity available for any of us in the near future. For myself, I feel that I will be obliged to wait until this cold spell is over before returning to my labours at Cranfield. I trust the wait will be of but short duration.

With the departure of the inimitable Cheadle, the atmosphere in the house has changed a little. The new man has an expressionless face and cold eyes behind which I felt I discerned a hint of mockery. I should like to watch him more closely for there is something about him that makes me feel a touch uneasy. He came, while I was at my work, ostensibly to put a little something on the fire, but in truth, I am of the opinion that he came to check up on me. I did not care for the way he glanced at me, nor indeed did I care for the insolent manner in which he addressed me, instructing me to leave everything as I had found it.

Priscilla bears up wonderfully under what must be very difficult conditions. She, with her indefatigable energy, her wit and efficiency, manages to radiate a special warmth and to enliven the very house with her vigour. I shall miss her during my absence, as I always do. She laughs at me for wishing to write about the Otterton family, so that occasionally I am minded to ponder once again on how she will react to my trifling melodrama. She in fact has asked no further questions about it of late and has perhaps put it from her mind.

### Sydney Otterton's diary

FEBRUARY 12TH

There's been an almighty bloody snowfall. The drive will be completely impassable unless they've managed to get the horses harnessed to the snowplough, which I doubt as most of the men will be snowed into their cottages. In fact what we could really do with at the moment is a confounded tractor. We can't even get out of this house as the snowdrifts come to half-way up the front door. Tony and I started to give Johnson a hand to dig a way out of the back door, but we didn't get very far because there was nowhere to go but into another drift. The telephone lines are down and, according to Mlle who heard it on the wireless just before the power was cut off, half the rest of the country is without power or fuel. Luckily Priscilla has quite a supply of candles and there's a certain amount of wood stored in the basement, but God alone knows what we'll do if this lasts for long and it certainly doesn't look like thawing yet. Things were bad enough during the cold weather in January what with Kipling risking his life every other day, climbing into the most impossible places to unfreeze frozen pipes with his blow-lamp, while that bloody fool of a Frenchwoman shouted from below, '*Bravo, le petit homme au châpeau rond!*' which only served to drive him on to further dare-devil exploits. And now with this lot, all I can say is, heaven help us when the thaw does set in and every vulnerable part of the roof gives way, which it surely will.

Despite the fact that Priscilla has always hated the snow which she says gives her a headache, there's a very jolly atmosphere in the house as we all feel ourselves to be in a state of siege. It's almost like being in gaol again. Johnson and Tony and I had a bit of a booze-up in the Japanese room to warm us up after our failed attempt to escape. There wasn't any booze in gaol but Johnson remembered a time in the desert when we thought we'd captured some whiskey off a retreating column of Italians, but it turned out to be scent which was part of their rations. That was a bitter disappointment. Then there was another time when we had better luck. I'd been on sick leave and was going back to join my squadron right in the south when our truck broke down, luckily not far from the rear echelons of the Indian Army Service Corps. The Indians were very kind, they entertained us in their dug-in tents, put us up for the night, mended the truck and sent us on our way. When we reached the squadron the next day, I found they'd also loaded us up with a whole lot of all the things we most valued, like beer, tea, sugar, tinned milk, tinned fruit and even some whiskey.

'Now here we are in t' bloody snowstorm without any Indians,' says Johnson. So then we spent some time discussing in a rather frivolous fashion whether we'd rather be in a snowstorm or a sandstorm. No conclusions were reached although all three of us agreed that at times we couldn't help missing playing fox and geese with Jerry in the desert, and yet we all three still have nightmares about it. Well all nightmares are obviously pretty confused, so that I sometimes dream that I'm at Villers Bocage, or back in gaol, having abandoned the Regiment to be destroyed by Rommel somewhere in Egypt, and that I can't escape and I panic, and everyone else is dead, and then of course I wake up in a bloody awful sweat. One of the worst things about being in gaol was not knowing what had happened to the Regiment and particularly to the rest of my Division after I was captured at Villers Bocage, although occasionally new prisoners would arrive bringing news from outside.

11 P.M.

There didn't seem much chance of getting out today so I was scribbling in my diary just after lunch when all of a sudden the power was reconnected for a few hours, which means that we have at least been able to hear the news. The weather forecast is dreadful, with no let-up in sight. In some parts of the country the R.A.F. is dropping food parcels for people and livestock in isolated villages, all the coal trains are stuck in twenty-foot drifts and the troops have been called in to help clear the main roads. All this with the country teetering on the verge of bankruptcy.

Anyway the good news is that they managed to get the snowplough harnessed down at the farm and they've begun to clear the drive where, luckily, the drifts don't appear to be too bad. In the end Johnson succeeded in digging quite a path from the back door, but I still fell into a snowdrift up to my waist because I couldn't find the damn drive. All the same I was able to get down to where the plough was and give the men a bit of encouragement. Of course they had to stop what they were doing by four thirty because of lack of light, but if it doesn't snow again tonight and if the wind doesn't get up, they should be able to go on in the morning from where they left off. But whatever happens, conditions will be pretty treacherous because of these sub-zero temperatures.

Annie was worried to death about old Jerrold on his own at the lodge and insisted on making her way all the way down there to see him. Priscilla told her not to come back tonight, so we don't know how she got on although I think Johnson went with her to make sure she was all right. I hope they've got some heat in that cottage, although I know Annie'll look after Jerrold somehow. I'm not sure about murder, but I don't doubt she'd steal for him. I must admit, it was a sad day when he retired. The new man seems like a decent fellow although of course the yield dropped as soon as Jerrold went. It'll be right down now, with this lot, and that's for sure.

There's one thing about Cranfield in the snow which always strikes me, though, and which, however dejected one may be and however appalling the circumstances, serves to lift the spirits. I was bowled over by it again this afternoon as I walked back up from seeing the horses pulling the plough. I have heard people describe the house as severe, even plain. Those who don't use their eyes sometimes dismiss it, superciliously comparing it to a red-brick jam factory. Why jam, I shall never know. But the truth is that when the snow lies on the ground, especially as thick and sparkling as it is at the moment, those bricks shine, each with a rosy warmth of its own. The whole great house glows and I, for one, know that I'll never want to leave it. This evening it was particularly inviting as I walked back up the hill for there was another power cut, but in some of the windows candlelight flickered.

# *Georgina's exercise book*

Our prayer was answered and it snowed but poor Thomas is at school. I bet he's playing snowballs. It's terribly cold and I've got chilblains. At first I wanted to go out in the snow but now I hate it and were allways being made to go out. We keep falling in it and we get wet in our boots and my gluves stick to my hands and it makes you cry. Mamzel says it gives her a cough so she keeps on having that green medcin. She says it keeps her warm. Mummy says snow gives her a headache and Father says the countrys going bankrupt which Mamzel says means we havent got any money. We cant have lessons because Major Doubleday cant get here so Mamzel gives us extra French and tells us how nice it is where she lives in some mountains with lots of snow and cheese with holes in it. The kettle takes ages to boil on the fire and Mamzel says that's because we arent alloud enough coal.

# *Annie's diary*

I don't know how we're going to manage if this dreadful weather goes on much longer. Her Ladyship let me have a couple of days off to go and stay with Father. Luckily Mr Johnson came with me because we found Father climbing up a ladder with a blow-lamp, trying to unfreeze an outside pipe and Mr Johnson was able to do it for him while Father and I held the ladder. Never mind climbing a ladder, the walk was bad enough, with the pair of us slithering all over the place, and then when we reached the bend in the drive we couldn't tell where to go next. The snowplough hadn't managed to get that far, so we just had to guess which way to go, which meant we kept falling into drifts. I was soaked to the skin by the time we got to Father's. He was pleased to see us both and teased me a bit. He wanted to know what we had to laugh so much about in these hard times. Mr Johnson had a good torch and a stick but I didn't envy him walking back on his own after tea while I remained inside. Father's managed to keep his kitchen quite warm and I think he would have liked me to stay more than a couple of days. Perhaps he feels a little nervous on his own under these conditions, but he must know that I can't spend all my time at his place although I do try to go and see him as often as I can. I have my work to do. What with all this snow and ice and all the slithering about and the power cuts and one thing and another, I'm beginning to see why Mr Johnson's so keen on Australia after all.

## *Sydney Otterton's diary*

Priscilla says the children are becoming obstreperous, which she puts down to the bad weather and the fact that Double-day has either been snowed in all winter or his car hasn't been able to start, so they've hardly had any proper lessons although she's been reading *Our Island Story* to them and making them learn poetry by heart to keep them quiet and Mlle's been giving them geography lessons about the Haute-Savoie or wherever she comes from. And after yesterday's snowfall, it looks as if nothing's about to change in a hurry. As it is, the whole country seems to be at a permanent standstill. I've hardly been able to get to London for the last six weeks and Tony's been stuck at Cranfield too, worrying about whether he made the right decision by coming here in the first place. The initial euphoria which we all felt when we started getting out the snowplough has all but evaporated.

Tony and I tend to sit up late by candlelight and reminisce about the war and drink, which only annoys Priscilla and doesn't really help us much either, even if it momentarily alleviates the depressing feeling of us all being trapped.

The trouble is you can't make any plans because of the weather and in addition to that, I can't make any plans because of my financial situation. We still haven't got probate which I had really hoped would have come through by now, and we still haven't got a tractor although the bank has promised me a loan to get one as soon as I can, but since tractors are like gold dust these days, we may have to wait for some time yet.

The good news is that they're re-raising the Regiment which since the war has been too short of numbers to function. A bit of peacetime soldiering with the territorials won't come amiss. Tony's pleased about it too. It'll involve one evening a week up in St John's Wood, one camp probably in the summer and the odd weekend I should imagine.

MARCH 31ST

I cannot think why we so longed for the thaw. The floods everywhere are dreadful and this morning the ceiling fell in in one of the top-floor bedrooms. We've got buckets out catching drips in almost all the upstairs rooms and this morning I received a letter from my solicitors saying that at last we have got probate. The sum I owe in death duties is formidable by any standards. Priscilla, when I told her, immediately began to make practical suggestions about what we could sell to raise some money and was quite encouraged by the fact that long-term, low-interest bank loans are available to people with death duties to pay. All I can do is put the letter to one side and not think about it, which won't do me any good, I know that. Whatever happens, I'll have to go and see both the bank and the solicitors at the end of the week, so I suppose I'll have to face up to the situation whether I like it or not.

The other bit of bad news this morning was that Johnson came to me and told me that he is more or less definitely going to Australia. I couldn't believe my ears because I think I've been telling myself that it was all a pipe-dream of his. But he's convinced that there's another, brighter life out there for him, and who can blame him? He said he's *hud inooff* of this effing country and there's not much he'll miss about it. We shook hands and I wished him well although I had a lump in my throat. Johnson's been one of the best friends I ever had and I told him so. He laughed that dry laugh of his and said, 'You'll be all right, M'lord, you've got this lot to look after.' Then he said, 'but mind you don't drink too much,' and left the room. It was as if we'd said goodbye to one another then and there, but of course he'll be here for another couple of months until he's got everything fixed for certain.

## *Letter from Dolly to Annie*

APRIL 2ND, 1947

Dear Annie,

I don't know what we would all do without you if you went to Australia, especially Father. He was so glad when you came back to live at Cranfield and I'm sure that you being there has made all the difference to his retirement. Of course the rest of us come to see him whenever we can, but you must understand how hard it is to get away when you have a family, not to mention the expense. I appreciate that what with them being nearer, Wilfie and Ethel manage to get over rather more often than we do, or than Elsie does, but then of course you've always been Father's favourite, ever since Mother died. People say you've almost been a second wife to him.

You will have to make your own decision, but what about

Bert? Have you thought about him? What would he say if you suddenly disappeared off to Australia with this Mr Johnson of yours? Now Annie, let me give you a piece of good advice from a younger sister, which is that they never marry you with the same face they court you. What would happen to you if you got all the way to Australia and Mr Johnson turned out not to be the man you thought he was? You would be stranded out there with no family and, never mind the assisted passage out, how would you be able to afford the passage home? I don't want to hurt your feelings but, at your age, it is unlikely that you will be having any children, so you could find yourself in a really lonely position. And how do you know that you would like Australia anyway? The children have been asking if Auntie Annie would have to walk on her head if she went there. Well, in some ways you might feel that you really were walking on your head with everything being so unfamiliar and there being snakes and things.

In the end, though, the decision is yours, but please don't make it without bearing in mind everything I have said. I haven't discussed the matter with anyone else and only told the children that you wondered what it would be like living in Australia. I certainly didn't suggest you would really be going there. If you do as I advise, no more need be said about it to anyone. Don't break poor Father's heart.

Love from
Dolly

## Annie's diary

I am not at all pleased with Dolly who has written me a most interfering letter suggesting that I am about to abandon

Father and go hurrying off to Australia. If I meant to go to Australia, I wouldn't need to ask Dolly's permission, I would just go whether she liked it or not. I did mention in a letter that the idea was quite tempting, but I hardly expected her to take it seriously. I suppose she didn't like the thought because she was terrified that if I went, then she would have to come and see Father a bit more often than she does. It's all very well her talking about the family and what it costs to get here. We all know about that, but she doesn't live so far away and I can't count how many months it is since she took the trouble to come. Some of my brothers are better than her, but you would think a daughter might think to bother about her old father. And what has Father ever done to deserve that kind of treatment I would like to know? She goes on about me being Father's favourite. Well, if you ask me, that's hardly surprising, and I reckon she must be jealous.

As for Australia, I think Mr Johnson has at last understood that nothing on earth would make me go there. Leave Cranfield? Not me. Not even for *his* big brown eyes. But it's nice to have been asked I suppose. Of course I'll miss him when he goes. Life won't be at all the same without him and I expect this huge house will feel quite empty with him gone. His Lordship will be altogether lost too. That's for sure. Nobody knows the countless things he does about the place. He gets a bit funny though if I ask him to write and tell me what Australia's like when he gets there. The other day he even looked quite angry and said pretty bluntly, 'If there's anything you want to know about Australia, you can come and see it for yourself, sweet Annie.' If he won't stay here for me, then I don't honestly see why I should go dragging all over the world for him, ironing his shirts and cooking his dinner. They're all the same in the end. And then there's Father. I could never leave Father.

# Zbigniew Rakowski's notebook

I did not think in January when I very nearly caught my death of cold at Cranfield, that my absence from the place that haunts me daily, would be so long enforced due to the Siberian conditions of our English winter. It is truly remarkable, I am inclined to think, that I, at my advanced age, should have managed to weather the storm (if that is not too facile a metaphor) and survive this fearful winter. Relentless hardship combined with the severity of the cold has carried many poor souls back to their Maker, causing unimaginable problems for undertakers caught in snowdrifts and for grave-diggers who were naturally prevented by circumstances from fulfilling their function. Fortunately for my dear daughter, I did not add to the confusion by joining the queue of corpses in the morgue. She, I fear, would have been sorely distressed, would have wrung her hands and told her beads. No doubt her tedious husband would have dealt efficiently with my demise.

But enough of this self-indulgence, for I wish not to die, but to live. So, not only did I weather the storm, but I am delighted to be able to say that I also managed during my prolonged incarceration in Wimble-on-Thames, to put the finishing touches to the *Whig Aristocracy* so that the manuscript is now with my publisher who appears to be both pleased with it and enthusiastic about my proposed history of the Otterton family.

Yesterday, at last, I returned to Cranfield, my passion for the house (and dare I say, for the chatelaine?) quite unabated, my curiosity concerning both its past and its present as alive as ever. Ah, but what did I find? The daffodils, crowning glory of Capability Brown's gently sloping incline to the lake, had, after so harsh a winter, not surprisingly hesitated to show their gentle faces to the elements, thus they were not yet, as might have been expected, nodding their heads in sprightly dance, but were merely in bud. 'Daffodils are late this year,' were the words with which Lord Otterton greeted me.

Yet it was not the absence of daffodils which I found distressing, so much as the atmosphere inside the house itself. Having, over the past two years, witnessed Cranfield rise, as it were, from the ashes under Priscilla's divine guidance, I was mortified to feel that it had somehow not come through the winter quite unscathed. I cannot say exactly to what I attributed this sensation. Perhaps I merely garnered it from the conversation of my hosts which was, in my opinion, unusually pessimistic. There was a woebegone look about the place, the carpets seemed noticeably more threadbare, the pictures in greater need of cleaning, and in the air there hung a depressing feeling of poverty. Although it is abundantly clear that living at Cranfield must be quite a struggle for Lord and Lady Otterton, formerly the atmosphere has been one of carefree optimism, of living for the day, with the wise Priscilla, doubtless less profligate than her husband, forever rising to the occasion as gracious hostess. Tuesday's budget, however, had no doubt done little to lighten the tone of the moment. His Lordship was bitterly cursing the fact that the Chancellor of the Exchequer has increased the price of a packet of twenty cigarettes by one shilling, so that he is now obliged to pay three shillings and fourpence for his Craven-A.

Nevertheless, I do not believe that it was the price of the Cravan-A alone that cast a blight over Lord Otterton's mood, for he lightly let fall that he has recently received a long-awaited demand for death duties. He only said, 'I can't pay them,' and laughed. I feared then for him and for the house and most of all for my *donna angelicata*.

It is very difficult to imagine what would happen to the Ottertons were they to lose, or for some reason beyond their control, be deprived of their essential framework which is

Cranfield. Of course they have not always lived at Cranfield and although I met them before they moved into the house, that house was already, as far as my perception of them was concerned, almost as much a part of them and of their reality, as were her Ladyship's hyacinth-blue eyes. From my own observation, I can only fear that, deprived of his house and estate (dilapidated though they may be), feeling quite lost and insubstantial, and knowing not whither to turn, the tempta-tion to surrender to Bacchus in order to boost his morale or, as the case might be, to drown his sorrows, might be too great for Lord Otterton to resist. In what kind of house might he live? In what English county? Would he not appear naked, dispossessed of all that is his, unsurrounded by the aura that a great house, however decrepit, bestows on one so at ease in it, one who has never, for a single moment since earliest childhood, doubted that he will grow up to inherit it and who has imagined no other path in life to be open to him? There must have been times during the war when his Lordship feared for his life, but nonetheless, knew to what he would return in the event of his survival. Such certainty must shore a man up, must give him confidence and infuse him with a sense of knowing who and what he is.

As for the beautiful Priscilla who has brought so much of herself, of her imagination, her intelligence and energy to bear on reviving the house, on transforming it from a dusty furniture repository, and home, or so I am told, of a deluded dope fiend, into a family dwelling, tattered but treasured, full of mirth and life and hope, how could she now bear to be torn from its elegant surroundings? How could she bear to abandon the Aubusson to decay, how could she suffer, now she has grasped them so adequately, to relinquish the reins of power, to leave that miraculous place quietly to decline?

This winter has already taken a toll of the house. How many empty, uninhabited winters could it withstand as rain and melted snow seeped through every conceivable part of the roof, as frost gnawed into the brick and the stone, as, blistered from the summer's sun, the unpainted sills crumbled, as the damp rose from the basement, the ivy crept up the walls, its tendrils working their way through broken panes to invade the inside of that lovely house? I see the eighteenth-century French flock falling in sheaths from the walls of the Palladio room, I see mildew spreading its way across the Mortlake tapestries in the Saloon whilst the ever-invasive moth gnaws its way through the delicious tapestries in her Ladyship's own Hunting Room. It would not be long before mice and rats and bats became the proud verminous inheritors of this lordly mansion, whilst my poor Priscilla eked out her existence in some suburban villa to which she was unsuited by both birth and temperament, her children mewling and puking at her feet whilst Lord Otterton tremblingly replenished his whiskey glass. How could she bear such a fate? Surely she could not, but would instead, one spring morning as a ray of hope filtered through cloudy skies, pack her few things and flee to the protection of an old but faithful admirer . . . How her delicacy would lighten my hovel, her wit awaken Robin Hood Way, her style set Wimble-on-Thames on fire! Ah me, what folly to be old and fanciful! Yet, after my recent visit to Cranfield I could not help but wonder whether the Ottertons would be able to cling on and whether they would still be there in a year's time, say. Or two.

Once again as I was bent over my researches in the Red Drawing-Room, I was made uneasy by the repeated intrusions of the man, Mason. He came, quite rightly, to announce that luncheon was served, but came, I felt, in what can only be described as an insinuating manner. He enquired, most unnecessarily, in my opinion, as to which drawers I had opened and as to whether or not I had left the room at any time during the morning. Later, in the afternoon, he appeared again, this time with nothing further to say than that he wondered whether or not I was still there. Having, I can only surmise, persuaded his Lordship to be rid of the picaroon Cheadle, Priscilla appears quite unconcerned about the faceless Mr Mason. He does not serve at table in a state of extreme intoxication, but moves his large frame quietly and with dignity around the dining-room which I suppose is all that she requires of him. Nonetheless, it is my intention to watch him, just as he watches me, and just as he doubtless watches the other members of the household. It is hard to imagine what may or may not lie behind this attitude of his and I am surprised that it appears to have gone unnoticed by the Ottertons who both smile at him and address him in a light, *dégagé* tone as if there were no problem attached to his incumbency.

For my own part, I am at present simply buoyed up by the promise of the hours to be spent working at Cranfield and the prospect of many interesting and no doubt delightful conversations to be held with Priscilla. Who can tell what the future holds for any of us?

## *Sydney Otterton's diary*

I thought after I'd seen my solicitor the other day that we really had reached the end of the road. I came away from his office thinking that if there were a handy bridge, I might just as well jump off it, but then I thought that to survive having my tank blown away from under me in the desert, only to jump off a bridge in peacetime seemed pretty futile, so instead, I came home and went to look for Tony who'd just got back from London. Tony was very sympathetic when I told him what blasted Littlejohn had said, which was, that taking everything into account, I ought to consider the estate bankrupt. He also said he couldn't see how I would ever be able to pay the death duties and that, for his money, the best thing I could possibly do would be to sell up and clear out.

Where, I asked him, is the bloody fool who's going to buy a damn great barracks of a place with a leaking roof like Cranfield in times like this? Oh, he says, some rich American. It would certainly have to be a bloody fool of a rich American. In any case, what rich American would think of settling in this country at the moment? We aren't allowed to light a coal fire or a gas fire from now until September, rationing is worse than it ever was in wartime, there are no building materials and there's no agricultural machinery, if you buy an egg, it's usually bad and cigarettes cost 3s./4d. a packet. Apart from anything else, I just couldn't sell up. I couldn't do it. Talking to Tony cheered me up a bit even though he doesn't have any good news to bring back from the Stock Exchange, but he did encourage me to hang on and we ended up agreeing that things can really only get better. I may even have to go and see Aunt Lettice. She might help. Perhaps she would be able to lend me some money.

Priscilla has this idea that we should have a sale. She's certainly right about the house being full of stuff we could sell. Not that we'd probably raise an awful lot of money because no one has any money to spend these days. But still, it would be something.

MAY IST

Priscilla and I spent the whole week-end going all round the house trying to decide what to put in the sale. We spent hours going through an amazing amount of dust-covered rubbish and occasionally falling on a long-forgotten treasure. Luckily Priscilla has a good eye and knows probably rather better than I do, what is what. Too bad if we have to sell one or two decent pieces because we need the cash, but, on the whole what we're flogging is masses of Victorian junk which unfortunately won't go for much, and some later, pre-war stuff. Most of the unused servants' rooms on the top floor are crammed with things, many of which I don't remember ever having seen before, and still I haven't found the undiscovered room of my dreams, about which I dreamt again only the other night. Perhaps it really is only a fantasy. Considering all the trouble Priscilla has taken over the house since we moved in, I thought she probably had a better idea than I did about what there was, but even she was amazed by some things we turned up.

God knows if my parents ever really knew what they had stuffed into the far corners of this house, and then during the war a lot of things must just have been stacked away any-old-how to make room for the public records when they were sent down here. All the really good stuff downstairs is entailed, so none of that will go in the sale because I couldn't hock it even if I wanted to.

Then this morning the people came from the auctioneers; a very excited, wispy little mouse of a man with bat ears and a quick, quiet voice, accompanied by a callow youth barely out of school who told me he'd just missed the war. I thought how green he was compared to all those boys in North Africa, but for all his inexperience, he kept interrupting the mouse in a most opinionated fashion. We went round the house again showing them what we wanted to sell and occasionally Mouse pounced greedily on something he'd seen and which we had no intention of flogging. I thought, thank God for Priscilla who's not only got a good eye, but is firm and determined. In fact we did give way over one or two things, but nothing important. But we're not nearly through yet. Mouse and his boy will be back again tomorrow with their little books of tickets, sticking lot numbers on everything and anything they can get their hands on.

MAY 8TH

When I got back from the House of Lords quite late last night, I found Priscilla still up in the Hunting Room, writing letters. Sometimes she's quite cross when I get back but she looked surprisingly pleased to see me and even a little relieved. She told me she'd been feeling very uneasy all evening on account of the fact that she'd been shopping in the afternoon, and just as she was coming out of the International Stores, who should she see disappearing down the High Street, but the Legros. Usually she comes back from the International Stores talking about some ruddy Uriah Heep of a grocer who's managed to charm her with his oily manner, but this time, she was so worked up about seeing the Legros (or thinking she had) that she even refused to laugh when I made a joke about her beloved grocer who's always trying to let her have a little more than our rations allow. I wanted to know how she could be so sure it was the Legros, if she only saw their backs. She said they had the dog with them and that she would have recognised that dog and the way they walked with it between them anywhere. I suppose it probably was them. But what if it was? If they're not in prison, they've got to be somewhere and I can see no very good reason why they shouldn't still be living around here.

I told Priscilla that it was unlike her to be so worked up and that I couldn't imagine what had got into her. I said that as far as I was concerned the Legros were past history. After all, they must have been gone for at least six months and there hasn't been any trouble of any kind since Mrs Arbuthnot moved in. I only hope she stays. Anyway then Priscilla began to get quite annoyed because she said she hadn't finished telling me what had happened and that the thing she had found most disturbing was the fact that she'd stood outside the grocer's shop, watching the Legros walk down the hill and just as they reached the bottom of the High Street, Mrs Mason suddenly appeared, walking up the pavement towards them. Priscilla swears that Mrs Mason not only acknowledged them, but stopped to speak to them. I told her that that had to be rubbish because the Legros left here long before Cheadle did and that there was then a gap of about a month before the Masons came, so they couldn't conceivably know each other. Anyway I don't see how

Priscilla could possibly have told from that distance whether or not it was Mrs Mason, although, I have to admit that it is a bit odd if what she says is right. But I can't help feeling she imagined it all.

## Zbigniew Rakowski's notebook

Both Lord and Lady Otterton were to be away on my most recent visit to Cranfield, and thus it was that I left home armed with a thermos of tea and some sandwiches for my luncheon. This I had intended to consume in the Red Drawing-Room during a short break from my labours, but the late spring having turned to summer almost overnight, I decided instead to take a walk in the grounds and to find an agreeable seat in some bosky corner of the garden where I could enjoy my simple picnic whilst admiring the south front of the house. That façade, with its stone pilasters and its swags above the first-floor windows, is unquestionably the most delicate of the four and the most Italianate. Below it there lies an elegant little formal garden which provides a delightful framework for the house when viewed from that side.

Forlorn though I may have been on account of Priscilla's absence, it was not without a slight spring in my tread that I walked past the Maori meeting hut (a hideous carved wooden edifice imported by Lord Otterton's grandfather from New Zealand where he served a term as Governor) and on up the slope of the lawn to a white-painted seat happily placed beneath two tall wellingtonias. Here I could sit, peacefully gazing on the lovely old house, its bricks now a rosy pink in the dancing sunlight, whilst I sipped my tea and consumed my usual fishpaste sandwich.

As I sat, I mused on past generations of Ottertons,

eccentric, flamboyant men and women, the vagaries of whose careers I had that very morning been studying, and attempted to picture them in this their proper setting. The Prince of Wales was a frequent visitor to Cranfield since it made a convenient stopping place on his journey from London to Brighton. Thus I envisaged Prinny, *embonpoint* and florid, trotting briskly up to the West front (so elegant then, before the addition of the monstrous Victorian *porte-cochère*), his brougham drawn perhaps by a dappled grey mare with arched neck, curly mane and flowing tail, snorting imperiously as the coachman up front is barely able to restrain her from breaking into a canter. Or perhaps, accompanied by Mrs FitzHerbert and some Whig crony, he might have travelled in a landau harnessed to four shiny black steeds haughtily tossing their heads and frothing at the nostrils. Then I turned to imagining the dark-eyed heiress from Jamaica whose money, a century earlier, had been used to build the house. Had she, two hundred years ago, wandered on this very lawn, admiring the same Italianate architecture that I now admired, yet heavy at heart, unloved and forlorn, missing the sunlit island home of her childhood as she stood, a diminutive figure in a silken gown, beneath grey English skies?

With such fond romantic thoughts as these was my foolish old head filled as I slowly munched my sandwiches under the wellingtonias, when all at once my reverie was interrupted by the sight of a dark-clad figure advancing towards me across the grass. I did not instantly discern the wooden features of the butler, Mason, but as he drew nearer, he looked straight at me and, at the same time, hastened his step, so that just as I recognised him, so did I realise that his intention was to seek me out. He then walked right up to where I sat and, with a gracelessness born of egalitarianism, but without what may be called a with-your-leave or a by-your-leave, stationed his not insignificant bulk on the seat beside me, pushing my thermos unceremoniously out of the way as he did so.

'Picknicking, I see,' were the words with which he first addressed me.

I fear that good manners did not then prevent me from instantly, but inadvertently, moving a little away from the man, towards the edge of the seat. But I soon recovered what I would like to think of as my natural aplomb and wished him good-afternoon, whereupon he rudely, and without more ado, waved an arm airily around and asked me my opinion of what he vulgarly referred to as 'this set-up'.

'Such houses as these,' he next saw fit to remark, 'are an anachronism.' He then went on to explain to me that there was no place for them in today's world. Since we were all equal, no one should be allowed to live in a house that was any bigger than anyone else's. In his view the stately homes of England should be nationalised and turned into council flats or conceivably used as palaces for the people, whatever such palaces might be. 'This monstrosity,' he said, jabbing a forefinger in the direction of Cranfield and with a sudden edge of anger in his voice, 'is a great redbrick blot on the landscape, a witness to all the injustices of the past.'

I am obliged to admit that as the man spoke, I was stunned into silence. With my solitary peaceful picnic so rudely interrupted and my fanciful thoughts abruptly banished, I had some difficulty in turning my full attention to the angry substance of the butler's diatribe. All history, he informed me, is nothing but the process of creating man through human labour, and in his struggle against nature, man finds the conditions of his fulfilment . . . the dawn of consciousness is inseparable from the struggle . . . man has irrefutable proof of his own creation by himself . . . On and on he went, quite carried away by the class struggle and how man becomes an alienated being in a capitalist society. I was not clear as to whether his favoured solution to all these wrongs lay in perpetual revolution or in one almighty conflagration; and neither, I consider, was he. He talked of the freedom which would come when the proletariat eventually succeeded in eliminating the bourgeoisie, thus producing a classless society, and he talked repeatedly of the oppressor and the oppressed, whilst allowing me no opportunity to reply. Coming as I do from a country that has suffered considerably from oppression throughout the ages, I felt that I might have something to contribute to a dialogue on the subject, but the man spoke uninterruptedly, as one possessed, almost as though he were oblivious of my presence, punching the air with his fist, as if attempting, by his rhetoric, to incite to action some imaginary crowd gathered on the lawn beneath us, or perhaps wishing only to work himself up into further flights of hyperbole. Yet I felt sure that his purpose in crossing the lawn that day and walking up the slope to where I sat, was to seek me out and to impart his bitter philosophy to me. He cannot have been unaware, as he spoke so passionately of history, that I was, in my own humble way, a historian, to some extent a maker of history since the version of events which I pass on to my readers constitutes but one man's perception of the truth. Perhaps I should have been bolder and made some valiant attempt to interrupt the flow of his discourse but, to be perfectly frank, as he sat there next to me, taking up so much space, I felt contaminated by his presence so that all I could wish was for him to depart.

Eventually, in my desperation, I gathered up my few things and with my customary apologetic manner, excused myself, saying that I had to return to my labours, thus, I added as a light-hearted quip which quite passed him by, to continue the process of creating man. He did not rise from the seat as I made my way back down the slope, but merely remarked in a gruff, unmannerly way that he would look in and see me sometime.

Much have I puzzled over this episode during the days since it occurred. Many aspects of it are to me quite incomprehensible; for instance, how, I ask myself, does this unmitigated villain imagine that he is going to achieve his dreamed-of revolution by working as a butler (most servile of all occupations) to the Ottertons? And what indeed did he hope to gain by informing me, humble pen-pusher that I am, of his political leanings? Does he not suppose that I will inform both Lord and Lady Otterton of his crude intrusion on my picnic? The imagination reels at the thought of what his intentions might be. Does he mean to burn the house down, to engulf his Lordship and her precious Ladyship in flames as they lie sleeping, or will he open the doors to allow the farm workers, armed with their scythes and pitchforks, to invade, to rip the tapestries from the wall and smash Rysbrack's masterpieces into smithereens? Yet how, one wonders, would that advance his cause? For the present, I remain dumbfounded by the whole episode but have decided that I will not instantly report it to Lady Otterton. I think indeed that I shall wait to see what happens next, wait until I can ascertain what precisely it is that the butler wants of me. Wait and watch.

## Sydney Otterton's diary

MAY 17TH

Just as I was beginning to think that everything was completely hopeless and that there was nothing any of us could do that would make any difference, things started to look up. For one thing the arrangements for the sale are going ahead quite well, and it's all rather exciting. Then yesterday, at long last, a tractor was delivered which my very generous aunt has offered to pay for. The sun's shining too, so that what with one thing and another we'd all be feeling pretty cheerful if it weren't for the bloody awful fact of Johnson's departure at the end of the month. Priscilla thinks Annie's in love with him and she may well be right, although I thought Bert was Annie's so-called 'young man'. It will be bad enough losing Johnson, but I don't know what the hell we'll do if Annie decides to go with him. She's Priscilla's right-hand man, so to speak, and as such, she more or less keeps the show on the road. Not that Annie's mentioned a thing about Johnson or Australia to us, so Priscilla may have imagined the whole thing, but, according to her, Annie hardly ever goes to see Bert these days.

## Annie's diary

MAY 31ST

So Mr Johnson has gone and left us. I somehow never really believed it would happen. He's sailing from Southampton on Monday and wanted me to go down there and wave him off. I certainly wasn't going to do that, and I told him so. Not on your life! I said. I've got work to do and I can't keep taking days off to go trailing down to Southampton, never mind the cost of the fare there and back.

It's a funny thing though, but when he said goodbye, I suddenly began to wonder what it must be like out there with all the sunshine and the wide open spaces and jobs for everyone. But then all these promises of a golden future never meant very much to me. Life's too hard for most of us and nothing wonderful ever drops into your lap as far as I can see. Well Mr Johnson dropped into mine, but he didn't stay for long of course. I told him I was sure he'd be back before he could say Jack Robinson. He only laughed a dry sort of laugh and stood there with his head on one side, looking at me with those big brown eyes of his. I can see him now. 'Sweet Annie,' he said in his flat Yorkshire voice, 'I'm not coming back. The sooner you get that fixed in your pretty little head the better.' 'Pretty little head, my foot!' I said. Well, he's not such a bad-looking man himself. I don't think I could wave him goodbye though. 'Not watch me sail out of

Southampton Water leaning on the taffrail and waving?' he said. 'My, you're a hard-hearted one.'

Now no one can call me hard-hearted, not after the way I've looked after Father, and Mr Johnson made me quite cross saying that. I had to turn my back as he left the room and the last thing he said was, 'If you ever change your mind, Annie, I'll be waiting for you, but we're neither of us that young any more, so don't leave it too long.'

I must say that I don't feel very happy at the thought of having to spend my days off with Bert from now on. But I expect I'll mostly go down to Father's. Father was funny about Mr Johnson. He wanted to know what all the talk was about Australia, and then one evening he said, 'If you want to go to Australia, Annie, don't you stay behind on account of your old father.' I can't imagine what made him think that I'd be going to Australia, unless Dolly had something to do with it. Then he went and said, 'I'll be able to manage, so long as you write home every so often.' He's a good man, my father, and I don't think I could ever leave him, any more than I could leave Cranfield which has been home for me all my life, even when I was away working for the Gowers. I'd miss the beech trees and the old elm on the corner of the drive and the walk down to the lake, and I'd miss the daffodils in spring and the primroses in the Big Wood and the cows lying down in the field because they know when it's going to rain. I can't imagine kangaroos having half that amount of good sense, and as for the wide-open spaces, well the park is good enough for me. I can stand by the bend in the drive and look out over the fields and the woods and not see another house and I can stare for ages out of my bedroom window across the gardens and the lake and never wish for a better view. I told Mr Johnson repeatedly that he would miss England. 'Never,' was all he would say. And then he'd go on about this country having done nothing for him and start again about all the wonderful things that would be waiting for him in Australia. The assisted passage out was only costing him

£10 and when he got there, they'd find him a job and it would all be marvellous. Well, we shall see.

## Sydney Otterton's diary

Johnson finally left last week. I wished him the best of luck but secretly hope he'll be back again before long although I very much doubt it. He'll probably make a go of it and all I can say is that, if the other immigrants are worth half of Johnson, then Australia's not doing badly. I think Priscilla may have had a point about Annie who's been in a filthy temper ever since Johnson left and is not at all her usual amenable self. She didn't even take much interest in the sale which is quite unlike her. She generally wants to know everything about anything that's going on.

In fact Priscilla was quite wonderful the way she organised the sale. She took it all right out of my hands and made most of the decisions. We planned on using the avenue for extra parking, at least we hoped it would be necessary although with the appalling state of petrol rationing as it is, we weren't sure that anyone would turn up at all. We also had to hope it would remain dry or someone would be bound to get stuck in the mud. As it turned out, we were lucky with the weather and the extra parking space was definitely needed. The auctioneers set themselves up in the hall, with the lots stacked around them and in the saloon behind them. I'm not sure how many chairs were put out, but they were all taken and there were plenty of people standing as well. I recognised half the village and was amused to see old Doubleday bidding 8s./6d. for a po cupboard. Perhaps the fellow is growing incontinent with age.

On the two days before the sale half the county must have turned out to view. I think that over the years, what with my parents cutting themselves off the way they did, the house had become such a place of mystery to everyone in the neighbourhood that they were all eaten up with curiosity about it. A good many people certainly came without the slightest intention of buying anything in the first place. All the same it went quite well; with nearly four hundred lots, the average price of the better ones being somewhere in the region of eight or nine guineas, we managed to raise nearly three thousand pounds. Considering there's so little money around, I think we must have been quite lucky to get that. At least it's something in the kitty. Not nearly enough, but a little.

So, one way and another, I was feeling on pretty good form the other afternoon when I bumped into Pammie in St James's. I hadn't seen her since the war but she didn't seem to have changed at all. She was her usual jolly self and all the more so, on account, according to her, of the fact that her divorce from Archie had just become absolute. I must say, I always thought of Archie as a very moderate fellow and could never understand why she married him in the first place. Anyway we had dinner together and what with one thing and another I didn't get back till the morning. I'm afraid Priscilla thinks that the Lords sat late and that I spent the night in my club.

## Georgina's exercise book

JUNE 7TH

You have to go to the hall to get cool because its so boiling hot but weve still got to do lessons which is boring and we cant collect snails because Mamzel says they only come out in the rain. I hate Mr Mason because he's allways creeping around behind us and he tries to tickle Jamie. I told Mamzel and she said I was silly and that she likes mr Mason much more than Mr Cheadle. When Jamie told Mummy she said hed imagined it and when he told Father Father just said why didn't Jamie run away because he can probly run faster than mr Mason anyway. Jamies jolly rude to Mr Mason but I think he is a bit fritened of him to.

## Sydney Otterton's diary

It's unbelievably hot which is very welcome after the winter we had, but of course they're already complaining about lack of rain on the farm. When I was down there yesterday I found that one of the men had seen fit to have a bonfire in this weather and had burnt the snowplough because it was taking up too much room in the old stables. Of course I immediately knew it had to be Goodfellow who'd done that. No one else could be such a bloody idiot. When I asked him what the hell he thought he'd been thinking of, he just said, looking at me moronically and scratching his head, 'Seeing it's so hot, I didn't think you'd be needing it again, M'lord.' I could have strangled the bugger. I was already in a pretty bad mood because the two old horses, both of which had been around a long time, went off to the knacker's yard in the morning. We've kept Violet who's got a few more years' work in her and who may well come in handy despite the tractor.

The children gave me a tortoise for my birthday. I've called it Adelaide although I haven't the first idea how to sex a tortoise. I don't know what the matter is with the children at the moment. They keep on complaining about Mason and saying they're frightened of him. Seems a perfectly decent fellow to me and anyway I don't see that they have much to do with him. Priscilla says they're getting bored and it's time they both went to school. Although I'll miss them, it'll be quite a relief not to have to keep bumping into old Double-day on the stairs. I always say he's like the Ancient Mariner, quite impossible to get away from and you have to listen to him banging on about India and Gandhi and the pros and cons of partition as if he, and he alone, held the solution to the problems of the sub-continent in the palm of his hand. Priscilla says he's taught the children very well up to now and that when they do go to school, they'll both be well ahead for their age. I suppose old bores like him are good at teaching because they don't mind saying the same thing over and over again.

Annie's still not her usual self. I'm sure she's pining for Johnson. I asked her the other day how she thought Bert was getting on and if he likes being here. She barely gave me a civil answer.

## Zbigniew Rakowski's notebook

The family is away and without its presence a strange aura of unreality hangs over Cranfield. I sense a sultriness about the park as I walk up the drive from the bus stop to the house. The trees seem bowed down by the weight of their heavy, dusty August foliage, in the air there is a stillness and the earth, after so hot a summer as this, is dry and caked whilst the fields are a colourless brown. I pass a mournful Guernsey herd clustered beneath a gigantic elm, tails swishing languidly in a vain attempt to disperse the flies. The atmosphere in the house echoes the melancholy outside. There is a silence about the place and many of the shutters are closed partly because there is no one at home and partly, I would imagine, in order to protect pictures and tapestries and carpets and fine furniture from the glare of the mid-day sun. I do not doubt that the butler who, in the absence of the Ottertons, must fulfil the role of guardian or caretaker, delights in not having to bother to open and close the shutters, or indeed to wait upon his employers. How he spends his day is a matter for conjecture.

Since that dreadful afternoon when the man, Mason, sought me out to harangue me as I sat innocently enjoying a sandwich, I have not found it easy to banish his odious image from my mind. On subsequent visits to Cranfield, I have carefully observed his demeanour and have not been in the least delighted by anything I have seen. He too is watchful and, since that day on the lawn, has taken to addressing me in a quasi-subservient, quasi-threatening and, to a certain extent, conniving manner as though he and I shared some guilty secret which gave him power over me. Indeed we do share a secret but certainly not one which causes me to feel the slightest twinge of guilt and if the man has the temerity to think that he has any hold over me at all, he is bound to be sorely disappointed. I am somewhat tempted to the view that his fanaticism leads him to see things in the narrowest possible way and that because of it, he has little, if any, understanding of those around him; thus he has quite mistakenly presumed to win me to his cause and, without having paused to wonder what my nature might be, has decided to co-opt my help in perpetrating his nefarious campaign, howsoever he might choose to do so. This morning when I reached the house, he had the impertinence to claim to be delighted by my arrival, flinging the great front door open and welcoming me as if he were Lord Otterton himself and master of all he surveyed.

I would gladly have been left to find my own way to the Red Drawing-Room with which I am, not unnaturally, only too familiar, but Mason saw fit to accompany me and to watch over me while I unlocked the cabinet where are kept the papers on which I am at present working. 'Should you find something of particular interest,' he addressed me with a sly grin, 'I have no doubt that you will let me know.' I am still at a complete loss as to what, if anything, I might find among the family papers that could be of any possible interest to the man.

Priscilla, accompanied by the good Annie, has taken the three young Ottertons to spend a few days beside the sea in Cornwall. The French governess has returned to her native land and his Lordship, or so Mason told me with a snigger, has been busy in London, but takes the night sleeper to Penzance this evening to join his family. I did not know, nor do I wish to dwell on what Mason might have intended to suggest by his snigger. If he was implying what I can only suppose that he was, then I would very much like to know by what means he is privy to his Lordship's secrets. Rather, I suppose him to be a person of mischievous intent who will stoop to any depths to undermine those who house him and pay his wages, thus to further his vile purposes and to bring his longed-for revolution one step nearer.

My little foible of a detective novel which so absorbed me a while ago has lain for some months now, untouched in a drawer of my desk. Little does Mason know how it is the very baseness of his behaviour which causes me to turn once more to that work. When I first wrote it, I cast the demon governess in the role of murderess, for such a wretch as is Mason had not yet entered the scene. But now, of an idle moment, my mind is unavoidably drawn back to that melodrama for there can be no doubt but that there is a part to be played in it by that detestable man. Having temporarily mislaid one of my notebooks, without which I feel denuded, I am sorely tempted to take a few days' respite from my serious work and return to that novelette and to tinker with it awhile.

Perhaps it was the unwonted atmosphere that hung about the house, or perhaps I should blame my carelessness on the fact that the butler's disagreeable behaviour did much to disturb my usual equanimity, but whatever the case, I was most distressed to discover on my return to Robin Hood

Way, that I had absent-mindedly left one of my notebooks behind. I can only imagine that I accidentally locked it away in the cabinet with the family papers that I had been perusing, once I had finished with them. I do not know if there is any key to the cabinet other than the one which Lady Otterton entrusted to my keeping before her departure for the Cornish coast. In any case, I would not be inclined to ask the butler to forward my notebook. I would wish neither to be indebted to him in any way, nor to have him involved in my affairs. Had Annie been at Cranfield and in possession of a key to the cabinet, I feel sure that she would have forwarded the troublesome object to me at my home, but as it is, I will have to suffer from the consequences of my own folly and do without that notebook until I next return to Cranfield.

## *Letter from Annie to Dolly*

Sennen Cove
Cornwall
AUGUST 4TH, 1947

Dear Dolly,

I expect Father will have told you that her Ladyship wanted me to come to Cornwall to look after the children for a week. We are having a lovely time and the weather is good apart from one day when there was a terrific storm and we watched the lifeboat put to sea. The children were very excited. I'm so glad her Ladyship asked me to come because I feel the change is doing me good. I love Cranfield, as you know, but there has been so much going on lately that it can begin to get you down.

We are staying in a hotel right on the beach. It has rather a noisy bar where all the fishermen come in the evening. Of course his Lordship finds that very amusing and is himself the life and soul of the party! There's one fisherman called Double George (his real name is George George) who they all think is wonderful. Double George has a very nice-looking son who is going to take the children mackerel fishing.

Father said that you would be coming over to see him while I am away. I hope you found him well. Did he tell you about the time back in June during that very hot weather when Goodfellow burnt the snowplough? You couldn't help having a laugh, but his Lordship was in a right tizwas.

Love from
Annie


## Georgina's exercise book

Mamzel has gone to France and she's not coming back. That horrid Mr Mason went into Thomas's room in the middle of the night when Thomas was in bed and looked at him. Thomas says he wasn't fritened and Mr Mason was in his butler's sute. Then Tony came along and said What the bloody hell do you think you are doing Mason or something and Mr Mason went away. Jamie wants to hach a plot to kill Mr Mason because he thinks hes a spy. We've got someone Mummy says is a holliday guverness now. She's called Tiz and is very nice. Yesterday she showed us how to disect frogs. I wish we could go back to the seaside.

# Annie's diary

If Mr Johnson has heard the latest news he'll certainly be glad to think he's left the country. Things seem to be going from bad to worse. The meat ration has been cut again and Mr Attlee warns us that we can only expect more cuts and more restrictions. We're all right here at Cranfield really because of the extra things we get off the farm like rabbits and the occasional pigeon, but I do sometimes wonder why I didn't decide to go to Australia too. Of course I would have missed Father and he would have missed me I know, but then he would have got used to it without me and I would have written every week and surely the others would have looked after him. I haven't heard a word from Mr Johnson, not that I would have expected to yet, but I wonder if he sometimes thinks about us.

The children have an atlas in the school-room and I had a quick look at it when I was in there the other day. Georgina wanted to show me a map of India because she and Jamie want to go there when they're grown up. That Major Double-day has been teaching them all about it and Georgina's been learning some poem about India which she wanted to recite to me. Anyway I had a quick look at Australia on the Q.T. because I wanted to see where Mr Johnson was. I know that after all those weeks at sea he was due to land in Perth. I suppose he got there safely and I hope he wasn't seasick. Mind you when I suggested before he left that he might be seasick, he was quite put out. If he wasn't seasick in a troop ship during the war, he had no intention of being sick in peacetime. But I simply don't know if he's still in Perth or not. He may have been found a job anywhere in Australia and it's a big place.

Now that Mamzelle's left, Mr Kipling spends his time hanging around the kitchen and getting under all our feet. I rather think he's got his eye on Mrs Laws. I suppose Mrs

Kipling's used to his carryings on, but I can't imagine how he gets his work done and he's supposed to be doing a lot of extra work now that Mr Johnson's gone. That's until the new man comes. He can be quite funny though, Mr Kipling, especially when he gets on to the subject of that so-called cough mixture Mamzelle kept up in the school-room. To tell the truth, I think he was tickled pink by her taking such a fancy to him.

There's a new governess, her Ladyship calls her a holiday governess, who's here until the children go to school in the autumn. I somehow don't think she will want to have anything to do with Mr Kipling, though. She's very young and nice-looking and I wouldn't doubt that she has a young man of her own somewhere.

I had a letter waiting for me from Mr Rakowski when we got back from Cornwall. He wants me to look out for one of his notebooks which he has mislaid although he thinks he may have locked it up in the cabinet down in the Red Drawing-Room. I've had a look for it and I've asked Mr Mason if he's seen it but neither of us has come across it. It would be unlike Mr Rakowski to mislay something like that, I should think. He is a most meticulous person.

### *Sydney Otterton's diary*

SEPTEMBER 5TH

It seems quite incredible that the war has been over for two years and the country's still in such a bloody awful mess. There's no fuel, no petrol, no coal, the miners are on strike and only a few weeks ago people were queuing in the streets of London for potatoes. My own affairs are in no better shape and as a result I swing between moods of extreme elation and near desperation and I've begun to have nightmares again.

There's some suggestion that it may be a good idea to get rid of the dairy herd and have sheep instead, but God alone knows if that will really work. Or we may keep the cows and have a few sheep as well. Whatever happens, it always seems to involve enormous outlay and very little return. If we want to keep the cows, we'll have to try to keep abreast of the times and install an electric milking machine. And where the hell does the money come from for that? At least we've got the tractor now and that does make a lot of difference. Thank the Lord and Aunt Lettice.

I found some excuse to go up to London yesterday, hoping, I suppose, to avoid thinking about my problems. I spent the evening with Pammie who was her usual cheerful self, crowing about her alimony and boasting about some coat she'd bought. It looked like a perfectly ordinary coat to me, but she just laughed and said that she was amazed I hadn't heard of the New Look. Nothing ever seems to get Pammie down and I have to say that after a couple of hours with her you can't help but feel your spirits lifting. I got back quite late to find Tony and Priscilla deep in some serious conversation in the Hunting Room. They looked almost surprised to see me. The three of us ended up having a drink together, then Priscilla went off to bed and Tony and I sat up till all hours. He told me that he, too, has been suffering from nightmares lately, then he started to bang on about the children's new governess to whom he appears to have taken a great shine. I didn't tell him that I'd been seeing Pammie but just laughed and said that, for my part, I was rather sorry to see the old Frenchwoman go. She must have been as ancient as the hills, but she was very spirited and she made me laugh with all her dandelion salad and snails. The poor woman hadn't been back to France since before the war and she couldn't wait to leave and make way for the lovely Tiz.

Then of course we started to get maudlin about Johnson and wish he'd never left and that led to reminiscing about the war and that kept us up most of the night which at least prevented either of us having nightmares for once. I still don't understand how we can be expected to throw the experiences of the war off just like that and get on with things as if nothing had ever happened. Tony feels the same. Sometimes I look back on those years and begin to see myself as if I were a completely different person to the person I am now. I seem to have been far better suited to leading a column of tanks across the desert than I am to dealing with the everyday problems of the estate, which is rather a pity, because the everyday problems are what I will have to deal with if we are to stay on here for much longer. And I sometimes wonder for just how much longer we will be able to hang on.

Priscilla, who, after all, was the one who hesitated to move into the house in the first place, is far more sanguine than I am at times. Perhaps that is because she has put so much energy into the place and, no doubt because of that, she has really grown to love it. She has certainly given it a face-lift and brought it back to life in a remarkable way which even I could never have imagined. After all, the house as I knew it in my childhood was always pretty gloomy because of the brooding presence of my mother and because of my father who was afraid of her and consequently permanently on tenterhooks when she was around. But you could always escape to some far-flung corner and there was always the dream of that imaginary room which I never found. I think our children now probably have that same feeling of being able to escape that I had as a child, down the back stairs or into the basement or the Blue Corner Room or to the West Room before we made it into part of the flat. I used to love the West Room with that sunken bath and the view across the lake to the temple. Anyway, no one ever knew where one was or what one was up to.

One rather odd thing came out of my conversation with Tony last night, which was that he wanted to know what I thought of Mason. I can't imagine why everyone is always going on about Mason. He seems like a perfectly harmless individual to me. He doesn't down all my best port like Cheadle did and he seems to do his job without much problem, but it struck me that Tony went on in rather an annoyingly insistent way, wanting to know what I *really* thought about him. I told him I didn't *really* think about the fellow at all. Then he said to me, rather pompously, 'Well, Sydney, I think you should.'

I had no idea what he was getting at, so this morning I asked Priscilla what she thought about Mason. To tell the truth, it occurred to me that she reacted a bit oddly to my question. She seemed to hesitate as if taken aback by it, then said, 'I don't like him, if you must know, but I can't tell you why.' Then she quickly changed the subject. I wasn't quite sure what she meant. Did she mean that she didn't know why she disliked him, or did she mean that she had cause to dislike him, which for some reason she could not tell me?

*Letter from Priscilla Otterton to Zbigniew Rakowski*

Cranfield
25.9.47

Dear Z.A.R.,

Thank you so much for your most amusing letter which arrived this morning and for the three others that I'm afraid I haven't yet acknowledged, but I have been very busy lately with the school holidays and one thing and another. Thomas went back to Westfields on Thursday, taking Jamie with him for the first time and at last I have found a moment to get back to the mountain of letters on my desk.

Annie tells me that she has looked everywhere she can think of for your lost notebook but has not been able to find it and Mason claims not to have seen it either. We cannot look in the cabinet as the only key is the one you have, but I feel sure that when you next come, you will find your notebook there. I hope that its loss hasn't been too much of a bore for you. You know we are all looking forward to reading your final assessment of the Otterton family. I'm sure you will manage to make them as interesting as anyone could, although I'm afraid that, as you must have realised by now, they are rather a Philistine bunch.

I know that although you occasionally write them, you don't often read novels, but I wonder if you have read the novels of Henry Green? A friend recently recommended *Loving* to me. I would be interested to know what you thought of it.

We look forward to seeing you as usual for lunch on Tuesday next, 30th September. I am sorry that no one was here to look after you when you came last.

Yours ever,
Priscilla


## *Zbigniew Rakowski's notebook*

OCTOBER 1ST

How lucky I consider myself to be during these hard times, when so many people have so much to put up with, to have my benighted existence blessed with such joy as my visits to Cranfield inspire perforce. It has been some time since the crowning joy of lunching with the exquisite Lady Otterton was mine. I had occasionally corresponded with her during the summer months as she is kind enough to say that my frivolous missives amuse her, but she, poor lady, has been so occupied by family duties that she did not, until most recently, have the time to respond. Unimaginable was my delight last week on perceiving her distinguished handwriting on a letter delivered to me by Friday's second post. Indeed I felt quite like a schoolboy as, with trembling hand, I inserted the paper-knife into the envelope to slit it open. I have not, I fear, read *Loving*, the novel by Henry Green to which she referred in her most amiable letter, although I am familiar with and have admired other works by the same writer. *Loving*. Yes, *Loving*. Loving as I do, I hastened to the Boots library on Saturday morning only to discover to my chagrin that they did not have a copy of the desired book, thus I would be unable to discuss it with Priscilla when next I saw her. Not unnaturally, however, I asked that they reserve the book for me, a request that I shall now be obliged to withdraw since, in her very great kindness, Lady Otterton lent me her precious own copy of *Loving* when I lunched at Cranfield yesterday.

Lord Otterton was not present at luncheon and since the children are now all at school and there is no longer a permanent governess, it befell the odious Mason to wait on her Ladyship with only my humble self for company. I could not but wonder what the man (if he was listening to us) made of our literary conversations, nor of the laughter we enjoyed, for I have to admit that, delighted to be back once more at Cranfield, partaking of the familiar rabbit stew and fired up by a quite unexpected *tête-à-tête* with my *donna angelicata*, I found myself to be on quite spirited form. There can be no doubt that there were moments when I was absolutely convinced that the butler, in most un-butlerlike fashion, attempted to catch my eye. I, of course, withstood his invitation.

It was not indeed until later in the afternoon that I had occasion to exchange more than a polite good-day with Mason. After luncheon her Ladyship kindly proposed that I take a stroll with her in the garden before returning to my labours, an offer which I was only too glad to accept. She is turning her attention particularly to the small formal garden by the South Front of the house which she intends to fill with roses.

However, not long before I was due to leave in order to catch my bus, and as I was somewhat anxiously searching once again through the drawers of the cabinet for my lost notebook (for I had, to my consternation, failed to find it on my arrival in the morning), the door of the Red Drawing-Room creaked open and who should appear, but the monstrous Mason, of course. And what did he have in his hand, but my precious notebook which, with his face contorted by the vilest leer, he held out towards me? Without a word, I crossed the room to where he stood and put my hand out to take the book, at which point, to my unutterable amazement, he withdrew his hand and whipped the note-book behind his back.

'You should not be so careless,' the dreadful man said. 'If you leave your notes around in this fashion, how can you be sure that someone won't read them?'

Were I of a different disposition, or of a different age or build, I feel I could have struck the man.

'My notebooks can be of interest to myself alone,' I said with all the dignity I could muster, 'since they contain only my notes for the work I have in progress.' I looked him straight in the eye, daring him to betray that he had read more than my scribblings about the Otterton family, that he had pried into my very heart and was thus privy to the secret flights of an old man's fancy. But what a senseless old dunderhead am I? For who but I would ever be so foolish as to intersperse his working notes with what other men confide only to a diary? I do it and have always done it because, for me, my work is my life, as is my love for Priscilla, and here the two go inescapably hand in hand; yet from that dreadful moment, as he and I stood there in the doorway to the Red Drawing-Room, I could no longer doubt that Mason knew of my passion for Lady Otterton, and that should the need arise, he would use that information to bring about my downfall.

It was hardly surprising that I was unable to sleep last

night, so consumed was I by hatred of the loathsome butler. I lay awake and attempted to read *Loving* which *she* had so enjoyed, but I soon found that I was turning the pages without having absorbed one word of what was written. Such a blight has Mason cast over Cranfield, that I shall never again, so long as he is butler, be able to go there with an easy heart, nor enjoy the pleasant, *dégagé* atmosphere to which I have become so accustomed.

I did not, however, allow the man to suppose for one instant that he had dismayed me in the slightest. I merely insisted that he hand over the notebook which he was of course obliged to do (having, no doubt, already perused it at his leisure), whereupon I thanked him graciously and enquired as to where he had found it. Her Ladyship, I informed him, had expressly told me that when asked, he had denied all knowledge of it.

'Aha,' he had the insolence to rejoin, 'I only found it after I had spoken to her Ladyship.' I could not help but notice that he pronounced the last two words in the most satirical manner imaginable.

All night I turned the matter over in my mind and it is my considered opinion that on my previous visit to Cranfield, that man sneaked into the Red Drawing-Room whilst I was answering a call of nature and impudently helped himself to my notebook, with what purpose in mind, I cannot imagine. I am, nonetheless, forced to conclude that what he found must surely have delighted him and indeed been more than he had any reason to expect, for I am indeed a very foolish fond old man. It always seemed most unlikely that I, who am normally so particular, should have muddled my own notes with the Otterton papers, and have put them without realising it into the cabinet. It is likelier by far that, not noticing that one was missing, I gathered my notebooks together and restored them, thus incomplete in number, to my basket before leaving the house.

I am intensely exercised by the incident, concerned as to

what will be the outcome and consequently quite unable to concentrate on my work. One way or another, however, I shall see that the butler reaps his punishment.

## Letter from Annie to Dolly

Dear Dolly,

I do hope that you will find a way of getting down to see Father soon as he has not been at all well lately. He is very tired and lacks energy even for his garden and is not at all his usual self. He won't see the doctor which is an added worry. I wonder if you would be able to persuade him. He certainly won't listen to me.

What with one thing and another I am finding myself very busy at the moment. I think I told you that Jamie has gone off to boarding school and Georgina is now at day school, so there is no longer a governess. I have to get Georgina ready for school in the morning and give her her tea when she comes home. She leaves her bicycle at the station and catches the train to the next stop down the line. As you know, I have always liked children so I am very happy with this arrangement. Georgina laughs at me because I say that I would really have liked to have been a nurse. It's not too late, she says. But I'm afraid it is. Then of course there's the extra washing and ironing.

I hope to see you soon at Father's. Give my love to Fred and the children.

Love from
Annie

## Georgina's exercise book

Sometimes it seems funny without Jamie or Mamzel but I like Annie looking after me. Schools alright and I like going by bike to the station but if its raining Tony usherly takes me in his car. Only the car often doesn't start and he has to get out and what he calls crank it up which takes ages. When I get home I rome about the house and no one knows were I am. Ive found lots of good books in a shelf on the back stairs and I'm looking for a secret room. Father thinks theres one somewere and he's allways singing us songs about annie get your gun which makes our Annie laugh. I hate Mr Mason hes such a spy.

## Sydney Otterton's diary

NOVEMBER 7TH

I had a most disturbing letter from my mother out of the blue today. I felt quite sick when I saw her handwriting on the envelope which, I observe, was posted in London, but the only address it gives is, as usual, the address of her bank. Nothing from her could possibly be good news and all she seemed to want to do on this occasion was to accuse me of stealing some of her possessions. She claims that a few pieces of furniture belonging to her were left here and that furthermore, according to her informants, I have had a sale and sold them. She is threatening me with some kind of legal action which is of course barmy as I certainly haven't sold anything which belongs to her, unless she plans to lay claim to the po cupboard old Doubleday bought for eight bob. Of course she's barking mad, not that that helps, and all this means is that I will find myself running up a whole lot of unnecessary lawyers' bills on top of everything else. She's also complaining about my having let the Dower House which she seems to think is hers by right. She certainly took all the furniture out of there when she left, some of which, I have no doubt was mine.

I bought a pair of Java finches last week to add to all the others in my dressing-room. Priscilla thinks they are a dreadful waste of money, and I think she tries to encourage Annie to complain about the mess, but they cheer me up and anyway I think Annie likes them, although she says that Mrs Summers won't go into my dressing-room because she's frightened of the parrot. Anyway the new finches make much less mess than Julia who not only talks quite a lot now, but can also imitate the noise of a vacuum cleaner, so someone must do the hoovering. Priscilla was furious when I told her that, because she thinks Annie does it, and it's not fair on Annie because it's not her job.

I don't know what to do about my wretched mother. I'm sure there's trouble in store.

## *Annie's diary*

DECEMBER 1ST

Georgina is very pleased at the moment because the government has announced that we're going to be allowed extra sweets over Christmas which is all very well when you think that only a couple of weeks ago they cut the bacon ration to one ounce a week. Perhaps things will get better next year. It's certainly high time something changed, although Princess Elizabeth's wedding was nice. Georgina and I looked at all the pictures in the papers and in *Picture Post*. The Princess had a beautiful dress and Princess Margaret Rose made a lovely bridesmaid.

And still not a word from Mr Johnson. I couldn't resist

asking his Lordship the other day if he had heard anything. I was clearing up after all those darned birds of his when his Lordship came into his dressing-room, grinning. 'That's very good of you Annie,' he says. 'Now don't you tell her Ladyship,' I said. 'She'll be furious with me.' Her Ladyship has forbidden me to clear up after the birds. So then I asked about Mr Johnson and I thought his Lordship gave me a funny kind of surprised, half-sad look. 'No Annie,' he said, 'I haven't heard a word. Not a word.' Then he wanted to know if I'd heard anything. I said no, I certainly hadn't and just got on with what I was doing. I can see me spending half of Christmas nursing poor Father who is still poorly and the other half with Bert, listening to him moaning on at me about wishing he'd never moved and complaining that I don't see enough of him. Perhaps Mr Johnson will send a Christmas card. The new man, Bob, isn't half as much fun as Mr Johnson was and not so nice-looking either. But then, handsome is as handsome does, as Father would say.

# 1948

# *Annie's diary*

What with one thing and another, I'm quite thankful to be into the New Year. Perhaps things will begin to look up a bit. Her Ladyship was wondering this morning if I'd had time to turn the collars on some of Thomas's old school shirts, so as to hand them on to Jamie. 'Well,' I said to her, 'you know what Christmas was.' It was one thing after another, what with the Christmas tree and the estate party and me helping her Ladyship with all that, and his Lordship roaring about and saying he couldn't afford any of it and carrying on alarming about Lilian one minute, and worrying about where the blasted tortoise was hibernating the next. Then there was the holiday governess who did less than nothing to help. She was very nice-looking, mind, but she could hardly speak a word of English and she spent most of the day lying in bed complaining about the cold. She should have been here last year if she wanted to know about the cold. Meanwhile the children were running wild all over the house and when her Ladyship asked that Francine what the matter was, she apparently just burst into floods of tears and said she had lied and she wasn't a governess at all but an out-of-work actress. Her Ladyship can be quite sharp at times, so she told her that she hoped she was a better actress than she was governess. In the end the young woman went back to France early which was just as well, but it meant that I was left with the children most of the time, not to mention all the washing and ironing and darning that that involved. Then on Boxing Day I had the most dreadful sore throat and his Lordship was going shooting with Mr MacIntosh upstairs and a few other friends and there was an awful hoo-ha at tea time because there weren't any birds. Never mind birds, I thought. He's got enough birds in his dressing-room, dropping seeds everywhere and attracting mice and all he can do is talk about putting pheasants down and starting up the shoot again properly, and her Ladyship isn't too pleased about that because she says he can't begin to afford it. And then, there was Father, not complaining, mind, but not at all his usual self. And Dolly came over with Fred and the children and she wanted to know if I had heard anything from Mr Johnson which is none of her business. Then she made me quite cross by saying that she expected I was really glad to have decided not to go to Australia. Really glad, my foot!

Bert wasn't too cheerful over Christmas either. I didn't particularly want him to come round to Father's on Christmas evening, but Father insisted. He said I wasn't being kind when the man was all on his own with no family. Me not kind? Well, I gave in and let him come, but he just sat there in the corner looking down in the mouth until Dolly started up about Australia and then he looked as if he was about to strangle me. He left pretty soon after that and went on home. 'Why won't you marry me Annie?' he said on New Year's Eve. 'Oh, come on, Bert,' I said, 'I thought we'd gone through all that.' Then he has the nerve to say to me, 'Oh, I know why. It's because your heart is in Australia.' 'Never you mind Australia,' I told him.

I've still got a rotten cold and her Ladyship's talking about the collars on the children's shirts. She ought to know that I won't forget them and they'll be done in time for the children to go back to school next week. Things might calm down a bit then.

I'm rather surprised that none of us has heard a word from Johnson since he went to Australia. I sometimes wonder if Annie wishes she had gone with him but perhaps he just never asked her to. She's a bit funny about him though and doesn't like it if you ever mention his name. In any case, it's certainly just as well for us that she didn't go. And now Priscilla's talking about taking the Golden Hind to Paris and going to stay with friends near Montluçon later on this year. She's got some scheme whereby we give pounds to our French friends when they come over here and they give them back in francs when we go over there. I'm not terribly keen to go myself but Priscilla loves the place and speaks the language and anyway always wants to go abroad.

I stopped at the village shop yesterday for some cigarettes and bumped into old Doubleday who, having just heard the news about Gandhi, had on a very long face of course. He's such a damn know-all about everything to do with India, that he insisted on telling me that he could have seen it coming. Then he urgently required me to agree with everything he said, as if my agreement somehow had the power automatically to confirm his rightness and the wisdom of all his opinions. The funny thing was that I'd hardly got home when Georgina came in from school and the first thing she wanted to know was why Gandhi had been shot, and was it true that they were going to burn his body on a bonfire. She was very pleased when I told her I'd been talking to Doubleday about it. If he taught them nothing else, he certainly taught those children about India and the British Empire. Even little Jamie informed me at Christmas that the new coins would no longer have *Ind. Imp.* on them.

All this nonsense with my mother is still going on. She remains quite convinced I've stolen and sold some of her things despite the fact that I've sent her the auctioneer's catalogue asking her to identify anything she claims as hers. If it could then be proved that some object or other was hers, I would have to pay her for it. But of course she makes absolutely no sense and is now threatening to come down here and go round the whole house. I'm terrified of her coming while we are out or away and have given the servants strict instructions not to let her in. Priscilla is very brave and prepared to meet her head on but what Priscilla doesn't fully realise is just how unreasonable my mother is. If you cross her she either narrows her eyes and with a wave of her hand dismisses what you've said as something not worth saying, or she flies into a towering rage.

Tony brought a very pretty girl called Lavinia down for the week-end. He seems quite keen on her but the poor devil is so hard up I can't see him marrying again in a hurry. I rather liked her but Priscilla wasn't so sure because she didn't think she was very bright. Anyway we're all so used to Tony being here now that I can't imagine what it will be like without him if he moves away.

Bloody awful time of year, but at least it's not as bad as it was last year and luckily we haven't needed the snowplough yet, although of course we had the buckets out on the upstairs landing again the other day when it rained so hard. Much as I love this place, I sometimes feel the need to get the hell out of it. Still, the weekly drill night helps. Once I've got through all the paperwork which naturally falls to the Colonel's lot, there's always a pretty jolly get-together in the mess to look forward to afterwards.

Then there's Pammie who is usually ready to cheer me up. She's a bit of a good-time girl, I suppose, which is perhaps why she enables one to forget one's worries for a while. And she doesn't demand anything beyond a good time. I dread to think what Priscilla would say if she knew about Pammie. I couldn't do without Priscilla. She does her best to keep me up to the mark but I'm not sure she realises quite how difficult it is to do anything when everything is such a muddle. Sometimes she makes me feel as if I am totally useless. Perhaps she's right.

## Zbigniew Rakowski's notebook

I had not been to Cranfield for some time and so, despite the fact that I feared the chill of the Red Drawing-Room, it was not without a certain thrill of expectation that I set out yesterday morning armed with a rug for my knees and a stone bottle for my feet, the which I trusted I would be able to prevail upon the good Annie to fill for me. I would not venture to ask such a service of the dreadful butler. Indeed I would be reluctant to ask one single favour of the man whom I half hoped might have been dismissed during the intervening weeks. I say 'half hoped', for I am forced to admit that one part of me wished once more to clap, as the saying goes, my eye upon the monstrous man. This no doubt because of my inordinate curiosity as to what it is that lies behind his strange and peculiarly immodest behaviour. I would like to know exactly what it is that the scoundrel is after. It would also interest me to know from whence he hails. How is it that Lord Otterton came to hire such a devious, deceitful man to be his butler? Has he not noticed that there is something profoundly disturbing about the man's presence in his house? What references did Mason have? Did he formerly work in some ducal residence from which he was dismissed? Did he then blackmail his Grace into giving him a good reference? Anything is possible and it is my intention to discover the truth. Quite how I will set about it, I am not as yet sure. Neither am I decided as to the wisdom of confiding my doubts about the man to her Ladyship. It is hardly my place to criticise the servants in a house where I have been made nothing, if not greatly welcome.

'Aha . . .' Whenever he opens the front door to me, the impertinent fellow has, I note, taken to greeting me in this fashion. On this most recent occasion, there followed an even more impertinent, 'It is none other than *our* Zbigniew.' I do not know by what criterion the butler has abrogated to himself the right to address me by my Christian name which he pronounces, either through ignorance or with the specific intention of sneering, I know not which, as Spig-new. I felt the hairs on my neck prickle as I struggled to control my temper, not quite sure whether it was this *Spig-new* or the awful use of the possessive pronoun which most enraged me. However, if I am to discover anything, it is in my interest to remain calm and on apparently good terms with this vile creature. 'Good morning Mr Mason,' I politely rejoined.

I was of course too proud to ask the man to fill the bottle for my feet and lived all morning in the hope that Annie might appear as she usually does to offer me a cup of tea. Yesterday, there was no sign of her and I cannot but suspect that this was somehow Mason's doing. So my poor feet froze although I was glad of the rug I had brought with which I managed to keep my legs and knees tolerably warm. Luncheon was a hurried affair since both Lord and Lady Otterton had to rush away about their various occupations punctually in the early afternoon. It was perhaps because of this that they both appeared a trifle distracted. I myself felt not a little uneasy being waited upon in a servile fashion by the man who, only a few hours earlier, had had the temerity to address me in such very different tones.

It was my intention to catch an earlier bus than usual home after luncheon, thus I was already engaged in carefully gathering up my possessions when the butler came sidling through the door, bearing aloft on one hand, just like any caricature of a butler, a large silver salver on which, to my horror, I discerned not one, but two cups. 'I thought our *Spig-*

*new* might welcome a cuppa,' he remarked as he oiled his way across the faded Persian carpet. Oh the vulgarity of the creature!

To my astonishment, the man's insolence did not this time enrage me, rather I sensed a thrill of excitement run through my old veins. It flashed across my mind that if I should partake of tea with the butler, I might make my first hesitant steps towards unravelling something of the mystery which surrounded him. This was an opportunity which I should at least not overlook. Mason deposited the salver on the table at which I had been working and, as he drew up an exquisite Louis XV *fauteuil* for himself to sit upon, asked me in a patronising manner whether or not I had remembered to lock the cabinet. 'I am sure you would wish to leave everything as you found it,' he added with a leer. Then, taking a seat on the *fauteuil* and tweaking his trousers at the knees as he did so, he gave me an almost humorous look which sent a chill right through me and said sweetly, with his head on one side, 'And be sure to take all your notebooks.' How I loathed the man!

How I detested the way he perched upright on the chair whose delicate, worn tapestry deserves in its decrepitude to be protected from the pressure of the human form, and most particularly so from the grotesque posterior of the infamous Mason. Knees placed firmly together, he sipped his tea from a bone china cup, crooking his little finger and simpering, for all the world like an elderly spinster at a clergyman's tea party. As I looked at the man, I decided that he was deranged. Quite deranged. But here, I thought, is at least something of an opportunity. I must make of it what I can.

'I think you must have been here now for over a year,' I opined with a hint of enquiry in my tone. 'Might I ask where you worked before?'

I instantly noted the man's body stiffen almost imperceptibly and there was a moment's hesitation before he replied with a question of his own. So I was not wrong in supposing that he had something to hide. Neither was I wrong in thinking that he had read my notebook which I so carelessly allowed him to purloin, for with his question which was so vulgar that I do not care to repeat it, he made it abundantly clear that he needed my help and that he would not hesitate to use blackmail in order to obtain it. So as to ascertain what I wish to know about the man and to discover the secrets of his nefarious plot, it occurred to me that for the present time at least, I should appear to go along with whatever the treacherous scallywag might suggest. Ultimately of course, he may act as he wishes, for the worst he can do is to cover an old man in shame, reveal his folly and have him banished for ever from the presence of his loved one. All of which things, I trust I would bear like a man.

Perhaps I should not have been totally surprised when Mason then told me that he was looking, on behalf of a person or persons unknown, as he chose to put it, for some important private letters which had gone missing in the house during the upheaval created by the war when the late Lord Otterton and his Lady moved out to the Dower House, leaving Leoni's triumph free to accommodate the nation's historic treasures sent there from the Public Record Office. Since, as he surmised, I had not only free access to the family papers, but in addition the ear of *his Lordship* and *her exquisite Ladyship*, which words he pronounced with such derision that I was barely able to contain my anger, he was satisfied that I was the person best placed to aid him in his search for the missing documents.

Thinking of these things, I am brought to mind of a day, not last summer, but the summer before when, in the village store, I came across Lord Otterton's driver, Johnson, a decent, apparently admirable man who used to work about the place, but who has since left to go, or so I am told, to the Colonies. There was then, as I recall, some intrigue concerning letters. I do not know what letter and nor do I know what the outcome of the affair was at the time. I only know that letters were involved and that they were in some mysterious way causing concern in certain quarters. I seem to remember that I made some reference to the incident in my notebook at the time. I must verify whether or not that was one and the same notebook that Mason temporarily purloined and from which I later observed he had carefully removed one or two pages in such a way that I was not at first aware of his perfidy. He left me yesterday like a trout with a fly hanging over my nose and refused on that occasion to enlighten me further, telling me only in a free and easy, off-hand manner that he would keep me informed. As I finally left the Red Drawing-Room yesterday afternoon, I sensed the presence of Laszlo's Lady Otterton looking down from the wall so that I could almost feel her cold eyes on my back, following me out of the room. I have much to think about in the days that lie ahead.

## Sydney Otterton's diary

I really haven't been making much of a go of anything lately which is probably why Priscilla is pretty fed up with me. I suppose the Regiment provides some sort of occasional discipline and to a certain extent so does the House of Lords which I do attend regularly and which has the added advantage of making me feel I'm doing something vaguely useful, if only by just going there. At home things seem much more difficult. There's the problem of the sheep for which we took out another enormous loan and which look as if they're not going to be very successful. I've never known animals have so many bloody diseases. If they don't have maggots, they have rotting feet and if their feet don't rot, they probably get scab, besides which, at this time of year they need an awful lot of fodder and that gives them intestinal troubles. Another minor inconvenience is that Peggy has taken to chasing them so I have to keep her on the lead when I go anywhere near where they are. I'm not sure that the man we've got looking after them knows a thing about what he's meant to be doing and I have a nasty feeling that instead of there being a pot of gold at the end of the road, the whole experiment is going to turn into an expensive failure. I keep thinking that sheep look wrong here in any case. They don't seem to have enough room and consequently need pampering, quite unlike the huge flocks I remember seeing in Australia before the war. Those sheep were apparently much more capable of looking after themselves even when they were lambing. Priscilla said it was a bad idea in the first place to go in for sheep, but since she doesn't know the first thing about farming, there didn't seem to be any very good reason why I should listen to her on the subject. She kept saying that she just had this feeling that it wouldn't work and it looks as if she was bloody well right.

On top of that there's been an outbreak of foot and mouth at Sharpe's farm down the road, so I'm just waiting for that to spread to us. We've got buckets of disinfectant by every gate, but I was coming up the drive only yesterday and I caught that idiot Goodfellow climbing a gate, obviously without having dipped his feet in the stuff which was right there under his nose. Thank God I never had him with me in an armoured car at Gubi or anywhere else for that matter.

Last night I woke up in an almighty sweat from one of those awful nightmares where you're trying to stand up and run and your limbs won't move. I got out of bed and went to talk to my birds in my dressing-room, thinking that that would rid me of the shakes. It didn't do much good because when I went back to bed about half an hour later, I fell into a restless sleep as soon as I'd turned the light off and the dream immediately recurred. I feel sure that that particular dream must result from the time my entire squadron was knocked out at a place called Belanda in a hilly part of the desert. After a few enemy reconnaissance planes had been over, everything had seemed perfectly calm and the attack in the early morning came very suddenly. I remember spending the whole of the rest of that day walking or running in the sand with a few other survivors. We were being chased and fired at by enemy tanks and kept dropping flat so as to hide in a hollow. God Almighty knows how we survived. I remember lying in one such hollow with one of my men and saying to him, 'It looks as if we've had it this time.' He didn't answer and it wasn't till later that night, after we'd been picked up and he'd been treated for burns that I realised he hadn't been able to speak because his lips had been sealed together by fire as he jumped from our burning tank. Of course we must have been terrified at the time, but it was all part of the day's work and one didn't have time to think about being afraid. Yet now, in a quiet country house in peacetime with nothing more to worry about than a few mangy sheep, it all comes back to haunt me. I don't understand it. It's not as if Cranfield isn't where I want to be. In fact it's so much part of me that it sometimes occurs to me that without it I wouldn't really exist although I also think sometimes that I'd like to burn the whole place down and be completely free of it. I wonder how Johnson's getting on in Australia. Perhaps he did have a point, going there to get away from it all. It certainly occasionally occurs to me to envy his being able to start from scratch. Starting again like that, a man is left with the raw material of nothing but himself or what he has made of himself.

Of course if I had been blown up by the Bosch, I wouldn't have to worry about the sheep or the cows, or the roof leaking, or my mother and death duties and the farm cottages and the fencing. That's another thing about sheep, the buggers break out of everywhere and contrive to do the most unbelievable amount of damage in no time.

# *Georgina's exercise book*

When I got back from school I couldn't be bothered to do my home work so I just romed about the house looking for that lost room that Father and I can't find. Mrs Arbuthnot was just going into her flat and she said would I like a sweet. Mummy says we cant bother Mrs Arbutnot but I said yes because I think the hiden room is somewere in her flat. Mrs Arbuthnot laughs a lot and calls you dear and is very nice. She's got white hair and is old. She says Cranfield is a *maaarvlous* place and she thinks there probebly is a secret room but she says its not in her flat. She wouldn't know. I bet horrible Mr Mason knows were it is. He's so nosey. He was on the back stairs landing yesterday rummijing in a drawer and he jumped out of his skin when he saw me and began to tell me off for coming upstairs. I wish Jamie or Thomas was there. They would be rude to him. I didn't dare. He looks so frightning. I think he hates us.

I didn't know Mr Rakofsky was here and he made me jump when I went into the hall this afternoon. He was standing so still in front of one of the fireplaces and he sudenly turned round and said good afternoon mairm. He said he was looking at the fireplace because he loves it and did I love it. I said I loved the hall and he said a lot of stuff about the hall and a lot of stuff about looking for some boring old papers. I think he's funny. He's more intrested not nosy like Mr Mason and I think he likes us but I think he likes the house even more.

# Zbigniew Rakowski's notebook

Yesterday afternoon I encountered the girl, Georgina, in the marble hall. I surmised from the beret on her head and the satchel on her back, that she was just returning from school. She informed me that she loved the hall at Cranfield which did not surprise me. The child must by now be nine or ten years old and no doubt the spirit of the place is already deeply embedded in her consciousness. She told me that she often roamed about the house looking for a secret room which she has not yet found. She wondered if I might know of such a place. I told her that I did not but proceeded to talk to her at some length about the beauties of the hall in which we stood. I spoke of Rysbrack and of the fine plasterwork ceiling, of the magnificent proportions and I even expostulated on the beauty of the shining mahogany doors. The poor child must have found such discourse tedious but she was good enough to listen politely to an old man's prattle.

I then suggested that she might miss her brothers who are away at school, but although she assured me that she looked forward to the holidays and to their return, she was, I opine, glad to be able to advise me that she never felt lonely in the house, there being so many places to hide and so many things to find. What sort of things did she find, I wished to know. 'Oh, books,' she said, 'and pills. Once Jamie and I found some old pills in a drawer in the Green Silk Room and we tried them but they weren't very nice.' I looked somewhat startled for, although I would not of course have mentioned the cause of my alarm to the child herself, I could not help but wonder what poison her depraved grandmother might have left lurking in some forgotten corner. She laughed, nevertheless, at what must have been my obvious concern and said that I was like her mother (oh, the bitter-sweet innocent words of childhood!) who had been quite *frantic*

187

when she heard of the incident. 'She made us swear never to eat anything we found lying about again.' I did not wonder at poor Priscilla's distress.

Before we parted company, it did occur to me to ask Georgina in as casual a tone as I knew how to muster, if at any time during the course of her investigations she had come across any old papers or letters. 'Oh,' she replied with a jaunty air, 'there are papers and bits of letters everywhere but they're awfully boring.' I felt at that moment obliged to enjoin her to keep her parents informed should she discover any further *awfully boring* papers which, although of no apparent interest to her, might well be of some interest to adults. I then humbly informed her that I was writing a history of her family (a fact with which she assured me she was already familiar) and explained that for this reason, I myself might be interested in her findings. I think that she was not displeased by the suggestion that she might be enrolled to play the part of a minor sleuth. I cannot deny that I was somewhat delighted by her parting shot, whereby she directed me not to seek the help of the butler. 'Mr Mason is too nosy,' she said, but I was also not a little distressed to hear her add, 'Anyway I think he hates us.'

In fact Mr Mason left me in peace yesterday. Or that is to say comparative peace. He refrained from taking tea with me and attempted to put no further pressure on me. Last time I saw him, he had had the temerity to tell me that time was on our side. I should take things slowly and quietly observe. The revolution would come in due course. He must, in my opinion, be a very stupid man for he appears to take no account whatsoever of the fact that I myself may not be wholly incapable of independent thought, nor that I might have some loyalty to Lord and Lady Otterton who have so kindly acted as my patrons over the last two years or so. How can he believe that the contents of my snivelling notebook can really be held as a threat over the head of a man of even the slightest integrity? Yet, I do declare that that is just what he does think. And so the game goes on with myself as deeply involved as he is, for I am determined to find whatever it may be that he seeks before he does so and to use it against him, and I am equally determined to discover how it is that he has come to be involved in such a fashion in this peculiar affair.

I become increasingly convinced that Lilian, Lady Otterton has a good deal to answer for. It is my intention gradually to ingratiate myself with the repulsive Mason, thus to gain his trust with a view to wheedling a little more information out of the man. What a truly splendid stroke of luck to have encountered the child who may prove to be an invaluable, hidden ally.

### Annie's diary

MARCH 21ST

Bert was quite full of himself yesterday evening because he had won 7s./6d. on Sheila's Cottage which won the Grand National. He never usually has a bet, only one on the Grand National and one on the Derby, just like me, not that I've ever been so lucky, although I think I did once win two bob on the Derby, but that was years gone by. In fact he made me quite cross because he straight away started to say that if his good fortune was to last, he would soon be able to afford to get married. I do wish he would take no for an answer. I was so put out that I left quite soon after I'd cleared up his tea. In any case I was fairly tired and didn't want to get to bed too late.

What with Easter being early this year, the boys will be back for the holidays in a day or two and that will liven us all up a bit. They'll be running around all over the place, acting the giddy goat and will be sure to get into trouble with his Lordship before long, with him in his present mood. He's

189

not been very happy at all lately and he flies off the handle at the slightest thing. We all know that when his Lordship's in a bad mood it affects everyone. Not that he's ever been anything but nice to me. But then I've always been very fond of him ever since he was a little boy, and I know that what with *Lilian* and one thing and another, he's had a dreadful time. I expect he's worried about the foot and mouth, but I'm quite sure it's not just that. I think he's got his mother on his mind again now. It's terrible the power that woman had over her family – she used to have his Lordship and his late Lordship quaking in their shoes. I reckon Lady Isley was the only one that never took a blind bit of notice of her.

They say that when his Lordship was seventeen or eighteen his mother was so angry with him over some incident or other that she tried to persuade the doctor to certify him and have him locked up in a lunatic asylum. She could never bear not to have her own way, besides which she was always said to bear some deep resentment against his Lordship. I've always thought it must have been something to do with the baby she had earlier that died. Perhaps that was what sent her off her head in the first place. All the same, what sort of woman would try to put her own son away? If you ask me she was the one that wanted locking up. Under the circumstances, I feel you can hardly blame his Lordship if he's a bit difficult at times. Mr Johnson always said he was marvellous in the war, very brave and he kept everyone's spirits up. Mr Johnson thought the world of him. Well, they thought the world of each other.

I often wonder how Mr Johnson is getting on. It's funny that he never wrote.

Her Ladyship says she can't wait to get away from us all. She's going off to France for a week as soon as the children go back to school and she says that once she has crossed the Channel she will be able to forget all her worries. 'I'll leave them behind for you, Annie,' she said to me. 'I know I can trust you to see that everything is properly looked after while I'm away.' Well, I thought to myself, I should certainly hope you can trust me. And there'll be Miss Wheel for company. She's coming for the inside of the week to mend some of the old curtains. I look forward to seeing Miss Wheel.

I expect Mr Rakowski will be here during the week as well and I know her Ladyship likes me to look in and see that he's all right. I always used to take him his tea in the afternoons, but lately Mr Mason seems very keen to do that. I don't know quite what's going on between those two. They shut themselves up together in that Red Drawing-Room for hours. Lord knows what they have to talk to each other about. I should hardly have thought that they were each other's cup of tea. In fact I'm beginning to wonder about Mr Mason. There's something about him that I don't quite like, not that I can put my finger on what it is exactly. There's something not altogether nice about the way he keeps turning up in odd places. I mean what business could he possibly have had to be going through the books in the bookcase on the top landing? And another time when the children were out with the governess I saw him coming out of the school-room. He looked a little surprised to see me and when I remarked that the children were out, he said something about a tray and having to take it down to the kitchen. Well that was odd because he certainly didn't have any tray in his hands, or anything else for that matter. It reminded me of the time the old mamzelle and Mr Cheadle had argued about who should take a tray downstairs. There was a tray that time of course because we all saw it sitting on the landing table for days on end.

## *Georgina's exercise book*

We all hate Mr Mason. Thomas says he is evil. When he goes to bed he puts a chair against the door to keep Mr Mason out and sleeps with a water pistol by his bed. We are planning our revenge but when we told Mummy we hated him she just said don't be silly but Tony looked very kind and said he quite understood the children. I don't think Mr Mason has any rite to go barjing into Jamies or Thomas's room. Why can't he stay in his own room. And he's always looking for things. Ive started to look for things for Mr Rakofsky. It's quite fun but I don't know what I'm supposed to be looking for. Perhaps there is some treshure in the secret room. Anyway I pretend I'm a detectiv and I hope I find something before Mr Mason does because I think he would steal it and do a midnight flit like the man in the story we heard on Children's Hour.

Father has bought us a pony called a strawberry rone. It's quite pink with a black main and tail and I can't catch it or make it go when I'm on it. Thomas and Jamie galop like mad. Thomas is going to put a stink bomb in the pantry to annoy Mr Mason. I hope he dares.

## *Letter from Annie to Dolly*

Cranfield Park.
APRIL 30TH, 1948

Dear Dolly,

I know you will be glad to hear that Father is looking up a bit, both in health and in his spirits. I think the warmer weather and the arrival of Spring have done him a lot of good. His being able to get back out in the garden has been a blessing.

He's been in a terrible state about all the weeds coming up and everything else that needed doing. I'm sure that won't be any surprise to you. As a matter of fact Bert did a bit of digging for him a while back so the place wasn't in too bad a way.

It'll be ever so quiet here for a bit now as the boys have gone off back to school and her Ladyship left for France this morning. She was all over the place. I'd done her packing and her suitcase was ready in the hall but first of all she couldn't find her passport and then she nearly left her handbag behind. Meanwhile his Lordship who was supposed to be driving her to London, was standing there laughing and saying it was a good thing she didn't have to get a squadron of tanks across the desert which made her furious. Anyway you would never believe what happened next, in fact no sooner than they were out of the door. I just went up to the kitchen for something and there was Mrs Laws with a funny look about her, I thought. She was standing there with that Lorraine by her side, holding her by the hand. It crossed my mind that the child should have been at school and then I wondered why on earth the woman was wearing her hat and coat at that time of day. 'Where are you going Mrs Laws?' I said. And then I realised she had a suitcase standing by her side. 'We're leaving Annie,' she said. 'We've had enough.' And all that without so much as a with your leave or a by your leave. I dread to think what his Lordship will say when he gets back. Never mind her Ladyship. Anyway the pair of them have gone and the Lord knows how we are going to manage without a cook. I wouldn't wonder if Mr Kipling didn't have something to do with it.

Miss Wheel is here which is company for me in the evenings.

No more news for now so I'll finish. I hope you are all keeping well and I look forward to hearing from you soon. Give my love to Fred and the children.

Love from
Annie

# Zbigniew Rakowski's notebook

As I trod the now so familiar path to Cranfield yesterday morning, enjoying the sweet scents of spring that filled the air, admiring, as I rounded the bend in the drive, the magnificent view of the house, so square and bold and yet so peaceful, at one with its surroundings, roseate against a background of tall, almost black wellingtonias and the newly sprung vivid green of the beech leaves, little did I imagine that a dramatic afternoon lay ahead.

Lady Otterton was, I of course knew, in France, enjoying as I hoped, a well-deserved visit to relatives. I picture her in some crumbling château whose pale *boiserie* and faded *toile de Jouy* are the perfect framework for her slender, aristocratic figure. I even imagine the washed-out blue of the cloth on which a little shepherdess, seated on a swing, hangs from the bough of a leafy tree whilst sheep graze at her feet and lambs gambol around her. I see Priscilla, seated no less elegantly on a cream and gilt *fauteuil*, conversing flawlessly in the language of Racine. But enough of that. I also knew that Lord Otterton would not be at home and that I was therefore not bidden to luncheon. Thus I had with me, as is my wont on such occasions, my picnic and my thermos. I hoped as I admired the gently sloping beauty of the park and mused on Priscilla's visit to France, that on such a pleasant day as this, the indescribable Mason would not interfere too grossly with my labours, although I was quite of the opinion that the time had come for me to oblige myself to pass some little time with his odious personage, if I was to progress at all in my investigations which, I was forced to admit to myself, had remained somewhat static during the preceding weeks.

By midday what had been a promising, fine morning had clouded over and there was a hint of rain in the dark clouds as I glanced out of the Red Drawing-Room window across the long lawn to where a hawthorn tree surprisingly leans and spreads its knotty branches. Not far to the right of it stands an old oak, more suited perhaps to the grandeur of its surroundings than is the little hawthorn. I have often wondered how and when these two trees came to be planted and had thought to take my rug and sit under one or the other to partake of my picnic, thus to admire for a change the East Front of the house.

In the event, however, I decided to eat my sandwiches speedily at the table where I work, to lose no time and thus to take an earlier than usual bus home. Like the weather, my mood had clouded over and, feeling weary, I did not for once feel equal to the task of battling with mystery or with Mason. When nature's own egalitarian had opened the door for me in the morning, he had not appeared to be quite his usual cock-a-hoop self. (I can think of no better way to describe this man's generally self-satisfied manner.) Rather he brushed me aside with a 'No one informed me that you were coming today', as if I were some tiresome encumbrance, and neither did he intrude on me all morning. Instead it was the good Annie who came to see if I was in need of anything. She, I am always glad to see. When I enquired on this occasion if all was well, she informed me of the disruption caused in the household by the sudden defection of the cook. His Lordship was in London and had not been seen for a few days and she was much concerned as to what her Ladyship's reaction would be when she returned to hear the bad news. Annie told me that she could not help but like the cook, yet, in her view, it was all wrong for anyone to leave in such a way without so much as a word to anyone. To have one's work interrupted for a while by Annie with her chatter is always a pleasure. She is, in my view, not only an honest woman, but shrewd, good-looking and humorous besides. I do not doubt her discretion for, as she herself is ever at pains to inform one, she likes to mind her p's and q's.

It was quite early in the afternoon when I collected my

belongings and made for the hall with the intention of leaving by the front door, and perhaps of lingering for a usual brief moment on my way, to admire yet again the nobility of the whole.

As I lingered in the hall, Mason suddenly burst through the door from the opposite side. He was walking fast, his hands clenched by his chest with his elbows sticking out behind him; on his face he wore an expression of concentrated urgency and, as he hastened towards the front door, he appeared to be completely oblivious of my presence, so that I was able to step swiftly back into the doorway at the back of the hall, from which I had emerged, and to stand there quietly without having been observed. Imagine then my amazement on seeing the treacherous butler advance towards the front door. Just before disappearing from my view into the porch, he stopped for a moment, still, as if to collect himself, and there he remained for a fleeting instant, straight as a die, pulling his shoulders back, smoothing his hair with both hands which he then proceeded to rub unctuously together before hurrying into the porch where I imagine he flung the door open, for I heard him instantly utter an unmitigatedly fawning, high-pitched 'M'lady!'

My heart missed a beat since, not unnaturally, my first thought was for Priscilla. Could she conceivably have returned early from her crumbling château? But just as the thought flitted through my mind, I became aware of the fact that under no circumstances would Mason have addressed the Lady Otterton that I know in such sycophantic tones. Nor indeed would his behaviour before he opened the door have remotely resembled that which I have described. The man's manner when addressing Priscilla can indeed be obsequious, and usually is, but nevertheless, I have observed a certain wariness in his attitude towards her as though, like an animal, he senses danger in her presence. When talking to Priscilla, Mason is very much on his mettle.

I held my breath as, from the sheltered alcove of my

doorway, I then observed a slight woman dressed in black and mauve step from the porch that so defiles the West Front of the house, into the hall itself. Having passed so many hours seated beneath Laszlo's painting, I would any-where have recognised the chilling figure of Lilian who now appeared, a little older than in her portrait, but otherwise just as though she had simply stepped down from the confines of the gilt frame which normally keeps her so safely incarcer-ated, to stand there before me, in flesh and blood, so tiny in the whiteness of the vast hall. Even from where I was, I could easily discern the pale face and hooded eyes, the straight nose, the pointed chin, the black, black hair (no doubt artificially aided by now in the depths of its colour). Round her neck she wore a long chain, just as she does in her portrait.

She raised an arm to wave autocratically towards the door on the side of the hall opposite me. As she did so, her sleeve fell back down her forearm to reveal a delicate wrist such as I would have expected to find on a porcelain figurine only. 'I'll go upstairs first,' she said grandly. 'See to the men, will you.' And with that she swept out of the hall by the far door. No sooner had she disappeared than Mason went back at once to the porch, from whence he immediately returned accompa-nied by two burly men attired in workmen's overalls. 'Come with me,' he commanded and without further ado, the three of them followed in the footsteps of the ghost-like Lilian and, as she had, disappeared from my view.

So alarmed was I by what I had witnessed, that I needed a moment to recover my equilibrium before daring to venture out on my journey home. At the same time, I was hesitant to remain in the house for fear of coming face to face with the dowager lady herself, yet, for the moment, I felt that there was no alternative but to withdraw back into the Red Drawing-Room from whence I had come, there to ponder on what my next move might be and perhaps, if I am honest, to ascertain that Laszlo's Lilian was still in her frame, that

Lady Otterton had not stepped out of the picture, and that what I had seen was no fantom, no creation of my heat-oppressed imagination, but a living, mortal being.

After some moments of consideration, and having re-assured myself that the painted Lilian was unquestionably still in her rightful place, I determined that what I had seen was enough; certainly enough for me to have a far greater hold over Mason than he could conceivably have over me merely on the evidence of a few paltry pages expressing the drooling fantasies of a frail old man. Eventually, on leaving the house through the basement and the back door, I was fortunate not to encounter a soul, but since my departure I have been quite unable to rid my mind of what occurred yesterday afternoon and am fearful as to what the eventual outcome of that dramatic event may possibly be. I lay awake last night, haunted by the idea that I, a cowardly old fool, may well have betrayed my good patrons by failing to spy (for spying it would indeed have been) on the further activities of her Ladyship and Mason, not to mention their burly accomplices. Yet at the time, it did not seem right that I should snoop. Snoop, ah yes, snoop. What an ugly word that is!

## Georgina's exercise book

MAY 4TH

A very frightening thing hapenned when I got back from school this afternoon. No one was about so I was just roming around as usual. I was in the galery looking down on the hall when all at once the front door bell rang. It was like a really spooky story and I was spying up above. First disgusting Mr Mason came running all bisily to the door and then in came guess who? GRANDMAMA!!!!! Who's not aloud here *at all*. Mr Mason looked as if he knew her and she just marched in looking like a witch with two great big workmen behind her.

I bet she knows Mummy and Father are away or she'd never have dared come here. I stayed spying for a long time even though I was afraid she might see me. After a bit these great big men started to carry fernicher out of the door. They were stealing our things! Father will be livid! Aksherly it was very frightening. Then Annie found me and was cross because she said she didn't know where I had got to. I asked her if she'd seen Grandmama but she wouldn't say. I'm writing this in bed after lights out but no one will know because I bet they're only thinking about Grandmama and what Mummy and Father will say.

## Annie's diary

I don't know what in the Lord's name her Ladyship will say when she gets back, and as for his Lordship, well, I should think anyone would be afraid to be near him when he finds out about what went on this afternoon. I'm afraid there'll be a bit of bad language. Anyway I can't get hold of him in London because there's no answer from the number he left. Luckily Mr MacIntosh came back quite early from work so I was able to tell him about what Lilian has done. I was really glad Mr MacIntosh was here. He was very kind and said I wasn't to worry and that he would go on trying to get hold of his Lordship for me this evening. I told him that it wasn't me who let Lady Otterton in just when his Lordship and her Ladyship are both away and he said he knew I wouldn't do a thing like that.

The Lord above knows what she's taken. She even went into her Ladyship's bedroom and emptied the contents of one small chest of drawers all over the bed and I had only this week relined those drawers and tidied them beautifully. Then these dreadful men came in and Lady Lilian told them to take the chest down and put it in their lorry. And that wasn't the end of it. There's no knowing what they didn't take. I was standing there saying that her Ladyship was away and Lilian just looked through me with that awful stare of hers and said, 'Oh, it's you. Simply do as I say, will you.' Then she dismissed me and there was nothing at all that I could do but stand there and watch her ransacking the place. I never felt so dreadful in all my life.

I don't know how she managed to get in unless she found the back door unlocked which Mr Mason thinks she must have done. Mr Mason says that Mr Rakowski left earlier than usual and that he saw him going down the basement stairs which means that he must have gone out through the back door and left it open. Mind you, I can't help feeling that there's something a bit funny about that. Mr Rakowski always goes out through the front door. I think he likes to admire the hall on his way. I've often seen him there just gazing up at the ceiling. Once he was even stroking the doors. It must have been on one of Mr Mason's days off because I remember I was going through to the Japanese Room to close the shutters and draw the curtains. And I know it must have been winter because fires were burning in those two big fireplaces and it was already dark although Mr Rakowski was still there. I remember he stopped me and said, 'Don't hurry through, Ma'am. You should stop to look at these chimney-pieces.' And I said something about not having any time to stand about staring at things because I had my work to do, and he laughed and said, 'Ma'am, pray feel the exquisite texture of these peerless glossy doors.' 'I don't know about peerless,' I said, 'but I have to say I've always liked the look of them.' Then, blow me down if he didn't say that I ought to keep a diary because according to him I'd have a fascinating story to tell. I never said a thing mind, but just gave him a look on the Q.T. and thought to myself that he was the one who was supposed to be the writer. Of course I've heard it all before. The servant's-eye view, my foot! So I left him there stroking those darned doors and went on to do my work. Then Bert goes and tells me, as if he knows a thing about anything, that some people love wood. And well they may.

So if Mr Rakowski didn't leave the back door open, which I doubt, how did Lilian get in? I have my suspicions. For one thing I didn't like the way Mr Mason was so sure that he'd seen Mr Rakowski leave early and I didn't like the way he talked about it, so fast that no one could get a word in edgeways, just like the children when they are telling fibs. Before long, I thought, you'll be swearing to me on the Holy Bible that you *saw* the poor man leaving the door open.

The other thing is that I was worried to death about Georgina. I didn't know where on earth she'd got to after she came back from school. She's supposed to come and find me when she gets in and I am always around waiting for her, but she loves to go off, roaming around all over the house so that it's quite impossible to find her. I didn't know what would happen if she came across her grandmother helping herself to the furniture, not to mention emptying her mother's drawers all over the place without so much as a with-your-leave or a by-your-leave. I thought she would be quite frightened. Besides, I didn't think that, as a child, she ought to know what was going on. Luckily I found her wandering along the gallery above the hall. I can't imagine what in the Lord's name she was doing there. Just mooching about was what she said. Mooching about, my good Lord! Where did she find an expression like that? I asked her if she wasn't supposed to be doing her homework. Oh no, she said, she only had a tiny bit to do. Anyway, never mind that, at least I was able to get her up to the schoolroom before she realised that there was anything funny going on and we managed to sit down and have our tea quite peacefully. I was really pleased to have Miss Wheel there with us. She was a great help with Georgina.

To tell the truth I don't know how I managed to get

through the rest of the evening. There was me trying to get in touch with his Lordship on the one hand and trying to get Georgina to bed on the other, worried sick about what had happened. Thank the Lord for Mr MacIntosh. I didn't know whether to mention Mr Mason to him. He knows just as well as the rest of us do that no one is allowed to let Lilian into the house and he must wonder, like I do, exactly how she did get in.

## *Sydney Otterton's diary*

I have never been so angry in my life as I was when I got home on Thursday and saw with my own eyes exactly what my mother had been up to. Mason denies having let the bloody woman into the house in the first place and poor Annie swears that she knew nothing about it at all until she found her ordering the contents of Priscilla's drawers to be tipped out onto the bed by two great thugs. It appears that Rakowski was here that day and he is being blamed by some-and-some for having left the back door open when he went. But that doesn't really ring true to me because my mother, after all, turned up here with a ruddy great furniture van, which she wasn't likely to have done if she had any doubts about being able to get into the house. Besides, someone must have told her that both Priscilla and I were away. She would never have been able to do what she did if either of us had been at home and she must have known that.

The children hate Mason, Priscilla thinks there's something funny about him and Tony mistrusts the fellow, but I've never had any problem with him. He's a dull dog as far as I can see, an impassive sort of man who says very little, a pretty typical sort of butler who does his job adequately and doesn't seem to have caused any trouble so far. I don't know why everyone's got it in for him. Annie won't commit herself but I'm not sure she's very keen on him either. In any case why the hell would he have let my mother in when I was away after I had specifically told him not to? He had absolutely nothing to gain from doing so, but the sack.

I find it quite impossible to understand what exactly motivated my mother to take what she did. She could have taken a good many things of much greater value. Perhaps she felt that she had a claim on that chest of drawers of Priscilla's which she emptied out because once upon a time it was, I think, in her room. But still that doesn't make an awful lot of sense. It's a pretty enough piece of furniture but my mother has masses of stuff which she took from the Dower House and I can see no very good reason beyond sheer malice as to why she should have decided to take that in particular. According to Annie, she not only took what she wanted, but she also wandered all around the house ordering cupboards and drawers to be opened for her.

However she damn well got in, I really don't see why Mason was unable to prevent her from taking things away. I have to say, he doesn't seem able to give a very good account of himself.

It's hardly surprising if Priscilla who doesn't cry easily was in tears when she came back from France. She said she'd had a wonderful time and getting home to find that Mrs Laws had walked out wouldn't have bothered her in the least because she was such a rotten cook, but it was horrible going into her bedroom knowing that it had been ransacked by my mother. I don't really know what to do about it. I suppose I could send my mother a lawyer's letter but I know for certain that it won't make any difference at all. I'm not prepared to take her to court and although I could threaten her, she's so mad that I don't think it would have any effect on her. What we have to do, is to find out how she got in and who told her that Priscilla and I were away. I wonder if Rakowski knows a thing or two.

# Georgina's exercise book

I don't dare tell Father that I saw Grandmama ariving at the front door. He's in a really bad mood and I think hed be livid with me. Mummy was crying when she came home and I think it was because Grandmama had stolen her things but she sent me back to the schoolroom and said it was nothing to do with children. If I told Mummy what I saw she'd be livid too and say what was I doing in the galery and why wasn't I doing my homework and it was none of my bisness and stuff like that. I bet Mr Mason told a wopper because I heard Annie say to Miss Wheel that Grandmama came in through the back door which I know she *DID NOT*. I wish Jamie was here he's very good at spying. I wish Mr Rekofsky would come back again. I like him.

# Annie's diary

It was awful when her Ladyship got home. I felt real sorry for her. She's never been one to go crying but when she found out about what had been going on, she just burst into tears and I can't say I blame her. I even felt like crying myself when I thought of all the trouble I'd taken to tidy those drawers. But her Ladyship wasn't a bit worried about Mrs Laws because she said she'd been a rotten cook all along. Mind you she's never said anything like that before, but of course she was full of talk about all this French food she'd been eating. Mrs Laws, she said, was very Anglo-Saxon. I wasn't sure what she meant by that but then she went on about Mrs Laws not wanting to cook those wretched snails. Well I must admit that I was on Mrs Laws's side about that. Not that I would have said anything.

His Lordship came back from London with this great big pink cockatoo called Brylcreme to add to the menagerie in his dressing-room. It seems to be the only thing that brings a smile to his face these days, not that her Ladyship or anyone else was particularly pleased to see it and poor Georgina is quite terrified of it. I think she pretends not to hear his Lordship calling her in case he's going to ask her to help him clean out the cage. As a matter of fact, I think her Ladyship was more annoyed about the arrival of *Brylcreme* than she ever was about the departure of Mrs Laws. What with Brylcreme *and* Lilian, you couldn't help feeling sorry for her.

I still think Mr Mason had something to do with Lilian coming here last week. It's at times like this that I miss Mr Johnson. He would have known what to do and he would never have let that woman into the house or allowed her to take away the furniture. I can't help remembering how he kept an eye on those Legros when they were in the flat and he was convinced they were up to no good. Well I hope he's happy now, standing upside down in Australia with all those kangaroos. It's funny that he never wrote.

As a matter of fact, I have an idea that her Ladyship thinks Mr Mason's got something to do with what went on too, but, how can it be proved? She says, 'Annie, his Lordship won't listen to me if I criticise Mason. I can't tell you why,' she says, 'but there's something about that man I don't like. What do you think?' Now I wasn't going to say a word. 'And what's more, Mr MacIntosh can't stand the man,' she goes on. 'Oh,' I thought to myself. I'm not saying anything about Mr MacIntosh either.

# Sydney Otterton's diary

My mother-in-law is here for the week-end driving poor Priscilla nearly mad so I've shut myself away for a while in the Japanese Room. Priscilla bears a good deal of resentment against her mother, with reason perhaps, but she doesn't look very happy when I suggest she tries mine for a change. One thing though that has cheered me up lately is my new cockatoo. It's absolutely beautiful but I'm afraid it does make a bit of a mess. Priscilla wasn't at all pleased to see it and even Annie looked at me 'askance', as she would say. 'Now then, M'lord,' she said, 'whoo' (with a drawn-out 'o') 'do you think is going to clear up the mess?' I just laughed because I know she won't mind doing it for me. After all, what's the hoover for? Sometimes Georgina can help, but she keeps saying she's frightened of the bird which is absolute nonsense.

As a matter of fact I've had rather a good idea. When I was going around the house to see what damage my mother had done, I found a lot of old beds stacked up in one of the unused servants' rooms and I thought I'd get Kipling to use the springs to make an aviary for the birds in my dressing-room. When I told Kipling what I wanted, he gave me a sly, somewhat insolent grin and said, rather as if he was putting me in my place, that he was busy mending the struts in the greenhouses at the moment. He was supposed to have finished that job months ago but he tells me the weather has prevented him from getting on with it. I know exactly what the weather has been like. I wish Johnson was still here.

I've sent my wretched mother a lawyer's letter to complain about her thieving and telling her to keep out of the house. I've told her that if she comes back and takes anything else which isn't hers all hell will be let loose. I don't suppose it will have any effect at all and was probably just a waste of money (more cash in those greedy lawyers' pockets), but I felt that something had to be put on paper about what had happened. And I still don't know what she was after. It can't have just been the few pieces of furniture which she took and which she certainly didn't need. She even took a rickety old bit of white-painted rubbish from one of the servants' rooms. I'd also like to know why she went round the house opening and shutting drawers and cupboards as if she was looking for something. What in God's name could she have been looking for?

Priscilla is adamant that I ought to sack Mason but I can't really see why. She almost gives me the impression that she's frightened of him, but as far as I can see he hasn't done anything wrong and he totally denies having had anything to do with my mother getting into the house. I can't help feeling that he must be telling the truth because if he weren't, someone else would probably have seen something and would have said so. In any case he could never be certain that he hadn't been seen, so one might imagine that if he were lying, he'd be a bit more uneasy. I think Rakowski's coming here some time next week, so when we see him, we might just ask him if he went out by the back door that day and left it open, for which crime he is endlessly being held responsible.

## Zbigniew Rakowski's notebook

It was certainly not without a degree of trepidation that I made my way to Cranfield on Tuesday morning. It was indeed some time since I had had the undiluted pleasure of conversing (let alone lunching) with Priscilla. Thus, but for the unsettling events of my last visit, I should have been walking with a spring in my step, anticipating with excruciating delight her Ladyship's account of her visit to France. I had already, in the solitude of Robin Hood Way, envisaged her seated in the dining-room at the head of the handsome mahogany table, heedless of the vile Mason as he hovered around and bent to hand her the rabbit stew, her manner, as ever, vivacious, her fine eyes shining as with histrionic gesture, much wit and a vivid turn of phrase she described her experiences in the crumbling château in the *Allier*. But eagerly as I dwelt on the prospect of Priscilla's conversation, I could not rid myself of the dreadful, intrusive thought of the treacherous Mason, not simply waiting at table as is his business, but listening, watching, deceiving. It did at times, however, cross my mind to wonder whether I might not find on my return to Cranfield that the sinister creature had been dismissed. I was not entirely sure that this would be the most desirable outcome and somewhat doubted that I would in fact discover it to be the case, since I felt convinced that he must have denied any responsibility for having allowed Lady Lilian to enter the house. Lord Otterton has never made a secret of the fact that he has forbidden the servants to open the door to his mother. On my frail shoulders, then, lay the burden of knowledge, for I alone had witnessed the door being opened, I alone had heard the butler's sycophantic cry of recognition and I alone had observed the violet-clad dowager sweeping into the hall.

Not only was I uncertain as to whether I should find Mason still at Cranfield, but I was not sure either as to the wisdom of informing Lord and Lady Otterton of all that I had seen. I was and am of course aware that I have a duty towards the Ottertons, but it is difficult for me to be sure as to the way in which this duty might best be fulfilled. To have told what I knew would inevitably have brought about the butler's dismissal which would in turn prevent me from making any further discoveries concerning the mystery at the heart of the matter. As things stood, I was of the opinion that I alone was in a position to unveil something of the truth, having, as I would do, should I remain silent, a unique hold over the obnoxious servant. Yet, for all my deliberations over the past days, I was, as I walked up the drive, still undecided as to the path I would take.

I rang the bell, and even as I did so, standing beneath the hideous *porte cochère* built so vandalistically and yet so lovingly in 1876 by his Lordship's grandfather in order that his lady wife might not alight from her carriage in the rain, my mind was in a turmoil as to how I should proceed. I held my breath as I heard the door being unlocked from the inside for I did not know whether, as it opened, I would be confronted by the awful Mason himself, by Annie in his stead, or perhaps by some newly appointed butler. Strange to say, it was not in fact without some degree of relief that, as the great door swung open, I instantly discerned the familiar if repulsive features of the unspeakable Mason. He did not look in the least dismayed to see me, thus confirming me in my belief that he had been completely unaware of my presence at the back of the hall on that terrible afternoon. I said nothing beyond a polite good-morning, considering it only wise to bide my time before in any way confronting the brute or even allowing him to suspect that I might have something distasteful awaiting him up my sleeve.

So concerned was I with the drama in which I had unwittingly become involved that I was, on Tuesday morning, most unfortunately, quite unable to attend to the work which is my business and the sole reason for my continued presence at Cranfield. I decided that should Mason seek me out in the Red Drawing-Room before luncheon, I would, at that early stage, say nothing, for I wished there to be no unnecessary complications when I conversed later with Lady Otterton and indeed with Lord Otterton, should he be present. It occurred to me that it was not beyond the realms of possibility that either his Lordship or indeed her Ladyship might wish to enlighten me as to the events surrounding the dowager Lady Otterton's recent monstrous behaviour, and under the butler's vigilant eye, I not unnaturally hoped to assume an air of polite interest and mild amazement, for I knew that he would be watching carefully and listening closely to everything that might be said. It is always a matter of surprise to me that, unless they address their servants directly, expecting them then, as the saying goes, to 'jump to it', the upper classes presume those self-same servants to have no ears at all.

As we sat down to the luncheon table we spoke of France; indeed as I unfolded my linen napkin and placed it on my knees, I enquired of Lady Otterton as to how her French trip had been. Somewhat frivolously perhaps, I even took the mild liberty of suggesting to Priscilla that I had imagined her staying in an elegant, if conceivably somewhat dilapidated château. Laughing gaily at my presumption, she nevertheless assured me that I had not been wholly wrong in what I surmised. 'It wasn't quite as dilapidated as Cranfield,' she jested, 'but in some ways less comfortable. The French don't have sofas, you know.' She added that she never found it very easy sitting for long periods, making *petite conversation* on those upright Louis XV or Louis XVI chairs, thus confirming the image I had had of her perched on an elegant *fauteuil*. But, as I had anticipated, we were not long at table before Lord Otterton himself turned to the subject of his mother.

'Mr Rakowski!' he addressed me earnestly, fixing me with his big brown eyes as he did so. 'Have you heard what my poisonous mother did while Priscilla and I were both away?' I did my very best to appear quite natural whilst sensing the unnerving presence of the butler hovering behind my chair with a dish of new potatoes.

'Pray, what did she do?' I enquired, carefully thus avoiding giving a direct reply to his Lordship's question. I was then told in no uncertain terms of Lilian's unforgivably deranged behaviour as, according to her son, she forced her way into the house in order to help herself to whatever she chose and, in his words, 'drove off with a bloody great cartload of my possessions.'

Completely unperturbed, the butler, forever with his dish of potatoes, leant to wait upon his Lordship.

'No one knows how the hell she got in,' said Lord Otterton as, with a nodded acknowledgement to Mason, he helped himself to the potatoes. 'Mason here didn't know a thing about it until she was half-way down the drive with the booty. Did you?' His Lordship turned to address the butler.

'Not a thing, M'lord.' Mason, still holding the dish, straightened himself up and looked his employer right in the eye as he lied. May the devil take the wretched man's soul!

'I don't suppose you were aware of anything?' Lord Otterton turned to address me. 'I think you were here that day.'

Now indeed was my chance to wipe the odious complacency from the butler's face, but as I have implied, I considered that too sudden an onslaught might ultimately result in no more than a Pyrrhic victory. Nevertheless I was at pains not to tell an untruth and consequently was careful to remark that, as is my wont, I had been occupied for the greater part of the day in the Red Drawing-Room which I had not left even for luncheon since, with the weather being changeable, it had struck me as unwise to venture into the garden where both I and my sandwiches would have risked being rained upon. There is nothing I dislike more than a damp sandwich.

'You didn't hear or see anything on the way out?' Lord Otterton then asked, but fortunately continued without waiting for me to reply. 'There is some suggestion that she may have come in through the back door and the basement, but you usually leave by the front door, I imagine?'

'Ah,' I was eager to reply, 'on this occasion, Sir, I left through the basement, but I can assure you that I encountered not a soul.' I further denied any suggestion that I might have left the door open behind me. The basement door has a

Yale lock on it and I would, beyond any question of doubt, have seen to it that I closed the door properly behind me. However, as I explained myself thus, a flash of intuition informed me that the two-faced butler had unquestionably attempted to lay the blame for Lilian's intrusion at my feet. I wondered if he had left it at that, merely implying that I, a careless old man, had absent-mindedly omitted to shut the door, or had he additionally suggested that I, miserable ageing writer that I am, forever prying needlessly into the affairs of others, was in cahoots (as the Americans say) with the dowager Lady Otterton. Was I, appallingly, under suspicion of treachery? Am I to be Mason's scapegoat? We shall see about that. Caution, I inwardly told myself, should rule my every action.

It was not until quite late in the afternoon, indeed shortly before I was intending to collect my things and leave, that I heard the door of the Red Drawing-Room open quietly behind me. I had not seen the butler since luncheon and had been asking myself what his next move might be. Would he come to torment me, or did he prefer to leave me, as he no doubt hoped, in a state of nervous uncertainty, thus further to have me, as he supposed, in his power?

The door creaked cautiously open. I affected to ignore the intrusion, hoping, by my insouciant demeanour to put the butler just a little on his mettle. On hearing what resembled a faint whimper rather than a whisper, I turned my whole body slowly round in my chair, to be confronted amazingly, by none other than the child, Georgina. I gazed at her for a moment solemnly over my half-moon spectacles. 'Good afternoon, Ma'am,' I said as she hesitated in the doorway. Two untidy pigtails stuck out from under her navy-blue beret which she wore at what can be described only as a raffish angle with the badge over her right ear. She was dressed in a blue-striped summer frock, with her customary brown leather satchel hanging loosely from one shoulder. My stern gaze appeared to do little to set the poor creature at her ease.

'Pray close the door and tell me how I may help you,' I continued, for I discerned from the tentative look on her face that she was not surprised to find me at my work, but had in fact sought me out.

The child shut the door as I had bidden her and slowly, with an undisguised degree of embarrassment, came towards where I sat. 'Mr Rakowski,' she began, 'Mummy says we're not allowed in here when you are working . . . Actually, I don't think we're supposed to come in here at all . . .'

'Never mind,' I interrupted, for I was curious indeed to know what had brought her. I informed her that I had finished my labours for the day and assured her that, as far as I was concerned, she was invited in and that I was delighted, indeed flattered by her visit. She stood rather awkwardly beside the bureau on which my work was spread out in front of me, fiddling with one of her pigtails in a fashion that I surmise was quite simply due to nervousness. I looked at her. She did not, I thought, resemble her mother.

'How, Ma'am, may I be of assistance to you?' I then enquired.

Did I remember, she wanted to know, ages ago asking her to look for some old papers? I was careful to reply that although I was aware of the conversation to which she alluded, I had not precisely instructed her to search for papers, but had merely enjoined her, should she come across any diaries or bundles of letters in a drawer or cupboard, to be so good as to inform her parents of that discovery.

She appeared to pay little attention to what I said, but continued in her own vein. 'I think,' she said, 'that everyone in this house is looking for something.' Then, as if she had gained confidence with speaking, she turned to look me straight in the eye and asked not a little fiercely, 'Can you keep a secret?' I naturally assured her that it would indeed be a sorry story if I, at my stage of life, were not able to do such a thing. 'Ah, dear Ma'am,' I sighed, 'many is the secret that I shall take with me to my final resting place.'

'You see,' she continued, heedless of my deliberations, 'an awful thing happened not last week, but the week before and you must absolutely swear on your word of honour not to tell anyone . . .' I placed my right hand solemnly on my heart as she hastily proceeded with her tale. 'Mummy and Father would be livid if they knew because I was supposed to be doing my homework, but I was in the gallery above the hall and the bell rang and I saw horrible Mr Mason,' here she narrowed her eyes, 'go to the door and let in my grand-mother. And do you know,' at this point the young lady contrived to sound immensely grand, 'that my grandmother is not allowed here at all because she's been so beastly to Father?'

Imagine my confusion on suddenly being apprised of the fact that I had not been alone in witnessing Mason's treachery! I immediately understood that this unexpected information could not but add an altogether new dimension to my dilemma. But my first reaction was to be wary, for I wished to be quite certain as to whether or not, from her vantage point in the gallery, Georgina had been able to discern the smallish figure of an old man standing in the shadow of the doorway at the back of the hall. I considered it unlikely since, in order to see me, she would have been obliged to lean right out over the hall, thus revealing her presence to anyone below. After considerable, careful en-quiry, I was able to satisfy myself that she had indeed been unaware of my presence and that she, as I had until this moment, believed herself to have been the only person to witness her grandmother's arrival.

I thought to question the young lady as to why she had chosen to entrust a stuffy, elderly gentleman such as I with this important information, for it occurred to me that her parents would surely overlook her minor disobedience in their gratitude at discovering the truth about Mason; yet I was not entirely sure that it suited my own purposes to have the child intervene, and thus it behoved me to hesitate before encouraging her to approach Lord or Lady Otterton with her story, something which she herself was, in any case, loath to do. However, as she continued speaking, one aspect of the matter, an explanation for which had so far eluded me, was clarified. What, I had been wondering, was the connection in her child's mind between the arrival of her grandmother and the conversation she and I had formerly held concerning old, lost papers.

In singularly animated mode she described to me how she had come across the vile Mason rummaging, as she thought, guiltily, through drawers on the back stairs; this, in a far from unintelligent manner, she connected to the fact that he, now revealed to be her grandmother's accomplice, was searching for something on Lilian's behalf. Did I know, she asked me, that Lilian had gone through the house with what she referred to as a fine toothbrush, looking for something and no one, not even her father, could imagine what. She had overheard her father talking about it to Mr MacIntosh.

I have to confess that whilst the child spoke, I was growing a little nervous as to what part I was to be called upon to play in the whole proceedings. And to think that all the while I have here in the drawer of my bureau a little work of my own imagination, *Death in the Dining-Room* or whatever, which begins to appear more trivial every day when compared to the real intrigue at Cranfield!

Before the young lady eventually took her leave of me to return to the schoolroom and, no doubt tea and cucumber sandwiches under the watchful eye of the good Annie, we had agreed that I would reveal her secret to no one and that she would institute a search in every conceivable nook and cranny. Should she find anything that might be of interest, she insisted that she would bring it to me, despite my assurance that I would be under a moral obligation to inform her parents of any such discovery. In my heart I did not, and do not, for one moment imagine that anything will result from her childish search. I am, nevertheless, only strengthened in my desire to ascertain the nature of the truth concerning this most mysterious intrigue, thus perhaps to reveal myself to her Ladyship as a knight in shining armour galloping to her rescue from the least expected quarter.

## *Sydney Otterton's diary*

I haven't heard a damn thing from either my mother or her lawyers which I suppose is just as well. What with the foot and mouth which, by the grace of God, we seem to have avoided, I have managed to put her right out of my mind, although I don't suppose for a moment that she will allow it to stay that way for very long. Priscilla has come to the conclusion that my mother's only motive in coming here was to make a scene and cause us as much trouble as possible because, for one thing, she thinks that my mother is horribly jealous of her and bitterly resents her living at Cranfield. I suppose she may well be right up to a point but my mother's desire to make everybody else's life a misery goes back far longer than any resentment she may have of Priscilla. Of course there can be no doubt about it that Priscilla is yet another person whom she somehow sees as being in her way. But it's impossible to say what my mother's way is or where, if she were to be satisfied, it would lead. Her trouble is that she sees the entire world as being in some sort of conspiracy against her and so she is full of hatred, resentment and spite. I find it quite strange when someone (say a man of my age) talks about his mother with anything approaching affection. To have had a remotely reasonable or fond mother, even one that occasionally appeared genuinely to like one the least little bit, is completely outside my experience.

Priscilla now thinks that Rakowski must have left the back door open, despite what he says, and she has decided that my mother has no ulterior, hidden motive for her actions. She says she's just mad and bad and probably does whatever comes into her head for no good reason. Perhaps this line of thinking makes things easier for her. In any case, she says that my mother probably decided on a whim that she wanted various things from Cranfield so she just came and helped herself, and more than likely took a spiteful pleasure in throwing Priscilla's things about at the same time. Funnily enough, when I do think about it, and about the way she apparently went through a whole lot of cupboards which simply could not have contained anything of interest, I'm beginning to suspect that she may well be looking for something that she really doesn't want us to find first. It crossed my mind that she might even think that my father left a last will hidden away somewhere which might have benefited ourselves. Perhaps he did. God alone knows!

Anyway, what with the House of Lords and the T.A. and problems over the sheep and the British Legion jamboree and everyone on the committee squabbling about the best ways to raise money for the new cathedral, I've had enough to think about without bothering about my mad mother. And what with the dock strike looming, Nye Bevan and the new health service, the row about capital punishment and, on a more cheerful note, the Olympic Games, you'd have thought that even she could have found something else to think about, but then she's never ever been aware of anything or anyone outside herself so that all of those things will pass her by as if they never were. I sometimes wonder how it will all end up.

I saw Pammie on Thursday evening and consequently came home quite late. She made me laugh because she was in such a fury about the government having what she regarded as the impertinence to suggest that women should wear shorter skirts because the so-called New Look is unpatriotic in its extravagant use of material. Pammie drove ambulances in the war with, she says, doodlebugs dropping all around her and that, she says, ought to be proof enough of her patriotism. I thought both Tony and Priscilla would be amused by that, so when I got back and found the pair of them having a drink together in the Hunting Room, I just pretended that I'd seen Pammie in the street and she'd told me all this. Tony laughed but Priscilla gave me a long, hard look. She probably doesn't trust me and I can't say I blame her, but we were married very young, then came the war, then after the war came the house and everything that that entails. I don't really see that a fling on the side with Pammie is the end of the world, but I couldn't help feeling a bit of a rat all the same.

Then Priscilla started to go on about Mason again. In fact I thought she'd given up on that one. I can't keep sacking butlers, after all, she made me sack Cheadle which was probably quite right in the end, although, I must say the fellow was far more amusing than Mason. In fact I some-times wonder what's happened to the old scoundrel now. I suppose he's drinking his way through some other poor so-and-so's cellar. Anyway I keep telling Priscilla that I can hardly just ask Mason to leave for no other reason than that her Ladyship doesn't like the look of his face. Then Tony joined in, talking in a very reasonable voice and making me rather annoyed. What the hell's it got to do with him? They've both got some damn fool theory about the fellow being sinister. I always thought it was in the nature of butlers to be either drunk or sinister. The butler my parents had before the war was permanently plastered.

I don't know what Georgina's up to these days either. She's plotting some secret of her own but I suppose it's pretty harmless. She keeps coming and asking me if there are any locked rooms in the house, or any secret passages or whether there's any piece of furniture with a secret drawer in it and she wants to know where I would hide something if I really didn't want somebody to find it. At first I thought that she'd just been reading some children's adventure stories, but she's so insistent and looks so earnest that I'm beginning to wonder if there isn't more to it. She says she's got a list in some exercise book or other of all the best places in the house to hide things. I've asked her what on earth she wants to hide and all she says is, 'Aha, wouldn't you like to know!'

## Georgina's exercise book

I keep forgeting to look for the stuff for Mr Rakofsky. I've tride to ask Father were he thinks is a good hiding place but he wont tell me. Mr Rakofsky wont say what he thinks about Mr Mason but I'm just sure he's on our side. I wish Jamie and Thomas were here. I think Grandmama was proberbly looking for some hidden mony because Father hasn't got any mony and she doesn't want him to have any and she's rolling in it. Its very hard looking for things here because the house is so big. I haven't even found the secret room yet. Perhaps the mony is in there. I hope Grandmama didn't find it when she came here. Mr Rakofsky says things about letters but I'm sure its mony or treasure they're looking for. What would Mr Mason want some boring old letters for?

## Letter from Annie to Dolly

Cranfield Park
JULY 4TH, 1948

Dear Dolly,
It was nice seeing you and Fred and the children when you came over to visit Father last week. Little Fred is a good boy. He has grown so much since Christmas that he'll soon be as tall as his father. Of course Father was thrilled to have you all over for the day and I was glad that you were able to see

for yourself how much better he is. I am writing this in his kitchen on Sunday afternoon while he is in the garden tying up his dahlias. He has a beautiful show of them this year. I hope you made sure to admire them last week, although I'm not certain they were quite out yet.

I wonder how you will all manage what with the meat ration being cut back again. I do think of you. We are very lucky here with all the rabbits and the odd pigeon but I'm not sure about the pheasant her Ladyship gave to Lord and Lady Williton last week-end. When Ellen (that's the new cook I think I told you about) went to put it in the oven, she discovered that it was crawling with maggots. Her Ladyship just said that there was nothing else to give them and that it didn't matter because it was all meat anyway. Then she washed the bird out with vinegar and made poor Ellen cook it. Ellen said she was glad that no one expected her to eat it. It didn't make her half sick, she said, to dish the darned thing up. As far as I know Lord and Lady Williton are still alive!

Do write when you have a moment. Things go on here much as usual despite the hoo-ha about Lilian, Lady Otterton, and I'm sure we haven't heard the last of her. I can't think what she wanted, coming here like that. And between you and me and the gatepost, I wouldn't be at all surprised if it wasn't Mr Mason who let her in. The trouble is that no one knows.

Love from
Annie

*Annie's diary*

JULY 24TH

Georgina broke up on Wednesday and the boys came home at the end of last week for their eight-week summer holiday. My good Lord, I could do with an eight-week summer holiday myself what with all the goings on! Tiz has come back to see to the children. She is a very nice person and I think everyone was pleased to see her including Mr MacIntosh. He was smiling all over his face when she turned up! Mind you, she is very nice-looking. His Lordship has bought the children another pony, a black one called Billy which he bought off the gypsies. Her Ladyship thinks it's really foolish of him to have bought it from the gypsies because she says it's a bad-tempered animal and you can't tell where it's come from or how it has been treated. I hear it all from both sides but I don't pay any attention as it's nothing to do with me. His Lordship says the ponies will keep the children occupied during the summer, and off he sends them, down to the farm to clean the tack. But Bert saw them at the stables the other day and he said they certainly weren't cleaning any tack. He says they spent the whole afternoon swinging on the stable doors and clambering among the hay bales. I wouldn't doubt it. They aren't going to the seaside this year because her Ladyship says they can't afford it, so I hope the children don't go getting into too much trouble.

## Letter from William Johnson to Annie Jerrold

'Cranfield',
Coolgardie,
W. Australia
APRIL 2ND, 1948

Dear Annie,

I was going to write yesterday but then it was April 1st so I thought you might think it was a practical joke after all this time. Don't think that I don't miss you, Annie, and that I'm not still waiting, it's just that I didn't want to write until things were settled.

When I got here, they sent me up to this place 350 miles inland from Perth called Coolgardie. Years gone by it used to be a gold mining town, but now it's mostly pastureland round about. They gave me a good engineering job with the railways and put me up with several others in some sort of a Nissen hut. There are plenty of kangaroos which I'm sure you would like if you saw them, and acacia trees everywhere.

Now I don't live in the Nissen hut any more because, dearest Annie, I have built my own bungalow. It isn't very big but there's plenty of room for two. I couldn't think what to call it so I just called it 'Cranfield' after the old place back home. It's not quite as grand, but at least the rain doesn't come through the roof.

Give my regards to his Lordship and tell him that I often think of the good times we had together in the war.

I don't know how long this letter will take to reach you, but I will keep waiting.

Love from
Yr. Bill Johnson
P.S. I think about you every day.

## Annie's diary

AUGUST 9TH

Mr Johnson was the last person I was thinking about yesterday afternoon when the second post arrived. I'd been to see if Father was all right after the dreadful gale we've had. There were trees down everywhere in the park with one across the drive and Father had lost a tile or two off his roof. He said he could fix them himself, but I didn't want him getting up that ladder so I told him to wait for Bert. Bert will do the job in no time. It's no good waiting for Mr Kipling. You could wait a month of Sundays for him. So I'd just left

Father's to come on home when the postman turned in under the lodge. He wanted to know if the tree had been cleared from the drive which it had more or less, but I said I'd take the letters all the same to save him the trouble. There's not usually much that comes in the afternoon post, only his Lordship's *Hansard*, but there wouldn't be any *Hansard* at this time of year, so I was a bit surprised to see the postman at all, but not half so surprised as I was when he handed me this letter with the envelope covered in all these great big foreign stamps and addressed to me. At first I couldn't think what the devil it could be. Then I realised that the stamps were Australian. 'My good Lord!' I thought to myself. I wasn't going to open the letter there and then with that nosy postman sticking his head out of his van and grinning at me like nobody's business, so I just put it in my bag and took it on back up to the house with me. I thought I'd read it quietly when I had a bit of time to myself.

Well, well, well, so there's Mr Johnson still wanting me to go out there and join him in Australia. I could hardly believe my eyes when I read his letter, and me thinking all the time how hard-hearted he was just going off like that and never writing. My first thought was, well, I've got over you now, so it's no good cropping up again just because you feel like it and talking about bungalows and kangaroos. Then I couldn't help thinking that it was nice to be asked and nice to know that there was somewhere else I could go, if I felt like it. Never mind it's the other end of the world. I shall think about it for a while before I answer and the Lord knows how long it will take my answer to reach him because I couldn't help noticing that that letter of his had taken nearly four months to get here.

I haven't said anything to his Lordship or her Ladyship.

## Gerogina's exercise book

We got taken down to the gates to watch the Olympic runner running to London with a flaming torch which comes all the way from Greese. Everybody cheered.

Its always pelting. Father was going to take us out in the pony trap yesterday but it absolutely pelted all day so we couldn't go. We were all mucking around in the room with the state bed in it were we are not aloud and we herd someone coming. Thomas and I ran away in time but Jamie hid in the great big wardrobe in their. Thomas and I saw Mr Mason on the landing and he said he'd tell our parents on us. Luckily he didn't catch Jamie because when Jamie was in the wardrobe his foot went through into a sort of hiden draw underneath. It wasn't his forlt. Anyway what do you think he found? As they say in storys. He found this huge great bundle of letters. We were very excited but they looked very boring and were all adressed to someone called Doris. Worse luck there wasn't any money in them. I asked Mummy when Mr Rakofsky was coming and she just said why are you always asking about Mr Rakofsky? We've hiden the letters under a floorbord in Thomas's room.

## Sydney Otterton's diary

I sometimes feel that nothing around here ever improves. Whatever you do goes wrong. Sheep, cows, crops, there's always a problem and nothing makes any money. My bank is forever hounding me and if it weren't for Aunt Lettice's help,

I don't suppose we'd still be living at Cranfield. It's an unending struggle. Priscilla is brilliantly resourceful. I don't know how she manages. She gives me quite a lot of stick for not pulling my weight, but what can I do about the cottages for instance? We had managed to get some repairs done at last, then that gale in August blew half the roofs off again. One thing that did cheer me up was the King opening Parliament last week. It was the first State Opening since '38 and it certainly made some of us feel that things were beginning to return to normal. Afterwards Priscilla and I spent a jolly evening with the Willitons.

Funny how empty the house seems when the children are all at school, particularly at this time of year which is always pretty gloomy anyway. There's something the matter with Annie too. I can't make out what, but Priscilla too has noticed that she's not her usual self. Priscilla thinks it may have something to do with old Jerrold being ill again. He was so much better in the summer but apparently he's gone downhill lately and Annie must be pretty worried because she's always adored her father. After her mother died, everyone said she used to look after him like a wife and she took care of all those younger brothers and sisters too. It's a mystery why Annie has never married. After all, she's a good-looking woman. Priscilla says she thinks it's because Annie sees herself as being above the likes of Bert, but I used to think she was keen on Johnson before he went to Australia. I often wonder how he got on and I sometimes wish I could go and join him out there one day, throw this lot in and start a new life. I might leave my clothes on a beach somewhere and let people think that I'd swum out to sea and drowned. I wonder what Priscilla would do? I sometimes think she might go off with Tony. Perhaps she will anyway. She'd probably be a good deal better off with him than with me in the end.

# Annie's diary

Jam rationing has come to an end. Not that bought jam is anything like homemade and in any case the quality is nothing like it was before the war. Princess Elizabeth has had a son but they haven't announced his names yet. I expect they'll call him Albert or Bertie after the King, but then perhaps that's a bit too German for these days.

Poor Father is not at all well again. I'd like to know how I could possibly go off to Australia and leave him now, even if I wanted to. I wrote to Mr Johnson by Airmail so I hope he will have got the letter quite quickly. I said I was downright surprised to hear from him after so long and I told him about Father and that otherwise everything was much the same here as when he left. I couldn't help adding that we all miss him. I still haven't told his Lordship that I've heard from him. I must do soon. I sometimes think about that bungalow though. You can't help laughing at it being called Cranfield. I don't suppose it's much like this Cranfield.

Things are quite quiet here at the moment. Her Ladyship's been busy with one thing and another, like the Red Cross and St Dunstan's, but his Lordship has been spending so much time in London and the children are off at school. This year seems to have flown by though, and it won't be many weeks now before they're all home for the Christmas holidays. Then her Ladyship's bound to be all over the place what with the estate party and the puddings and the cake and the Christmas tree, not to mention the wrapping up and the rest of the whole darned caboodle to boot.

# 1949

# Zbigniew Rakowski's notebook

It has been some months since my last visit to Cranfield during which time I have indeed been quietly and most studiously sitting here at home in Robin Hood Way, concentrating on my history of the Otterton family. On the couple of occasions that I returned to the house during the summer and early autumn, I saw no one. That is to say that on both occasions the family was absent and on both occasions it was the good Annie who opened the door to me. Thus the drama of last spring with Lilian, Lady Otterton's arrival and all the monstrous Mason's devious dealings had perforce retreated into the background of my imagination.

I have to confess that I am not entirely displeased with the work on which I am at present engaged, for during the winter months I have made not inconsiderable progress, drawing together the threads of the disparate members of this family to reveal, as I trust, some kind of homogeneity. I have become quite engrossed in the earlier Ottertons and of some of them, trimmers and rapscallions though they may be, I have even grown inordinately fond. There was one Lord Otterton who so disliked the sight of his plain spouse's face that he caused a screen to be placed on the dining-room table, that he might not be obliged to look upon his wife as he dined. The screen was of a variety that could be raised or lowered at wish and he was frequently heard to shout at the footman, 'Higher, you damn fool, higher, I can still see her Ladyship's face.' Such a character as he, uncouth and ribald, living as he did, surrounded by great architectural magnificence, cannot but attract my attention and fascinate me. Did the beauty of his surroundings in no way gentle his condition? Did he not wish to stroke those silken mahogany doors or gaze in wonder at Rysbrack's masterpieces? Did he not look in awe at his surroundings? Sometimes I marvel that such a house as Cranfield can have been built by a family who produced so many Philistines. Or, am I perchance a little unjust? Perhaps the exquisite nature of her surroundings so highlighted the said Lady Otterton's ill-favoured countenance, that the contrast between their beauty and her ugliness made it unbearable for his Lordship to dwell upon her features. Who is to know? What is sadly not in doubt, is that she was an heiress whose fortune must, at least momentarily, have caused his Lordship to disregard whatever aesthetic sensibilities he may have had. But where, the present Lord Otterton may sigh, is that fortune now?

As for my little work of fiction, that too, has been relegated to almost forgotten territory, although I am in no doubt that as soon as the family history is completed, I will feel the urge to return to it, for with what reluctance will I eventually be obliged to turn my back on Cranfield and its inhabitants, both of which have done so much to thaw an old man's chilly heart, to lighten for him the burden of age and to restore in him a zest for life? For so long now have I been engrossed in Cranfield that its absence will surely create a void.

Crowned as it is by a forlornly crumbling balustrade, the house, when I returned to it yesterday, struck me as melancholy indeed, almost forbidding beneath the louring grey clouds. The winter hedgerows, appearing to have taken their cue from the skies above, seemed themselves to be devoid of colour. Beyond them, a solitary, leafless oak, under which I had picnicked one summer, its bleak black branches reaching to the unyielding heavens, stood desolate and abandoned amongst the brambles of an unkempt field. It seemed to me, as I walked up the drive, that for this particular family of aristocrats, even without the intervention of their treacherous butler, Nemesis was at hand.

I need hardly say that, despite the door being opened to me by the odiously servile Mason, I had no sooner entered the hall and gazed aloft once more at the incomparable plasterwork of the ceiling, than my spirits soared again. Referring as I do (and rightly so) to Mr Mason's odious servility, I am nevertheless obliged to confess that, at the sight of the man, although my hackles, so to speak, rose, I felt a not unwelcome surge of blood in my veins, a tremor of almost youthful excitement provoked, no doubt, by my coming face to face once more, and after so many months, with my enemy – nay my quarry. The hideous man was still employed at Cranfield then!

What work I had in mind to do I was able to accomplish quite speedily and was therefore more than ready to be invited to the dining-room for luncheon when I eventually heard the summons from the gong at the foot of the oak staircase. After the usual quiet Christmas spent at home, interrupted only by the customary brief visit from my daughter, her husband who remains as tedious as ever and their pale child, I was delighted by the prospect of a little company, particularly of course, company that included the lovely Lady Otterton. There was, as it so happened, a not inconsiderable gathering already assembled in the dining-room when I arrived there. Lord and Lady Otterton were both present with their three children and a young governess; Lady Isley and Mr MacIntosh were also present. Lady Otterton welcomed me most cordially, saying what a long time it had been since I last lunched at Cranfield. I was indeed honoured to be placed beside Lady Isley who showed ample interest in my work and was kind enough to say that she could barely wait for me to complete it. Lord Otterton was his usual jovial self, iconoclastic and bawdy of humour, thus in his buffoonery reminding me once more and not a little of one or two of his ancestors with whom I have lately grown so familiar.

So concentrated was I on my conversation with Lady Isley

and so eager to hear what she had to say to me, that I scarcely paid any attention to the butler as he handed around the food. I did however notice that the young Georgina appeared at times to be looking at me across the table in a somewhat concentrated fashion, gazing at me earnestly as though wishing to attract my attention. I was just a little disconcerted at the thought of what she might wish to confide in me. She might conceivably, as I very well knew, have something of value to say, but she might equally have only childish prattle to convey. I had intended to collect up my papers and leave as soon as luncheon was over, but decided instead to idle away half an hour or so in the Red Drawing-Room just in case the child saw fit to seek me out for, all of a sudden, I felt myself once more immersed in the excitement of what I had begun to think of as last year's drama.

Despite all that has gone before and despite my renascent interest in the peculiar goings-on at Cranfield, I could not have been more surprised, *bouleversé* indeed is the word that springs to mind, than I was by the information brought to me by the two children that afternoon. Shortly after luncheon I was quietly reading a book at the table I am accustomed to use for a desk in the Red Drawing-Room when there was a hesitant knock on the door accompanied by some kind of unintelligible murmurings and a stifled giggle. There were further giggles in response to my invitation, 'Pray enter!' On this occasion the child, Georgina, was escorted by the younger of her two brothers, James, a humorous-looking boy who, if my ears do not deceive me, is commonly referred to by the sobriquet 'Jamie'. I rose to my feet to greet the young people as they advanced gauchely, nudging each other with their elbows and still, or so it seemed to me, nervously verging on the edge of laughter. It was not for me to enquire as to the object of their mirth. 'Ma'am. Sir,' I merely said, addressing them with a little bow in my customary manner, for who should say that *politesse* be reserved for adults alone? 'How can I be of assistance to you?'

At my few short words, the pair of them, incapable of composing themselves any longer, burst into a crescendo of futile, childish laughter. When this at last subsided, I was not displeased to hear them both apologise, which apology all but set them off again on a further wave of hilarity, but Georgina, managing to pull herself together, so to speak, began to explain the reasons for their having sought me out. Thomas, she opined, should have come with them too but he had gone out shooting with their father. 'Thomas was with us when it happened,' she explained mysteriously, 'and anyway, it wasn't Jamie's fault but we daren't tell because Mummy and Father would be livid.' The children had gone, or so it transpired from the girl's somewhat incoherent and, to say the least, unchronological account of the events which had occurred during the summer holidays, to the state bedroom in order that Thomas who had acquired an early fascination with history, might enact the part of Henry VIII at the Field of the Cloth of God, with the four-poster bed necessarily serving as the King's tent. Thomas was perforce to portray Henry VIII in their game. 'I always have to be the enemy,' Georgina explained crossly. 'Indeed, Ma'am,' I spoke, as I hope, in tones expressive of my understanding of her plight, thus to encourage her to continue with her tale. At her side James, having quite regained his self-control, occasionally interrupted to agree with her or to urge her to further disclosures, remembering nevertheless to reiterate that what-ever had happened was not his fault and that I must promise not to tell their parents of the occurrence.

Naturally I was and am in no position to connive with the children against their parents, nor would I conceive of doing so, but by the time it was eventually revealed to me that, as a result of the children's disobedience, a pile of hidden letters had come to light which since last August has been residing under the floorboards of Thomas's bedroom, I was of a mind to suggest that should the letters which the children sought to hand over to me, then be passed to their parents which, I hastened to explain, was inevitable, it would be politic to suggest, without resorting to a falsehood, that they came from under Thomas's floorboards. In truth, I was surprised that neither Georgina nor James had fallen upon this way out of their difficulties, the art of deceit being in no manner alien to the childish mind.

'We don't think the letters look very interesting,' James advised me with a touch of bathos in his tone. 'They're all to someone called Miss Batty.' The pronouncement of which name reduced the boy once more to a state of helpless mirth.

'Actually,' young Georgina interjected in the blithest of tones, 'we haven't really read them.' It was not her wish, or so I surmised, to allow her brother to cast an air of despondency upon the proceedings; rather, she wished to keep me on my proverbial toes, eager for delivery of the secret bundle which she hoped would reveal a thrilling tale of intrigue, and death no doubt. She meanwhile would be cast as some precocious latter-day Sherlock Holmes of Cranfield Park.

Most unfortunately, considering the time that has already elapsed since the discovery of these letters which may indeed prove to be of as little consequence as Master James suggests, neither of the children thought that they would be able to retrieve the bundle without the help of Thomas and it was therefore not possible for them to hand them to me yesterday afternoon. Conscious of the fact that my behaviour might be regarded in certain quarters as somewhat dubious, I hastened to tell Georgina that I would be returning to Cranfield two weeks hence. This, I am forced to confess, would not be strictly necessary for the purposes of my work, but curiosity as to the contents of the *letters to Miss Batty* tempted me to behave in a way that is totally out of character. For what indeed am I, a humble scribbler, friend of the family, entrusted with the family papers and given the *entrée* to Cranfield Park, doing, making secret pacts, and entering into puerile alliances with the children of the house? Is it not my duty to refer them at once to their parents, or indeed to inform their parents of their discovery if they persist in refusing so to do?

My mind goes back not only to the unpleasant incident when the wretched Mason sat with me on the lawn, spouting his unequivocal revolutionary views and sneering at his employers, but also to the remarkably unpleasing sight of the man rubbing his hands unctuously together before opening the front door to the mauve dowager. I truly feel that, because of my hold over Mason, of which he is as yet unaware, I am in the singular position of being able to discover something which may well be of considerable assistance to the Ottertons, and it is with this in mind that I allow myself to fall in with the peculiar commerce of these two young scallywags at the risk of being thought to deceive those I seek to serve.

## *Georgina's exercise book*

Thomas and Jamie have gone back to school but I've got the letters under my bed and Im going to give them to Mr Rakofsky tomorrow. They were in my jersey draw but Annie saw them when she was getting my school uniform reddy and said Whats all this rubbish then? She had them in her hand and I just grabbed them and she said not to be rude. I told her they were something I had to do for school but I don't think she even looked at them but just said 'Well don't keep dirty bits of paper in your clothes draw.' Phew!!!

I took the letters to school in my satchel for fear that Annie would find them and gave them to Mr Rakofsky when I got back. He said 'thank you mam' very grandly and put them in his basket. I think he is a bit exited but all he said was 'I shall peroose them at my liesure.' I'm dying to know if there really good. Jamie thinks there boring.

# Sydney Otterton's diary

In spite of the filthy weather, the eternally leaking roof and all the other problems, none of which seems to have been satisfactorily resolved (nor, for that matter is likely to be), I have been feeling in pretty good form lately. Priscilla and I are going to Copenhagen next week-end. When the Jørgensens invited us, I didn't think Priscilla would want to go. She hasn't been very pleased with me lately and who can really blame her? Perhaps I was beginning to think that she wasn't even prepared to put up with me for much longer and, all I can say about that is that I couldn't survive here (or anywhere else for that matter) without her. She makes this whole place work, in so far as it works at all. Aunt Lettice thinks she's marvellous, and I'm sure that everybody on the farm and in the house likes and respects her, although I expect they're quite frightened of her, but then so am I when it comes to the point. I often wonder if she really will run off with Tony, but then that would probably only create more problems than it would solve. Tony hasn't got any money and she could hardly run to his flat on the top floor. Perhaps in the difficult circumstances of our marriage, we are doing as well as can be expected. In any case I'm really pleased about Copenhagen. We haven't seen the yolly Yørgensens since before the war and neither of us has ever been to Denmark. Priscilla keeps talking in a sing-song voice about something she says is called *smørrebrød* and which she claims is all they ever eat in Denmark. She's already started telling me to go steady on the schnapps.

I haven't seen Pammie for a while which may be just as well. In fact, I think she's got another feller. The thing about Pammie is that, being what you might call a good-time girl, she's quite keen on sheckles, in which commodity I am remarkably deficient. Anyway I've been in the Lords most of the time, keeping myself out of trouble, and I've managed to prevent myself from getting too gloomy as well. One thing that's probably helped to keep me cheerful is that I haven't seen the bloody bank manager for a while, but I can't imagine that happy state of affairs lasting very long.

A world without a bank manager or my mother would be a truly wonderful place. I could even bear all the recurring nightmares if those two weren't lurking in the background. Although when the nightmares come, I wake up sweating like a pig and with my heart pounding, I have in some peculiar way grown almost attached to them. It is as if I feel them to be necessary, not so much because I don't want to forget the war, but because they remind me that the war was real. People sometimes talk about the war now as if it never really happened, or at least as if it were somehow all over, ready to be forgotten, and yet if you walk about London you can't fail to be devastated by the bomb sites which are a permanent reminder of the Blitz and all the lives lost. I don't know why we weren't more frightened than we were at the time. It's all the belated fear that visits me now at night I suppose. Then I think of some of my friends, the poor sods who died and who aren't even here to feel afraid.

I often suspect that the Regiment is the one thing that keeps me sane at all. I always look forward to my one night a week with it. In a way those evenings are a kind of escape but at the same time they provide some sort of balance to life and, if they have served no other purpose, they have certainly made the transition from war to peace at least more comprehensible. For six years the war seemed to be everything; it was our entire existence and sometimes it still feels that way even though it's been over for nearly four years now. You can't just put it behind you, and neither in a way does one really want to. Most of the others feel the same and several of them have told me that they too suffer from nightmares, which they generally treat as a laughing matter.

As for my mother, there's absolutely no knowing when she will suddenly make herself felt again. I've never been able to work out what in God's name she could have been looking for last year when she marched in and turned everything upside down. Perhaps she found whatever it was. In any case, she's gone remarkably quiet since then. The extraordinary thing about her was that she ran this place as a hospital during the First World War. I was too young to know much about it then, but, on looking back, it's quite impossible to imagine her doing anything of the kind. As I grew up, I can remember her either lying in bed, doping herself to the eyeballs, or mysteriously appearing at meals, only to cause a tremendous scene. She must have made a terrifying matron. There's no member of the family I have ever spoken to who has a good word to say for her. Aunt Lettice maintains that when she married my father she was thoroughly spoilt, very selfish and already half mad, but that she really began to go right off her rocker after her first child died. She always told me that if that child had been a son and had survived, she would never have had another one. That would have saved me a lot of trouble!

Sometimes when I think back on what the house was like before the war, I am amazed at what Priscilla has achieved. Then, for all the lavish way of life and for all the servants, the atmosphere was one of holy dread brought about by the brooding presence of my mother and the perpetual fear of her rages and her irrational orders. My poor old father who, at the best of times could be incredibly funny and very good company, was generally reduced to a gibbering wreck by her and consequently fewer and fewer people came to the house. Now, with Priscilla and Annie and the children and the great fires in the hall and friends to stay and my parrots and Peggy, it's turned into the real home it ought to be, despite rationing, the leaking roof and the mice keeping you awake at night. Priscilla blames me for the mice which she claims wouldn't rampage nearly so freely if it weren't for my birds. I suppose she could be right. Annie certainly sides with her on that one.

Tony and I have been doing a bit of rough shooting at week-ends and we even took the boys out once or twice over Christmas. There are plenty of rabbits and the occasional pigeon but I'm afraid that pheasants are few and far between. I certainly can't afford to start putting any down, but neither, come to that, can I afford to go on paying a keeper so I'm coming round to the idea of forming a syndicate which would be the only possible way of getting the shoot off the ground again properly. Perhaps I'll look into that after we come back from Denmark. One thing at a time is what I say although Priscilla complains that I never stick to any of them.

## Letter from Horace Pink to Doris Batty

7 Back Alley Lane.
JUNE 25TH, 1910

Dear Miss Batty,

Please excuse the liberty I take of approaching you and allow me to humbly thank you in advance for being so kind as to read this letter. I am sure that a fine woman such as yourself must realise that the unfortunate recent events at Cranfield Park have given rise to what you might call a lot of talk. Being as you're the one what's so close to her Ladyship you must know what really went on. I myself have some information her Ladyship would give a king's ransom to know and I am of a mind to advise you of the said information for a consideration. Since I lost my position I am not exactly flush and a small consideration would come in handy.

You will find me residing in lodgings at the above address where I could meet you at your convenience on any day that you could arrange a ride into town.

I remain her Ladyship's trusty and obedient servant,

Yrs. Very Sincerely
Horace G. Pink

## *Zbigniew Rakowski's notebook*

Considering the baffling circumstances which have constantly attracted my attention at Cranfield, not to say
distracted me from my work, nothing could have been more
instantly intriguing than the remarkable parcel of letters
handed to me by Georgina Otterton on a colourless January
afternoon in the Red Drawing-Room. I had not arrived at the
house that day until after luncheon, hardly wishing to impose
myself upon the Ottertons under anything resembling a false
pretext and had indeed been feeling uncomfortable throughout the afternoon, even somewhat fraudulent, having no
great business to attend to among the archives that day. I
found myself impatiently and not infrequently glancing at my
watch, anxious for the hour at which the child might return
from school and not a little apprehensive lest she forget the
arrangement by which we had agreed to the handing over of
the *letters to Miss Batty*. However, I need have had no fear, for
young Georgina appeared most promptly in the half dusk at
four o'clock and, without more ado, she extracted from her
somewhat tattered school bag (for I have noticed that
children these days have a tendency to drag their bags along
the ground behind them in a most unmannerly and, one
would have thought, uncomfortable fashion) an even more
tattered bundle of brownish envelopes. I carefully wrapped
them in a sheet of newspaper which I had had the foresight
to bring with me, placed them in my basket and assured the
young lady that I would take the greatest care of them and

that I would peruse them at my leisure. I further felt the obligation to add that there would inevitably come a moment when I would be compelled to inform her parents of her discovery. This information she accepted with good grace. I fear, however, that as I packed away those letters, the shaking of my infirm old hand could not but have made manifest even to the most obtuse observer, the emotion the occasion had aroused in me. For at last I had my hands on what I presumed to be unread letters concerning the Otterton family. It was not until I reached home that I discovered the date of those letters, but whatever the date, here was a biographer's dream come true. A secret cache of letters had come to light and fallen miraculously into this old scribbler's hands!

Need I say that during the days that have since elapsed, I have to the most irresponsible degree neglected the work on which I am supposed to be engaged in order to concentrate on the amazing evidence that has so inadvertently landed in my undeserving lap? The letters, not unnaturally, raise a few questions which I am not immediately able to answer. Who for instance is, or was, the nefarious Mr Horace Pink? Miss Batty, I can only surmise, must have been Lilian, Lady Otterton's personal maid.

At a glance, from the moment I cast my eyes on the very first of Master Pink's odious missives, I was instantly aware that what I had unwittingly unearthed was a case of the basest and most vile blackmail.

I have now perused the letters with the greatest care and with my accustomed attention to detail, and have furthermore transcribed them into a notebook for my own keeping. Now it is, alas, my unquestionable duty to hand the offending documents over to Lord Otterton. I shoulder this responsibility, not with any pleasure, but rather with a deep sense of foreboding, for the contents of the letters, the discovery of which so excited me, are of such an unpleasing nature that the reading of them will but cause the greatest distress to

Lord Otterton. So unpalatable indeed are the contents, that it has even crossed my vacillating old mind to place the lot of them on a bonfire. But my training is that of a historian whose whole being recoils at the suggestion of suppressing evidence, burning papers, hiding the truth. Besides, there is the not inconsiderable element of the children's awareness of the existence of these papers. It is not inconceivable that one of them will one day enquire as to the contents of the bundle they so fortuitously (or not so fortuitously) discovered or may even wish to know of its whereabouts. These papers, I have constantly to remind myself, do not belong to me and it is as much as my honour is worth not to hand them over to their rightful owner, whatever the outcome may be. In my greedy desire to be the first to cast an eye over newly unearthed documents, I have perhaps already overstepped the mark, even betrayed the trust of my benefactors whilst inadvertently putting one foot in a quagmire.

*Sydney Otterton's diary*

FEBRUARY 18TH

There was the usual pile of rubbish waiting for me when we got back from Denmark. Bills, a bloody awful letter from the bank manager, complaints from the tenants about the condition of their houses, a letter from Mrs Arbuthnot saying she was leaving because she finds the flat too draughty in winter. She says she's been very happy here and that she loves it in summer because of the view. Cold comfort to me! Then there was this barmy communication from old Rakowski. I was rather surprised by that because he usually conducts all his affairs to do with Cranfield through Priscilla with whom he has been conducting a lengthy (and no doubt on his part verbose) correspondence for years. He wants to see me on my own as he says he has something of 'the gravest importance to communicate', which he wishes to do in the strictest of confidence. He accompanies this, as is his wont, with a good deal of metaphorical bowing and scraping. I can't imagine for the life of me what the fellow has to say; after all he's been coming here for so long now that he can hardly suddenly have turned up some new piece of shady family history with which to scandalise us. Perhaps the great Speaker of whom we are all so proud will turn out to have been a bugger. But who cares? In fact, I've often wondered how Rakowski's managed to spend quite so much time as he has among those archives. I should think he must know them all back to front by now. Perhaps he just uses them as an excuse to come and fawn at Priscilla's feet, but it annoys her when I say so. In any case, he's quite an entertaining old boy and if he wants to come and see me he can, but I can't believe there's any urgency, so I've dropped him a line suggesting a day next month. As a matter of fact I couldn't help laughing at Priscilla because, for all her indignation when I tease her about Rakowski, when I showed her his letter she was quite incensed that he had written to me instead of to her.

The trouble with going away is that you forget all your troubles and then when you get back, they always seem to have multiplied a thousandfold. It seems unfortunately to be a fact of human nature that people love to greet you with the news that there's a tree down in Beggar's Bottom, the tiles are off the gardener's cottage, the cows aren't giving enough milk and that a mouse has given birth to four babies in the bread bin, which babies it has subsequently eaten. That last piece of information sent Priscilla wild. I wouldn't have liked to be in Ellen's shoes, whose lame excuse was that it must have been a very strong mouse to lift the lid off the bread bin. Annie thought it all very funny and was, I suspect, quite pleased to see Ellen put on the mat.

Poor old Annie's been a bit down in the dumps again because of Jerrold's health. He seemed so much better in the summer but, according to her, he's had some sort of lapse while we've been away. So I expect the mouse in the bread bin provided a bit of a distraction.

A yolly good time was had by all with the yolly Jørgensens who were extremely lavish with their schnapps. An enormous amount of it was drunk which no doubt added to the yeneral yollity. Anyway I certainly wouldn't mind going back there one of these days yust to get away from this lot for a while.

One thing that does cheer me up is the arrival of Otto. I simply couldn't resist him when I found him in the local pet shop yesterday afternoon. I don't know how old he is but they told me he was about three months. Surprisingly enough, young otters are quite easy to train and there's no doubt about it, but this one is an amazingly friendly little chap, so that even Priscilla who usually complains about my animals, has been won round to him. I took him out for a walk in the garden this morning and he was already following me like a lamb.

## Annie's diary

MARCH 6TH

I sometimes think you might as well live in Whipsnade Zoo as at Cranfield Park. But you can't help quite liking his Lordship's otter. Even her Ladyship walked down to the farm with the pair of them the other day. But then her Ladyship doesn't have to clear up the mess it makes in the house. His Lordship just laughs as usual.

There's no two ways about it, but poor Father has taken a turn for the worse since Christmas. I always say that it's the winter that does him in. It brings back the bronchitis every time. Perhaps if we get some warmer weather when the spring eventually comes, then he'll look up a bit. It's funny how often all through the winter I've been thinking about Mr

Johnson's letter and how, if I had wanted, I could be in Coolgardie with the kangaroos now. Well I didn't want. No fear. There are enough animals here in what her Ladyship calls his Lordship's *menagerie* without anyone needing to go all the way to Australia to look at kangaroos. I wouldn't be surprised if we didn't have kangaroos here in the garden before long, to judge by the way things are going.

I wouldn't say a word to anyone mind, but when the weather's bad I can't help sometimes wondering what it would be like in Australia, and when Bert gets on my nerves, I tell him that for two pins I'd be off. But I've always said I couldn't leave Father and I certainly wrote and told Mr Johnson as much. In fact I told him he was plain daft to go on thinking that I would or ever could come and join him. Even if he has called his house 'Cranfield', I doubt it would be very much like home.

Mind you, it was pretty quiet around here with his Lordship and her Ladyship away, which was just as well as it gave me a chance to go down and spend more time with Father. But it's all go again now they're back, what with Otto, and guests to stay every other week-end and his Lordship going on talking all the time in what he says is a Danish accent. It sounds plain silly to me but it makes him laugh and even though it annoys her, I've noticed it sometimes makes her Ladyship laugh too. To tell the truth I was really glad to see them back because what with them both out of the way, I was a bit worried that Lilian, Lady Otterton might put in an appearance since she seems to have some downright peculiar way of knowing what's going on here most of the time. I was particularly anxious because no one has yet explained satisfactorily how she got in last time. Not to my satisfaction at any rate. But I have my suspicions. And I don't think Mr Rakowski is to blame either. Mr Rakowski is a gentleman. I am quite sure he would never dream of leaving anyone's back door open.

I haven't liked what I've seen of Mr Mason at all while his

Lordship and her Ladyship have been away. Not that I was ever very fond of him, come to that, and I know the children don't like him in the least little bit. I have a suspicion that Mr MacIntosh isn't all that keen on him either. Mr MacIntosh is always very kind to me when Lord and Lady Otterton are both away, coming and finding me every day to ask if everything is all right. He was ever so considerate that afternoon when Lilian did come and you can't help feeling that he's someone who will always back you up. I shall be really sad to see him go if he ever leaves Cranfield, not that he looks like wanting to leave at the moment, as far as I can see.

Mr MacIntosh said to me only the other day, 'Now, Annie, you don't want to bother yourself about Mason.' Then he gave me a rather old-fashioned look and said, 'If you ask me, his days here are numbered.' I think that must be because of her Ladyship. She hasn't said much lately but I know that she used to go on to his Lordship about Mr Mason and about how she never trusted him. I can't stand the way the man's for ever snooping. Wherever you come across him, he's always opening a drawer or looking in a cupboard. The Lord knows what he's after. Apart from that, he's quite unfriendly and never has been one to pass the time of day with you.

MARCH 12TH

Goodness gracious me, what a hoo-ha there was this morning! There was her Ladyship all dressed up, as smart as anything in her Red Cross uniform, ready to go off to her meeting while his Lordship was putting that darned otter on a lead and planning to take it God knows where. And what was Annie Jerrold doing? Picking up the birdseed the wretched parrots had thrown out of their cages all over the dressing-room floor, while one of the cockatoos was sitting on a picture frame, only making matters worse by screaming its head off. Her Ladyship was in a very brisk mood, telling his Lordship about this, that and the other that needed doing and wasn't he worried about that bird which was going to ruin the picture frame and please would he not waste Annie's time by asking her to clear up after his wretched animals. And his Lordship was messing around all the while with the otter which isn't supposed to be in the house anyway, and saying Annie didn't mind. And Annie said nothing.

Anyway all at once, there was this terrific din of pounding feet and a banging on the door and in burst Mr Mason. I couldn't think what had come over the man, barging in like that and it took me a moment to take in what he was saying. Then I realised he was talking about a burglary. At that point even his Lordship had to stop fooling around with that otter. Well his Lordship went to ring the police and her Ladyship had to go off to her meeting. When the police came, there were two of them and they spent the whole morning interviewing everyone in the house and asking if we'd seen or heard anything, which of course no one had, so they decided the burglar must have come at night. The funny thing was, he didn't take anything, only the coronets which were kept in glass cases in the Red Drawing-Room. Whoever it was had thrown something through the Red Drawing-Room window and then must have put a ladder up to it to get in.

His Lordship was swearing and blinding about it like nobody's business although in the end he decided it was quite funny because according to him the coronets weren't worth a tinker's cuss because were only made of base metal and a bit of old velvet. The burglar probably thought they were made of gold so he must have been downright disappointed. I just hope he doesn't come back and take something that is valuable. Anyway, what with the otter and the burglary and the police, today was quite a day. And I don't know what we're going to do about Ellen, she's been quaking in her shoes at the thought of burglars ever since the police came, and seems quite sure that next time they'll be wanting to murder her. Why her? I really don't know. She already thought the house was haunted, so perhaps she won't be with us much longer and then we'll have to be looking for another cook.

## Sydney Otterton's diary

Clothes rationing ended yesterday which seems to have resulted in a great deal of rejoicing in certain quarters. Georgina, much to Priscilla's annoyance, is demanding a velvet dress like one some other child has, but I'm not sure she's going to get it, rationing or no rationing. Meanwhile my coronets are probably sitting at the bottom of the lake since the police regard the whole burglary as remarkably suspicious. For one thing they think it was an inside job with the window having been broken from indoors, and for another, they can't understand why the burglar took nothing except the coronets, although, of course he may have been interrupted by someone or by something even if no one seems to know anything about it, or to have been around to interrupt him. As a result the police have pretty well lost interest, but as far as we're concerned, suspicion inevitably falls on Mason, but there is absolutely no hard evidence to point to him. Tony has a theory that Mason has always been very resentful of us and that he might have taken the coronets to cock a snook at us. The only thing for him to have done with them then would have been to dispose of them as quickly as possible, and the nearest and best place in which to dispose of them was the lake. It would be one thing, if we were looking for a dead body, but I'm damned if the lake needs dragging for the sake of two tin coronets. In any case it all seems pretty odd to me because I can't really see what Mason, or anyone else for that matter, could hope to gain by such tomfoolery. However, I've told Mason to make sure that the shutters are closed on all the downstairs windows every night in future. He looked at me with his dead eyes and said, 'Yes, M'lord,' as cold as ice.

Annie's looking pretty gloomy about her father who seems to be going downhill, poor devil. Those were the days, when he was cowman. Nothing has been quite the same since he retired; in fact it's a pity he's not feeling a bit better at the moment or he might have been able to help out in the present crisis. Apparently a lot of funny things were going on while we were in Denmark, but no one said anything till a couple of days ago when all the men on the farm began to complain about some sort of dreadful wailing that they claimed was coming out of Wilkins's house all day long. Apparently Bert, who lives in the next-door cottage, said it went on all night as well, and Annie who's been down to see Bert, was full of it. She says it was like some kind of terrible howling and everyone thought Wilkins must have been beating up his wife. Anyway, yesterday Priscilla decided to find out what the hell was going on, only to discover that the noise made by the pair of them was quite horrific. So the upshot of it is that both Wilkinses have been carted away to the local looney bin by men in white coats and I haven't got a cowman. Or a coronet, come to that! According to the quack, they're suffering from some weird kind of lunacy known as *folie à deux* which seems to have manifested itself on this occasion in a bloody awful din. Anyway Bert's taken over the milking for the moment until I can find someone else. I'm frankly amazed by the unexpected things that manage to crop up one after another to put a spanner in the works; so much so that I'm more than ever convinced that it's a great deal easier to lead a column of tanks across the desert than it ever can be to run a country estate. I somehow thought that when we got rid of the sheep which were a short-lived and totally uncommercial experiment, things would miraculously begin to get better, but that hardly seems to have turned out to be the case, although I can't deny that whatever else may happen, I'm damned glad to have seen the back of those moth-eaten creatures. At least I don't have to worry about them any longer.

I must admit that what with the wailing Wilkinses and the stolen coronets probably having been thrown in the lake, I thought I'd heard it all. Then along comes Rakowski with his piece of newly discovered family history. To tell the truth, I hadn't really given him a thought since I got his letter saying he wanted to see me. I'd imagined that all he wanted was to discuss some nit-picking detail about the house or my great-grandfather which would be unlikely to make what Annie would call a ha'p'orth of difference to any of us. He's a tidy, meticulous little fellow, Rakowski, and fastidious to a fault where detail is concerned, which is why it vaguely occurred to me that he might want me to put him right over some minor incident about which I would, in fact, most probably know considerably less than he. Anyway, having refused to come to lunch, he turned up here yesterday morning with a bundle of letters. Priscilla had gone off shopping in a bit of a huff because I think she was annoyed at the old boy wanting to see me on my own, and by the time she got home, I'd left for London.

Rakowski started telling me some long rigmarole about how the children had found the letters and handed them to him which struck me as pretty odd. I can't think why they didn't give them straight to me or Priscilla. As it turns out, it would have been better for them not to fall into the hands of an outsider, although, I have to say, I'm quite sure Rakowski is an honourable fellow. I am convinced that he is most unlikely to mention the contents to anyone other than myself. He maintains that the children, having found them, never bothered to read them, assuming them to be of little interest and that they only handed them over to him as part of some sort of game. As a matter of fact, I'm quite surprised that they'd ever spoken to him other than to say good-morning or good-afternoon.

Then of course Rakowski wanted to know if I knew who Horace G. Pink and Miss Doris Batty were. He may be the soul of honour, but he is also a nosy little beggar. After all he could have handed me the letters without having read them, or he might have discreetly claimed not to have read them, even if he had, but that would have been more than his curiosity could bear, because he also wants me to fill in the missing details for him. In fact I couldn't help him about Horace Pink, but, as for Batty, well enough I know the fiendish Batty! Monstrous woman. She was my mother's lady's maid before I was born and as far as I know, she's still with her now. If there was one woman I hated more than I hated my mother and of whom I was more afraid, it was Batty. When, as a child, I displeased my mother, it was always Batty who was told to take the cane to me. Or the riding crop. Whatever came to hand.

Without explaining the exact contents of the letters, Rakowski told me that I would find their tone profoundly distasteful. He implied, without however being specific, that an element of blackmail was involved. I would advise you, he said, to lock the letters away where no prying eye can see them. Then, very much to my amazement, he rather pompously informed me that whatever I chose to do with them was entirely up to me. He would, he said, enquire no further. He then began somewhat raffishly to talk beside the point, dropping a few heavy hints as he did so. He, as a historian, would never recommend the burning of letters or family papers, however insignificant those papers might appear to be. Indeed, in his humble opinion, the burning of historical evidence was a moral crime, 'dastardly behaviour, Sir!' Some people, he conceded, did not hold these views and would rashly and indiscriminately burn anything which they supposed might bring themselves or their families into disrepute. He banged on for quite a while, then Mason appeared with the drinks tray. In fact, I thought Rakowski gave Mason rather a funny look, perhaps because he suspected him of listening at the door, which, had he been, would not have surprised me in the least. Anyway, the old boy accepted a glass of sherry from the salver that Mason, with a basilisk stare, offered him, and having downed it remarkably quickly, took his leave.

I don't know if it had anything to do with Mason's furtive, darting eyes, or if it was in response to Rakowski's overt warnings, but I was careful to lock that parcel of letters away in my desk, and to pocket the key, rather than leave it as I generally do, in the keyhole. I had no time to read the letters before leaving for London, but I did have time, thank God, for another large gin and tonic.

### Letter from Horace Pink to Doris Batty

7 Back Alley Lane.
JULY 10TH, 1910

Dear Miss Batty,

Seeing as how I have not had the pleasure of a reply to my earlier communication with yourself, I have it in mind to approach you again. I am of the opinion that you did not fully understand the nature of my request. There is informa-tion what I know about that would put your precious Ladyship's pretty little nose out of joint. For a consideration I would be prepared to discuss the aforesaid intelligence with a view to it not going no further.

You will appreciate that it is the loyalty of a humble servant which prompts me to approach you over this matter. I would not like to see her Ladyship, nor yourself neither, get into a mess on account of what I knows. I would of thought that as one what is still in her Ladyship's employ you, yourself, Miss Batty, might of been inclined to be as trusty a servant to her Ladyship as is

Yr humble and faithful freind
Horace G. Pink

## *Sydney Otterton's diary*

Christ Almighty! I don't know what the hell to do about these awful letters of Rakowski's. I wish to God I'd never set eyes on them. For the first time in my life, I've even begun to feel a little sorry for my mother, although not for Batty. That woman deserves to be hanged! And to think that my mad mother still employs her, probably, I now suspect, because she's been blackmailed into doing so.

Priscilla, surprisingly, is rather less shocked than I am. Perhaps because it's not her family which is involved and also because she so loathes my mother that she most likely believes her to be capable of anything from a white lie to genocide. Of course she also rather likes evidence of my mother's perfidy (as if any more were needed) in order to shore up her strongly held opinions, and perhaps, even to explain my own lack of filial sentiment. But in fact we don't yet know the truth of the matter. In my opinion, if there is any truth at all in Pink's filthy allegations, then Batty has to be the guilty party. I remember from my childhood how evil that woman was. I'm even beginning to think of my mother as a victim in Batty's clutches. Whatever one feels about her, there must be certain things of which one can never believe one's own mother to be capable.

One thing I have discovered is the identity of Horace Pink. It wasn't very difficult. I only had to ask Jerrold. He's a man who keeps his own counsel, but he's also always had his ear to the ground and I was certain (quite rightly as it turned out) that he would remember the name of anyone who had ever worked in the house or on the estate, so I went down to see him. The poor devil was looking a bit green about the gills, but sure enough, he did remember, although he scratched his head for a while and complained about time running on before he came up with anything. Then he said that there'd definitely been a Horace Pink at Cranfield 'years gone by'. A footman who hadn't lasted long, he seemed to think. But he couldn't put a face to him, nor could he remember exactly when he was here, but he thought it might have been around the time I was born, or even a few years earlier. Of course Jerrold never knew why he'd left, nor what had happened to him later. Or if he did, he wasn't going to say. I need to ask someone who actually worked in the house at the time but I couldn't at first think of anyone whose whereabouts I knew, except for Batty, and she's about as likely to answer my letters as she was Horace Pink's. Anyway, it suddenly crossed my mind that I could drop by the almshouses and look in on old Nanny McFee to see if she knows anything. Priscilla's always going on at me about not going to see my old nanny often enough, so she should be delighted to hear that I'm going tomorrow afternoon. Not that I'm really sure of what use it will be to learn very much more about Pink. The fellow may well be dead, for all I know, or in prison. For that matter he may still be blackmailing my mother. Perhaps he can afford to live in a stately home by now, which may well have something to do with my being so bloody broke all the time.

## Annie's diary

Bert quite got on my nerves when I was cooking his tea yesterday evening. He would go on about how this horse he had his money on in the Grand National fell at the third fence which according to him he shouldn't have done. Just because he won 7s./6d. last year, he seems to think that he's going to win something every year. Well, I told him not to be so sure. He ought to know better than to think he can count on any darned horse in the Grand National. Anyway he would carry on so, that I had to make it quite plain I could think of better ways to spend my Sunday evenings than cooking his tea and listening to him complaining about a horse. For one thing, I could have been down at Father's, but my little sister is stopping with him for a week, so I took pity on Bert for once. I think Bert's quite full of himself now, what with him taking over the milking which he seems to think impresses me, just because of Father having been the cowman. I reckon that Father was a better cowman than Bert would ever be in a month of Sundays. Never mind the milking, he's as pleased as Punch too about the Wilkinses being carted off, poor things.

I never heard such a noise in all my life as those Wilkinses were making next door last time I was at Bert's, and I can't help admitting that last night I was downright relieved to know they'd gone away. Bert saw them leave. He said it was terrible. First of all some relations came to collect the children who were all crying and not wanting to go, and kicking up an awful shindy and then an ambulance came for the parents and they were both wailing like nobody's business. I told Bert that I always thought there was something funny about those two. They never did look you in the eye, either of them.

His Lordship went to see Father the other day. I wasn't sure if it was just a friendly call or if there was something he particularly wanted to talk to him about. Father wasn't saying anything. Only that he was real glad to see his Lordship. I suppose it might have had something to do with this Horace Pink his Lordship keeps wanting to know about. The funny thing is that the name rings a bell to me for some reason, not that I can think for the life of me who he might be. But if he worked here when his Lordship was a baby, I wouldn't have been much more than seven or eight years old so I wouldn't have known anything about him. After all we never went into the house in those days, although Mother would have known the people who worked there because she used to go up once a week to collect and deliver the mending from the servants' hall. One thing I learnt from my mother was how to mend and how to darn. I'll always think of Mother doing the mending, either for all of us or for the big house.

And it's just as well I did learn how to darn, what with all the sheets and pillow-cases and socks that I have piled up at the moment waiting to be mended. There's been so much going on lately what with the burglary and Father, and one thing and another, that I've got quite behind.

## *Sydney Otterton's diary*

I've been brooding all week about Horace Pink and his filthy correspondence. I'm not yet at all sure what I want to do about it. I suppose I could just put all the letters in a parcel and send them to my mother, or, come to that, to Doris Batty c/o my mother, via the bank, but I'm not convinced that that would be the best solution. For one thing, I'd like to know if Pink is alive or not because if he is, he may well still be living off the proceeds of his blackmail and to tell the truth, I wouldn't mind seeing the fellow in gaol. If he's dead, I suppose that casts rather a different light on things. If I find that he is dead, I might simply throw the letters on the fire, although I wouldn't mind letting Batty know first that I have discovered her secret, and leaving her to sweat a bit.

Priscilla, for once, is as undecided as I am about what we ought to do next. She came up with the idea, though, that these letters may have been what my mother has been looking for so desperately. After all, she presumably knew of their existence, and must have been incensed at Batty leaving them around for someone else to find. I can't imagine why Batty was such a fool. Or why the bloody hell she kept them at all when they could only have incriminated her. I suppose she's a very stupid woman and perhaps she thought that if she kept them, she might eventually be able to get the man for blackmail, or, more than likely, use them in some vile way for her own ends.

Nanny turned out to be very useful. She moaned a bit about my never coming to see her, but then when I asked about Pink, she quite cheered up. She never knew what happened to him in the end, or even if he was alive or dead, but she certainly remembered him quite clearly as the second footman. But that was before I was born. Nanny left after my mother's first child died and went to work briefly for another family before coming back to look after me. Pink, she remembers, was at Cranfield when she first arrived. He sounds like a very moderate fellow. According to Nanny, the servants' gossip was that on his days off he used to dress up in women's clothes, stays and bloomers, the lot. She heard that from the butler and she says she wouldn't wonder if it was true. She never liked the man because he reminded her of a spiteful schoolgirl, but there was something about him which made it difficult not to notice him. He was a small man, pale and dark and what she called foreign-looking, with a narrow mean little face, a huge nose and small black eyes. Looked like a Spanish rat, she said. The sort of man who, according to her, was always there when he wasn't wanted, forever turning up in unexpected places, poking his nose into other people's business, looking at you askance. Nanny said that she always thought he had a thing about Batty. I was a bit surprised by that, I have to admit, but she insisted that Batty had been a good-looking woman in her day. She couldn't remember why Pink left, although she thought there might have been some kind of scandal that might have involved Batty. But then it all happened immediately after the baby died when everyone was in a bad way and she, of course, was leaving too. 'It was a dreadful thing when we lost that baby,' she said. 'It happened on my day off, and when I came back, the poor little thing was gone.' Funnily enough I had never heard her mention it before. Then she began to cry and to tell me that in all her years as a nursery-maid and then a nanny, that was the only one she'd lost.


## *Letter from Horace Pink to Doris Batty*

7 Back Alley Lane.
AUGUST 7TH, 1910

Dear Miss Batty,

I do not doubt that you yourself, Miss Batty, must be enlitened as to the fact that since leaving Cranfield Park I have been unemployed which is not a comfortable position for an honest man what is innocent to of fallen into. I have been most patient with yourself and with her Ladyship who I hoped would of sent me some small consideration by now in the lite of the information what you must have told her I knows of.

I was interested to read in the newspaper last week as how the doctor what poisoned and dismembered his wife was arrested on a ship going to Canada. I expect he and his accomplice was both hoping to go scot free whereas it now transpires that the pair of them will as like as not swing for it. Have you ever considered how a man, or a woman come to that, must feel standing on that there trap door waiting for the noose to be slipped ever so gently round his acursed neck?

I remain, Miss Batty, as ever
Her Ladyship's devoted servant and your loyal friend
Horace G. Pink

# Sydney Otterton's diary

Priscilla and I have reached a point where we are really having to ask ourselves quite seriously how much longer we can manage to stay here with things going as badly as they are. The results of the local council elections have certainly put a smile on the face of the Tories, but I don't think my circumstances will alter much even with a change of government. This government seems to be getting into deeper and deeper trouble every week and perhaps I ought to feel some sort of sympathy for them since my affairs appear to be in very much the same sort of state as the country's as a whole. For all the loans and concessions on agricultural land, and for all Aunt Lettice's immensely generous help, I'm beginning to think that I will never be able to pay the death duties or work my way out of the morass of debt and decay in which I find myself. Most people (especially my bank manager) are of the opinion that I'm raving mad even to consider trying to go on living in Cranfield. Sometimes I try not to think about what will happen and then I go off to London and get drunk and see Posy and she gives me hell and calls me a two-timer and then I have another drink and come home and go to bed and wake up in the small hours sick to the gills and in a bloody awful panic.

My nightmares have taken on a new, rather macabre dimension. I'm either in the Western Desert, or at Villers Bocage or somewhere in Italy and I've got this baby with me and I have to save it from the enemy whose lines are forever advancing, and the turret of my tank jams and under their tin hats every single German has the face of Doris Batty. It's extraordinary that anything quite so ridiculous can cause one to sweat so much.

Tony and I had lunch together the other day in London

because he very kindly offered to go round to Somerset House with me to see what we could find out about Horace Pink. We looked up his birth certificate and discovered that he was born in Bermondsey in 1885 which means that he's only in his mid sixties, if he's alive, which I imagine he is since we didn't find a death certificate. I'm beginning to think that my only possible line of action is to approach my mother and Batty directly which I am certainly loath to do. Otherwise I burn the letters. After all, those letters must have been lost for years and have only been found by chance. Of course it would be one thing if they had never been found, but having come to light, they cannot be entirely ignored. All the same, I think I'll do nothing for a while, nothing always being the easiest option and anyway I've got plenty of other things to think about, not to mention a couple of weeks' soldiering at Lulworth coming up soon. There's nothing like playing with tanks to take one's mind off one's troubles.

## *Georgina's exercise book*

MAY 6TH

Everybody's in an awful bate these days which is very boring of them. Mummy keeps saying we haven't got any money and Father's always shouting. I think he's cross with the government about something. Mr Rakowski never comes any more and I bet he went and lost those letters and stinky Mr Mason's still here. I wish he would go. No one likes him and he's still always snooping.

JULY 19TH

Its better now the hollidays are here and Thomas and Jamie have come back from school. Father says we can take a picnic to the big wood in the pony trap tomorrow. We've got a French governess for the holidays. She's jolly young but she's going to be a nun so we're supposed to be good.

## Letter from Horace Pink to Doris Batty

7 Back Alley Lane.
AUGUST 16TH, 1910

Dear Miss Batty,

Not having received no reply to my former letters, the situation has considerably deteriorated. As you know I am unemployed and consequently I who am an honest gentleman, am having a awful deal of trouble rubbing two pence together as you might say. I find as I am obliged to write to you again to beg of her Ladyship's mercy that she might send me a consideration in view of what I knows. I think you should understand that I have evidence of the facts what the police might be interested in.

I await your gracious reply,
Yr ever faithful friend
Horace G. Pink

## Zbigniew Rakowski's notebook

SEPTEMBER 4TH

Pine. Indeed I do for the beautiful Lady Otterton. She of the hyacinth eyes. It is now some six or seven months since I last visited Cranfield and since I handed Mr Pink's offending letters over to Lord Otterton. I have in all honesty had no good reason to return there in the interim, for I can barely claim to require any further access to the Cranfield archives. I have done all the research that I need, and have furthermore, during the course of these last months, managed to progress so considerably with my work that I am in truth nearing its conclusion. I have on occasion exchanged the briefest notes with Priscilla who has been so kind as to inform me that she looks forward to my returning to Cranfield in the near future since she feels that it would be most unfortunate were we to lose touch. She has, she avers, enjoyed our luncheon-time discussions. I am indeed more than gratified by her sentiment.

There yet remains the unsettled business of Mason. Alone in Robin Hood Way, I have dwelt at length on the perfidy of Mason, and on what appears to me now as my own defective handling of the matter and my own inadequate dealing with the information that I have. I have had no communication with Lord Otterton since that sunless morning in February when I handed him Pink's nefarious correspondence, nor, for that matter, did I truthfully expect any. No doubt his Lordship has dealt with the letters according to his own lights. I meanwhile am left with the uncomfortable thought that Lilian, Lady Otterton, in cahoots, as modern idiom would express it, with the repulsive Mason, was probably looking for the letters which so inadvertently came into my possession. Such a supposition leads me to ask a good many questions regarding the nature of Mason's employment and the degree of knowledge he may or may not have concerning the Pink letters. I have indeed become a very slow old man, both vainly deluded and cumbersome in my thinking. Overwhelmed in my dotage by a foolish passion for a lovely lady, not to say over-excited by the faintest suspicion of Gothic intrigue, I have perhaps not acted as I should have done, with such prudence and sagacity of which I could reasonably have been proud.

If, as I half suspect, Lord Otterton is still in ignorance of the part played by Mason, and if Mason is still employed at Cranfield, I am inclined to think that the time has surely come for me to apprise the Ottertons of everything of which

I am aware. Indeed the time is long past when I should initially have done so and, mulling as I do over the events as they occurred, I find myself somewhat confused in my own mind as to why I acted then as I did. I can only surmise that at the time I felt that the hold I had over Mason would eventually enable me to unravel his dark secret which, I am now of the firm opinion, must have revolved entirely around the lost letters. Thus I have this morning penned a letter to Lord Otterton begging him to allow me to call at Cranfield to discuss one or two important matters with him. I have not intimated what these important matters might be, leaving him to suppose that they are most likely connected with *The Otterton Family*, towards the conclusion of which work, I reiterate, I am now drawing, and with which I am not wholly displeased. I cannot but dwell on the fact that the end is nigh for, satisfied although I may be with the work, it will surely be with a heavy heart that I survey the vacuum into which its completion will condemn me to live, unless I return, as I have often intimated that I might, to my unfinished little crime novel, the which, in my heart of hearts, I know on reflection can of course, for reasons of loyalty, never be published. But no doubt it will nevertheless provide me with a little *divertimento* during the lonely days that must inevitably lie ahead.

SEPTEMBER 19TH

Today I lunched once more at Cranfield. I was deeply touched to receive a gracious note from Priscilla written, as she was kind enough to explain, in response to my letter to his Lordship, which had arrived during his absence in Scotland where I gather he had repaired with friends on some sporting venture. She suggested that I come to see his Lordship in the morning and insisted that I stay to luncheon since, she maintained, she has missed my regular visits and both she and Lord Otterton would very much like to hear how I am progressing with the family history.

My initial reaction was one of dismay since it occurred to me that once I had divulged my knowledge to Lord Otterton, which eventuality would inevitably occur before luncheon, I might very well be no longer *persona grata* at their table, around which table, to make matters worse, there would presumably be lurking, *coûte que coûte*, the abominable Mason. How would Lord Otterton react to the information that I had witnessed the butler opening the door to his violet-clad mother all those months ago? Would it not be natural for him to enquire as to the delay in my keeping him informed? Would he not inevitably see me as party to the dreadful dealings? It is hardly surprising, that with this in mind, I therefore set out for Cranfield on this occasion without my usual lightness of step, and not without a little trepidation.

As after so many months, I once more wound my way up the drive, and as the great house hove into view, reminding me suddenly of a gigantic liner in a sea of green, my heart gave a lurch at the realisation of what that house had come to mean to me and of what she must mean to those who sail in her. How all our imaginations are captured! Even the children's own awareness appears to be woven inextricably into the warp and the weft of the life of the house, from which they would seem to see their own young lives as being inseparable.

Yesterday, after many months of denial, the government devalued the pound and I could not but reflect as I walked on towards the house, that like the country, Lord Otterton most probably teeters on the edge of bankruptcy. For how much longer would he and his exquisite consort be able to continue in the aristocratic style, albeit threadbare, to which they are accustomed? I felt a sudden sinking of the heart as it occurred to me with a peculiar rapier-like certainty that this, for whatsoever reason, might be the very last time I would be invited to my beloved Cranfield.

It would be no falsification to add that when, a few

moments after I had rung the bell, the front door was opened by none other than the detestable Mason himself, still employed to wait upon the Ottertons and to hand sweetmeats to my Beatrice, I again felt a sickening shock to the system, which resulted partly from my having had no contact with the man for months and partly from a sense of guilt, that were it not for my delay in acting, the dreadful creature should surely have been given his cards many weeks ago. And yet, who else had I expected would open the door? There was nothing for it but to steel myself to the encounter and thus I instantly straightened my back and looked hard at the brute, confident in the knowledge that, although my days at Cranfield might be numbered, so indeed were his.

Lord Otterton received me in the Japanese Room where he offered me a glass of sherry and invited me to sit down before a blazing fire. Much as I did not like the thought of the inevitable reappearance of Mason bearing a drinks tray laden with decanters of sherry and gin and no doubt bottles of tonic for what I have observed to be his Lordship's preferred tipple, I was glad of the offer of a little something which I felt could not but give me Dutch courage for the task in hand. A task, the performance of which I had, over the past days, many times rehearsed.

Since no situation ever eventually bears the least resemblance to that which has been previously imagined, it remains a mystery as to why men and women are ever wont to concern themselves with such unavailing rehearsals. Not surprisingly, Lord Otterton did not react in any way for which I might have prepared myself. After a few brief pleasantries concerning the weather and his recent visit to Scotland, I gently broached the matter of Pink's letters and then, emboldened by my sherry, informed his Lordship that I had some further distressing news for him. Whilst I perambulated around the subject, trying, I fear, to justify my delay in coming forth with the aforementioned information, I noticed his Lordship's large dark eyes wandering away from my gaze, anxiously seeking the corners of the room, as if it were he, not I, who had something to fear. He stood up and with hunched shoulders, but without a word, strode to the table where Mason had left the drinks tray and swiftly replenished his glass. It crossed my addled old mind that the contents of the letters must have shocked him so profoundly, that now he dreaded what I might have to say next. Eventually I came to the point.

His Lordship was standing in front of the fire and, as I finished speaking, he said not a word, but loured at me in apparent incomprehension before, without tarrying even to put down his tumbler, he crossed the room on his cat-like tread, flung open the door (another of those fine mahogany doors) and without so much as a moment's hesitation, without pausing, *même*, to close that door, he left the room. I, quite at a loss, appalled to say the least, at what I might have unleashed, leaped nervously from the armchair in which I had been seated and stood where his Lordship had been standing in front of the fire, knowing not what to do. To go or to stay? To be or not to be . . . ?

It seemed to me then that I remained a long while in a surreal state of suspended animation in front of that fire. In the silence that appeared to have been occasioned by Lord Otterton's sudden departure, I had the impression that I was alone, all alone in that great mansion, that it and I were both anachronisms which might at any given moment be swept up together by some supernatural whirlwind, blown away, disintegrated, annihilated and finally consigned to nothing more substantial than the fallibility of human memory, which I suppose is where we belong.

When the whirlwind came, it was not quite as I had anticipated it would be. It manifested itself rather, in the form of such a thundering and a shouting from the hall, such an exchange of oaths, such a bawling and such a *hollering* (for want of a better word), as I have never before experienced. My immediate reaction was to cross to the door and gently close it, for it was indeed no business of mine to be eavesdropping.

I stood for some time at the window, gazing out over the formal rose garden, up the grassy slope to the Victorian grotto beneath the trees, and back along the top of the bank to the dark wellingtonias under which I had been partaking of a humble sandwich on that fateful occasion when I was first approached by the perfidious Mason. It seemed so long ago that all at once I was shocked by what appeared to me to have been my own inertia. The dreadful whirlwind of noise which the mahogany doors themselves were unable to block out, and that reached me even as my back was turned, should long ago have blown over, had I behaved as I ought to have done. Had I not been blinded by an old man's hopeless love and by the romance of Cranfield itself.

Later Priscilla came to find me. No doubt, she said, I was aware that there had been something of a rumpus, but we had better have luncheon all the same. Luncheon was an uncomfortable meal. His Lordship scowled and spoke little, her Ladyship made some attempt to converse, asking me my opinion of André Gide in whose *Journal* she is at present engrossed. There being no Mason to wait at table, we helped ourselves from the sideboard to rabbit pie and mashed potatoes, followed by stewed plums.

## *Sydney Otterton's diary*

SEPTEMBER 23RD

I can't imagine that many people were taken completely by surprise when, none too soon, and after a massive amount of twisting and turning, umpteen denials and a good many outright lies, Stafford Cripps finally announced the devaluation of the pound. Apparently, so as to stop the news from leaking out early, and after the Chancellor had acquainted them with the new exchange rate, the leaders of the Opposition were locked up for hours with a whole bunch of lobby hacks in some government offices or other. Next the banks and the Stock Exchange were closed. What with all that and the milk ration being cut again, the entire country appears to be in a terrible state of turmoil. My blasted cows, under Bert's aegis, are certainly doing nothing to help boost the milk supply at the moment, but in my present circumstances, I really don't want to have to employ another hand, so I'm just hoping that Buttercup III and her pals will soon knuckle under. According to Annie, Jerrold's pretty fed up with what he's been hearing about it all, but then Jerrold blames everything that goes wrong with the cows on the electric milking machine and nothing anyone can ever say will change his mind on that score.

So what with all that going on, I'd almost completely forgotten about Rakowski wanting to see me again, when along the bloody old fool comes with another well-timed bombshell. I cannot understand why the hell the blithering imbecile never told me before about Mason and my mother. He spun me some futile rigmarole about why he didn't say anything at the time, none of which seemed to make very much sense to me. All Priscilla says is that she told me so, which she didn't. Well, I know she never liked Mason although she always refused to say exactly what it was that she objected to about him, but she certainly didn't suspect him of having anything to do with my mother, as far as I know.

Anyway Rakowski came and sat himself down opposite me in the Japanese Room, gibbering and talking nonsense so that I hadn't the faintest idea what he was getting at, then all of a sudden he made this bloody silly announcement about having seen Mason open the door to my mother. I just looked at him sitting there bolt upright in his mittens with a scarf tied round his scraggy old neck, fingering his little goatee beard, and the sight of him made me so angry I couldn't speak. I couldn't imagine what the fucking idiot thought he'd been up to all this time, squatting in the bowels of the earth, writing some damn silly book, talking about literature to Priscilla and pretending to be everybody's friend. He even tried to bring the children into it somehow. I think at the time it was my intention to go and find Priscilla, anyway for some reason I simply left the room, only to walk straight into Mason who was coming across the hall to announce lunch.

I was so angry when I saw him that I just bawled at him and told him to f— off there and then. In fact in the end I managed to get a surprising amount of information out of that bugger. I think he must have been completely taken by surprise when he met me. In any case, I thought the man must be right off his head to judge by the way he started to bellow back at me, calling me a parasite and yelling about man's struggle against nature and the evils of capitalism and how it served me right if my coronets were rusting at the bottom of the lake. It was where they belonged. As for me and my family, he said he'd like to see us all, along with Annie (poor Annie), cleaning the lavatories on Waterloo Station. I've never seen a man so disturbed, purple in the face, his eyes swivelling in his bloody head and his jowls quivering. He was almost foaming at the mouth and I doubt that my mother would have been very pleased with her henchman if she could have heard the way he talked about her so that even I felt obliged to defend her. Anyway, I saw the man again in the evening when he appeared to have come to his senses although in some ways he was almost odder than he'd been in the morning. I told him that in fact I never wished to clap eyes on him again although before he left I wanted an answer to one or two questions. Most uncharacteristically he kept wanting to shake my hand and to tell me that we were 'mates'. I've no intention of being his mate.

Priscilla was annoyed with me for getting so angry. She goes on about it being undignified and she keeps saying that it would be more 'telling' if I kept calm. Or some such bloody rubbish. But she also says that I seem to have to get angry before I'm prepared to sack anyone, which to my mind is a perfectly reasonable sequence of events.

I don't know what Mason thought I could do to him beyond sacking him, which I had already done, but when I saw him before he left, when he kept on wanting to shake my hand, I had the overwhelming impression that he was terrified of something. Which, I imagine, is the only reason why he was prepared to tell me as much as he did.

I have to say I was amazed when he announced that Mrs Mason and the awful Mrs Legros dit Courrier are sisters, although when I thought about it later, a bell rang somewhere in the back of my mind. Then of course Priscilla reminded me of how ages ago she'd seen the two of them waving or nodding at each other outside the International Stores. In fact I do remember her telling me something of the sort at the time, but I didn't pay any attention which perhaps I should have done. Priscilla says I never pay any attention to anything she says which is absolute cock, and, in any case I don't really see what difference it would have made in this instance if I had. After all you can't stop people nodding at each other in a public place nor can you count it as evidence of appalling treachery if they do. Priscilla says we could and should have found out all about Mason months ago which would have saved us from being spied on for all this time in our own house. I have to say the thought, first of those creepy Legros with that bloody big dog of theirs and then Mason snooping around is pretty unpleasant. I do remember being delighted when the police came and removed Legros. The ruddy flat's been empty for ages now, but perhaps it's just as well with people like the Legros around.

Like every other feckless coward, Mason is a man of little loyalty. He told me that Legros who was planted here in the flat by my mother (and I have yet to find out exactly what the connection there is), later tipped him the wink to apply for the job of butler, but after I'd sacked the bugger, there was nothing bad enough that Mason could find to say about Legros.

'Now that you and I are mates, M'lord,' says Mason, clinging onto my hand with both his sweaty mitts, and trembling like a jelly, 'I think it only right to tell you that my brother-in-law, that is to say the *wife's* brother-in-law, is a crook.' Thank God he let go of my hand at last, in order I suppose to draw himself up before going on in his vile wheedling tone to call Legros every name under the sun, from a forger to a paedophile. 'And,' he said, his eyes rolling in his head like a madman, 'he's out to smash the capitalist system.' All of that would have been bad enough without the fellow, who's much taller than me, having to bend over me and push his revolting great face into mine so that I caught a gust of his stinking breath that almost made me gag. What with the Wilkinses at the farm and the Masons in the house, I began to think I was doing a public service by running a looney bin.

How I long for Johnson and the voice of sanity, not that he'll ever come back from Australia now, but funnily enough, he was the one who was initially on to the Legros. I don't know why we never listened to him at the time.

The luckiest thing of all is that none of these idiots bribed by my mother ever found what they were presumably sent to look for, and instead, by some miracle the children were the ones to discover Pink's letters. I don't think I have been told the whole truth about that either, but then that is the least of my worries. One thing that I am quite curious about though, is how much Mason or Legros knew about what they were looking for. But that isn't something to which I could easily expect an answer. I certainly didn't want to hear much more about Legros, but Mason insisted on telling me with peculiar satisfaction combined with a spiteful snigger that the man is back inside. 'To think what the wife's sister has been through,' he added sanctimoniously, rubbing his hands together and then pursing his lips. It struck me that neither the wife nor the wife's sister had shown any great perception in their choice of husband.

The funny thing is that now, in retrospect and with the Masons gone, I find that it's Rakowski who really makes me angry. I was rather fond of the fellow and always quite pleased to see him when he turned up. He's an affected old booby, a bit unctuous at times and obviously besotted with Priscilla, but he's unusual and he's got a sense of humour and up until this happened, I always thought he was on one's side. Now I feel that he has just been watching us, or looking at us like specimens under his microscope. For two pins he'd pull all our wings off. Merely to think about the fellow makes me reach for the gin. I've told Priscilla that I don't want to see him here again. I don't give a toss about his ruddy book. He can finish it as he pleases but without any further help from me.

## Letter from Annie to Dolly

Cranfield Park
OCTOBER 2ND, 1949

Dear Dolly,

As I write this I am sitting at Father's kitchen table, with Father having a quick forty winks in the armchair by the stove. I'm worried about his cough which seems to be getting worse rather than better and am sure that it cannot be helped by the coke fumes that come billowing out of that stove. The whole house smells of coke. All the same he seems to be in quite good heart and never complains. To tell the truth, he thinks about nothing so much as his Michaelmas daisies!

There's been terrific goings on at the house recently what

with Mr Mason getting the sack. I think everyone was pleased when that happened. If you ask me he was a nasty piece of work. Anyway, it turned out that it was him who let *Lilian* in last year against his Lordship's orders. Mr Rakowski, the gentleman who is writing a book about the family, saw him opening the front door to her, but no one seems to know why he kept quiet about it until now. Well you can imagine what a fury his Lordship was in when he heard!

Bert is still managing the cows and very pleased with himself about that. I expect he's hoping his Lordship won't find another cowman. Father grumbles about it and worries about his cows and goes on alarming about the electric milking machine. He says that Bert's not the right man for the job anyway and that if his Lordship wants the yield to go up, he'd do better to hire an experienced cowman.

Father's just woken up and will be wanting his tea, so I'll stop now. Give my love to Fred and the children.

Love from
Annie

## Georgina's exercise book

SEPTEMBER 29TH

The boys have gone back to school and it's quite boring. I was helping Father feed his parrots and he was awfully angry with Mr Rakofsky. He says he can't come here any more and it's all something to do with those letters we found. I admitted that we'd found them and given them to Mr Rakofsky and Father was quite cross and said we should have given them to him. He wanted to know if we had read them but I told him they looked boring so we hadn't and he said they were nothing to do with us anyway. When I asked what they were about he got really annoyed and said 'None of your b—y bisness!!' Then he said something about children having little minds and I know he was only trying to bait me so I said he was lucky that I helped him with his birds. Then he got in a better mood.

I'm really sorry about Mr Rakofski because he was very nice to us and I liked him. I'm sure he hasn't done anything wrong and I wish Father would let him come back. I asked Mummy when he was coming again but I think she smelt a rat. She said something like 'What's that got to do with you?' and I said I dunno but I like him and she said 'He comes here to do his work and he doesn't want children interrupting him all the time.' That was very unfair because I never interrupted him *all the time.*

## *Zbigniew Rakowski's notebook*

Alas another bleak Tuesday dawns without the prospect of a visit to Cranfield. I no longer remember how it came about that my outings to Cranfield always took place on a Tuesday, but since the very earliest days of my association with the Ottertons, that has ever been the way. My history of the family is all but completed and indeed I should be engaged in writing those final pages now, rather than in yielding to these my feelings of despair and bitter disappointment.

Only yesterday I received a most courteous note from Priscilla. Ah, how my cracked old heart missed a beat when I recognised her fair firm hand on the light blue envelope, but how dashed were my hopes when I read what she had to say! She wished me to know that she shared her husband's incomprehension at what she chose to call my 'secretive' behaviour and she was indeed appalled that I had endeavoured to involve the children in what she referred to as my machinations. She was, she claimed, at a loss to discern to what ends I had acted as I did. She and Lord Otterton had, she opined, regarded me as a friend and had both enjoyed my company on the many occasions I lunched with them, which made it all the more painful for them to realise that I had not been straight with them. Straight indeed. She wished me luck with the *Ottertons* and assured me that she and Lord Otterton were looking forward to receiving a copy of the book when it is eventually published. She then reminded me, in a manner that I can regard as nothing less than insulting, that I might be so good as not to forget to send Lady Isley a copy as well. She closed her missive with the chilling observation that our paths might cross again at some future date.

This hurtful letter left me in such a distressed state that I was quite unable to concentrate on my work for the rest of the day. How unjust I found it, for I had only acted out of love for her and loyalty to her family, tempered, as I now see, by vanity, for it was not young Georgina, but I who so fondly saw myself as a latter-day Holmes. What folly indeed to suppose that I, brittle-boned old buffoon that I am, had the makings of a great detective, that I would be able to solve the imponderable, unmask the treacherous, kill the dragon and save my Beatrice, to the echoing applause of her family. Let *dithering nincompoop* be the words inscribed on my tombstone, for now this dithering nincompoop finds himself, by his own hand, destined to a disappointed and cheerless future, bereft of the delights of Cranfield, of rabbit pie and mahogany doors, of Georgina and Annie, of Laszlo's scornful Lilian and Rysbrack's sacrifice to Bacchus, of Lord Otterton's extravagant humour and exquisite eccentricity, but most surely bereft of the joy born of friendship with Priscilla. *Freude, schöner Götterfunken* . . . Ah me! If only . . . the saddest words indeed.

Priscilla and I have had a long discussion about these ruddy letters of Pink's and for once we seem to be more or less in agreement as to what we ought to do, which is, thank God, nothing for the moment. As Priscilla points out, they were written nearly forty years ago and have probably lain undiscovered under the floorboards for nearly as long. They raise a hell of a lot of questions, some of which don't bear answering and we both feel that it would be madness to act rashly which, in Priscilla's eyes, would include burning them. For my part I would happily burn them, but she has made me promise to keep them till after Christmas and then to think again. I vaguely thought of putting them back under another piece of old floorboard and leaving them there for future generations to discover but Priscilla has taken them and locked them away with her jewellery in her bedroom safe.

One of the things that worries me about the blasted things, is not knowing who else has read them. Priscilla is sure that Rakowski must have. He had them long enough as far as I can make out, although he never really came quite clean about exactly when they were found. I refuse to discuss the matter with the children although Georgina volunteered that they never read them. She could of course be lying but I do in fact believe her.

Then there remains the problem of Mason and the Legros and the whole network of spies imposed on us by my mother. How the hell can I ever employ anyone again without suspecting them of being in her pay? And what do I do about that bunch of crooks out there? What do they know? Or think they know? Priscilla says ignore them. Forget all about them, she says, because they can't do us any more harm. But I sometimes think that the only way to put a stop to all this nonsense would be to send Pink's letters to my mother and let her got on with it. And I sometimes think that the vile creature Batty deserves whatever she might have coming to her.

Anyway, it's agreed that we won't think about it all again until after Christmas. And God alone knows where we will be by then. In the debtors' gaol I should think, judging by the way things are going. Never mind Pink's letters and my mother, there are far more important things to think about at the moment, like how long we can seriously consider going on here. Priscilla has begun to think quite a lot about the Dower House, which is a relief in some ways because I'm afraid that if we had to leave here, she might take that opportunity to leave me. The Dower House would certainly be a possibility for us as the tenants there only pay a pittance and in any case their lease is due to come up for renewal in the New Year. Even Aunt Lettice, the one person who more than anyone else would hate to see the Ottertons leave Cranfield, is beginning to think that we will eventually have to decide to move out. You could say that under the circumstances, the sooner we do so, the better. Or perhaps we'll hang on until after the election before we decide, not that I can really see what difference that will make to my affairs either way.


## *Zbigniew Rakowski's notebook*

TUESDAY, NOVEMBER 15TH

Woe is me, for it is forever Tuesday and I am forever banished. *The Otterton Family* is with the publisher who has been kind enough to say that he is delighted with it and who now pesters me to know what my next project will be. I am quite unable to consider any further undertaking at the moment, so heavy is my heart, so great the void that surrounds me. The book I have dedicated, with her permission, *to Priscilla*. How well I remember humbly begging her, in those now far-off halcyon days, graciously to accept this mark of my respect and admiration! How well I remember too, her obvious delight at the suggestion, for she was, I dare opine, somewhat flattered by the notion. I have not seen fit, under the present circumstances, to withdraw this badge of my esteem.

So here I sit, alone in Robin Hood Way, twiddling my thumbs as it were, dreading once more the long winter ahead, the advent of Christmas and the arrival of my daughter with her tedious husband, who will no doubt regard it as their bounden duty to 'cheer me up'. I feel myself sinking into a terminal state of depression for the world no longer holds any gladness for me; I anticipate nothing now beyond gradual decay, a loosening of the muscles, a stiffening of the joints, a dimming of the light, a numbing of the senses and a softening of the brain. Ah, Beatrice, to what have you reduced me? Even my little novel, my so-called *divertissement*, has lost its savour.

## Annie's diary

DECEMBER 15TH

I was quite surprised yesterday morning when, along with a letter from Dolly, the postman delivered this Christmas card from Mr Johnson. A lovely card mind, but I never thought to hear from him again after what I wrote last year, telling him downright cruelly that I would never dream of going to Australia, not for all the tea in China. Not that he went on about me going there any more but he did enclose a short letter, saying that he was getting on all right and that although he never regrets his decision to leave this country he sometimes misses it. He quite made me laugh, saying it's the drizzle he misses most and what he called 'them soft grey days'. The drizzle and the elm trees. Never mind the drizzle, I would definitely miss the elm trees myself. He says he still often thinks about Cranfield and would like to hear how his Lordship's getting on. He ended up by saying that he's come to consider himself quite a good cook, but he does occasionally wish he had someone to share his bungalow with. I suppose that was a bit of a dig at me, but then I reckon that by now he must have given up any hope of seeing me again. He certainly should have, although I don't mind writing back and telling him all the news, but I think I'll add (just to be on the safe side) that neither do I have any regrets about staying here in spite of the grey skies and the drizzle.

We still haven't got a new butler, or a cowman come to that. I sometimes think his Lordship is frightened to take on anyone new after all the trouble there's been. In any case, it means that I have a lot of extra work trying to make sure things get done properly and seeing to it that the dailies clean the silver. When there are guests Bert smartens himself up and comes in to wait at table. I reckon he's a darned sight better at that job than he ever is at milking the cows. He certainly seems to enjoy taking everything over. Father was furious when I told him. He wanted to know who on earth had ever heard of a cowman waiting at table? Well, I told him, times are changing. He said there was no doubt about that.

Poor old father he's not at all well, always coughing and spluttering and finding it hard to get about. It breaks my heart to see him like that, not that I think he's really lost interest in life, nor, come to that, has he lost the twinkle in his eye. When I complain about the winter, he just laughs and says, 'Now don't you go moaning on my girl, for it won't be long afore the snowdrops is up!' He seems quite sure that when the snowdrops come up, he'll begin to feel better, and then, he says, there'll be the daffs and before you can say Jack Robinson it will be time for him to prune the roses again.

# 1950

# Sydney Otterton's diary

An abysmal meeting with my bank manager on Friday only confirmed what in fact I already knew which is that we are going to have to leave this place. The farm accounts are like something out of *Alice in Wonderland*, completely topsy-turvy. The only thing about them that is abundantly clear is the fact that we are losing money hand over fist.

Priscilla and I went over to lunch with Aunt Lettice and had a long talk with her just after Christmas. Even she was beginning to think that things couldn't quite go on as they are, and that was before this last disastrous meeting with the bank manager. There's no possible way in which I will ever be able to pay off the death duties and keep my head above water, never mind run the farm, start up the shoot (even to do it as a syndicate will require an injection of capital which I don't have), pay the servants, keep the bloody roof on the house and pay the school fees. I've already had to sell most of the houses I had in the village, the tenant farmers are buying their farms and it's still costing me an arm and a leg to try to keep the cottages here in any sort of condition for human beings to live in.

It seems to me that, much as I shall feel a failure having to move out, perhaps it will be a relief finally to have made the decision to go. And to tell the truth, that decision is now all but made. I just need to sleep on it for a little while longer so as to accustom myself to the idea before I announce it to the world.

The new butler moved in immediately after Christmas, which might be a bit awkward, but at least I had the foresight to warn him that we might not be here for ever and that if we did move out he might consider staying on as caretaker since we wouldn't want to leave the house empty. He seems like a decent enough fellow with a wife who doesn't say much and a pair of grown-up children.

There's the election coming up on February 23rd but I know perfectly well that not all the elections in Christendom would make a pennyworth of difference to my state of affairs.

It's funny about Priscilla. She was so reluctant to move into Cranfield in the first instance, but now of course, partly because she's done so much for the place, she loves it and feels tremendously sad at the thought of moving out. All the same, I regard her as infinitely more practical than I am, so I feel sure that she must have faced up to the reality of the situation long before I did and so of course knew that we would inevitably have to go. She is quite keen on the thought of the Dower House and declares very positively that we are lucky to have somewhere so nice to move to. She's also talking about having another sale which would make sense and raise a bit of money too, and then she talks about our opening the house to the public.

I, on the other hand, sometimes think that if we are to leave the house, we might as well sell up altogether and go somewhere else. Be shot of Cranfield, lock, stock and barrel: start again from scratch. Excise the past which would most likely be impossible because, for one thing which I don't think Priscilla can ever fully understand and, silly though it may sound, the house is like a part of myself. That's probably why I feel so strongly. It's in my blood for whatever reason. It always has been and always will be but I can't tell if that's because of the hall which is about the grandest and most beautiful one in England, or because of the mean little dark back stairs leading to the basement where I used to hide as a child, or if it's because of the top landing where I went to play and to escape my mother's wrath. I had a bloody awful childhood I admit, but there were always the servants who were invariably kind to me and I think sorry for me too. I remember an old cook we used to have, feeding me on little cakes, and the butler who'd take me to the pantry when I was only about twelve years old to ask my opinion on a bottle of my father's port he had seen fit to open. In those days the house, too, felt like a friend. It was certainly a place of refuge. So for whatever reason, I love it. I love the way it stands; I love its solidity, its grace, the welcome it extends, the treasures in conceals and I have, to boot, always assumed that I would end my days here. In the Western Desert I often dreamt about it, sometimes about that imaginary undiscovered room, or just that I was standing in the hall or the saloon with friends, brother officers who might never even have been to Cranfield, and laughing, always laughing, because, despite my monstrous mother, the house has never struck me as an unhappy place. It has too great a character of its own to be affected by one or other of its temporary custodians.

My family built Cranfield. To have to abandon it now after they have owned it for two hundred years must be a mark of defeat and the thought of seeing it standing here empty day after day while I struggle on with a failing farm and an ailing bank account seems infinitely depressing. But Priscilla is amazing. She just turns her mind to the opening of the house and sees it as an enjoyable challenge rather than a miserable reverse. Or perhaps she's just trying to buoy me up. In any case we haven't yet decided exactly what to do in the end. Whatever happens, I suppose we'll have a furniture sale and that awful ass of a mouse from the auctioneers will be back again, delighted by my misfortune and twitching to get his hands on all my possessions.

# Annie's diary

I can't really make out what's going on at the moment. His Lordship seems to be in a bad mood all the time. Not at all his usual self and her Ladyship has barely spoken to me since Christmas. I was drawing her bath this morning and only asked her which dress she wanted ironed for this evening when she quite snapped my head off. I thought to myself, you don't have to talk to Annie Jerrold like that just because things aren't going your way, but I didn't say a word. I've got my own problems to dwell on, what with Father and one thing and another, and then there's Bert starting up all over again about getting married. If I had as many pounds in the bank as I have had proposals, I'd be a rich woman by now.

It was only the other day I wrote to Mr Johnson to thank him for his card and to tell him all the news. I simply hadn't had a minute to sit down and write before but I knew he would be glad to hear about his Lordship and perhaps even be quite surprised to learn that the family is still living in the big house. After all, it was never any secret that his Lordship was broke. 'Don't you realise, Annie, I'm stony b—y broke,' he always used to say from the very start. Anyway I couldn't help adding that Mr Johnson ought to be back here right now as we have had nothing but the grey drizzle he loves so much for the last three or four weeks. And him out there in all that sunshine. Never mind sunshine, I could do with it being a little less muddy under foot. And fancy them not having any elm trees in Australia. I can't imagine anywhere without elms.

Georgina was asking about Mr Rakowski the other day. I can't for the life of me think why she's got to be so interested in him, but she's forever wondering why he never comes here any more. I told her that I supposed he'd finished his book, not that that was a good enough reason for her. Now I don't mind admitting that I like Mr Rakowski and always have done. He was very nice to me and a perfect gentleman, not that I wanted to say anything to Georgina about his Lordship being so furious when he discovered about him knowing all about Mr Mason and not saying a word. I, for one, doubt we'll be seeing much more of Mr Rakowski in the future. As it was, I thought Georgina gave me a funny look and I wondered if she knew more than she should when she immediately said that she was very pleased Mr Mason had left. She says she hated him. I've told her not to go on about hating people but she says she doesn't care because she and Thomas and Jamie all hated him and he was disgusting. I'm not quite sure what she meant by that but I told her that none of them need think about him any more since he's gone now. All she says is, good riddance to bad rubbish.

Mr Marshall, the new butler, seems quite a nice man and his wife is a much friendlier person than Mrs Mason ever was. She asked me in for a cup of tea soon after they arrived and told me all about her family.

## Zbigniew Rakowski's notebook

FEBRUARY 14TH

Ah me! I note the date: Saint Valentine's Day! The day on which, according to ancient legend, every bird 'chooseth a mate', for neither Valentine the bishop nor Valentine the priest, holy martyrs and wise men both, manifested, in so far as we can tell from the relevant hagiography, the slightest concern for worldly passion or romantic love. I too have finally turned my back on such things for what use is it to me now to dream of hyacinth eyes and fine aristocratic looks, to ache for witty repartee, to yearn for rabbit pie? These things are not for me. Priscilla has made it quite clear that I have served my purpose, that in the end I have not pleased her and she no longer has any use for the funny, ageing little Pole who used to come to Cranfield and talk to her about literature, praise her good taste and laugh so gaily at her wit. Thus, mortified by what I now see as an old man's gullibility, have I consigned a once-precious bundle of letters senselessly tied up in hyacinth-blue ribbon to the flames.

I have finished my book and my publishers have not refrained from badgering me continuously to know what I will write about next. Before Christmas my spirits were so low that I never envisaged putting pen to paper again, but now I feel my own gloom, rather than being reinforced by the gloom of an English February, has gradually turned to scorn and from scorn it is but one short step to anger.

My daughter came fleetingly as usual for Christmas and, as I had predicted, attempted to 'cheer me up' with little anecdotes about her life in the north, about her neighbours and their imperfections. I enquired of her, not without a measure of sarcasm which I fear she did not detect, how it felt to be the only sane person in her village. My daughter bears, I fear, a strong resemblance to her late mother. The late Mrs Rakowski was a dour woman, pretty enough and demure in youth, whose limited imagination was responsible for her turning as the years passed into a narrow-minded, puritanical person, addicted to her religion and profoundly contemptuous of the foibles and weaknesses of her fellow beings. Thus she found her cantankerous husband, whose writing she rarely read, a trial, and her daughter an irksome duty. After a long illness, bravely borne as they say, she was relieved to shuffle off this mortal coil and to die in the odour of sanctity. To this day many is the rosary said by my daughter with a view to shortening the duration of her mother's stay in Purgatory and hastening her arrival in the land of milk and honey, there, I suppose, to take her place among the congregation of saints from whence she will look down at those less fortunate than herself, confirmed in the rightness of her belief that the greedy, the mean and the adulterous should perish, or like Dante's Paolo and Francesca, be buffeted about eternally in a stinking wind that keeps them forever apart. The late Mrs Rakowski, as I learnt to my cost, was nothing if not uncompromising.

It was not, however, without a flicker of pleasure, that I noticed for the first time a streak of rebellion in my young granddaughter, the which, I cannot but surmise, must denote an awakening intelligence and a desire to question some of her mother's assumptions, not to mention the platitudes that spring so readily from her father's lips.

The child went so far as to display a certain curiosity with regard to the scribblings of her old grandfather, and so fired was her imagination by the no more than pallid description of Cranfield and its inhabitants with which I regaled her, that she repeatedly requested further information as to the lives of the children, the age of the house, the size of the rooms, the pictures on the walls. No admonition from her parents who, showing no interest whatsoever in the subject themselves, pressed her to refrain from asking so many questions, could silence her. She desired even to know my opinion with regard to the rights and wrongs of people living in such large houses in these post-war days of hardship. Equality, she informed me, was what the war had been all about. She then went on to declare with what I deemed to be an incipient and indeed precocious revolutionary zeal, that the fathers of some of the children with whom she is at school are unemployed.

For once, I am forced to admit, that number one Robin Hood Way felt disagreeably empty after the three of them had left. Not that my son-in-law's departure could ever be anything but a solace to me. The man, a tax collector whose every utterance is greeted with nods of approval by his unquestioning wife, is both opinionated and preternaturally ignorant, and it is therefore a sorry truth indeed that neither my daughter nor her dreary husband could ever be in possession of the wherewithal to 'cheer me up' in the slightest degree, but I am forced and certainly happy to admit that where they failed, my admirable little granddaughter succeeded. The child has come a long way from being the silent, pallid creature I remember and I shall henceforth look forward to seeing how she is to develop.

So with the young lady and her cheerless parents back in the no doubt equally cheerless north, and provoked by the memory of the child's most pertinent questions, I have sat brooding, nay pondering on my experiences at Cranfield over the last few years. I have considered every aspect of my relationship to the house which I will always hold in deepest affection and to the family with whom I became so defencelessly involved. Alone in my front room in Robin Hood Way I have castigated myself out loud for the folly whereby I permitted myself during those years to lose all judgement, to abandon reason and to dream. And that, all for the love of a lady . . . Priscilla is undoubtedly a fine woman in many ways; legion will be those who have fallen, or will fall for her charms, beguiled by her wit and dazzled by her looks, as indeed was I, yet I am firmly of the opinion that at some point it behoves realism and rationality to take romanticism by the hand so as to lead it resolutely away. For me that moment has now come. And as I suggested earlier, scorn is but a short step away from anger. I fear that scorn has, not unnaturally, resulted from my contemplation of Priscilla's high-handed behaviour whereby, true to the traditions of a *grande dame* such as I fear she considers herself to be, she has taken me, a poor humble foreigner, squeezed all the juices from my soul and thrown away the husk.

Lord Otterton, on the other hand, I regard as a likeable, engaging scallywag, a ribald man, a chancer, what-you-will, an indisciplined person not to be taken too seriously on any level. I am told that he fought bravely in the war, the which I do not hesitate to believe and for which reason I am bound to admire him. Originating, as I do, from a country which for generations has been fought over, divided and subjected to the whims of its predatory neighbours, I would be the first to hail the intrepid man who fights for his country's freedom and certainly I have no reason to doubt Lord Otterton's considerable courage, not to say his daring, even his bravado. It would hardly surprise me if his experiences of war, culminating as they did in prison, had not made him unable or unwilling to adjust to the humdrum demands of everyday life in peacetime. Not that his life strikes this humble observer as being of a notably humdrum nature, nor as one deserving sympathy. Whatever his privations may have been, he does not know and has never known, as my own poor dear father did, the rigours of total displacement, he has not suffered the loss of home, of country, of friends, nor has he had to abandon the daily use of his native tongue, a far more grievous wrench than it is commonly supposed to be. No, the Ottertons, despite whatever qualities they may possess, have, I fear, come to deserve my scorn.

Thus, as I sit twiddling my thumbs, has my mind returned to the little *divertissement* with which some years ago I fondly teased my brain. I have now taken from the drawer of my bureau the manuscript of that sometime tale of murder, adultery and betrayal, conceived, as it was, of an intelligence clouded with romantic dreams. Despite, or perhaps on account of my altered mood, it strikes me once more as being infinitely full of possibilities and, with this in mind, I have begun to rewrite it, to reshape it indeed according to my present pragmatic view of things. It is to be a humorous, not to say witty set piece, a precise account of life at Cranfield, incorporating all the drama, all the hatred, all the passion, all the weaknesses of the family who still, although who can guess for how long, inhabit that captivating place. Once again, as I pick up my pen, I feel the sap rise in me and the creative urge is reawakened.

# Annie's diary

I can't help worrying about Father's health. We had all hoped that with the winter nearly over he might begin to feel a bit better, but every time I go to see him, I feel he's spiralled down even further. He never complains of course, just the same as usual, but he's looking so tired and thin and his cough never lets up so that sometimes when he's gasping for breath, I think he's going to choke to death. Worst of all, he seems to have lost interest in the garden. It was all I could do on Sunday afternoon to persuade him to put his overcoat on and poke his nose out of doors just to take a look at the daffodils which were all in bud, and the japonica which was quite covered in bloom and which he's always loved. Mind you, I think he was quite pleased when I picked some of it and put it in a jug on the table in the kitchen for him. 'Japonica,' he said. 'Now that was always your mother's favourite shrub. "Promise of Spring" she used to call it.' Well it's only another week before the first day of Spring now, but you'd never believe it, not to see Father huddled over that dusty old coke fire. Other years he'd have been out and about, digging the garden, pruning his roses, anything but sit indoors with the mild weather we've been having these last few days.

Then there's his Lordship telling me that he can't afford to stay at Cranfield any longer, not that that entirely surprised me. 'Annie,' he says, 'we can't go on. I've tried to keep the show on the road but I'm afraid the party's over now.' Then he says no one knows yet so, 'don't go spreading it around.' See me spreading anything around. 'Now who on earth would I tell?' I asked him. He says, 'I think we'll go to the Dower House. You'll come too, won't you, Annie?' I told him it only seemed like yesterday that he was calling on me down at Father's, begging me to come to work for her

Ladyship, and there was me trying to get on with the ironing and that darned puppy was piddling all over the floor. I asked him what he was going to do with his *menagerie*. 'Oh,' he says, as bright as a button, 'take the animals with me of course.' I can picture her Ladyship's face when she sees all those parrots and the otter, not to mention the giant squirrel he's just been and bought, all moving house with her. She can't stand them as it is, and then the other day there was poor Georgina crying because the squirrel had bitten her. All his Lordship did was laugh and say it didn't hurt. I dare say it didn't really, but I wouldn't fancy being attacked by a huge great squirrel whether it came from India or not. I can't think what his Lordship wants with an Indian squirrel after all the trouble they've been having on the farm and in the kitchen garden trying to keep the ordinary grey squirrels down. I've told him that I for one am not going near the blasted creature, not for all the tea in China.

So what with this and that, it's hardly surprising if I haven't been sleeping much lately. For one thing, I know for sure that if we move out of Cranfield, it will only give Bert an excuse to go on at me again about getting married. I doubt he'll ever take no for an answer, but of course being in the Dower House won't be the same as living here. Not that I can make up my mind about anything until her Ladyship's said something to me and she hasn't said a word as yet. All the same, I couldn't help looking around my room this morning and thinking how I would miss it and particularly how I would miss the view from the window, out over the lawns and the park to the distant hills. I can spend hours just staring out of that window. Georgina who's always learning something by heart knows a poem about the sheep and cows, and us having no time to stand and stare. She laughs when I go on about it. I tell her it's just like me, I don't have half enough time to stand and stare and then she tells me the poem was written by a tramp. I should have thought he had plenty of time to stand and stare, if anyone did.

I wonder what will happen to Mr MacIntosh if we leave Cranfield. I'll miss Mr MacIntosh and I should think her Ladyship will too. As a matter of fact I expect we'll all miss Mr MacIntosh.

## *Sydney Otterton's diary*

The government was defeated in the Commons for the first time yesterday and it doesn't look as if it will be able to survive much longer. People can talk about nothing else although I have to admit that my mind has really been on other things. We've at last made the firm decision to move to the Dower House in June, taking Annie with us I hope.

I was rather surprised by Annie's reaction to leaving Cranfield. She knows I haven't got a brass bean to my name, but it made her very cross when I told her we would definitely have to go. Then when Priscilla talked to her she was apparently quite huffy and announced that she wasn't saying what she would do. I'm sure she will come with us. For one thing, where else would she go? And for another, she's got her father here. Poor old Jerrold, I fear he may not be long for this world. Then there's Bert too of course.

There can be no doubt about the hold the house has on us all. Everyone's unhappy about the turn of events, even Georgina was in tears when Priscilla told her we were leaving. She says she doesn't like the Dower House at all. In fact she says she hates it. In a way, I've felt much better about moving since our plans became more definite and since we made them known publicly. Although to begin with I played with the idea of going right away to Shropshire or somewhere, I'm glad Priscilla convinced me of the folly of that line of action. I need to be near London, not only for the House of Lords, but for the Regiment too, that is, so long as I remain with it. I also happen to know that I couldn't in fact really bear to be far from Cranfield which is after all where I belong, if any of us belongs anywhere. It was just that at one point I found the idea of living here, but not in the house, unbearable as if it would have been a daily reminder of my inability to manage my own affairs with any degree of competence at all.

We're going to hold another sale before we go, but we'll do it through Sotheby's this time, and then we're planning to open the house to the public. Priscilla is full of how I'd be too illiterate to write a guide book, so she intends to do it herself which suits me because I'm quite sure she's right and that she'll do it far better than I could. She's also very busy thinking of how to do up the Dower House and talking about getting Miss Wheel back on board to make the curtains. In a way it's all quite exciting. I'm thinking of building a large aviary in the garden for some of my birds which Priscilla says is a waste of money. She didn't think it very funny when I told her that my motto has always been, 'Spend your way out!' Anyway, as I said, we'll be saving money on so many things when we do move, like not hiring some bloody fool to wind the clocks once a week, that I don't see why I shouldn't have an aviary.

Then we rather changed the subject because she suddenly wanted to know what on earth we were going to do about those damn letters from that frightful fellow, Pink. In fact I hadn't given them a thought for months. Not since Priscilla locked them away in her safe. Anyway, she rather flew off the handle, saying that before I spent my way into the debtors' gaol, she would like to know what to do about those blackmailing letters. She said she'd been thinking about them lately and that it bothered her having them in her safe. She wanted to be shot of them, certainly before the move, and as far as she was concerned she had finally come to the conclusion that the best possible thing to do with them was to send them to my mother, care of her bank. We would probably never hear another word about them and at least the ball would be in my mother's court where it belonged. And, talking about balls and courts, Priscilla may think my aviary is a waste of money but she's full bent on having a tennis court at the Dower House. I expect she will get her way. Not that I ever intend to play tennis. The last time I went anywhere with a tennis racquet was when I smuggled some love-birds back to England from Australia before I was married. All the way home on the boat I kept them in a tennis-ball box with holes punched in the side and when we reached Southampton I swanned off the boat with the box tied to a racquet as if I were Fred Perry himself. No one asked any questions.

In the end I told Priscilla to do what she liked with those letters. I don't want to have to think about them and wish to God we'd never found them, so I suppose she will send them off to my mother which may, as she suspects, mean that we never hear any more about them, or it may create one hell of a shindy. She is convinced that if we either burn them or keep them we'll never be shot of interference from my mother who, she says, must have been looking for the letters all this time. Why else, Priscilla wants to know, did she come here that time when we were away, and why was she always trying to pay people to snoop on us? She must have known of the existence of the letters and have been living in dread lest they were found.

## *Georgina's exercise book*

It is very sad because we have got to leave Cranfield. When Mummy told me I cried and she said not to be silly because it didn't matter to me but it does and I do *not* want to go. Jamie and I wont have anywhere decent to hide from the grown-ups in the horrid old Dower House which is a silly house

296

anyway with gohsts in it I bet. And Thomas will be absolutely furious because he thinks he's going to live here when Father's dead and turn me and Jamie out. No one is at all pleased. I'm sure Annie wants to stay because she looked really sorry when I asked her what she thought. She's not happy anyway because her father had to go to hospitle today and he's very ill. I may have to go to boarding school after we move which is another thing I do *not* want to do, but Mummy says children always have a wonderful time and they have no idea what grown-ups have to put up with. It seems to me that grown-ups always do what they want like moving house whenever they feel like it and dragging the poor children behind them. I don't think Father really wants to go but he says he's going to build a special aviery for the birds at the new house and he's looking forward to that. I hope we don't have to take that vile squirrel which bit me with us. But I suppose we will.

## *Extract from Zbigniew Rakowski's work in progress*

*How fondly did the beautiful Hyacinth imagine herself to be a liberal and intelligent woman unfettered by the customary assumptions, not to say prejudices of her class. With her beauty and natural wit, it was in truth not impossible for her to persuade those of lesser birth or lesser understanding that she was indeed what she wished to appear, a generous-hearted, open-minded Renaissance princess. Yet she ruled her stately home with a rod of iron and, it was she, rather than her jocose if irascible, nay volatile husband who, like the Queen in* Alice in Wonderland, *dispensed justice, mercilessly banishing old favourites, beheading, so to speak, the innocent, promoting the vain and treacherous, ever confident in the rightness of her own judgement. It was hardly surprising then, that there were those of her entourage who would gladly plot her downfall, even some of those closest to her might have wished to be rid of this turbulent high-priestess . . .*

## Letter from Annie to her sister Dolly

Dear Dolly

You left so soon after the funeral yesterday that what with one thing and another I hardly had a chance to see you, but I did want to say how glad I was that you were able to get over to see Father before he passed away. He went very peacefully and I am sure it was a blessed release for him even though I feel that nothing will ever be the same again. I've spent so much time with him, particularly recently, that I know I will miss him terribly. I was very fond of Father.

Of course I knew there was bound to be trouble from Bert. Can you believe it, but he has already decided that he would like to move into Father's cottage! What a cheek, I thought to myself, even though I'll grant you that it's much nicer than his own. No doubt he would like to have me there with him, but what with the Ottertons moving out of the big house in June, I have other things to think about. Her Ladyship goes on at me about going with them to the Dower House. We'll see, is all I have told her for the moment.

I'll be going up to the churchyard at the week-end to see to the grave.

Give my love to Fred and the children.

Love from
Annie


## Sydney Otterton's diary

APRIL 15TH

The British Legion do in the village last night was full of nosy buggers wanting to know every damn thing about our move.

Old Doubleday and one or two others were overflowing with disingenuous sympathy for my impecunious state, blaming the Labour government, but no doubt behind my back rubbing their hands in glee at the thought of my misfortunes. Somehow the news has got about that next year we are planning to open the house to the public and three quarters of the retired majors in the Home Counties want to be at the door with their wives selling tickets and showing the *hoi polloi* around, whilst commiserating with me about the horrors of letting the public into one's home. It took the wind out of their sails when I told them I was rather looking forward to it.

It's only a few weeks now before we move and, funnily enough, I've very quickly become accustomed to the idea. We've been spending a good deal of time going round the house and choosing what furniture and pictures to take with us and what to put in the sale. All the better and larger things will of course have to stay here to be put on show. The Dower House under Priscilla's aegis is beginning to look very nice indeed and it'll certainly be warmer and a great deal more comfortable than Cranfield is in our present circumstances. This morning we took the children to see how it was getting on and even Georgina was quite excited by the prospect of her new bedroom. The one she's in at the moment is certainly falling apart. The rain came in above her bed last winter and the wallpaper which must have been put up at least fifty years ago has almost come away from one wall. Thomas was quite happy too. And so he bloody well ought to be since Priscilla has seen to it that he has one of the nicest rooms.

And it's perfectly true that the whole idea (which I didn't find at all appealing at first) of opening the house has begun to take quite a hold with me. After all we won't be the first people to do it, and as far as I can see, it's just another way of keeping the roof on the bloody thing.

Old Jerrold was buried on Monday and there wasn't a dry eye in the place. He was part of my childhood and a thoroughly good fellow for whom I had a great deal of affection. I will miss him and will certainly feel that Cranfield won't be the same without his quiet wisdom and watchful eye. Priscilla had a soft spot for him too and keeps claiming that he was very good-looking. You could have fooled me. He had a nice, friendly face, but as far as I was concerned, he was just a very decent country sort of man and a damn good cowman.

Annie, not surprisingly, has clammed up and is very unhappy so it's no good asking her about her plans at the moment. 'I was always very fond of me father,' she told me yesterday in an understatement typical of her. And that's about as far as she will commit herself. Priscilla, who has now decided that Annie is tremendously insular and would never ever want to go abroad, was once afraid that she might run off to Australia with Johnson, not that I ever thought she would leave here as long as Jerrold was alive. In fact not long ago she told me that the one thing she would like to do if she won the football pools, would be to travel. She'd particularly like to go to Italy. Why Italy, I have no idea. Anyway Priscilla obviously hasn't got it quite right for once.

I still think Annie will stay with us in the end, although she may easily decide to move in with Bert and marry him. Poor old Jerrold was hardly cold in his grave before Bert formed up to me to say he wanted Jerrold's cottage, which was what made me think he and Annie might be planning to get married. I wouldn't have put it past Annie to have told Bert all along that she wouldn't marry him until after her father died. For one thing she would never have put up with living where Bert is now. Annie quite likes her creature comforts. Priscilla always says that Annie's room is warmer and more comfortable than her own. In any case I can't really see why she shouldn't look after herself. If she doesn't no one else will. Anyway I haven't made up my mind what to do about Bert yet which may in a way rather depend on what Annie decides to do.

Priscilla finally got me to send those bloody letters to my

mother. I just enclosed a note with them to say that they had turned up and that I would be grateful if she would be so kind as to return them to Batty. Not surprisingly, I haven't heard a word, but at least I suppose my mother may now decide to leave us alone, although half of me feels that we should have burnt the wretched things and been done with them. I rather think Priscilla, who's always got an eye for a story, still has a sneaking curiosity about the whole Pink/Batty saga and longs to know the truth of it. For all the high-faluting literature she reads, I've often caught her with her nose in a Margery Allingham or a Raymond Chandler.

## Annie's diary

It's hard to believe that it's already a month since poor Father died. I don't think I'll ever get used to his not being here. I'm always thinking about him and about how he was in days gone by when he was young and fit. It was different when Mother went somehow because for one thing there was Father then and for another, I didn't have time to think about anything then but getting along on and looking after the family. I certainly never had time to stand and stare. Not like the sheep and cows. I don't like going down to Father's place now, although I've had to go and tidy up his things. And I certainly don't fancy living there with Bert. Bert gets on my nerves the way he always thinks he'll be able to make me do whatever he wants in the end so long as he wants it badly enough. Well, all I can say is that he doesn't know Annie Jerrold if that's what he thinks. I decided to drop Mr Johnson a line just so as to let him know about Father. Now I always thought Mr Johnson a very nice man and I know he liked Father. He and Father got on very well together.

I also thought Mr Johnson would be interested to know

how the move was coming along and I'm certain he'd like
to hear all about the family and about Mr MacIntosh.
Mr MacIntosh was talking to me only yesterday morning.
They'd all just come back from church and were in the
saloon. I was looking for his Lordship because one of his
parrots was out of its cage, sitting on a gilt picture frame up
there in his dressing-room, attacking it with its beak. It was
making a dreadful mess. Anyway I think his Lordship must
have been reading the lesson because there he was, prancing
up and down laughing and going on about Nebuchadnezzar
and a burning fiery furnace and her Ladyship was telling him
not to be foolish and Georgina was giggling and then he
started to recite some rhyme which her Ladyship said was
unsuitable for children. Of course I wasn't paying a blind bit
of attention, I'd only come to say about the parrot. Then
just as I was leaving the room, Mr MacIntosh came over
and asked me how I was. He said I must be missing Father.
He's ever so kind, is Mr MacIntosh. Anyway, he then went
on about how sad all these changes were, and leaving
Cranfield was like the end of an era. He'd loved living
here, he said, but he was looking forward to his new cottage
in the village. I've got an idea that it's one of his Lordship's
he's bought. He said I was to make sure and go and see him
there when he's settled in, which I most certainly will, if I'm
still here.

I haven't yet said anything to her Ladyship about staying
on indefinitely although she will keep telling me about the
bedroom I'm to have at the Dower House, which I have to
say is very nice although of course it doesn't have the view.
To my mind neither she nor his Lordship seems to think that
there is anywhere else I could go. Well, we shall see about
that. I haven't said a word about Bert and Father's cottage
even though his Lordship was trying to sound me out about
it the other day. I said to his Lordship, 'It's your cottage, you
must do as you please with it.' I thought to myself then that it
was a darned good thing I knew how to mind my p's and q's.

I don't know what he's going to do about Bert and I've no idea who else he might want to put in that cottage.

## *Georgina's exercise book*

Yesterday afternoon I was just mucking about down by the lake after school when I saw this really spooky person. When I told Mummy about her, she said I was being silly because the public footpath goes past the lake so there's nothing odd about anyone being down there. I still thought this woman was spooky. She was very old and ugly and she gave me a vile look. I didn't want to talk to her because she gave me the creeps but when she gave me this vile look she said something about 'I'm on an erand child.' I hate people who call you child. We're not alloud to call them woman. I don't know what she was doing. I wish Jamie or Thomas had been there. I told Annie about her but she just said not to worry. These days Annie's in a bad mood and doesn't talk nearly so much. She probably doesn't want to move and nor do I but Mummy's made my new room look pretty so I suppose it will be all right in the end. I'm aloud to choose the wallpaper and I'm having some of the stuff out of my old room. I began to sort of exagerate a bit about that spooky woman to make Mummy believe me but I think she just decided I'd made the whole thing up. Perhaps it was a gohst but I think it looked too sort of solid.

# Letter from Zbigniew Rakowski to Priscilla Otterton

1 Robin Hood Way
MAY 26TH, 1950

Dear Priscilla,

It is not without considerable misgivings that I tremblingly submit for your and Lord Otterton's generous scrutiny the enclosed humble offering, the fruit of my protracted labours at Cranfield. How sincerely do I hope that you will look charitably on these pages and that in them Lord Otterton will be pleased to recognise some of the more picturesque members of his family into whom I have attempted to breathe new life. I hope that it will not be with a jaundiced eye that he views the juxtaposition of saint and scoundrel and that both you and he will derive at least some pleasure from the perusal of this volume.

To work at Cranfield was as great a pleasure as it was a privilege, its beauty will perpetually nourish my imagination and I shall forever cherish my remembrance of the place. It was with a great sense of doom that I learned of your intention to abandon it to trippers, but I now take this opportunity to wish you every success as you venture to open your exquisite house to what I fear may prove to be an undeserving public.

It remains only for me to thank you both for the notable forbearance with which you permitted me to pore over the Cranfield archives and for the generosity with which you so graciously extended your hospitality to a lonely old pen pusher, one who is now engaged in the writing of a mere novel which dwells, with, I pray not too heavy a hand, on the darker side of human nature.

I remain, humble chronicler of the Otterton family
yours most sincerely
Z.A.R.

# *Sydney Otterton's diary*

For some reason which I don't understand I have started having nightmares again. I had begun to think that I had got over them, but I've had some horrible ones recently. Last night I dreamt we were landing in Salerno Bay, except of course it wasn't Salerno Bay as I remember it, it was more like Woolacombe and my legs had been shot from under me so I couldn't think how I was going to run up the beach. Then of course I woke up in a dreadful sweat. In fact when we did get to Salerno in real life, I and another young officer had a lucky escape. We'd landed under cover of darkness and were horrified when dawn broke to see the destruction around us. Village after village had been reduced to rubble and as we progressed we came across huge numbers of dispossessed and wounded civilians, men and women, old and young, and there were everywhere piles of dead cattle and horses, lying on their backs, killed by the shelling. Anyway, just after breakfast I was sent out with this other fellow to reconnoitre and after a few miles we found a blown-up bridge where the pair of us came under a salvo of German artillery fire. We dived for cover and crept back, I can't imagine how, to where I had left my driver in the scout car, fully expecting to discover that he'd been blown up. In fact he too had, by some miracle, been missed and had accelerated back to take cover round a bend in the road. Despite the passage of time, these images still haunt me and I imagine they always will.

Anyway everyone else is pretty cheerful this morning what with the sun shining for the Whitsun week-end and petrol rationing ending at the same time. People have been queuing at the garages since before midnight so I should imagine the whole world will be on the roads over the Bank Holiday.

I have a niggling feeling of unease somehow connected to

my mother and Pink and Batty and the fact that I haven't heard so much as a squeak since we sent off those letters. I don't really see why we should have heard anything, but instinctively I feel that such a shock as they must have given my mother (assuming her to have received them) would have provoked some kind of reaction from her – if only rage and, as is common knowledge, she's not one to keep her anger to herself.

This morning's post brought a copy of Rakowski's book, dedicated to Priscilla and enclosing an unctuous letter to her of course. I thought it rather lacked his usual humour but he's probably still feeling hard done by or uncomfortable about the bloody silly way he carried on. The book looks all right and is decently illustrated with a few well-chosen pictures of the house, the Speaker and so forth. Priscilla has requisitioned it for the moment and seems quite to have forgiven Rakowski his sins. She's decided that the old fool is just a bit of an ass, that he wasn't really thinking about what he was doing and that we ought to take a lenient view considering the trouble he went to over the book. For all I know she'll be asking him back for lunch again before long. That's all right by me. I hold no grudges even though it may strike me that there remain a couple of things he has manifestly failed to explain.

## Annie's diary

A funny thing happened yesterday afternoon just as I was coming back from seeing Bert. It must have been about half past four and as it was such a lovely day, I thought that instead of walking straight up the drive, I'd go the long way round, down through the field to the lake, over the bridge and up the path to the house. There's a dreadful blanket of duckweed on the lake so that it hardly looks as if there's any water in it at all, but there must be because I saw a heron standing on a bit of old tree that's fallen across the surface and, as Father would have told anyone, where there's a heron there are sure to be fish. So I was simply standing there, just like the sheep and cows, staring at the heron, wondering about the fish swimming about down there under all that weed and thinking what a shame it was that his Lordship would probably never be able to afford to drain the lake and clean it out. As it is you can only walk along one side of it at the moment. The other side where the old boathouse is, is completely overgrown with bamboo and elder and brambles, you'd barely know there had ever been a path there. In fact you can scarcely see where the boathouse is any more because it's almost hidden behind what look like giant rhubarb leaves. It must have all been so different years gone by when there were dozens of gardeners and no doubt swans and lilies on the lake as well. Anyway I was just looking at that darned heron when I suddenly noticed something sticking up out of the water underneath the branch on which he was standing. Blow me down if it didn't look exactly like a lady's shoe. Then I thought it must be a bit of old wood stuck at a funny angle, not that I could be quite sure, but as there was no means by which I could have got round to the other side, I just stood as close to the edge as I dared and squinted at this thing from across the water. Of course I couldn't see it very well, but I'd eat my hat if that wretched bit of wood didn't turn out to be someone's shoe in the end. Anyway there it was for all the world to see, pointing up through the duckweed some of which clung to it in greenish streaks. I was just wondering how in the devil's name it got there when there was a rustling in the undergrowth behind where the boathouse is and a trembling in the bamboos as if they'd been caught by a sudden gust of wind. Well there certainly wasn't a breath of wind yesterday. I can vouch for that. In fact it was so warm that I'd taken my cardigan off and was carrying it over my arm. To be honest I felt a bit nervous, almost as if I'd seen a ghost. Anyway the heron must have felt the same because it suddenly rose from the branch and flapped away towards the lower lake which, if you ask me, is in even worse condition than the upper one. To be perfectly frank it's no more than a swamp now.

As I walked on up to the house I tried to put what had happened out of my mind and began to think about the move which is only a couple of weeks away now. The house looks ever so grand standing above you against the dark trees as you come up from the lake below and I suddenly felt really sad at the thought of leaving it. Not that I'll be going far yet as I've agreed to start off at the Dower House with her Ladyship and just see how it goes. His Lordship was overjoyed when he heard I'd decided to stay, for a while at least, I said. 'Neither of us would be any good without you, Annie,' he said.

It was lovely and cool inside the house and I was on my way up to my room when I came across Georgina sitting cross-legged in a corner on the half landing with her nose in a book. I was surprised to see her because her Ladyship was supposed to have gone to collect her from school and take her to buy some new shoes. 'My Good Lord,' I said to her. 'I wasn't expecting you back so early and now you'll be wanting your tea.' Well her Ladyship had fetched her from school but had decided against going shopping so they'd come straight home. Georgina explained all this, and then gave me quite a turn by saying that as she'd supposed I was at the farm she'd started to walk down the drive to meet me but had got scared, as she put it, because she'd seen some peculiar woman coming up onto the drive from the overgrown side of the lake. So she'd run back to the house to hide. I couldn't make head or tail of what she was talking about at first, but she can be quite obstinate and was absolutely full bent on telling me that she'd seen this woman snooping around the lake before. As a matter of fact I do remember her saying something of the sort a little while back but I didn't take much notice at the time. Anyway this time I wanted to know what that woman looked like, but all Georgina could tell me was that she was very old and very ugly and rather frightening. I never mentioned a word about the wind in the bamboos mind, but I did say that she really must tell his Lordship or her Ladyship, especially now she's seen this person twice. She says she told her Ladyship the first time and her Ladyship said she was imagining things, so she doesn't want to say any more, besides which she seems to think she'll get into some sort of trouble. What for, I can't make out, but then Georgina always thinks she's going to get into trouble for nothing.

As a matter of fact I wondered if the woman she'd seen might be the wife of the mad cowman we had for a while after Father retired, come back to pester us. I reckon she was pretty well as strange as her husband, that Mrs Wilkins, but I don't suppose the pair of them remained locked up for all that long. Or perhaps she has escaped from the asylum. But of course I didn't say any of that to Georgina because I didn't want to frighten her any more. I have decided though, that if she won't tell her parents, I will certainly have to say something myself. We don't want lunatics roaming around the place just when we're moving. And we don't want another burglary either, thank you very much.

### Georgina's exercise book

I saw that horrible spooky woman again this afternoon. Annie says I've got to tell Mummy and Father but I think they'd just say I was silly. Mummy wasn't intrested when I told her the first time. The witch woman gave me another vile look just like last time but she didn't say anything because

I ran away too soon. I think Annie was a bit frightened when I said she'd been snooping about down by the lake but she would *not* admit it. She just kept saying, 'Now then Georgina you tell your parents what happened.' And Annie will *not* say who she thinks this ugly woman is or what she thinks she's doing. I think she could be a kidnapper but as Father says he hasn't got any money he'll never be able to pay the ransom. I bet I'm going to have nightmares now.

## *Sydney Otterton's diary*

Bert found my mother's body on Saturday morning. Apparently Annie had been talking to him about a shoe she thought she'd seen in the lake. Something about the way she went on about it made him curious, so as soon as he'd finished milking the cows that morning he went along to investigate. Now I expect the poor blighter wishes that he'd never been near the place. I suspect that no one had been near the lake for a couple of days, during which time the body had somehow floated right up against the bank and it was lying there half exposed when Bert found it. All I can say is thank the Lord Georgina never found it. She's always playing down by the lake. The police came and I had the unpleasant task of having to identify the body which they say must have been in the water for two or three days. Now there's going to be a hell of a lot of trouble. For one thing there obviously has to be a post-mortem so we can't yet arrange a funeral, and for another there are going to be a great many questions which will have to be answered.

I am of the opinion that my mother did herself in, possibly as a consequence of receiving the Pink letters, or perhaps for some other reason of which we are unaware, but then both Annie and Georgina swear that there was someone else involved. Georgina actually saw a woman near the lake on Thursday afternoon whom she describes as old and ugly and on that same day Annie thought not only that she saw a woman's shoe poking out of the water but also that someone was moving about in the bamboos behind the boathouse. That naturally had to be told to the police, which of course means that we are now all about to be involved in a possible murder enquiry. But it goes without saying that if my mother did decide to kill herself she would, without any question of doubt, have chosen to do so in the way most calculated to cause us the maximum possible distress.

The worst of it is that I can't see how I can avoid telling the police about the letters. If I honestly thought I could get away with it, I'd say nothing. None of us wants all that horror from the past dragged up, what with the stuff about the dead baby and so forth. But on the other hand, if Batty killed my mother, I don't see why I should let her get away with it. I loathed my mother, but that isn't a reason for allowing that filthy bitch to murder her. Priscilla thinks we'll all be under suspicion but, as I told her, I at least should be off the hook. I can hardly have killed my mother for gain since, not surprisingly, it appears she's left all her money to a cats' home. She told me long ago that that was her intention and my lawyers are in possession of a letter informing me that I have no expectations from her. Not that that has prevented the police from giving me a pretty unpleasant grilling and I don't doubt that there will be more of the same before we're through. All the servants have to be questioned and all the farm workers. Poor innocent Bert has been given a dreadful time and the only one that seems to have disappeared into thin air is Batty.

Priscilla in fact is absolutely furious about the whole thing which, rather untypically, she sees as an evil omen for our move. 'All the same,' I heard her say to Annie, 'as far as my mother-in-law is concerned, she won't be any loss.' 'Well no one was very fond of *that* Lady Otterton,' Annie replied.

For some reason best known to herself Annie thinks that the woman Georgina saw must have been the mad cowman's wife, but although Georgina isn't much good at describing her, I'm still convinced it was Batty. I can't think of any reason why Mrs Wilkins would want to come back and haunt us.

Bert really has been given a thorough going-over by the police when all he's done is to come across a dead body floating in the duckweed and come up here as green as grass to raise the alarm. I was in the bath when he arrived. Apparently he was out there for ages, banging at the back door, ringing the bell and hollering for help. Marshall eventually heard the din, let him in and brought him up to the hall. Then I think Annie heard something going on. I suppose she heard Bert's voice and must have wondered what on earth he was doing here at that time, so she went down to see what in God's name the shindy was about. By the time I got to him, the wretched fellow was sitting on a hall chair with his head in his hands, shaking from head to foot and saying he'd never seen the like of it in all his born days. It took me a moment or two to make out what it was he had seen and I have to say that when he told me, I was at first quite unable to take it in. All I could think of in some sort of totally irrelevant way, was that after all this I'd have to let the fellow have Jerrold's cottage if that was what he really wanted, and that that would mean having to spend a bit of money on his because I can't imagine anyone else being prepared to live in it as it is.

In any case, we're all in some bloody awful sort of limbo at the moment, waiting, as far as I can see, for the police to lay hands on Batty. The sooner they find her the better.

## Georgina's exercise book

The grown-ups didn't want me to know about Grandmama being drowned in the lake but they had to tell me which was sucks to them because this police woman wanted to ask me about that creepy old witch I saw. I think the witch probably murdered Grandmama but Annie says I've no bisness saying such things. The grown-ups are going about with very long faces and always stopping talking when they see me. And Mummy just keeps saying 'pas devan' which she thinks I can't understand but I can. So this police woman was very nice and she kept on asking me what the witch looked like and what colour was her hair and stuff like that and then she said she didn't want me to be upset. Actualy it's very exciting!! I wish Jamie and Thomas were here but I heard Mummy say the other day something about it being just as well the boys were at school. I hate the way grown-ups always think children are a nuissance.

## Annie's diary

Father wasn't a man of many words but, if he said it once, he said it a hundred times that Lilian, Lady Otterton meant trouble. If you ask me he never liked her from the word go and I think he felt quite sorry for his late Lordship having to put up with her. Now fancy her choosing to go and drown herself in the lake just now, what with us all busy moving out of the house, and her Ladyship's having so much on her plate and his Lordship with plenty of things to think about. I reckon she did it on purpose just to spite them. I think it would be a darn good thing if the police could find Miss

Batty and get the whole thing sorted out once and for all. I reckon that woman knows what happened. Then perhaps the rest of us might be given a little bit of peace and quiet. There's Mrs Marshall up there in the butler's flat, she's quite indignant, saying that when Mr Marshall took the job here he was supposed he was coming to work for a respectable family, he certainly hadn't expected to be questioned like a common criminal. I thought to myself, oh Lord, they'll be off again before you can say Jack Robinson and his Lordship will be looking for another caretaker. The police have been all over the place for days now. It's much worse than when we had the burglary.

You can't help feeling sorry for Bert. It was such a dreadful shock finding her Ladyship's body like that. He's really shaken up still and has been questioned over and over again by the police. As if Bert would go pushing anyone into the lake! And if he did, where would be the sense in his rushing up to the house to tell us all about it? Mind you, I've no idea what took him down there in the first place. He says it was something to do with my talking to him about a shoe and the wind in the bamboos which made him wonder what had been going on, but really, I think it was just that it was a nice fine morning so once he'd finished with the cows, he felt like a bit of a walk. It's beautiful at that time of day with no one about, and peaceful, especially down by the lake. I expect he went there almost automatically, never mind the shoe. Come to that, it chills my bones just thinking of that there shoe and of me only standing on the bank in the sunshine with my cardigan over my arm and not knowing what on earth I was looking at. His Lordship's convinced Miss Batty was involved and I have to admit now that it was probably her that Georgina saw on the drive. I don't know why I was so set on its being Mrs Wilkins.

# Sydney Otterton's diary

They've done the autopsy and established that death was by drowning so at least we can bury my mother now. There'll have to be an inquest of course and I suppose the verdict will be accidental death. There's been no suicide note and no sign of Batty for the moment, not that I imagine she will find it very easy to lie low for long. She may well have killed my mother but how can we ever know? I turn the thing over and over in my mind, sometimes feeling relieved that my mother is dead, sensing the removal of an enemy and of a whole area of spite directly mainly towards me, but I'm always appalled by the manner of her death and the uncertainty surrounding it, and yet in some sort of way I can almost feel sorry for her, which was something I never did when she was alive. Batty now surfaces in my dreams. I've seen her being taken prisoner with me after the Normandy Landings and I've seen my mother driving a Honey through the desert, searching the barren landscape for water to drown in, with hundreds of flies settling on her arms and her face. My God, will I ever be shot of these dreams?

In the midst of all this Marshall came to see me yesterday morning to give me his notice. He said that Mrs Marshall didn't care for what he referred to as the police presence in the house. I asked him who the bloody hell she expected to find in the house after a three-day-old corpse had been discovered in the lake. We were hardly likely to be entertaining King Farouk and Rita Hayworth. As he left the room and just as he was closing the door, he said, 'I can appreciate that you're upset, M'lord.' Patronising bugger. He had the nerve to add graciously that he'll stay until he finds another job. I never really thought he was much of a fellow. I gave myself a large gin and tonic after that.

According to Priscilla, Mrs Wilkins who came under

suspicion for some reason, is out of the bin and living with her children in a council house up the road. The husband's still inside but she's apparently perfectly all right, in which case she must have been a bit put out on coming back from visiting her mother in Basingstoke to find P.C. Plod on her doorstep, wanting to know if she'd killed my mother. I had to tell Annie. She's been convinced all along that Mrs Wilkins had something to do with it all. I can't think why unless it's because Bert whipped her up against the woman when she was wailing in the cottage next door to him. I imagine that it was only because Annie mentioned her to the police in the first place that they bothered to go looking for her.

JUNE 10TH

Batty's turned up at last. Stark staring mad, if you ask me. Thank the Lord Priscilla was here at the time. I don't know how the hell I would have dealt with her on my own. In fact Priscilla had just come back from the village shop and was taking her shopping out of the car round by the back door when she heard a kind of wail or whimper. She looked round and who in the devil's name should she find standing by her shoulder, but Batty. One thing about Priscilla is that, although she can get quite worked up about minor things and quite carried away at times, when there's any kind of real crisis she always manages to remain magnificently calm. She brought Batty into the house and met me crossing the hall with the dog. The undertaker had been to see me and I'd been showing him out. A bit of a Uriah Heep of a man who'd been full of unwelcome condolences, bowing and scraping and saying how sorry he was and it being not so many years since he had the honour of burying his late Lordship. I couldn't wait to get rid of the fellow.

Anyway the last thing I was expecting was to turn round and find Batty walking across the hall with Priscilla. In fact Batty, as if nothing untoward had occurred, stopped to admire the flowers Priscilla had arranged in the big vase on

316

top of that pillar in the hall. Very nice flowers, but I had no intention of standing and discussing roses with Batty, the woman I have most hated all my life. The mere fact of seeing that woman makes me feel queasy because she instantly evokes so much of the fear and horror of my childhood. I can still see the expression on her face when she used to take a birch to me or a belt, or whatever she thought would inflict most pain on a small child. But Priscilla said later that one look at her now was enough to make anyone realise that she had finally completely taken leave of her senses and whether or not she had been before, she was clearly now certifiable. Priscilla even went so far as to say that she could feel sorry for her because she was wandering around like a lost soul in hell. I told Priscilla she'd feel rather differently if she'd known her as I did.

Anyway the long and the short of it was that Priscilla called a doctor and the police and while we were waiting for them all to arrive, we managed to get the beginnings of an explanation from Batty about everything that has happened. It was difficult to make much sense of what she said because she became appallingly distressed whenever my mother's death was mentioned. I thought that must mean that she'd pushed her in the lake, but Priscilla, who fancies herself as an amateur psychologist, is convinced that the woman was in love with my mother and that with her dead, the bottom's fallen out of Batty's world.

## Letter from Annie to Dolly

JUNE 11TH, 1950

Dear Dolly,

I'm sorry I was unable to come up and see you last week-end but as you must have gathered, it's been one thing after another here what with Lilian, Lady Otterton falling in the lake and Miss Batty disappearing and poor Bert finding the body, and us being supposed to move house. The funeral is on Tuesday but it's not to be a big affair. Do you remember all the things we used to hear about Lilian and the way she carried on? Well I know we shouldn't speak ill of the dead, but I can't imagine his Lordship is going to miss her very much. Now no one can say I don't miss Father. I think of him every day that passes and there are all his roses blooming in his garden and him not here to see them. It breaks your heart.

Would you believe it now? Who should turn up yesterday but Miss Batty? And, if you ask me, there's more to it all than meets the eye. We haven't heard the end of it yet. You mark my words. Well her Ladyship called the police who'd been looking for her and they stayed here questioning her for hours, but then in the end she was taken away to the lunatic asylum.

I hope we will be able to get back to normal again once the funeral is over. There's going to be a lot to do what with all the packing up. We shall see what happens after that, but I will let you know as soon as I can get away to come and see you.

Give my love to Fred and the children.

Love from
Annie


## Zbigniew Rakowski's notebook

JUNE 10TH

If truth is to be my helmsman, I am forced to admit that it was not without the faintest tremor of excitement that I read in the press of the retrieval of Lilian, Lady Otterton's body from the weed-infested waters of Capability Brown's once limpid lake at Cranfield. What discovery could better have suited my mood just as I handed the finished manuscript of my little *divertissement* to my publishers? My publishers are not only delighted, but, dare I say it, tickled pink, by my new *œuvre*. It is full of lust and envy, hatred, guilt and pride, all couched in a veneer of exquisite refinement. The tale is a simple one of betrayal and murder, but told, I trust, in a vein such as to carry the reader light-heartedly on, whilst ever ensuring that beneath an apparently frivolous surface, there lies an awareness of the baseness that is mankind.

I deemed it only suitable that I should pen a line to Lord Otterton, to commiserate with him on the loss of his mother, but I was not able to distance myself from the remembrance of the manner in which he was wont to refer to that lady, under whose daunting portrait and disdainful eye I worked for so many contented hours. However I acquitted myself with a brief acknowledgement of the distress the circumstances must have afforded him, wished to be remembered to Priscilla and, at the same time thanked him for the kind words he had written to me on receiving *The Otterton Family*. I did not consider it suitable to inform him of my latest work which, *D.V.*, will be published in the Autumn. I fear that this little tease may not delight the Ottertons quite so much as did my lively and scholarly account of their eccentric ancestors. I can only hope that before they lay eyes on that little volume, I may have the opportunity of discovering the truth behind Lilian's death from her of the hyacinth eyes. Alone in my humble dwelling, many are the hours I spend pondering what might be the connection between those blackmailing letters that passed through my hands and the subsequent, recent, fearful events that are reported to have befallen at Cranfield. If I am not very much mistaken, her Ladyship has of late taken a more lenient view towards me and, appreciating, as she surely does, my interest in the family, she might, perhaps, even be so gracious, were we to meet, as to inform me of the outcome of the drama which has occurred.

## *Sydney Otterton's diary*

We buried my mother this morning in that bloody awful vault. There's only one place left in it now. For me I suppose. We took Thomas out from school but didn't think the other children needed to attend. Apart from ourselves, one cousin, Aunt Lettice, a couple of the older men from the farm and my mother's solicitor, there were one or two representatives of local organisations and that was all. Aunt Lettice said that as the door of the vault closed behind the coffin, she felt it was a blessed relief, not, as is usually the case, for the one who had died, but for those of us left behind. We went back to the house and had a few stiff drinks, then everyone left except for my cousin and Aunt Lettice who stayed for lunch. And that, I suppose, will be the last lunch party we ever hold at Cranfield. I felt like blubbing. Not for my mother but for the house. Next week we'll be in the Dower House.

Tomorrow morning I've got the local chief bobby coming to see me. He seems to think I'd like to know exactly what they managed to get out of Batty, which indeed I would. It sounds as though they're not going to charge her.

## *Letter from William Johnson to Annie Jerrold*

'Cranfield',
Coolgardie,
W. Australia
MAY 9TH, 1950

Dear Annie,

Thank you for your letter. I was very sorry to hear about your father. He was a good man and I had a great respect for him. You will miss him very much. I was also interested to hear the news about his Lordship. Please remember me to him. I often think about the war and all the good times we had together.

To go by what I hear the old country is in a bit of a mess at the moment so I think I did the right thing by coming here.

Now Annie, why didn't you write sooner? I waited a long time but I was lonely you see and I don't know how to put this, but when I met Sarah, she was lonely too. Her husband was killed a year ago in a mining accident and she was all on her own. They'd come from Yorkshire like me and it was nice to meet a lass from Yorkshire and talk about the places we both remembered. Sarah didn't have no children and I didn't have no one either, only you, and you said you would never come so Sarah and I got married Christmas time. You'd like Sarah. She keeps the bungalow nice and tidy and feeds me well. I think I've put on weight since we married.

I've still got the photo you gave me Annie, of you in your father's garden holding a great big bunch of daffodils and I'll never forget the jokes we used to have together and your laughing eyes.

Love from
Bill


*Sydney Otterton's diary*

The Chief Constable, a man with the good old-fashioned name of Wapshott, came to see me yesterday morning. Priscilla found him rather annoying because she said he was too smooth and too good-looking for his own good, but as far as I could see he was a perfectly reasonable fellow. I think she took against him because she decided he was arrogant. She also said he was delighted to be at Cranfield. I didn't see why he shouldn't be. It's a damn nice place and we won't be here for long now so he might as well have made the best of it. In any case, the man wasn't really that interesting. It was what he told us that really mattered. He was here for quite a long time and I think almost as amazed as we were by the whole sorry story.

The first thing he told us, which I have to admit rather took the wind out of my sails, was that within the next few days, they would be taking a team down to the lake to look for Pink's body which, if Batty is to be believed, lies there in a shallow grave. He then, to my considerable relief, announced that it was most unlikely there would be enough evidence of any kind to justify a charge of murder. The question arises as to whether Batty is or was criminally insane. Whether or not she is in any condition to be charged with manslaughter is another matter. It's not that I wish Batty well. In fact nothing would give me greater pleasure than to see her behind bars, but I think Wapshott and I both feel that some skeletons are best left in their cupboards. My mother's dead, Pink, it appears, is dead and Batty's locked up in a loony bin where she's likely to remain for some time. Of course Mason and Legros and various others of my mother's henchmen are still out and about but I can see very little reason why they would wish to return to haunt us now.

No one can be quite sure that Batty in her present condition is capable of telling, let alone recalling, the truth, but it appears that by the time she turned up here, dropped, as it happens, by Mason with whom she'd been in hiding since my mother's death, she was so confused and so indiscriminately angry with everyone, that she didn't mind what she said to anyone. Nevertheless, not surprisingly, it took them a long time to make much sense of what she was saying.

Funnily enough Priscilla was obviously on the right track about Batty because, according to the trick-cyclist at the bin, she had a pathological obsession with my mother whose death has consequently left her completely unhinged. Such was her obsession that she had difficulty in separating her thoughts and her actions from those of my mother. She seemed to think that the two of them were activated by one mind, all of which sounds pretty rum to me although, when I was a child, in a funny sort of way, I did see them as peculiarly united. I wouldn't be at all surprised if my father didn't feel the same.

As to the baby that died, there is some doubt as to whether Pink ever had any real evidence to suggest that either my mother or Batty had anything to do with its death. Batty swears that neither she nor *her Ladyship* would have ever done anything to harm what she apparently referred to as 'the mite'. Who knows? And who knows what gave Pink the idea that he could blackmail them? And why did they react as they apparently did to the blackmail unless they had something to hide? But I really didn't want to question Wapshott too closely about any of that. He, I suspect, wants to let sleeping dogs lie almost as much as we do. But of course things may change once they've exhumed Pink. In any case, if Batty is to be believed, and there's no one else who can tell us anything different, she eventually agreed to meet Pink down by the lake where she thought they would be out of sight in the boathouse. She claims that my mother never knew of the meeting. That again is something about which we shall never know the truth.

Of course, all this happened forty years ago now, so even if she was perfectly clear-headed, Batty's memory would have been likely to play her false after so long. But what she does claim to remember is meeting Pink under the bamboos and going with him into the boathouse with the intention, I suppose, of coming to some kind of agreement with him. Perhaps my mother had even given her money to pay him off. All she is able to articulate now, apparently, is that she just wanted to give him a talking to. Once they were inside the boathouse, he drew a knife and began to threaten her. For some reason a lot of tools had been left in the boathouse, probably left around by some lazy so-and-so who had been doing a few repairs down there. Anyway, Batty, in self-defence, grabbed a hammer with which she hit Pink on the side of the head.

Pink was a small man, but it is still difficult to imagine how Batty managed all alone to drag his body out of the boathouse, up the slope further into the bushes and there, with the help of whatever tools she'd found, to bury him in the shallow grave where he presumably remains to this day but which is shortly to be disturbed. A surge of adrenalin would, I suppose, have given her extra strength.

It is unclear as to whether or not my mother ever knew what had happened, whether or not she was indeed an accessory after the fact, but it is my belief that she must have known and that the weight of it all, from the baby's death to Pink's, only served to intensify her dependency on Batty and on heroin.

Whatever else she did or didn't know, she must at least have known about the letters which for obvious reasons she was so desperate to find. Batty claims to have hidden them in a succession of places. Why she never destroyed them I can't think, unless she thought that she herself might one day want to use them against my mother. She apparently thinks she hid them in some cupboard just before the war, which I told Wapshott couldn't be true because the children had found them under the floorboards on the top landing. In any case when the war came and my parents moved out of the house to make way for the public records, she never took them with her. She thought she knew where they were and that no one would find them, but when my father died immediately after the war and we came to live here, she and my mother began to panic. Of course we moved all the furniture around so she no longer knew where she thought she had put them. Perhaps she just lied to my mother because she never really wanted my mother to get her hands on those letters. Anyway that was when all the fun started and all the snooping.

We were sitting in the Japanese Room and at a certain point, before Wapshatt had even touched on my mother's death, a glacial silence suddenly descended. Even the smooth Chief Constable was briefly discountenanced. It was as though an evil gust of wind had all at once blown through the room, wrapping its icy fingers around each of us in turn. For a moment I wanted to be shot of Cranfield and everything it represents, but then I can hardly blame the house. I looked nervously at Priscilla who was looking at the floor and back at Wapshott who was running his long fingers through his lank hair. I stood up nervously and rang the bell for Marshall to bring the drinks tray.

## Annie's diary

His Lordship was in a dreadful state after that policeman came to see him the other morning. Cursing and swearing all over the place and talking about his b— mother and b— Doris Batty. I reckon he'd had one or two drinks by the time he came up to change for dinner just as I was drawing her Ladyship's bath. I wasn't feeling too happy myself but I wasn't saying anything about that. Anyway he heard me in the bathroom and he came in to tell me that he thought it was a darn good thing they were moving out. He'd had enough of everything. Mind you, I think he was just being awkward. I told him not to take on so but he wasn't going to listen.

'How would you like it Annie,' he said, 'if you'd had my mother?' I couldn't help laughing at the very thought of it, but his Lordship wasn't seeing the funny side. They don't know, he told me, whether she killed herself or if Batty pushed her in the water. Then when her Ladyship went to have her bath, he followed me into the bedroom, and there was me trying to lay out her Ladyship's clothes for the evening and him striding up and down in a dreadful state.

Now Miss Batty wasn't likely to admit to murder was she? I have no idea what he was going on about, but he kept saying that it was all because of some letters he'd sent to his mother. Her Ladyship wasn't very pleased to find him still there when she came out of the bathroom. 'Oh Sydney,' she says, 'do go and get changed.' Lady Isley was coming to dinner and we all know how punctual she is. Anyway his Lordship went off to his dressing-room still mumbling and swearing.

## Sydney Otterton's diary

Priscilla kept on telling me this morning that I had bad blood from my mother's family. That may well be the case, but it didn't seem to occur to her that if I have bad blood then so do her children. Perhaps she thinks theirs is diluted, but I reminded her of an ancestor of hers who took a pig onto the roof of his house and then threw it down as a punishment for not admiring the view. He can't have been all that sane, but Priscilla didn't think it funny. No one seems to think anything funny any more. Even Annie. She's been really down in the dumps for the last few weeks. God alone knows why.

Of course I can't think about anything except my mother at the moment. And the more I think about her, the more confusing I find everything. I know that I was right in thinking that Mason and Legros were planted here in order for them to find those incriminating letters. What no one will ever know now is the degree of my mother's guilt and although I was initially convinced that she had killed herself, I am now not so sure. What on earth, one wonders, were she and Batty doing down by the lake? They must have gone there as a reaction to receiving the letters from me and I can only imagine that they went to see if Pink's grave had been disturbed. It may or may not have been the first my mother heard about Pink's death or there may even have been some incomprehensible reason of her own whereby she followed Batty to the lake that day. After all my mother was certainly quite as deranged as Batty, so who can say what her reasons might have been? Batty of course says that my mother slipped on the bank, fell into the lake and drowned and that she, Batty, was powerless to save her. That may well be true. The only problem is that Batty appears to have been involved in rather too many unexplained deaths.

One of the most unsettling aspects of the whole affair, is the connection between Batty, the Legros and Mason. All right, so Mrs Mason and Mrs Legros are sisters, and we knew that, but as if that weren't enough, it now turns out, according to Wapshott, that Batty is Legros's sister. And Legros, who uses five or six different names, has a record as long as your arm. He's spent a good deal of his life in and out of gaol and has repeatedly been in trouble for sexual attacks on young children. The police suspect Mason and Legros of being part of a ring involving sexual molestation of young boys, not that it's so simple to pin anything on them. I felt quite uneasy when Wapshott told me about that because I couldn't help remembering the violent reaction the children always had to Mason and how they always called him disgusting. I thought they were being silly at the time and I paid no attention, but now I wonder if he tried something on one of them. it wouldn't surprise me. There have always been a lot of buggers around and children are easy prey because they never tell. I can remember a gardener I used to avoid like the plague.

Priscilla quite rightly says that we've just got to try and put all this behind us now and concentrate on the move, the sale and then, opening the house to the public next year. But there remains the grisly problem of the exhumation of Pink's body which may result in some kind of case against Batty. And that will make it quite impossible for us to put the whole thing behind us for a while. Aunt Lettice, needless to say, is quite delighted by the whole saga. She finds it *moost* interesting. Probably more interesting than anything else she's heard for a long time.

## Georgina's exercise book

When I got back from school today my bed had been taken away because it's going in the sale. I wanted to take it to the Dower House but Mummy said it was too big which made me very sad. I wonder who will have it next. It's our very last night in the poor house and I've got to sleep on a mattress in the peacock room tonight. Father and Mummy seem quite excited about everything and Father's laughing rather a lot and Mummy keeps saying, 'You're such a fool Sydney,' and laughing too. Yesterday she said, 'Your father has so many ideas that one of them must sometimes be good.' Father was really pleased about that. But Annie's not in a good mood at all. In fact she's been in a bad mood for ages now. Perhaps she feels like I do that nothing will ever be the same again. After the summer holidays I've got to go to boarding school and Thomas has got to go to public school and no one seems to know if Annie is even going to stay with us. When I asked Mummy about Annie she told me to mind my own business. Anyway my new room's all right, but it's really boring compared to my old one which I will never forget for as long as I live.

# Annie's diary

There's no doubt about it, but his Lordship is as cheerful as a cricket. He seems to be really pleased about the move. He's been hanging pictures all day and moving the furniture about in his study and in his dressing-room. I was expecting him to be quite depressed about moving, but I reckon it must be a weight off his mind to have left the poor old house. Perhaps what with all the recent goings on, he was reminded too much of the past so he'll be glad to have moved out. After all he must have some horrible memories of years gone by which he may feel won't be troubling him so much now he's left the house.

It's funny to think of the Marshalls up there all alone on the top floor. I rather think they wish they hadn't given their notice now. I wonder who his Lordship will find as a butler and caretaker. We haven't had much luck with butlers so far what with Mr Cheadle and then Mr Mason. Her Ladyship always hated Mr Mason but she never said why and I've wondered if it wasn't something to do with Mr MacIntosh. Mr Mason may have known something he had no business knowing. Anyway Mr MacIntosh has gone now, too, not that he's very far away. Only in the village.

I never said her Ladyship hadn't given me a nice room. I expect she thinks that if I have a nice room, I'll want to stay. Well I'm not going anywhere now, so that's that. Not that I've said a word to anyone.

# *Sydney Otterton's diary*

Priscilla went charging off to see old Rakowski this morning. His daughter rang on the day we moved to say he'd had a stroke and was in hospital. I couldn't really see why she rang us but Priscilla felt sorry for the old boy so she agreed to go and see him. Apparently he's not too bad but his daughter thinks he won't be able to go on living alone so she wanted to know if Priscilla knew of any reasonable old people's home in the neighbourhood.

I'm surprised by how glad I am to have moved. For one thing the Dower House is a very decent house and for another, in some peculiar way, I almost feel as if nothing has changed. The house is still there for me to see through the trees every time I step outside the front door, and what with the grant from the Ministry of Works which we're hoping to get for the roof, the future is looking up for Cranfield. Priscilla seems quite happy too. Only Annie remains moody. I can't laugh her out of it.

# 1995

# POSTSCRIPT

I first went to Cranfield on Easter Monday three years ago. Easter was late that year and with the sun shining throughout the Bank Holiday week-end, England was briefly the loveliest country in the world. John Major had surprisingly just won a fourth successive Conservative victory at the polls, and for the first time a woman was about to become Speaker of the House of Commons. The country was so changed from the one inhabited by my grandfather during the years immediately after the war when he used to spend so much time at Cranfield, that I doubt he would have recognised it.

It seems likely that my grandfather never returned to Cranfield after his first stroke early in 1950. All I do know is that when he moved from the Edwardian terrace house at Wimble-on-Thames where we used to spend Christmas during my childhood, to a residential home for the elderly, surrounded by laurels and rhododendrons and situated in a sprawling village three miles from the gates of Cranfield Park, Lady Otterton was briefly good to him, visiting him at comparatively regular intervals until the dreadful day when she discovered how he had lampooned her and her family in *Hyacinth's House*. *Hyacinth's House* was the last book he ever wrote, and in it he describes Cranfield just as clearly and with just as much passion as he does in *The Otterton Family* or in his own private diaries. The characters in the book were as easily identifiable as was the house.

Unfortunately after my grandfather moved to The Laurels, he only recorded a few rare details of his daily life. Perhaps he found writing difficult or perhaps he had entered a period of deep depression. On the few occasions I visited him there, I felt that he had changed and although he appeared to be pleased to see me, he was never so talkative or so entertaining as I remembered him to have been earlier. I do, however, recall his once making a remark that led me to suppose that he regretted having alienated Lady Otterton. After all, he was a lonely old man who could ill afford to lose the few friends he had. 'Her Ladyship,' he remarked, 'was not amused by my little *persiflage*.' Then he said something about it having perhaps been a mistake to cast Annie as the butler. He would never have wished to offend Annie whom he regarded as an intelligent and worthy woman with a finely tuned awareness of the droll.

Although I remember, at a very young age, being fascinated by my grandfather's tales of Cranfield which, then, in my imagination, seemed to be just as real or unreal a place as Rapunzel's tower, it was not until four years ago when my mother died and I inherited his papers that I fully appreciated the depth of Grandpapa's romantic attachment to the house.

My mother's relationship with her father was such that neither he nor she appeared to show any real interest in the other. She steadfastly refused to read his books, claiming that, since he was a free thinker, they could not but contain blasphemous material. To her dying day she maintained that through his cold-heartedness he had sent her mother to an early grave. She dutifully visited him once, or perhaps twice a year and on Sundays prayed for his reconversion to the fold. Consequently when he died, she had many masses said for the repose of his soul, but never once had the curiosity so much as to glance at one page of the many notebooks he left behind. Lady Otterton attended the funeral.

When I came to think about it, it struck me as remarkably lucky that my mother had even kept those notebooks. She might so easily have burnt them or thrown them in the dustbin. But then she in turn died and I returned home to help my father sort out her personal effects. In the loft I came across a battered old leather attaché case marked with

334

the initials Z.A.R., and on looking inside discovered it to be full of exercise books, every page of which was closely covered in my grandfather's neat, old-fashioned hand. Of course I knew my father would have no use for my grandfather's diaries, indeed that he would be glad to be rid of them. My father hates anything that he refers to as 'clutter', which for him includes ornaments, novels or keepsakes of any kind. He also dislikes my chosen profession. 'You're supposed to be the writer,' he said rudely. 'You had better take that rubbish away with you, or dispose of it.'

Initially I had a certain amount of difficulty in making much sense of what I read because of my grandfather's rather unusual habit of keeping what amounted to his personal diaries amongst whatever notes he was making for a work in hand. But as soon as I began to read the notebooks for the year 1945, my imagination was engaged; so much unexpected feeling did Grandpapa express and so vivid was his description of Cranfield and of the Ottertons, that I began to be as captivated by them as he had been. The more I read, the more obsessed I became until I finally decided that I had to investigate the family further. I had not only to go to Cranfield and to see it for myself, which was easily enough done, but I had also somehow to decipher the truth behind the half-told story in the diaries.

In a strange way, I felt my grandfather's spirit urging me on, urging me to ignore a biography of Piłsudski which had been commissioned and which I should have been researching, in favour of a story about a crumbling mansion and an improbable eighty-year-old tale of blackmail and possible murder. It was all quite unlike anything that I had been involved in before, or that had ever come my way, but it so aroused my curiosity that I decided to beg for an extension on Piłsudski, on the grounds that some new letters of his had come to light; in reality so as to pursue my researches into what I had come to think of, not as the Ottertons, but as *the house*, with a view to writing a book about it. A sequel to *The Otterton Family* perhaps, or to *Hyacinth's House*. Who knows?

In the event, the book wrote itself in the form of all the diaries and papers that so fortuitously came my way. My thanks are especially due to the present Lord Otterton for all the help he has given me, most particularly in so kindly allowing me access to his father's diaries. I would also like to thank Georgina Otterton for speaking to me freely and at length about her early years at Cranfield and for her generosity in permitting me to include in this work extracts from her childhood notebooks. I would like to thank Dolly Quick for the letters and diaries of her late sister, Annie, and for William Johnson's two letters. My attempts to trace Mr Johnson resulted in the discovery that he died of a heart attack early in 1974; his wife, Sarah, survived him briefly. I am grateful to Mr Johnson's niece, Carly Paine, for permission to publish Mr Johnson's two letters.

Of course there would have been no tale to recount without those people who lived at Cranfield and who in these letters and diaries tell their own stories. People with whom, over the last two or three years, I have become more familiar than I could ever have done had I known them in person. People whose lives and attitudes, like every one of ours, depended very much on the times they lived in and the attitudes of their day. All of them, in some way victims. All of them conditioned by Cranfield. I see the house as the protagonist of this tale. It is the house that shaped their destinies, directed their thinking and held them all entranced. For every one of them the house appears to have been of paramount importance.

So it was with bated breath that I made my first expedition to Cranfield. I had learnt that the late Lord Otterton, with the enormous support of his wife, struggled for several years to make a success of opening the house to the public and that it was eventually the good Lady Isley who came to their help and who, by generously endowing the house, made it possible for it to be handed over to the National Trust.

As a result of a huge grant from the Ministry of Works, the house was given a brand-new copper roof shortly after the Ottertons left, and in the heady early days under the National Trust, the ground floor and main staircase were entirely redecorated by a fashionable interior designer of the day and the basement was completely renovated, ready to house a shop and a tea room. With so much money spent on the house, with it saved for posterity, given a new lease of life as a piece of history, a museum, made into somewhere for holiday-makers to go on a rainy day, or somewhere to take a visiting mother-in-law or a guest from the Antipodes, I wondered how I would recognise the crumbling old house that had so enchanted my grandfather.

My first impression of the house was of its sheer size and of course of the redness of the brick. I could see at once, from the car park which had formerly, as I later learnt from Georgina, been a bulb park, that this was a house at which you needed to look carefully before you could begin to appreciate its grandeur or indeed its beauty. Yet I immediately felt familiar with it, as if it were an old friend. As I stood there in the car park, queuing at a wooden hut for my ticket, surrounded by rows of parked cars, off whose shiny red and green and blue roofs the sun glinted mockingly, was the house already beginning to work its ineffable magic on me?

I bought my ticket and began to wander slowly in the direction of the house. As I came out of the car park, with Cranfield standing at an angle to the left of me, I looked down across a field towards the lake. There should have been daffodils, although because of the early spring, they would already have been blown, but the daffodils so loved by Sydney Otterton and Annie were no longer there. All the same, as I looked over towards Capability Brown's lake, I could not but feel that I knew it already and I supposed that were I to walk down to its shore, I might encounter Annie making her way back from the farm, or there I might find young children at play. At the very least, I would see, protruding from the water, a rigid foot shod in delicate black calfskin. A pointed little shoe, I imagined, with a narrow strap across the front attached by a small round black button.

Involuntarily I shuddered, and then, like a dog emerging from the water, shook myself so as to bring myself to my senses. By profession I am a historian and therefore have no business fantasising about the ghosts of footmen, faded daffodils and murdered chatelaines. I had come to Cranfield in search of the truth, not to write a ghost story. I turned to walk up the short incline to the front door sheltered as it is by the Victorian excrescence, or *porte cochère*, built, as I knew, by Lady Isley's father, Sydney Otterton's grandfather. Even that was familiar to me.

Within a few moments, I would be inside the marble hall, gasping at the magnificence of the ceiling, awed by the beauty of Rysbrack's chimney-pieces. There, as I stroked the silken polished mahogany of the doors, I would conjure up the past, attempt to visualise the stark post-war era, imagine Sydney Otterton striding with his golden labrador across the great white marble floor and think of my grandfather, huddled fifty years earlier, in the cold of the Red Drawing-Room, concentrating, not as he should have been, on earlier Ottertons, but on Priscilla Otterton's blue eyes.

I was suitably impressed by the magnificence of the interior at Cranfield. As many have done before and as others will do in the future, I gasped at the hall ceiling. For all the money thrown at the house, for all the pseudo-eighteenth-century, fussy, ruched curtains, for all the elaborate and often jarring colours that betoken the exuberance of a runaway horse or a decorator out of his element, the house manages to retain its dignity and an aura of its past. I was reminded of something Sydney Otterton wrote in his diary about the house: It has too great a character of its own to be affected by one or other of its temporary custodians.

Since that first visit, I have returned on several occasions to Cranfield and on one occasion I was kindly shown behind the scenes and taken to the top floor where Georgina had had her bedroom. There was the school-room with the old wallpaper peeling off the walls, there was the landing I had already so clearly envisaged from the diaries, the lavatory concealed behind a bookcase, the spiral staircase to the roof and Annie's favourite view over the lawns and the park to the distant hills. Water dripped through the roof, just as it had done after the war, for the copper roof had been incorrectly laid and Cranfield was about to receive its second new roof in forty years, its original one having lasted for over two hundred.

The contrast between the grand downstairs rooms which the visitor normally sees and the musty old top floor seemed to summarise for me the history of the house and to encapsulate its essence as a home and a museum and as an integral part of British social history.

Only one act of vandalism truly made me weep and makes me weep again to think on it. Those silken mahogany doors have been painted cream, or fawn, or beige – and the paint dragged to produce a striped effect. How could anyone wish to stroke them now?

Elizabeth Rakowska Walters
1995